SILVER SERENADE

NANCY J. COHEN

OGP
ORANGE
GROVE
PRESS

Silver Serenade

Space pilot Jace Vernon flees his home after being framed for murder. He seeks justice, but a lovely S.I.N. agent gets in his way. Not only does she distract him with her silvery hair and violet eyes, but she counters his every move in the quest to clear his name. As he attempts to sway her to his cause, he doesn't count on falling for her charms.

Rookie assassin Silver Malloy refuses to abort her deadly mission even if it means killing the man Jace needs alive to prove his innocence. Ever since Tyrone Bluth, the leader of Tyrone's Marauders, murdered her parents, she's dedicated her life to getting revenge. Now that she has it within her grasp, she won't let Jace stop her. But as his sincerity melts the barriers around her heart, she realizes they'll have to work together to expose Bluth and prevent a galactic war.

*Best Book in Romantic SciFi/Fantasy at
The Romance Reviews*

"Fans of Nathan Fillion and Firefly are sure to enjoy this futuristic romantic fantasy." *Coffee Time Romance*

"Silver Serenade is an exciting, action-packed space adventure." *Two Lips Reviews*

"Nancy J. Cohen has written a thrilling fantasy with compelling characters. You won't want to put the book down!" Traci Hall, *USA Today* Bestselling Author of the Scottish Shire Mysteries

"From start to finish, *Silver Serenade* throws an action-packed thrill ride. It's fun and adventurous, and left me begging for more!" *Siren Book Reviews*

"With a touching love story, a great blend of humor, action and passion, and a great cast of characters, this is a book that won't let you go until the very last page." *The Romance Reviews*

"A fun romantic science fiction thriller." *The Romantic Post*

"This is an exceptional, fast-paced, futuristic book that takes you to different worlds and introduces you to a whole new outlook on this genre of writing." *Babes in Bookland*

Chapter One

Despite the coolness of the woods, sweat dribbled down the back of Silver Malloy's neck. Her muscles ached from hours spent in a crouched position, but stealth mattered more than comfort. She'd waited for this opportunity for months—no, make that years—and wasn't about to lose it due to a lapse in technique. This first kill might be her last, but at least she'd complete her revenge.

Using her rifle scope, she scanned the dusty street that stretched below her hillside vantage point. The few scruffy inhabitants who trudged between the ramshackle buildings didn't interest her.

A lucky tip had brought her to Al'ron, a watering hole for space travelers. Those who visited here were not welcome elsewhere. They came to buy arms, men, and equipment to carry out lawless raids against innocent victims, and Tyrone Bluth had earned the reputation as the cruelest bandit of them all.

Silver couldn't wait to end his reign of terror. Raucous bird cries and the drone of insects rang in her ears, augmented by the auditory sensors in her gold drop earrings. Her concentration centered on the only saloon in town as she waited for the slightest hint of movement from the double swinging doors.

The spicy scent of tangleberries tickled her nose. She stifled a sneeze, unwilling to lose focus, even for a moment.

Her pulse accelerated as someone staggered from the saloon. She recognized Bluth, the leader of Tyrone's Marauders. He sported a wide-brimmed black hat, militia-style clothes, and a weapons belt bristling with armaments. A hostile scowl creased his ugly face, a face that had haunted her dreams for decades.

Shutting one eye, she took careful aim through the targeting sight of her TechVix LD-6 Sharpshooter Special.

Her gut clenched, and she steeled herself to fire. Just as her finger twitched on the trigger, a shadowy figure dove into her. The impact knocked her to the ground. She dropped the rifle, but not before it discharged a wild shot.

A heavy weight toppled across her body, forcing her spine against the packed earth. Tiny pebbles dug into the small of her back while brittle pine needles pierced her skin. So much for the protective jumpsuit she'd worn.

"Let me up." She shoved at the bulk immobilizing her. Unable to break free, she aimed a string of expletives toward the man whose furious green eyes glared down at her.

"Who the devil are you?" he demanded, his thick dark brows drawn together.

"I could ask you the same." Silver's hand scrabbled in the dirt, searching for her fallen weapon. "Are you one of Bluth's men?"

"No." His thighs pressed her firmly to the ground.

"Then get off me so I can finish what I started."

"Only after you tell me why you're here."

Panic seized her as she faced the possibility of failure. "All I need is one clear shot, then we'll talk." She thrust at his broad chest, but he wouldn't budge.

"If you're worried about Bluth getting away, it's too late."

"What?" Silver lifted her head to peer over the crest of the hill. Sure enough, Tyrone Bluth was nowhere in sight.

The villain had torn apart everything meaningful in her life, and now she'd lost her chance to even the score.

Rage clouded her vision. "I don't know who you are, but you've no right to interfere."

His lip curled. "Is that so?" His attention shifted to a spot beyond the ridge, then he lowered his face close enough for her to see the brown flecks in his irises. "Be quiet. Bluth's patrol is searching the area."

Gritting her teeth, she gave him an appraising glance. Taut angles highlighted his bone structure, emphasizing a patrician nose and a jaw set at an arrogant pitch. Jet black hair swept in tousled waves to his nape. Slicked back from a wide forehead, its style proclaimed he was a man who couldn't be swayed from his purpose.

With her smaller frame, she doubted the defensive tactics she'd learned during training would be effective. He looked like a guy who could counter her every move.

Minutes ticked by while he pressed against her in a manner that made unwanted awareness flood through her.

He raised himself to peer over the rise. "All right, it's clear. Get up and identify yourself."

You wish, mister. As soon as his weight lifted off her, she rolled to her side, snatched her rifle, and stood. The stranger appeared unarmed. From the tight fit of his vest and leather pants, she didn't see where he could hide a weapon unless one was tucked inside his polished black boots.

"I should shoot you for what you've done." She aimed her laser rifle at his chest. "I've waited months for this opportunity to kill Tyrone Bluth."

"Why are you after him?"

Maybe if she explained, he'd let her finish the job. "Bluth is a ruthless outlaw. He leads a band of terrorists who prey upon colonists. His raids destroy entire settlements, killing thousands of innocent people. I mean to end his tyranny."

They both spoke in low tones, aware that Bluth's men still scoured the woods.

The man's jaw clenched, exposing a slight cleft in his chin. "I need the man alive, not dead. Fortunately, I caught a gleam of your weapon and stopped you in time."

Before she could respond, a flurry of birds fluttered into the air. Silver's head tilted sharply as she read the sign of unwelcome visitors. She hadn't detected the stranger earlier only because she'd been so focused on her target.

"Someone's coming," she said. "I'm outta here." Slinging her rifle strap over her shoulder, she sped down the slope, twigs and dead leaves flying in her wake. The man's footfalls pounded behind her.

At the base of the hill, the forest swallowed them. Late afternoon sunlight filtered through the branches, illuminating cobwebs suspended in the air. Pine needles swatted her face, but she ignored them, icy prickles of fear clawing her spine. She'd heard what Bluth did to captives.

The man pushed past her to take the lead, swerving by a cluster of bramblejuice bushes. Silver couldn't help admiring his agility as he skirted rocks in their path. For a big man, he moved fast.

She easily kept pace. Her feet dodged a fallen log as she charged after him down a grassy decline to the bank of a small stream.

Halting, he whipped around to face her. "These woods don't go much farther. Beyond that rise, the terrain changes abruptly. We won't find many places to hide in that barren landscape. Let's circle around toward the spaceport."

Since she was headed in the same direction, Silver didn't argue. She hopped across a jagged row of slimy rocks to cross the stream. In her haste, she slipped on a pile of wet leaves coating the opposite bank.

The man dashed forward and offered a hand to assist her. Surprising herself, she accepted, feeling an odd tingling when his large palm enveloped hers in a firm, warm grip.

Once they reached the top of the embankment, he dropped her hand as though he'd touched fire.

His gaze darkening, the stranger turned away and charged across a ridge riddled with tangled kurl vines that made progress difficult. She watched her footing, careful to avoid snagging her ankle. They'd gone a short distance when she sniffed the distinctive scent of crushed marlberries.

"They're directly in front of us." She tugged on his arm to stop his forward momentum.

He glanced at her, his eyebrows raised. "How do you know?"

She smirked. "I've done my homework. Fallen marlberries cover the ground during the summer here. They emit a distinctive musty aroma when broken. Someone is on the trail ahead of us."

His appreciative grin might have charmed her under other circumstances, but anger still drove her. Bluth would be dead now if not for him.

"We'll change direction," the stranger said. "Follow me."

"Why should I?" She stood her ground.

"Because we have a better chance of alerting each other to danger if we stick together."

He had a point. All right, she'd go along with the guy for now but only until the coast was clear.

Footsteps crashed through the brush behind them. Her pulse racing, Silver darted after the man toward an outcropping of boulders that bordered the woods on the eastern edge. They'd circled the perimeter of the town to approach the spaceport from the opposite end but still had a distance to go.

The man gestured toward a crevice in one of the larger rocks. "It looks like we can just squeeze through."

"We're not far from the port. I say we take our chances." She could still catch Bluth before his ship lifted off. Once she'd killed him, it didn't matter if his henchmen caught her.

"They'll overtake us first. Do as I say."

"No, thanks. You can hide in there, but I'm on my way." Small, dark spaces held no appeal for her, and that gap in the rocky mountainside looked as inviting as a bear's den.

She ducked past him but wasn't fast enough. His eyes glittered as he blocked her path.

"You're not getting captured. I can't trust you to keep silent about meeting me. Inside." Grasping her arm, he hauled her toward the crack in the granite.

"Let go of me." She struggled for her rifle but couldn't reach it. Nor did her attempts to kick him succeed.

He tugged her closer to the yawning black space that reminded her of… no, don't go there. Memories surfaced anyway, bringing home the reason for this mission. Bile rose in her throat at the thought of Bluth getting away.

Forced into the narrow opening, she sucked in her stomach and flattened her back against one side of the boulder. The tight squeeze proved a challenge, but she emerged into a small chamber beyond. The ceiling lowered as she progressed, forcing her to crouch in order to proceed through a gap at the other end.

Her rifle scraped the rock. She hoped it wouldn't be damaged, but the space was too small for her to adjust it. Besides, the man followed directly behind.

Iridescent cilica crystals imbedded in the granite provided illumination. After a few paces, the passage widened.

Her lungs ached, and she let out the burst of air she'd been holding. She breathed in a cool, rustic scent.

"Keep moving." The man poked her arm.

Unable to retreat, she advanced forward, gasping in awe as the passage opened into a large chamber with a high ceiling and sprays of gypsum festooning the walls. Glittering stalactites and stalagmites and huge gnarled calcite columns added to the impression of height. Her glance halted on the streaks of red gleaming along the walls.

Rubilite formations.

Her resentment toward the stranger temporarily forgotten, she stepped onto the flowstone floor to examine one of the glowing veins which lit the interior like fire. Trickling water sang a steady rhythm in the background.

"Look at this!" She drew a finger along the streak of ruby red, its surface rough but cool to the touch. "Can you believe it?" She stared about the room, overwhelmed by its richness.

Behind her, the stranger gave a grunt of appreciation. "A hidden treasure of Al'ron. I wonder if anyone knows. This sector might be riddled with these caves."

"This lode could be worth a fortune, when properly cut and polished. Whoever stakes a claim wins the mining rights."

"I cannot take advantage of such a find, but you can."

Puzzled by the bitterness in his tone, she pivoted to face him. Her gaze slid from his thick hair to his broad shoulders and muscled arms, lingering on his partly exposed chest and bronzed skin. Her pulse thrummed in her ears as a compulsion to learn more about him crept into her mind.

Forget it. Nothing else matters except your mission.

"Let's not waste time," she said, hoping to impress upon him a sense of urgency. "We still have a good chance to catch Bluth before he reaches his ship."

Annoyed by her loose hair, she twisted it into a braid, fastening the ends with a cord from her pocket.

The man had been studying her face. Now his glance drifted to her hair, making her take perverse delight in slowing her movements.

He tightened his lips. "We'll wait a few minutes to let those goons pass."

Awkward moments ticked by while they listened for signs of pursuit. During the interim, Silver's nerves reacted to every movement he made. Tension crackled between them, eliciting a sheen of sweat on her skin. Risking a glance at his stern profile, she was consoled to note a muscle twitching in his jaw. So he wasn't immune to her after all.

"I'll reconnoiter the entrance," he suggested. "Wait here."

I may have screwed up my first kill, but I'm not that dumb. The man might desert her in order to reach the terrorist first. Or he could plan to expose her position and use her as a decoy for his own escape. Either way, she wouldn't give him the opportunity. Ignoring his command, she followed him.

"What is your business with Tyrone Bluth?" she asked while they edged through the cramped passage.

"Why do you want to kill him?" he countered.

"I told you. He's a menace to society."

"So are a lot of other people."

Again she heard that bitter note in his voice and wondered at it. "Who are you?" When he didn't respond, she said, "All right, I'll go first. I'm Silver Malloy."

"Pleased to meet you," he drawled as they reached the entrance. He stretched to his full height, tilting his head when muffled voices sounded outside. "Quiet, they're nearby. Get back inside." He darted deeper into the cave.

Silver followed, her heart thumping when she realized how close they'd come to being discovered.

The stranger stopped abruptly and pivoted to face her. When he placed his finger on her mouth to warn her against talking, she stiffened. She didn't need the reminder. If they were caught, Bluth wouldn't show any mercy.

As they waited, her body warmed to the man's touch. Bad timing, but that seemed to be her fate. She'd had little luck in the men department. Either they viewed her as a sexual object or as a comrade in arms. Only dear Burrell had treated her with true affection. Now her fiancé was gone along with her family.

No room remained in her heart for anyone else, only for revenge against the pirate who'd caused her sorrow.

The stranger dropped his arm. "I'll see if they've left," he said in a gruff tone. Without sparing her a backward glance, he retreated toward the exit. "It's clear," he called.

She trailed him outside, wincing at the bright sunshine. A brilliant flash drew her attention toward the spaceport.

"Oh no, that might be Bluth's ship." Disappointment colored her voice.

"He'll leave an ion trail. We can follow him to his next destination."

"We?"

"I have a fast scout ship on the launchpad."

"So do I, and I prefer to work alone." She started to sidestep beyond him, but he blocked her path.

"We're both after the same man. We'd have a better chance of catching him together."

"I'll think about it. Stand aside."

No way would she tag along with this guy for much longer. Not only did he want Bluth alive for his own purposes, but he played havoc with her hormones. Once they safely reached the launching platform, she'd fly solo.

Their trek through the woods was effortless since Bluth's henchmen had cleared the area. It wasn't long before they stood on a hillside gazing at the spaceport. Dust swirled in the air, clogging her nostrils, while heat rose from the rocks like an outdoor oven. Her parched throat cried for a drink. Beyond the hill, an array of launch sites interspersed with maintenance sheds dotted the flat expanse of reverrock.

"You didn't say who you are," she mentioned. "I gave you my name."

Facing her squarely, he gave her a searching glance. "I'm Jace Vernon." His jaw clenched when her expression registered shock. "Listen to me before you pass judgment."

"Judgment has already been passed." She couldn't help her involuntary step backward. Ignoring the wild thumping of her heart, she raised her weapon. "Everyone knows about the high price on your head. What worse crime could there be than murdering your parents and selling your sister into slavery?"

She took aim. "Under the authority vested in me as a member of Earth Centrum's Security Integrated Network, I hereby place you under arrest."

"You're an agent of S.I.N.?" he said, pronouncing it as one word rhyming with bin. "I should have guessed." His scorching glance raked her from head to toe. "I suppose you've been assigned to assassinate Tyrone Bluth. His Marauders have been terrorizing Earth's colonies, and you did say you meant to end his tyranny."

"My job is no concern of yours. Now move." She gestured with her rifle. "We'll take my ship and tow yours. I hear quite a few bounty hunters are on your trail. I'll look forward to receiving the reward for your capture."

Chapter Two

Jace's muscles tensed. Scanning the field below the rise of the hill, he searched for a sign that Mixy was outside his ship. His loyal valet must have chosen to remain aboard because Jace didn't spot him anywhere. That suited him fine. Mixy would sense his feelings soon enough and wouldn't interfere in his game to play the docile prisoner.

Since he and Silver were both after the same target, he'd decided it would be wise to stick close to her. Maybe he could convince her to help him. God knew he could use an ally.

"My ship is the GW Nova 14 next to that cargo transport," Silver said at his back. "Which one is yours? Turn around so I can see your face."

Jace rotated until he stared down at her. Wisps of platinum hair had worked loose from her braid, and they floated about her face like strands of fairy silk. He'd never seen such an unusual color. Like polished silver in a bright light, her lustrous hair gleamed in the sunshine.

Her determined violet eyes impacted him like a gut punch. Well, not a punch exactly, judging from the response in his lower regions. In his situation, he couldn't afford to be distracted by a woman. If only his body would listen, but certain equipment had a habit of defiance.

Giving her his most disarming grin, he noted smugly that her lips parted ever so slightly in response. "We could pursue Bluth in my ship. She's the latest KDY Model 10 Torris."

"Nice try, but we'll still take mine. It's fitted with a magna beam, and I'll be needing it. Let's go."

Obediently, he trudged down the hill, the fragrant scent of pines poignantly reminding him of the forested preserve on his ancestral estate. With the memory, his throat constricted from grief. His parents dead, his sister Shanna missing. Would he ever right the injustices done to his family?

Although Tyrone Bluth had carried out the attack, evidence left at the scene pointed to Jace as the instigator. The judge had stripped his inheritance away in one dreadful swoop just like he'd lost his family.

Bluth was the only man who could clear his name, but not if this woman killed the Marauder first.

****

Silver indicated to Jace that he should ascend the ramp to her ship. She noted the rigid set of his shoulders as he complied. If she were in his boots, she'd be figuring a way to escape. He faced a death sentence on Kurash, but then he'd brought that punishment upon himself by destroying innocent lives. He didn't deserve special consideration.

Her tone curt, she ordered him inside after keying in the entry code on a raised panel beside the closed hatch. The door slid open, and he preceded her without responding.

"Hold it," she said, her gaze scanning the interior.

They stood just behind the forward command console. An array of blinking lights indicated the various ops and navigational stations. Two seats faced a wide viewscreen in front, while a hatchway to the rear led to sleeping quarters and a small galley. Access to a turret-style gunnery module led from a companionway off the port side. The main engineering deck resided on a lower level along with the cargo hold.

"Where should I put you?" she said half to herself.

"I can help you pursue Bluth," he offered. "My training included tactical combat maneuvers."

She arched an eyebrow. "Really? So did mine." Careful to keep her weapon aimed at his chest, she strode to a storage cabinet and withdrew a pair of manacles.

"Turn around," she commanded, ignoring his dark scowl.

His powerful back muscles made her catch her breath. In the confined space, his height stretched so that he appeared a pillar before her eyes. Her gaze surveyed his wavy hair, roamed down his torso, and fixated on his tight buttocks.

"Put your hands behind your back," she ordered in a softer voice than intended. Fastening the handcuffs on his wrists necessitated touching his skin, and a thrill of warmth shot through her at the contact. "Now sit in that corner."

She indicated a position by the rear bulkhead, believing it unwise to put him near the controls where his presence might prove to be an unwelcome distraction.

Taking the pilot's chair, she began the preflight warmup.

The launch sequence activated, and she leaned back in her seat, preparing for the gut-wrenching lurch of liftoff.

Five... four... three... two... one.

The powerful engines shifted from a low whine to a pulsating roar. With a bone-jarring shudder, the vessel leapt into the air. The anti-grav system made for a fairly smooth ascent, but the steep angle always caused Silver's head to reel dizzily. Her fingers danced over the controls, keying in the sequence for a towing lock. Satisfaction warmed her skin when she observed Jace's vessel rising in their wake.

"How do you know I don't have a full crew aboard my ship?" Jace said from behind, startling her.

Risking a glance in his direction, she grimaced at the sight of his hulking form crouched by the bulkhead. A frown creased his face, as though he were uncomfortable in the cramped space. She had to remind herself that he was a criminal who deserved his fate.

"If anyone were aboard your ship, he would have broken my magna beam by now," Silver replied. A chime sounded, indicating they had entered orbit around Al'ron. "What do you call your ship?"

"She's the Stinger because she packs a punch and leaves before you know what hit you."

"Mine is the Avenger." Silver began a sensor sweep of the area, hoping to pick up Bluth's ion trail. A couple of other ships approached their vector, but they didn't look like the Marauder's sleek Pamorian T-80 Corvette.

"Try looking for omincron particles," Jace suggested. "Sometimes Bluth uses a foticular generator when he's under attack."

"I know what I'm doing." Glancing back, she meant to ask how he'd acquired that piece of information when alarm flashed in his eyes.

"Then I expect you'll be initiating evasive maneuvers," he drawled.

Her ship rocked with impact. She whipped her head toward the viewscreen, gaping at the sight of laser batteries firing from the two vessels in the vicinity. As they closed into visual range, adrenaline rushed into her blood. Gunships! Armed with lethal firepower for close combat, they'd make mincemeat of her ship. A ship better suited for speed than battle.

Both vessels converged upon the Avenger. Her fingers manipulated the controls as another blast rattled the ship.

She broke orbit, plunging into a series of defensive moves that strained the fabric of her vessel.

"Brace yourself," she yelled, firing her portside thrusters.

Jace struggled to rise. "Let me help. They're regrouping into dockwing formation. If you don't—"

Too late. Caught in their crossfire, the Avenger took a direct hit. The impact knocked Silver from her seat and spewed sparks and noxious fumes throughout the bridge deck. Thrown clear, she crashed against a bulkhead wall, a white-hot explosion of pain shattering her skull before all went dark.

****

"Silver," Jace called as he rushed to her side, alarmed by her ashen complexion.

Long, dark lashes shaped in delicate crescents shadowed her pale skin. Her lips, slightly parted, sang of sensual promise.

In anguished frustration, he struggled against his bonds before remembering she had the key to unlock them. His gaze fell to her breast pocket, where he spied the telltale outline. What other choice did he have?

A shudder rocked the ship as another hit registered. He toppled over the lovely assassin, his cheek crushing against her chest. Just a few inches more, and he could reach her pocket. He'd have to use his teeth. As his mouth moved across her taut jumpsuit, more than his frustration grew. By the moons, she was so soft and yet so firm. Warmth flooded his groin as he nuzzled her bosom to achieve his goal.

His breathing became more labored and not from the effort involved. Ignoring the effect their intimate pose induced, he entwined his legs with hers and pushed the fabric out of his way with his lips. With a careful grip on the key between his teeth, he slid the small disk from its insert with utmost care.

Reluctant to move aside, he jolted into action upon a sideways lurch of the ship. He dropped the key on the floor then fumbled it into his hands from behind. His fingers managed to hit the universal release code. Thankfully, Silver hadn't added an encryption lockout circuit. The restraints released, and Jace tossed them to the floor.

He turned his attention back to the motionless woman. Stooping down, he gently searched her head for injuries. Blood oozed from a gash on her temple.

"Comet dust," he cursed as another laser bolt found its mark.

Smoke stung his nostrils from a filament smoldering on the main console. He'd better do something to get the attackers off their tail. Mixy could help fight off the assault, but only if Jace disengaged the towing lock first.

At the command station, he cut the magna beam, did a quick damage assessment, then programmed in a defense sequence he'd learned during the Dorian war. Fortunately, Silver's ship was easy to fly, requiring the most basic skills. He doubted she'd made many modifications. That knowledge might come in handy later, but right now he was glad to locate a first aid kit mounted on the port side in accordance with standard regulations.

After spraying Silver's wound with a healing gel, he lifted her in his arms and staggered toward the sleeping quarters. It wasn't easy considering the gyrating moves of the ship that followed his prescribed commands. He'd seen the Stinger veering away. Mixy would handle matters until he secured Silver in her cabin.

Her quarters held a double bed, computer station, and utilitarian chest of drawers in an off-white clastine material. As he carefully placed her limp form on the mattress, he wondered at the lack of family holos or feminine frills. A few hair ornaments sat in a receptacle on the bureau, but like the command deck, nothing else personalized her space.

Curious about the type of woman who'd work for S.I.N., he swung his gaze to her arched brows, darker than her swirls of platinum hair. Tearing his eyes from the silvery strands fanning the pillow, he studied her features. Her pert nose tilted upward at the tip, hinting at a defiant nature. He liked her firm chin, and the faint blush of sunburn on her cheeks. And her mouth… an incredible urge to taste her swept him.

Bad idea. She'd tried to kill the one man who could clear his name. Then she had taken him into custody, planning to turn him in at the nearest starbase. If he were smart, he'd snap the restraints on her before she awakened to cause trouble.

A soft moan escaped her lips, causing his throat to tighten. He should check her pupils. Inequality would indicate neurologic impairment. Wishing the medical skills he'd learned in battle were more complete, he leaned over, brushing her arm in the process.

****

Silver's eyelids fluttered open at his touch. "What's happening? Where am I?"

She struggled to rise, her temples throbbing painfully. Panic seized her when she spied Jace staring down at her. Stars above, he'd undone the manacles she'd locked on his wrists.

"You hit your head when you fell. How do you feel?"

Touching her head, she grimaced at the healing gel's sticky texture. "I'll be okay."

Color suffused her cheeks when she noticed her disheveled state. Jace must have riffled through her jumpsuit for the key while she was unconscious. He hadn't taken advantage of her immobility, which earned him a few points in her estimation. Unless he'd added acting to his skills, the man actually seemed concerned for her welfare.

"Thanks for your help. What's our status?" She decided to defer any action to arrest him again until after their situation stabilized.

"We've escaped the Marauders. I expect they were Bluth's rear guard. Now that he knows we're on his trail, we'll have to be more careful."

"We?"

Jace sat himself on the edge of her bunk. "I have a proposition for you."

"Go ahead." She kept her tone level.

"Our vessels suffered extensive damage. After we make repairs, we'll track Bluth together. As a government agent, you have access to resources I could use."

Oh, so now I know why you didn't disable me when you had the chance. You need me to accomplish your goals. Well, two can play the same game.

Waving away his assistance, she swung her legs over the edge of the bunk and slid to her feet. "How bad are things?"

"The coolant generator coils are down on my ship. I could see the vapor trail from here. Worse, your hyperdrive actuators are fused. We can't make a jump until they're fixed. I say we should transfer to my vessel and tow yours."

"I'm not leaving the Avenger."

Nor would she shirk her duty. However, which option should take priority—catching Tyrone Bluth or turning Jace in?

I don't have a choice. The mission comes first.

"My cousin Remy is Chief Mechanical Engineer at Gravicom Wells Shipyards." She scrubbed a hand over her face. "He'll help us without asking any questions."

Jace raised an eyebrow. "Gravicom Wells is on Earth, and negotiations between our governments are delicate right now. Hostilities could erupt at any time—we're on the verge of war. I'd be taking a big risk by showing my face there."

For more than one reason. Diplomatic relations may have soured between their people, but the authorities of both worlds still honored extradition treaties. Jace's arrest on her home planet would lead to his deportation to Kurash.

"You might not be recognized as a Kurashki. By Earth standards, your skin just looks tanned." *And by my standards, the rest of you looks pretty damn good.*

"Our security forces have distributed my hologram."

"So we'll give you a disguise."

Her jaunty response didn't amuse him, judging by the way his eyes narrowed. "I suppose you want to put in a claim for the mining rights to Al'ron's substantial rubilite lode," he said.

"Well sure, why not?" No wonder he couldn't take advantage of the find. As a wanted criminal, he had to stay under cover.

The deck jerked beneath their feet. Startled, they stared at each other for a brief moment before plunging through the hatchway toward the bridge deck.

"What the—?" Silver gaped at the viewscreen. Jace's ship, no longer caught in her magna beam, flew parallel to the Avenger. A stream of vaporous gas emitted from its mid-section, venting into space. It looked more serious than he'd indicated.

Jace shoved her out of his way before pouncing on the controls. "Mixy!" he shouted into the comm link. "Respond."

"Who is Mixy?" Silver queried, annoyed that he usurped her command so readily.

He spared her a quick glance. "Mixy is my valet. I have to get him out of there."

"You mean he is your accomplice. You didn't say anyone else was aboard."

"If you recall, I mentioned that I might have a crew, but you didn't believe me."

A garbled transmission came through, then clarified enough for Silver to distinguish the words. "Oxygen leak… little time left… must transfer over."

Jace's fingers frantically worked the controls as he edged the Avenger closer to his stricken vessel. "It's a good thing your docking module is on the starboard side."

Silver's heart skipped a beat. "You must be a better pilot than I thought. That's a tough maneuver even with a high level of training."

"I was a combat pilot in the Dorian war." His brow wrinkled in concentration as he barked directives at the hapless Mixy.

Silver admired his skill as he closed the distance between the two ships. "I'll ready the grappling locks."

She hustled toward the rear companionway, where she skipped down the steps toward the cargo bay. After locating the massive levers, she struggled to unlatch them.

Better put in a request for hydraulics during my next refit.

Sweat dripped down her face as she strained her arms, clenching her teeth against the exertion-induced pain.

Determination won, and she swung the levers into Receive with a final grunt.

Taking a breather, she leaned against a wall and listened for the series of thumps that would indicate docking.

Who was this Mixy they were rescuing? Jace claimed he was a valet. Laughter bubbled into her throat at the image of an accused murderer roaming the stars with his valet in attendance. At least Jace had an active imagination.

A teeth-jarring vibration followed by a grinding noise told her the other ship had successfully docked. Watching the blinking red light above the levers, she snapped the controls into the Lock position. The light changed to green. She turned, waiting for the airlock to open. Her mouth dropped when she spied the figure waiting just beyond the hatch.

"You're an Elusian," she said as he loped forward.

Mixy's tall, reed-thin frame, pale complexion, and cobalt blue robe confirmed his origins. From Jace's speech, she had gathered he was male, although one couldn't tell from his delicate features. A pair of wispy eyebrows rose above large coffee brown eyes. His nose, straight and narrow, could easily belong to a person with finicky tastes. His lips, a bit wide, curved up at the corners in a pleasing shape.

She shifted her gaze to the Elusian's elaborate hairdo. He'd piled his masses of rich mahogany hair atop his head in a swirling style like an ice cream sundae. Added to his already tall height, it made him seem a giant.

Mixy bowed, then raised his head and grinned. "I am attuned to Master Jace's feelings, madam, so it gives me great pleasure to make your acquaintance."

Silver's brow furrowed. "Thanks, I think."

He turned to lift two heavy valises from the airlock section. "Can you show me to Master Jace's quarters? I'll explain along the way."

"Sure." She proceeded toward the companionway. As they climbed the stairs, Mixy chattered in his peculiar soft voice which was neither deep like a man's nor higher pitched like a woman's. His modulation varied depending upon the topic under discussion.

"How much do you know about my people?" Mixy inquired.

"Not a whole lot."

"We Elusians lack the hormones that give humans certain characteristics. For instance, we do not mate. We reproduce by budding. Therefore our sexual attributes are nil."

Silver's eyes widened at this revelation. Of course she noticed he had no chest to boast about and his slim shoulders indicated a lack of muscular prowess. But no sex hormones?

"The disadvantage is the low level of stimulation for our emotions." Mixy's skirted robe rustled at his ankles. "It has long been our custom to bond with an individual from another species so we can experience stronger feelings. If you think about it, much of human aggressiveness can be attributed to testosterone. As for females, you demonstrate sensitivity and compassion. Most of my race craves to share these emotions."

You've got it wrong about this female. I lost my compassion when Tyrone Bluth destroyed my family.

Silver pointed down the corridor toward the crew quarters. "So what is your relationship to Jace?"

"He saved my life during an attack on Elusia by the Dorians. In my culture, we form an empathic bond with a compatible being during a moment of extreme distress. Thus I became his atrani, his bond-mate for life. He is a kind and generous master."

The blue of his robe paled, becoming interspersed with streaks of tangerine as he spoke with true affection. Silver glanced at him curiously as they strolled down the short passage.

"Neither one of us has regretted his action," Jace's voice boomed from behind. He clapped a hand on Mixy's shoulder, a happy grin animating his face.

Mixy set down the suitcases. Tears welled in his eyes as he regarded Jace. "Milord!" he cried. "I am ecstatic about seeing you as well. Thank the stars you are safe." The Elusian's robe deepened its orange tint.

Jace's face flushed. "What have I told you about displaying your emotions in public?"

"But they're really your feelings, Master Jace." Touches of scarlet invaded Mixy's robe. "You need not be embarrassed if your reactions are exaggerated when I experience them."

Jace rolled his eyes. "Let's stow your gear."

Silver watched them with a bemused tilt to her lips as they entered the spare cabin. So whenever she wanted to know what motivated Jace, she merely had to interpret the hues of Mixy's flowing robe? Ingenious garment.

Too bad she had to turn Jace Vernon in at the completion of her mission. He and his valet were the only ones in a long time who'd given her a reason to smile.

Chapter Three

Silver was running a diagnostic when Jace entered the bridge deck a short while later. Plopping into the adjacent copilot's seat, he gave her a sheepish grin. Her heart did a somersault when she noticed he'd changed into a long-sleeved blue shirt open at the collar, revealing a sprinkling of manly hairs. Her glance slid downward to his hip-hugging denim trousers.

"Mixy can be quite a handful, but I've learned to rely on him." Jace gave her a sexy grin.

"Is that right?" Appalled at herself, Silver glanced away. She shouldn't allow his damnable good looks to distract her.

"At least Mixy has faith in me. That's more than I can say for most people." When her gaze swung back, his riveting eyes captured hers. "Maybe you'll become my ally when you hear my story."

"Oh? And what's that?" No doubt he'd concocted a tale to win her sympathy.

His lips compressed. "I was framed. The night it happened, our servants had leave to attend a holiday festival. I'd stayed home, along with my parents, my sister Shanna, and her friend Yvette. Soon after dinner, I dropped into a deep slumber.

"In the morning, I awoke to find my parents dead and the girls missing. The butler had already summoned the enforcers. He'd found me with… the murder weapon in my hand."

She kept her expression neutral. "So how did Tyrone Bluth get implicated?"

"His ship registered on the logs, plus the way the fatal

wounds appeared…" He shook his head. "Likely Bluth sold the girls to slave traders. I think my cousin Garth hired him."

"For what purpose?" She got a kick out of his lies. They almost sounded believable.

His gaze slid away, focusing on a console dial as though it might provide answers. "Garth opposes my views in the Parsate. I had been about to cast the deciding vote in favor of a peace treaty between the Kurashki Alliance and the Terran Consortium. Garth leads the hardliners who are pushing for war. Now he'll sway Ruler Hurat to take by force what could be ours through peaceful trade."

"You're a politician?" She hadn't pictured him in that role.

He frowned. "Not exactly. As I said, I flew a combat ship in the Dorian war. My father summoned me home when problems developed on our estate. Each prominent family, like mine, holds a seat in the Parsate. When my father became ill, I took his place as Parsator for our district."

"So why would your people believe Garth rather than you?"

Jace's mouth twisted in a grim smile. "The evidence condemned me. What about you? How did you get involved with S.I.N.? If we're to be partners, I need to learn more about you."

Partners? As if!

"My parents were agricultural specialists on Altuis Three where they ran the aquaponics farm. Our settlement prospered until Tyrone's Marauders attacked the colony. I was twelve years old when it happened. My parents hid me in a conduit during the assault."

She squeezed her eyes shut, remembering the confined space, the darkness, the sound of explosions shattering the world above.

"I was the only survivor." She steeled herself to meet his gaze. "My aunt and uncle from Earth became my guardians, and I went to live with them and my cousins. Thirteen years later, my path crossed Bluth's again. He led a raid on the colony where I worked as an agronomist."

Her lips clamped tight, sealing the discovery she'd made on Roth Colony and how it would tip the balance in Earth's favor if war erupted. Bluth must have been paid to target her research, but Silver had no idea who had leaked the information.

Maybe she and Jace had more in common than she'd realized. Both of them, if he spoke the truth, had been betrayed.

"So then you trained to become a S.I.N. agent, and your first mission was to kill the terrorist leader." Jace's burning gaze bore into hers. "I need Bluth alive to clear my name."

"He deserves the same treatment he gives his victims."

"Since when is murder a form of justice?"

Silver cut off her reply when the overhead lights faltered. "What now? Blast, it's the secondary drive modulators. They've shut down. Now we won't have enough power to make it to the Shipyards." Her fingers flew over the touch pads as she shifted the flow of energy to the feeder conduits to get them back on line. After a moment, the lighting improved.

Jace leaned forward, his posture tense. "We'll have to put in for temporary repairs."

Silver examined their coordinates on her nav computer. "We could reach Bartlett Station by tomorrow. That's a lot closer than Earth, but we'll still have to visit the Shipyards for a complete overhaul."

He gave her a keen glance. "A stopover might work to our advantage. We can fish for information about Bluth."

Her eyebrows lifted. "Can your valet assist us? He has good flying skills." At his nod, she added, "Then let's meet later to discuss strategy."

And don't even think about deserting me at the space station. I'll be watching your every move.

****

Mixy, unpacking the cases he kept ready for emergencies, glanced up when Jace entered their quarters. Most of the clothes he was carefully placing in the open drawers were Jace's.

"I won't be needing all of those." Jace folded his arms across his chest and leaned against the hatchway.

Mixy straightened his spine, shooting Jace an indignant glare. "You have no idea what situations you'll encounter, milord. It is my duty to make certain you are properly attired."

"Comet dust, Mixy. I'm not a privileged member of the upper classes anymore, remember?"

"Bah! Your blood still runs true. Woe be to those who betrayed you." He beat a hand against his forehead. "If not for your cousin Garth's perfidy, you would still be an esteemed member of the Parsate, not an outlaw"—he spit the word—"hunted throughout the galaxy."

He wrung his hands in the air like a priest summoning the ancient gods. "Let us pursue revenge. Let us reap the rewards of justice!"

"Let us not get carried away." Jace's lips curved downward. "I'm not after revenge, unlike someone else I know. Being selfish would benefit no one except myself, and it won't bring back the dead. Better to serve others by preventing further abuse."

Mixy's robe, which had turned mellow orange at Jace's arrival, exhibited a hot pink tinge. "Ah! Sexually attracted to Agent Malloy, are we? Fingers of guilt are reaching out, milord. Remember, you have an obligation to your family."

"My parents can no longer arrange a marriage for me. My only obligation is to restore my honor."

"You would do well to ally yourself with Yvette's clan," Mixy advised, tossing a shirt with creases onto a separate pile.

"I've known Yvette all my life; she's like another sister to me. I was never interested in such a match."

"I've sensed more than sisterly affection on her part, plus her parents were amenable to your suit."

"Not anymore." He'd learned quickly who his true friends were after being accused of a crime. Now his cousin would have enough clout to influence Hurat to declare war. The merchants opposed hostilities, fearful any escalation might disrupt their trade routes. Jace could see the advantages of gaining support from Yvette's powerful merchant family, but her father had refused to visit him in detention.

Fortunately, he'd had a few friends left, including Yvette's brother who shared Jace's broader view. Jace only hoped that once he cleared his name, Connor wouldn't expect him to declare for his sister.

"Damn Garth for sinking me into this predicament." Jace clenched his fists.

Mixy's robe darkened to black. "He'll rue the day he dealt this blow to us. We'll pummel him. We'll level his monstrosity of a manor house. We'll—"

"Easy does it, my friend. Restraint is what we need, not a hot-headed charge into battle."

"Forgive me. I grieve for your losses. Of course we must focus on finding Tyrone Bluth. But beware your lust for Agent Malloy. It could sway you from your purpose." Streaks of hot pink infiltrated his garment.

"Mixy, stop it."

"I am merely following my duty to advise you."

Jace regarded him with a fond smile. The Elusian could get on his nerves, but at least Mixy understood his views. He just didn't care for it when Mixy put his emotions on display… or reminded him of feelings he'd rather not acknowledge.

****

Sharing command had its advantages, Silver considered as she relaxed in her cabin. Since Jace had relieved her at the bridge, she looked forward to an evening on her own.

Her temples throbbed. Careful to avoid the spot where

she'd cracked her head earlier, she released her hair from its braid and brushed it out. The repetitive strokes eased her tension.

She put the brush down and opened a drawer. Inside rested a box of kewlwood sticks. She took a long taper, lit it, and inhaled the moldy scent that drifted into her nostrils. Then she placed the candle in a vertical holder.

Bowing her head, she chanted a mournful prayer for the dead. For her parents, for her fiancé, and for all those unfortunates lost in battles long past. Her low, wailing tone rose and fell while she recalled the warmth of her mother's smile, the comfort of her father's arms.

A loud rap on the door startled her. "Who is it?"

"Mixy. May I have a word?"

Silver coded a keypad and the door slid open. Mixy stood hesitantly in the hatchway. "Forgive me if I am intruding. I heard your singing and thought you'd be awake."

Embarrassed to be caught at her nightly ritual, she gave a snappish reply. "What do you want?"

He fingered his robe, tinged with scarlet. "If you wouldn't mind, madam, that peculiar scent… I have a delicate nose."

"It's not supposed to be pleasant. But then you didn't come here to interrupt my prayers, did you?"

"Master Jace informed me of your plans to stop at Bartlett Station. I was wondering if you could recommend suitable attire so I can prepare his wardrobe." The valet gave her a supercilious look over his long nose.

Silver stared at the elaborate hairdo piled atop his head and got perverse pleasure from her next remark. "I figured Jace would make a passable Mynoran trader."

"Certainly not." The horrified expression on Mixy's face made her stifle a smile. "Master Jace would never agree to impersonate such a rogue."

Silver arched her eyebrows. "The Mynorans trade in high tech goods that will interest the science staff at the space station. Jace will agree with me."

"We'll see about that." With a swish of his robes, the valet made a dignified bow. "I must turn down his bed. Good evening, madam."

****

"Mixy said you had a disguise in mind for me," Jace said when the threesome sat in the galley for a quick meal during their approach to Bartlett Station.

Silver's cheeks flamed. She'd imagined different modes of dress on him… and undress, ever since Mixy's unwelcome visit to her cabin.

"You'll wear the garb of a Mynoran merchant." She surveyed his features, too good looking by far. "We'd better lighten your hair and add contact lenses. That should do the trick."

Mixy snorted. "I cannot believe you are agreeable to the prospect of displaying yourself in such a manner, milord. I am ashamed to share this emotion."

Silver ignored him. "After we arrange repairs for our ships, Jace can scope out information on Tyrone Bluth. Liquor loosens tongues. You might hear gossip about his next destination if you play your part well."

"Bluth has likely issued an alert for our vessels. The Stinger is registered under a friend's name, so he won't be able to trace my identity. What about you? Your hair is a dead giveaway, and as for the rest of you, men will notice."

A quiver of warmth rippled through her at his pointed glance to her breasts.

"Don't worry about me. I'll supervise the repairs to make sure they're done properly. Mixy can obtain provisions."

"Thank the stars." Mixy's hands fluttered in the air. "I could not possibly continue this journey without restocking our lamentable pantry. The store of foodstuffs on this vessel is pathetic. And if I may say so, Master Jace, you could use a new supply of shirts. I have been laundering the same ones for days. It is unseemly for you to lack the proper apparel."

Jace threw back his head and roared with laughter. "We're running for our lives, and you're concerned about my wardrobe. Mixy, I'm glad you give me a reason to smile."

Silver frowned, curious as to how a convicted criminal had escaped with the generous supply of money Jace seemed to possess. Perhaps Mixy or the friend who'd helped him escape had tapped into his available resources.

"I thought you were unable to experience your own emotions," she said to Mixy in an accusatory tone. "You certainly seem capable of expressing personal feelings. Am I missing something?"

Jace clasped his water glass. "Elusians have trouble filtering human emotions. Sometimes it's difficult to understand whose feelings he's exhibiting, his or mine. He does have his own reactions, but they're mild compared to ours." A teasing gleam entered his eyes. "I must say, however, that I agree with Mixy concerning our cuisine. This repast has been less than desirable. Your meat is tougher than my boots." He held up his empty wrapper.

Silver's mouth drew taut. "It took me longer than expected to locate Bluth, and I ran out of regular rations."

"What if you'd succeeded in killing him? You barely have enough supplies for a return trip." His face registered surprise along with dismay. "Don't tell me… you expected to be caught by Bluth's men. That's why this ship is so bare. You went on a suicide mission."

****

The truth of his assessment hit Jace in the gut as Silver strode from the galley. What did life mean to her if she hadn't formulated an escape plan? Did she care about nothing except her job? Or had sorrow so darkened her heart that the thirst for revenge had displaced her grief? And when she accomplished her goal, what then? She faced an empty void bereft of purpose other than to welcome death.

He understood her thought processes, having visited those dark places himself. However, he'd decided to work for the benefit of others rather than wallowing in self-pity.

His gaze fixed on her taut bottom as she disappeared through the hatchway. She had so many assets to offer, if only she'd appreciate that fact. *Like I'm appreciating her rear end.*

"Not again!" moaned Mixy, whose robe changed hues from orange to hot pink. "This hormone rush you experience every time we discuss the woman is most disturbing. I wish you would restrain your baser impulses."

Jace poked his shoulder. "I thought that's why you bonded with me. You want to feel my deeper emotions. Besides, I can't help it if the lady's hair reminds me of the snows atop the Klondo Range. Her violet eyes speak of lupella blooms in the Valley of Rainbows. And her body makes me wonder what it would be like to bed her."

Mixy wiped his brow. "See that you don't forget your obligations at home."

Jace's mood sobered. "As if I could, with your constant reminders. First I need to clear my name."

"You're not a murderer, milord."

"You weren't there. You don't know."

"We've been over this before. The servants had the night off for the holiday. You fell into a deep sleep after dinner. It's obvious you were drugged."

His lips thinned. "Too bad the wine bottle went missing so its contents couldn't be tested. I don't remember what happened. Maybe I went berserk as a result of my war experiences, like the magistrate suggested. Maybe I did commit those horrible acts."

"You cannot convince me."

Jace gave him a grim smile. "I need evidence, my friend. Otherwise, I'll never prove my innocence."

To myself, as well as to everyone else.

Chapter Four

"How did you find out Bluth would be on Al'ron?" Jace whispered to Silver as they strolled the main concourse at Bartlett Station. "I had a hard time tracking his movements."

"S.I.N. received an anonymous tip." She pronounced her agency name in one word like Jace. "Now stop looking at everyone as though they're your enemy. Smile as if you're enthralled by my conversation."

"People are staring at us. You might have chosen a less remarkable disguise."

"Mynorans are flamboyant dressers. No one should suspect we're here for anything other than trade." She spoke patiently, like to a child, unexpectedly touched by his anxiety. "It's better than slinking around as though we have something to hide."

"Maybe so, but this is outrageous." He lifted an arm encased in a white ruffled shirt. His scarlet waistcoat with its turned-back cuffs, loose-fitting breeches tucked into tan leather boots, and low-crowned hat trimmed with feathers drew snickers from the crowd. "What about my face?" he asked, rubbing his jaw.

She smirked. "The shadowing I applied makes your contours appear thinner. Don't worry—no one will recognize you with your blond hair, either."

"You're attracting more attention than I am." He didn't sound pleased by that observation.

She patted her daffodil silk gown with its fitted bodice and full gathered skirt. "The idea is to display our supposed wealth. Merchants will be eager to do business with us."

His glance fell to her exposed cleavage. "With you, maybe. Aren't you showcasing the wealth a bit too much?"

Her cheeks warmed under his regard. "The more skin they see, the more men will treat me like a bubblehead. It's part of my disguise."

"Oh, right." His forehead creased while he digested her words. "So what happens if someone does a credit check and taps into your true identity?"

"That won't be a problem." Her employer should have covered her tracks.

They steered through the throng. Silver played her role by nodding at passersby. Humans from the colonies mingled with aliens from neighboring confederations. The space station belonged to the privately owned Hoatch Foundation, a scientific firm that transcended planetary boundaries. Members staffed the trading post and repair stations as a means to bring in extra income. Security details patrolled the corridors, mainly concerned with keeping the peace and allowing only authorized individuals into the science modules.

"That lounge looks busy." Silver indicated the boisterous crowd spilling from an open-air bar. The heady scent of Talusican ale mingled with pungent smoke from outlawed joyfa bars. "It might be a good place to glean info on Bluth."

"Mixy should have come with us. He serves no useful purpose hanging around the hangar bay." Jace's morose tone told her what he thought of that plan.

"He's making sure our repairs are completed on time. Besides, you never know what you can learn by chatting up the technicians. I'm confident Mixy is doing his job. Let's get on with ours."

Originally, she'd meant to supervise repairs and watch their ships so Jace didn't launch without her. But he'd been concerned about strolling the corridors alone. With an attractive woman on his arm, bounty hunters might not give him a second glance, especially if they searched for a lone criminal.

She held up a list nearly as long as her arm. "It will take me all day to shop for this stuff. Mixy requested enough provisions for the next year. I doubt I'll find half of these items. Do you really think they'll have pickled ochart's tongue on this station?"

Jace snatched the list from her fingers. "I have a better idea. I'll do the shopping. You check out the bar. The guys in there are more likely to approach a single woman."

"I thought you didn't want to be on your own." She'd gone along with his change of plan so she could keep an eye on him. Fortunately, she'd had the foresight to attach a sensor device to his clothing, in case he took it into his mind to bolt.

"I'll be careful."

"All right, good luck."

After Jace strode away, she grabbed a seat in the lounge and ordered a Melarian brandy through the input screen on her table. As the botdrone delivered her drink, she twiddled her earrings to pick up snatches of dialogue spoken in the common Basic language.

"There's no way I'll move to that dust bowl. You're out of your freakin' mind. So what if the boss pisses on your shoes? Better the devil you know than one you don't."

"… you keep eating like that, and I won't be able to roll you out the docking port."

"She said if I wanted to see her again, I'd have to bonk her friend at the same time. Ho, jive that one, will ya?"

"He made me this deal, see, like I'm gonna get sixty percent if I do the run."

"And ye believed him?" someone replied. "That's just as good as his offer to pay fifty thousand for bagging that woman. A laser bolt in the back is what yer likely will get."

"Be that way, but I'll find out because she's here. Her ship docked for repairs just like Razor predicted."

Silver's head jerked up. Razor was a street name for

Tyrone Bluth since he sliced away anyone in his path. Were these men talking about her?

She fumbled in her pocket to pull out her credit chip, inserting it into the appropriate slot on the table before rising. Her long skirt snagged on an edge, and she yanked it free with a trembling hand. Her stomach roiled at the rancid odor of fried sorgut bellies as she strolled toward the entry.

"I need to look for her," continued the first man. "Razor was right mad that some slip of a gal with silver hair could get that close to him. No one like that got off the Avenger because I waited at the airlock. Some Elusian fellow and a couple of Mynoran traders debarked to the concourse."

"Ye think she sold her ship and them was the new owners?"

"Dunno. Who'd want to buy a damaged vessel?"

"Didn't you say the ship towed another craft?"

"Yep. Owner is Kurashki, a fella who claims it's leased. Look, there goes that Mynoran woman. She must know something."

Quick as lightning, the man knocked back his chair and shot over to her. Silver barely had time to register her surprise before he sprayed something in her face. She stumbled in the archway, spots dancing in front of her eyes.

A strong hand grasped her arm, propelling her forward.

"This way, lady. We have some talking to do." The second man flanked her other side. Wedged between them, Silver shook her head. If only her brain didn't feel like sludge. She couldn't formulate a clear thought.

"Ye works fast, Kev. No wonder Razor keeps you on."

"Wanna job? He's looking for newcomers."

"Mebbe. Make way, folks. This gal ain't feeling well. Drank too much of her brandy. Har har."

Silver struggled to twist away, but her limbs wouldn't cooperate. She made out Jace's voice coming from somewhere ahead. Dragged along, she scraped her heels to provide resistance. Bodies bumped into her, and she caught murmurs of disgust.

"Ish not drunk. Need hep," she muttered. Saliva pooled at the corner of her mouth. No one paid her any heed.

Jace. She spied him inside a boutique selling evening wear. What in Zolifer was he doing there when he was supposed to be buying food and other necessities?

No matter. She had to get his attention.

"There's her mate," warned Kev. "Head him off if he spots us. I'll meet you at delta level by the transient hostel."

"You want him, too? Or I should just crash him?"

"Crash and burn, Otto. We don't need two of `em. She'll tell us what we need to know."

Silver loosened her arm enough to twist one of her earrings. That should activate the transmitter in Jace's sensor, the one she'd planted on him. "Watch your back," she murmured.

His blond head lifted as he scanned the corridor. She could tell by his widening eyes the instant he noted her situation.

And then he did something that astounded her in return. He turned his back on her.

Her stomach clenched. She should have known better than to trust him. Had he tipped off these goons? Now he could leave with Mixy after the techs fixed their ships.

Sickness roiled through her gut. They'd made a bargain. She could have exposed him, but she'd kept her word.

That's what you get for counting on someone else.

Kev yanked her upright and hauled her toward a transport tube. When she kicked him in the shin, he backhanded her across the face. Her head snapped back, making her wig slip.

"You," Kev cried. "Lookey, Otto, we got us here a prize. Guess we'll take you to Razor himself, lady."

She heard the whine of the levelator. Once they got her inside that tube, she had two choices—kill or be killed. Another riskier, more dangerous option presented itself. Let herself be taken, and eliminate Bluth when she faced him in person.

"How'd you trace the Avenger to me?" she asked her captors.

"Razor has friends in high places." The door in front of them hissed open, and Kev thrust her inside. Otto leered when she didn't put up any resistance. In the confined quarters, he emitted an odor like smelly feet. Her skin prickled. The enclosure's shielding cut off her auditory sensors from outside. An ominous silence hung in the air, punctuated by Otto's heavy breathing. She didn't like the way he ogled her chest. Catching her glance, his grin broadened.

"Why we goin' down here?" he asked his partner. "Shouldn't we be headin' for yer ship?"

"Not yet." Kev picked his teeth. "I gotta check with Razor to see where he wants to hook up. You coming along?"

"Mebbe ye could contact him during pre-flight, ask if I can join the ranks. Or is he outta range?"

"Last I heard, Razor planned to hunker at Stacktown. Relays out that way been down for weeks."

Otto grunted. "Ain't nothin' in that hole `cept spooks. Why he wanna go there?"

Kev cleared his throat and spit on the floor. "Got wind of an auction. That's the only place where you can get carolla nuts."

"What's that?"

"You know, the crop that's refined into pure grade carollium. The nuts are harvested once every five years."

"I've heard tell that people who go to Stacktown don't come back. Don't seem worth it to me."

"We'll meet the boss elsewhere. If we have to wait for him, we might as well have some fun in the meantime. Razor will want this lady alive, but he didn't say nothin' about us tasting her first."

Silver's spine stiffened. *Touch me that way, and you're dead.*

Her mind might be foggy and her reflexes slow, but her limbs had regained agility. She'd fight when the time came.

Her breath hitched when the levelator dropped abruptly,

slowed, and came to a grinding halt. The door slid open. Kev tugged her into a smoky district where a raucous din overloaded her auditory sensors. Transient passengers, some stuck here indefinitely, roamed the labyrinth-like sector where cables snaked overhead and conduits belched steam.

She jerked her arm free, reaching up to twist her earring. "Jace?" she said, hoping he wasn't purposefully ignoring her. Maybe she'd been too hasty in assuming the worst about him. "If you can hear me, we're on delta deck."

Kev grabbed her elbow. "Whaddya doing? You got some kind of transmitter?"

Otto wagged his eyebrows, which didn't take much effort, considering they grew like a bush nearly to his bulbous nose.

"We'd better search her, don't ye think? Ye make yer call to Razor, and I'll take care of her."

Kev raked a free hand through his spiky blond hair. "I know a corner we can use. Nobody goes there 'cause it smells bad."

Like you? A shudder rippled through her while she considered her next move. Was it worth it to be used by these two hoodlums in order to reach Bluth? Even if she did get to him, she might be restrained and unable to carry out her mission. Wouldn't it be smarter to wait until she confronted the terrorist on her own terms?

"Help," she croaked to a passerby. "They're kidnapping me." Her voice sounded hoarse. The drug had made her throat dry.

The scruffy fellow glanced at her, averted his gaze, and scurried away.

"Shut up." Kev reached into his pocket and withdrew a syringe with a nasty inch-long needle. "You say one more word, and I'll use this. I'd rather have you awake, though. I like a woman squirming beneath me."

She kicked and scratched as they hauled her ahead, but her reactions felt lame, as though she slogged through mud. They entered a restricted area, part of a waste recycling center. The stench turned her stomach. No wonder visitors avoided the place. Evidently Kev had been here before, though, because he knew exactly where to take her.

Amidst pipes oozing filth and leaking sludge, he thrust her into an alcove. "I'll report to the boss after we're done," he told Otto. "You go first. I like to watch. Better make sure she doesn't have any hidden weapons." His scarred face stretched into a lecherous grin.

"Take off yer clothes, girlie," Otto ordered, his bulk looming over her. A feral gleam lit his eyes.

"Over my dead body." Crouching, she assumed a combat stance, elbows bent and hands stiff.

"If ye don't cooperate, we'll do it for ye. Ye may get hurt."

"Damage me, and your boss will be upset."

Her words didn't deter him. When Otto reached for her, she lashed out. Her foot caught him in the gut, but it didn't stop him. He tore at her dress. Ignoring the ripping noise that ensued, she thrust her palm at his face, intending to blast his nose into his brain. He deflected the blow, knocking her head with such force that she toppled onto her side.

In an instant, he was on top of her, tearing off her gown while forcing her onto her back. Kev knelt above her head to grasp her wrists with his meaty paw. With his free hand, he primed the syringe. Panic seized her as she watched a drop of liquid dribble from its tip. If she got stuck, forget it.

A rush of adrenaline cleared her mind. With a roar of rage, she bent her knee and brought it home into Otto's groin. His howl of pain reverberated in her ears as he jerked back. Cool air hit her bare flesh even as she twisted sideways and yanked her arms from Kev's single-handed grasp.

She leapt upward and kicked at his temple, but he dodged in time to avoid the blow. As he straightened, he took a swing at her. His elbow met her stomach, and she doubled over, gasping for breath. The next impact hit her jaw. She went down, stunned and helpless.

Kev's triumphant cry became a strangled choke.

"Need some help?" Jace called.

A body thumped to the floor. Silver concentrated on inhaling short breaths of air and slowing her heart rate. She ignored the sounds of fists thwacking and men grunting in the background as she regained her senses.

If she'd been operating on all cylinders, she might have realized the fighting had stopped. As it was, the resultant silence compelled her to push herself upright.

Kev lay immobile on the floor, his neck twisted at an unnatural angle. Otto lay close by, a dagger embedded in his chest. Jace stood over him, blood dripping from his hand.

****

Jace noted her dismayed expression. "Don't look at me like that. The guy lunged at me. I reacted automatically."

"You killed them. We could have gotten more information if you'd kept them alive." Refusing his offer of assistance, she struggled to her feet.

Stung by her words, he aimed back in kind. "Well, pardon me for not considering the options while I saved your sorry ass."

She rubbed her chin where a red blotch showed a bruise forming. "I only kill in battle when there's no alternative."

"Good for you. I tend to do what's necessary." Rage twisted through him, remnants of his fury from the sight of Silver on the floor, straddled by that thug. Images of his sister had popped into his mind. He could only imagine what horrors Shanna was experiencing as captive to some slave lord, assuming she was still alive. It had been enough to throw him over the edge.

Don't go down that road.

Bending, Jace retrieved his dagger and wiped it on the big thug's shirt. His loins tightened as he surveyed Silver's disheveled state. "Your gown… it's torn." She didn't appear overly shaken by the attack, merely annoyed with him for eliminating their witnesses.

"It'll hold together until we reach our ships."

"I wouldn't count on it. Here, take this."

She accepted his sash, drawing the edges of her garment together and securing them. Then she took off at a brisk pace just as a flashing strobe light pierced the gloom, accompanied by a shrieking siren. Jace jumped over a pair of cables snaking across the floor to catch up to her. Water splashed from a loose pipe joint. He stopped to rinse his hands. It wouldn't do to emerge in public covered in blood.

"Where's your hat?" Silver asked, halting to wait for him.

"I lost it in the fight." He loped toward her and they resumed their pace.

"And you left it behind? Good move, flyboy. Station police will use it as evidence linking you to the crime scene."

"Doesn't matter now. Keep moving."

They'd made it out of the restricted area and into the crowded transient sector when an armed security team emerged from the levelator tube. The bulk of the troops rushed toward the recycling plant, but a detachment broke away to question people. Smells of sweat and liquor penetrated the smoky haze as Jace watched them move from person to person.

Panic bloomed in his chest. Would they notice him? Vagrants surrounded him, grabbing at his finery. Surely he'd stand out in this crowd. He jabbed his elbow into a man attempting to detach his timepiece, then glanced at Silver who'd darted ahead of him.

His breath hitched when she changed vectors to approach the guards on a direct path. Her cool gaze met his for a brief instant before she turned away. She gave the tallest soldier a cloying smile and said something that absorbed his attention.

Jace's veins chilled as he experienced a sharp stab of betrayal. So this was the way of it. She'd expose him as a wanted criminal and collect the reward for his capture. He should have known he couldn't trust her. No doubt his killing rampage hadn't helped, but he'd been rescuing her. Gratitude must not count for much in her book.

He gave his wrist a sharp wrench, and a slicer disk slipped into his palm. He'd defend himself if necessary. His pulse thrummed in his ears while Silver spoke to the guards. Then she pointed toward a side corridor, gesturing fiercely.

His jaw dropped as the uniforms took off in the opposite direction. What had that been about?

He spotted Silver scurrying his way and hastily shoved his weapon back into its hidden sleeve.

"Get in the levelator before they realize what I've done." She pushed the button, and the door slid open.

"Yes, ma'am." Jace trailed her into the transport tube while his mind digested what he'd just seen. "You didn't give me away," he blurted after the stomach-lurching lift shot them several levels higher.

Thankfully, they were the sole occupants. Inhabitants from delta deck didn't often rise above their squalor unless they had the proper credits to move somewhere else. Station scientists couldn't afford to be charitable. They had their own problems with funding.

Silver tightened her sash, making Jace's gaze inadvertently slide to the swell of her breasts. He imagined his hands there, drawing the edges of her dress together, slipping his fingers inside to feel her soft flesh. In these close quarters, he could smell her subtle perfume. His senses must be fogged. He hadn't even noticed she'd lost her wig. Waves of platinum hair spilled over her shoulders.

"Don't think I care about you." Silver's blunt statement quelled his libido. "I deflected them to give us time to reach our ships. You're free to go, Jace. I've got more important things to do than turn you in."

"Oh?" His eyes narrowed suspiciously. "Like what? The only thing that interests you is finding Tyrone Bluth."

"Same as you." She lifted her eyebrows in challenge.

"You wouldn't let me go so easily. You've learned something, haven't you? Those men who attacked you, what did they say? Were they members of Bluth's gang?"

A shifting play of emotions crossed her face. "Kev was waiting for me." Silver spoke in a low tone, her violet eyes showing a flash of decision. "He works for Bluth, and they'd identified my ship. What bothers me is how they connected the Avenger to me so fast."

"Maybe they had access to a networked database."

"Kev said his boss had friends in high places, but I'm wondering if there's a snitch back home. I would have been assigned a ship by S.I.N., but I wanted to use my own. I'd already bought the Avenger with insurance money. So I asked my employer to lease the vessel from me. That arrangement should have been buried in their records."

"We're going to Earth from here to finish repairs. You can make inquiries then."

Silver opened her mouth to respond, but just then the levelator jerked to a stop, and the door slid open.

Chapter Five

"Tell me," Jace commanded when they emerged from the transport tube onto the main concourse, "why are you so eager to get rid of me, especially after I helped you?"

She sidestepped around a quartet of boisterous children playing tag while their parents shouted in vain to control them. "Stars, flyboy, I don't need any delays, and I'd have to file for your bounty if I turned you in. Why didn't you abandon me to those thugs?"

"I'm not in the habit of sending my partners to slaughter." *No, just your parents and sister.* The unspoken words burned into his brain.

"I'm not your partner."

He caught her hand, swinging her to face him. Her silver mane cascaded over bared shoulders where her gown had slipped from its makeshift fastening. Tearing his gaze from the pleasing view, he met her scornful eyes.

"You can't deny there's something between us. That's why you want to believe me."

"Ha!" She yanked her hand free. "The only thing I believe in is the justice of my mission. Besides, after that explicit demonstration below, I'd say you definitely have a tendency toward violence."

"Excuse me?" She'd turned away, and he hurried after her. "Thank you would be more appropriate. I saved your skin."

"And I saved yours. One word to those security guards, and you'd be on your way back to Kurash with an armed escort."

Jostling through the crowd, he glanced down the corridor to gauge the distance to the exit. He stiffened involuntarily upon catching sight of two Dorians. Tall, rangy, and unmistakably alien with their speckled skin, they swaggered toward an open café while everyone in their path moved aside.

"Comet dust," Jace muttered.

Silver, two paces ahead, halted as if she'd heard him. "Behave," she said as though she stood at his shoulder. "The war is over. Don't let them notice you."

"How do you do that?"

She beat a retreat and landed next to him, clinging to his arm like a proper Mynoran trader's woman. Careful to maintain his stride, he peered into shop windows with pretended interest.

"I put a locator sensor with an audio link on your jacket. Keep moving. As soon as security views its loop on what went down on delta deck, they'll be onto us."

"Did you inform the guards that you're a S.I.N. agent?"

"You think I would have blown my cover so readily?" she retorted, answering his question with a question. He recognized it as an annoying habit. "I said we'd seen a pair of pirates who have been plaguing the space lanes, and they were headed for beta sector. You seem to think I'm some sort of amateur."

"I just assumed you'd use your clout to get us off the hook." *Or to betray me.* "You're in jeopardy because I'm with you. If station forces realize who I am, they'll nail you as an accomplice."

"Then I'll flash my badge and claim you're under my custody."

"After we're caught on security cameras with two dead men? You'll have a lot of explaining to do. We both need a quick way out of here." He sniffed the fragrant aroma of fresh baked bread. His stomach growling, he searched for the source.

"Hey, where are you going?"

"We missed lunch. I'm hungry." He veered toward a bakery.

"You would think of food at a time like this. Did you manage to get the items on our shopping list before coming after me?"

He glanced back at her. "Most of them, but not all. I ordered everything to be sent to the ship. Wait here. I'm going to run in for a chaklah bread and some of those chocolate swirl rolls."

His fingers groped empty space inside his overcoat pocket. "Oh, no. Where's my credit chip?" He patted his other pockets before giving her a startled glance. "I must have left it in the clothing shop."

"We'll stop there on our way out. Let's hope the clerk is honest, and that he still has it. In the meantime, you can use my disk, but be quick." Her expression changed to confusion when she reached a hand into her skirt folds.

"What's the matter?"

"It's not here. I've lost mine, too."

"You mean we have no credits?" Jace knew he sounded incredulous, but he couldn't help it. This was the first time he'd found himself without funds. It was almost worse than facing Bluth's henchmen.

Get a grip. You can always tap into your reserve fund.

"Hey, you there," called a deep voice from behind. "The Mynorans. This is Hoatch Security Patrol. Stop where you are, and raise your hands in the air."

****

Dingbat's tail. They hadn't warded off the station police for very long.

"This way," Silver cried, veering in another direction as laser bolts whined past them. "There's a levelator on the other side of the wheel."

"How do you know?" Jace took off at a trot beside her.

"I studied the schematics. We'll go down to epsilon, cross

over to blue segment, then enter the spoke at that level. We can get to alpha from the science node. They all have emergency extension arms in case of separation. We should be able to reach maintenance from the rim."

He gave her an admiring glance. "You did your homework. Good job."

Her heart somersaulted at his compliment. She'd expected him to abandon her earlier, when it would have been easy for him to take charge of their ships and depart, leaving her behind. Instead, he had risked his life in a rescue attempt. It said things about his character and changed her perspective. When their roles reversed, she'd been unable to expose him as a hunted felon.

Don't get soft. He could only be using you for your resources. Trust no one. Yet her body had different ideas. Remembering his perusal of her cleavage earlier made her breath come short. Or maybe it was the laser beams sizzling through the air that heated her blood. Regardless of the cause, her heart thumped erratically.

Dodging weapons fire, they stumbled into a service levelator behind a hardware depot. After jabbing the button for epsilon deck, she sagged against a wall. The doors shut, and they descended precipitously.

"Now what?" Jace asked, hanging onto a safety strap.

A lock of bleached hair had fallen across his forehead, giving him a rakish look. Combined with his blood-streaked sleeve and stubbled jaw, he looked every bit the reputed criminal. An anticipatory gleam in his green eyes betrayed a reckless love of danger.

"We have to lose these clothes," Silver said, not realizing the innuendo until his smirk gave her the direction of his thoughts. "I mean, we're targeted as Mynorans. Let's look for a pair of worker coveralls. Labor crews reside on epsilon, so we shouldn't have any trouble finding new disguises."

"Milord, are you all right?" Mixy's anxious voice pealed from Jace's comm device when they emerged from the lift.

"Yes, I'm fine," he said, tapping his wrist unit for two-way communication. "That is, except for the goons I killed, the security people who are after us, and the fact that we are five decks on the opposite side from where we need to be."

"I see." Mixy's breathless tone reflected his master's excitement. "Our supplies arrived, but we are lacking the pickled tongue, inox truffles, and capsilon spice sticks."

"That's not important. Are the repairs finished?"

"Nearly so. The technician is fusing the last actuator as we speak."

Silver gave Jace an annoyed glance. "Can't you have this conversation later? We're being monitored." She gestured at a bank of holovid cameras.

Jace waggled his eyebrows. "Fine. I'll catch you later, Mixy. Signing off." He turned to Silver. "Tell me, my lady assassin, what other tricks do you have up your sleeve?"

"You'll see. Trust me."

He blocked her path, hands on his hips. "If we did it my way, we'd blast our way out of here."

"Oh, sure. Firing weapons is just what we need to get everyone off our tail. What happened to your diplomatic skills?"

"I'm not good at sneaking around. I prefer the frontal approach."

"The one that kills off the most opponents? So I noticed."

"Don't knock it. My action saved your life."

"Unless you want your efforts to be wasted, we'd better move on. We have to get across to blue side."

"Where do we go? This corridor branches in two directions."

Silver's pulse accelerated as a contingent of troops rounded a corner ahead of them. "Down there." She pointed to the other path as disruptor fire cut the air.

Her feet stumbled on the long skirt swishing about her ankles. The motion made her bodice sag open. Aware of her fate should those soldiers catch them, she surged forward. They needed to acquire more practical outfits without delay.

Multiple doors opened off the wide corridor. They'd have one chance to escape, before the soldiers had them in their line of sight again. Her vision zeroed in on a door lacking a coded entry. She rushed over and pushed it open.

After stepping across the threshold, she peered about the room in surprise. Clothing on hangers hung on tracks winding along the ceiling. Different colored bins stood beneath gaping openings, presumably chutes coming from upper levels. In the rear, machinery hissed and steamed like a mythical dragon. Workbot drones shuffled between sonic cleansers, oblivious to the intrusion. Eyeing them warily, Silver hoped they weren't fitted with security nodes.

"It's an automated laundry," Jace observed, his brows knitted. "We could hide in those containers under the shirts."

"Not good enough. The guards might come in here, or someone else might show up to check operations." She advanced toward one of the round chutes. "How are you at climbing?"

"Learned it in basic training. Watch this." Levering his hands on either side, he plunged feet-first into the aperture.

His grinning face dangled upside-down. "You coming?"

Angry voices reached her auditory sensors. "Right behind you."

She leapt after him, yanking a sheet into place to cover their trail. Jace twisted his body into a semi-upright position, thighs braced against the tunnel walls. She huddled by the entrance, straining to hear while her fingers touched cold duranium alloy.

Her muscles ached as she held her position. From her lower vantage point, she caught a tantalizing view of Jace's bottom. Now there was a butt worth the wait. She imagined him in tight-fitting jalobies and moistened her lips.

Speaking of a tight fit, the walls on their tunnel seemed to close in, especially when the sliver of light from the laundry room blinked out.

"No one here. They must have moved down the passage," a security trooper said in a gruff voice. "Let's post a guard outside anyway."

The sound of a door latching made fear grip her in its cold vise. Her body trembled as unwanted memories surfaced.

"Mommy, where are you? I'm scared. Why is everything shaking, and what are those loud noises? Why did you leave me here?"

Smoke drifted in through the cracks of her hideout. Her throat constricted. Her lungs burned for a breath of fresh air. If she dared to cough, one of the bad men might hear her.

"Mommy, I can't breathe. When are you coming back? Ow, my ears. I can't hear above the explosions."

Sweat beading her brow, Silver pushed aside those haunting images of her past.

"They've left a guard." She forced the words beyond her dry tongue. "We'll have to climb to the next level, but my legs are twisted in this damn dress." Gulps of air failed to calm her. She pressed a hand to her rib cage, her heart pounding.

"Too bad we didn't have time to snitch a couple of utility outfits, but we'll find some later." Jace's reassuring tone helped her to focus. He squeezed upward. "At least these walls are ridged. Can you get a grip?"

"Piece of cake."

"Cake? Where?"

She sighed. "It's an Earth idiom meaning easy."

Using her legs for leverage, she stretched her arms until her fingers found depressions in the metal tunnel. She tightened her thighs and propelled herself higher by a few notches. Their grunts resounded in the laundry drop. Silver's hands grew warm from friction as she progressed. Soon it became painful to touch the walls.

"Comet dust," Jace proclaimed, jerking back and nearly knocking her from a precarious perch. "Is it my imagination, or are these confounded panels heating up?"

Silver licked her raw fingertips. "We'd better wrap our hands."

Even as she spoke, the heat intensified. Droplets of perspiration trickled down her face. Bracing herself against the tunnel wall with her legs, she tore strips of material from her bodice.

"Here, use this cloth." She held up a handful for Jace.

Once she'd wound enough fabric around her own palms, she ordered him to move on.

Her breath came short, the hot air searing her lungs. She felt like a slice of beef in an oven. How much longer would this last? Tamping down her panic, she concentrated on her trembling muscles. *Find the next ridge to hold on, brace your legs, push.*

A wave of lightheadedness almost made her pass out. *Stop hyperventilating. You'll make it. You have to survive, so Bluth can pay for his wrongs.*

Gritting her teeth, she inched after Jace another measure. His taller length carried him farther into the black void. She heard the sound of his boots scraping against metal mixed with his labored breathing. Hearing and touch became the only sensory input available. No, there was something else. A smell. Familiar, but at the same time, elusive.

"The heat's off at this level." Jace sounded relieved. "Silver? Are you okay?"

"I'm coming. Do you see any sign of light yet?" She cursed when her foot tangled in her skirt. It was a miracle the silken material hadn't caught fire from the heated walls. If only she could get rid of the encumbrance.

"Get up here, then we'll rest a minute." Jace's voice cracked, and she imagined his throat felt like sandpaper, same as hers.

Finally, she ascended to the cooler zone. "Ah, I can breathe again." She sucked in a breath of fresh air.

"I have to remove this frigging overcoat. It's hindering my movements besides being hot as Zolifer," Jace said from above. "Watch out." Rustling noises sounded in the dark, followed by a heavy weight of brocade fabric falling onto her shoulders. "Sorry about that," he said when she cried out.

She scrunched against a wall, then swept his coat into the

drop. His action motivated her to do the same. Digging her fingers into her skirt, she tore at the waistband until the material fell away. The remnants of her dress followed his overcoat. She wriggled her legs to the extent possible in her cramped position. The sudden freedom felt wonderful. She unwound the shredded fabric around her hands without losing her balance, and tossed it after the other items.

"Here comes my shirt," Jace added in a wry tone. "Might as well get rid of that, too. We're too conspicuous in these clothes."

"You think?"

He chuckled, a low, deep rumble. "I'm glad you're a gal with a sense of humor. You're a real trooper, you know?"

She warmed to the admiration in his voice but would never let him know it affected her. "I'm a trained operative. Escaping from sticky situations is part of my job."

"That's good, because the walls are sticky up here. It's damp at the section just beyond the curve."

"Keep moving." She grunted with effort, scraping her elbows against the metal walls. "Someone might enter the laundry room and spot our clothing below."

She could think of worse companions. Jace didn't act like a hardened criminal. If he'd wanted to get rid of her, he could have done it several times over. Even now, he could kick her head in and make his own escape. Yet he waited for her to catch up to him, inquired about her well-being, and even cracked jokes. His behavior didn't jive with the violence he'd unleashed in the transient hold.

"Look out!" Jace cried suddenly.

She heard the dripping water before it plopped onto her exposed skin. Ping… ping. It hit her shoulders with all the subtlety of a dentist's sonic drill. Ping… ping… ping. She inhaled a sharp breath, catching the fresh scent of rain. Rain, in here? Before she could consider what it meant, her auditory sensors detected a roaring noise.

A waterfall gushed past, and her back began to slide. She

lunged for a handhold while gasping for air. Water clogged her nostrils and sloshed past her face. Wet strands of hair lashed her skin as she struggled to climb past the barrage.

"It's not far. Keep going," Jace called, his voice faint.

If not for her earrings, she would have missed his words. They'd lost the audio link on her sensor along with his jacket.

Water streamed down, pounding her shoulders, beating her shaking limbs. With a loud groan, she pushed her strained muscles another few notches. Just as quickly as it started, the downpour vanished. "Thank the stars." If they ever reached their ship, she wouldn't move for a week. Her body felt like it had been through a wash cycle. "Hey, I get it. Jace, do you hear me? These chutes must be a cleansing device for their industrial laundry. I'll bet they use it for cleaning standard issue uniforms, judging from those shirts we saw down below."

"That's just terrific. I'm in the detergent section. It's too slippery to get a grip." His voice edged with panic.

"Can you see an opening yet?"

"There's a light up ahead. Wait, I brought something that may help." A sharp crack ensued, followed by scraping noises and then Jace's triumphant cry. "We're outta here. I hooked a line. See if you can reach it."

Without his help, she would never have gotten a grasp on the slimy walls where soapy detergent oozed from tiny pores. Jace let her edge past him where the chute widened, giving her a boost before following at her heels.

Before long, Silver reached the yawning aperture above. She grabbed the rim, swung herself over, and tumbled onto a cold floor. She rolled to her feet in an empty room. Every body part ached. No time to worry about that now. She'd better secure the place from station personnel.

She sped to the exit to check the corridor outside. All clear. After shutting the door, she latched it before inspecting the room for vidcams. Plenty of soap jugs, laundry carts, soaking tubs, and supplies, but no security monitors.

Glancing down as her skin chilled, she realized she had nothing on except her underwear. Her body was sopping wet and slick with soap. They didn't dare leave a trail of water in their wake. Getting dried and clothed took precedence over everything else.

****

Getting clothed was the farthest thing from Jace's mind when he emerged from the laundry drop and caught a glimpse of Silver. Clad only in her lacey undergarments, she presented a tantalizing view, especially when he remembered nuzzling her bosom to get the restraints key.

Raising his glance to her face, he caught her staring at his bare chest. She flushed at his perusal and averted her gaze, but not before he noted the interest in her eyes.

"I don't know about you, but I have to wash this glop off." He indicated the suds clinging to his skin. "Want me to hose you down first?" At the nearest tub, he held up a flexible tube attached to the faucet. Without waiting for a reply, he flicked it on and directed a spray in her direction.

Instead of shrieking in protest like he'd expected, she squared her shoulders and lifted her chin. "Don't forget my hair," she told him in a breezy tone as though this ritual were routine.

She rotated slowly until she faced him again. Her curves sent his pulse racing. As if that wasn't enough to arouse him, she unhooked her bra and flung it to the ground. His jaw dropped at her bold action.

"It's not as though you haven't seen me half-naked before, so we might as well get this over with." Her panties joined the pile on the floor.

Jace lowered the hose, his breathing ragged. The stream of water slowed to a trickle, its force dependent on direction. A familiar pressure built inside his sodden trousers.

"What are you doing?" He swallowed as she sauntered closer. His gaze slid to her firm breasts and taut nipples before roaming lower to the juncture between her thighs.

"Giving you the thanks you deserve."

She sidled up to him, scraping her knuckles across his navel. He sucked in a sharp intake of air, aware that his response was quite evident. Her lips parted as she tilted her face, bringing her mouth inches from his. Her brandy-scented breath warmed his skin.

Uttering a groan, he pressed the small of her back to draw her near. Torn between wanting to admire her lithe body and needing to savor her soft skin, he bent his head for a taste. Just as he touched her lips, she jerked back.

"Never let down your guard," she admonished while he stared at her in confusion. "And don't let yourself get distracted when you're working with me. Understand?"

His spine stiffened. "What is this, some sort of lesson?" A chill entered his voice. "You're the one who is afraid of letting down her guard. You don't dare let your feelings show. Do you think it will make you less effective as an agent? Well, allow me to demonstrate where you really stand."

He jammed her against his chest, lowered his head, and pressed his lips to hers. Frustration and fury mixed to fuel his onslaught. Captivated by her boldness and enraged by her withdrawal, he ravished her mouth with brutal force.

She fought him at first, trying to wrestle him down, but this time he used tricks from combat training. Sparring with her slick body only raised his ardor. Their tussling affected her as well, because when he plunged his tongue inside her mouth, her effort weakened. She stretched her arms around his neck and relaxed her jaw.

Elated, he explored deeper, tracing the contours of her teeth. Molten fire thrummed through his veins. She smelled like hot, sweet sex. When his fingers lightly caressed her breasts, she sagged as though her knees had buckled. Masculine pride surged through him, and he dared to trail his hand south. Her moist response almost unraveled him. Almost.

He stepped back, lowering his arms. "You've been frozen for so long, you've nearly forgotten how to live. Hatred can do that to you, Silver. But now I see the volcano you're hiding under all that ice. You're no killer. Help me catch Tyrone Bluth and turn him in for trial."

Her beautiful face hardened into a mask. "I'm sorry to disappoint you, but my purpose remains clear. Just because I'm attracted to you doesn't mean I'll forfeit my goal."

At least she'd admitted there might be something between them. But her problems went deeper than her mission assignment. She needed help getting over the traumatic events in her past. Unfortunately, the woman wouldn't let anyone near enough to break the shell she'd built around herself.

Nor was he the best person to try. Maybe he didn't murder his family, but he had been guilty of not keeping his guard up as she'd said. Had he been more alert, he might have prevented the carnage from taking place at all. Then there were those two guards he'd pounded to pieces on delta deck. Yep, she had plenty of reasons to keep her emotional distance from a man like him. Trying to force a response from her only proved how low he'd fallen.

"You're absolutely right," he replied. "Now that we've established how we're using each other, let's find some clothes and get out of here."

Chapter Six

Silver dried herself with a couple of rags before pulling on a utilitarian gray jumpsuit she found lying across a chair. Aware that each minute increased their risk of discovery, she dressed with haste. The coarse material grated against her skin, reminding her with a swell of warmth of how Jace's touch had seared her body. She'd wanted to mash her lips to his, to feel his hands stroking her skin, to inhale his manly scent. Why had she responded to him when no one else in recent memory had been able to stir her?

His statement that they were using each other added a log to the fire. If he truly had not committed the sins for which he stood accused, he had every reason to seek justice. She couldn't blame him for taking advantage of any means possible to achieve this goal. A surge of sympathy overtook her. They both carried enough emotional baggage to fill a cargo hold.

Cold feet reminded her to replace her sodden slippers. She tugged on a pair of handy worker shoes. Her blood quickened when she stole a glance at Jace, folding his pant cuff over a knife strapped to his ankle. Why did he have to be such a handsome devil?

Forcing herself to focus, she strode to the door, unlocked it, and peeked outside to see if the corridor was clear.

Jace didn't seem in any hurry to join her. Using a metal trim shield as a mirror, he ruffled his fingers through his strands of lightened hair as though preparing for a political speech. If he wasted more time preening, she'd move on alone.

"Will you put that thing down?" she said. "We need to get out of here."

He plunked it on a counter and threw her an irritated glance. "I'm trying to make myself decent so we don't stand out in a crowd. You should do the same."

"Grooming is the last thing on my mind."

"Is that so? You're the one likely to get caught. You look like the Snow Queen."

"Excuse me?"

"One glance in your direction, and every man in this facility will remember you. Can't you tuck your hair into a knot or something to make yourself less noticeable?"

From his wry expression, it appeared he was more concerned with the notion of her being a disturbing influence on himself rather than the station's crew. Nonetheless, he'd scored a point. She separated her damp strands of hair, quickly twisted the sections into a braid, and tied the ends with a gray shoelace found on a shelf.

A final search revealed a row of hats. She snatched a cap and stuck it on her head before slipping into the corridor. Now they only had to reach blue side to access the science module. From there they could elevate to the rim and the docking bays.

"Do you suppose Mixy is holding off the hounds?" she asked, experiencing a twinge of anxiety. "We haven't updated him on our situation."

"Security is looking for two Mynorans. Mixy would have told them the ships were stolen from their rightful owners, whom he represents. They'll confirm his story with my ally on Kurash."

Voices alerted her to a group ahead of them at the next junction. Silver just had time to give Jace a warning poke when a team of four maintenance men and two women strolled in their direction.

"Heya, aren't you two going to the meeting?" a lean fellow said. His thick eyebrows nearly grew together, looking incongruous on his narrow face.

"Sure, we'll be there soon." Jace gave a two-fingered salute. "Gotta couple of errands to do on the way."

The man tilted his head, as though not quite buying their excuse. Thinking fast, Silver drew him aside.

"We're new here, so cut us some slack. These corridors are confusing. It's hard to get oriented."

Tension eased from the man's shoulders. "See that you're not late. Hammersan has a fit if the seats aren't filled, and he'll dock you the day's pay."

One of his pals heard and snorted. "That's not such a big deal after what he's going to say. Those pirate raids in the Kaloran sector have delayed shipments. Revenue is down, so we're gonna get a pay cut anyway."

"Work more, and get paid less," grumbled the taller woman. "Ain't it a bitch?"

Silver knitted her brows. "What do you mean by shipments? I thought the repair bays and shops brought in revenue."

The crew man scratched his arm. "Spare parts ain't coming in. Can't do no ship repairs if you ain't got the equipment."

She gave Jace a worried glance. Hopefully, their ships had been fixed enough for them to reach Earth. Mixy would have notified them otherwise.

"It's not fair to dock your… our pay," she remarked while Jace tugged impatiently on her elbow. "Why doesn't the dockmaster find another supplier?"

The lean worker guffawed. "Suggest that to Hammersan. You'll be outta here before you take another breath." He slapped a teammate on the shoulder. Laughing, they proceeded down the corridor.

"What in Zolifer is the matter with you?" Jace snarled as they strode through the winding corridor without meeting any more workers. His shoulders hunched like a bear stalking the woods. "You have no right to offer your opinion on the affairs of this station, nor do we have the time to waste. Who cares why their pay is being cut?"

She studied the gray walls striped with a horizontal blue line. "I have my reasons."

"Oh, yeah? I hope your act is good enough to get us into the science module. If you've noticed, we're in blue sector. The entry chamber is just ahead. How do you plan to get us through the validation process?"

"Easy. I'll use my super secret spy gadgets. Watch this."

****

Jace grabbed for her sleeve to halt her progress, but she nudged him out of the way and edged past.

One wrong move, and she'd be history. If this entry held the standard encryptions, she'd have three chances to hit the right code. If she missed, toxic gases would reduce her to a puddle on the floor. With horrified disbelief, he watched her slip inside the circular chamber. The transparent door sealed shut behind her.

She frowned with concentration as she punched numbers into a keyboard, spoke into a voice analyzer, and stuck her hand into a formatron.

Several quick paces brought him flat up against the panel. He spread his fingers on the clear, hard surface, wondering how to save her if she failed.

She withdrew her hand and tried again while her lips drew back in exasperation. Her features expressed relief at the third attempt.

She'd passed? But how, unless they had her prints on file?

That left the retinal scan, and he didn't know how she'd get by this one, unless she wore a disguised contact lens. She bent forward, fit her eye to the device, and waited for the instrument to measure her parameters. Jace jerked back when the light inside the chamber switched to a bluish glow.

Silver straightened, then cocked her head as though listening to instructions. While Jace shifted his feet impatiently, she mouthed something to the wall, as though talking into a speaker. Then she turned toward him with a triumphant grin. Two doors slid open simultaneously—one in front of him, and one at the opposite end of the chamber.

He squeezed her elbow when he reached her. "That was remarkable. How did you do it?"

"Tricks of the trade. Let's go."

Her smug expression erased when she stepped across the threshold into an airlock where they suited up. Thus garbed, they entered the outer spoke, floating in zero gravity. Jace followed her lead, pulling himself along on the grip bars. It would have been easier had they donned magnetic boots, but this saved time.

Past the next airlock, they stood in a small vestibule once again in their borrowed utility outfits. Footsteps sounded from around a corner. Jace's heart lurched when four people strode into view. Judging from their white lab coats, they were scientists. Silver gave them a broad smile.

A middle-aged woman addressed her. "Welcome to Bartlett Station, Miss Malloy."

Jace gaped at his companion. "They know you?"

"They recognized my entry code. I've been here before."

"What? And you didn't think to share that nugget with me?"

"I'll tell you more later. Guys, meet a friend of mine. His name is Jack Guess." She swept a hand at Jace.

"I'm Dr. Caldwell," stated a fellow with a white beard. "It's a pleasure to meet you, Mr. Guess."

Jace shook the man's hand, resisting the urge to shake his head instead. Silver seemed to be a few steps ahead of him. Not only had she sent the guards below decks in the wrong direction, but she'd been smart enough to present him to her friends with a false name. Despite her leaving out certain critical details, the lady could be handy in a crisis.

"We didn't expect your visit," Dr. Caldwell said, "or we would have made better arrangements. I'm sure you'll find your spot inspection to be satisfactory. Let's make the rounds."

Silver showed real interest, asking questions as the researcher took them on a cursory tour of a microbiology lab, aquaponics center, filtration matrix, and vats swarming with live anhunda. Viewing the large scaly fish fascinated Jace, especially when Caldwell explained how the nutrient-rich water from the tanks fed the vegetables growing in the garden. Hmm, maybe he could adapt these techniques on his home world.

"I'd like to know how you control the overpopulation problem in the fish tanks," Silver told the group. "Doesn't the average female hatch over three hundred fingerlings every month? That's a tremendous harvest. It could easily get out of hand."

While Silver discussed fish breeding techniques with the scientists, Jace bent to sniff a tomato on the vine in the vegetable section. He couldn't believe the produce they grew here. Mixy would love to get hold of some fresh lettuce, peppers, eggplants, or squash.

"I don't suppose we can buy some of these crops?" he began. He caught Silver's glare aimed in his direction. Oh, right. No credit chips.

Her eyebrows arched when a red strobe light flashed over the door. "I'm afraid we have to cut this visit short. Our ship is waiting. Next time, I'll be sure to give you advance warning of our visit. Thanks so much, Dr. Caldwell."

Anticipating her move toward the rim lift, Jace punched the call button while waiting for her to join him. The chief scientist wouldn't let her go so easily. After the other members of his team murmured platitudes and dispersed, Caldwell trailed in her wake.

"Allow me to give you a small token of our appreciation. You have no idea how many people you're helping by funding our work here."

"Doctor," cried the woman researcher from a console by the wall. "A security team is requesting entry into this spoke. They're threatening to override our protocols if we don't comply."

"What do they want?" Caldwell demanded.

"We, uh, got involved in a slight incident down below," Silver said, casting Jace a warning glance.

Caldwell stuffed some vegetables into a wire basket and handed Silver the goods. "You'd better move along. I'll stall them." The lift door hissed open. "Come again soon," he shouted as they leapt inside.

The doors shut, and they rocketed upward in a teeth-jarring ascent.

"What was that all about?" Jace had shared his background with her, but apparently she hadn't been totally honest with him. Gripping the safety straps, he stared at her while the levelator buffeted their bodies.

"I have an interest in the Hoatch Foundation." Her shoulders lifted in a carefree shrug.

"That's a scientific organization. I thought you gave up your former career when you joined S.I.N.?"

"I quit my job as a research agronomist, but that doesn't mean I gave up my investments."

"But I figured you were—"

"Poor?" Her derisive tone of voice told him what she thought of this assumption.

"A colonist on Altuis Three when your parents were killed," he finished.

"Just because my parents chose a roughshod way of life doesn't mean they came from poverty. What else would I expect you to believe, though, when Kurash endorses a political system based on hereditary titles?"

Ignoring her barb, he persisted to draw her out. "But if you have wealth, and you use it to fund this station, why would you throw yourself away by going after Bluth when other people depend upon your support?"

Her eyes narrowed into slivers of amethyst. "No one is safe until Bluth's raids stop. You heard what that crewman said today about the Kaloran sector. Shipments aren't getting through due to pirate attacks. That's brought revenues down, caused delays, and reduced morale. It has a cyclical effect on the researchers in the science modules, because they depend upon income from the repair facilities, as well as from the merchants, to offset expenses. My foundation only supplies basic operating capital."

"I see." Admiring her generosity, he realized she felt a sense of responsibility toward these people but not enough to supply a reason to live. Her wounds must be so deep as to encase her heart in stone.

He wanted to ask what had happened to her after Altuis Three, when she'd moved in with her relatives on Earth. Had she expressed her grief, or had she bottled it up, only to be dealt a second blow later on Roth Colony?

Perhaps he'd get a chance for answers if he met her family. That is, assuming their ships were in condition to take them to Earth. Assuming Mixy had gotten launch clearance. And assuming Jace wasn't recognized and detained as soon as he stepped foot on Silver's home planet.

Those were a lot of assumptions, including the one about why he cared. If he were smart, he'd look after his own skin. He'd rescue Shanna and Yvette and then face his own demons. Someone had killed two men down on delta deck, and he wasn't sure he recognized that man as himself. If he harbored seeds of violence that burst out of control and even out of his own cognizance, he didn't deserve to judge Silver's life or anyone else's, because his own should be forfeit.

****

Silver sensed Jace's mood swing before the levelator doors opened and they emerged onto rim deck. Noting the clanging klaxons and amassed troops, she hoped Mixy had readied their ships for immediate departure.

"Milord!" Mixy hurried toward them, his elaborate hairdo askew. "I sensed your imminent arrival, but I have the most grievous news." His robe faded into jade, which Silver took to mean agitation.

"What is it?" Jace queried, his tone curt.

Silver glanced at their ships, moored within viewing distance. She should have picked up the sound of rumbling engines, if Mixy had completed the pre-launch procedures.

Her heart sank. "There's no vibration. Fusion hasn't even begun. Mixy, how do you expect us to get out of here?"

"That is what I'm trying to tell you, madam. Follow me." He led them away from the nearest cluster of troops. "Our vessels have been appropriated by station security. They're looking for the two Mynorans who docked here. It was only through cunning, plus a couple of bribes, that I avoided being detained and was able to secure us another ride."

"Don't tell me we're boarding someone else's ship as passengers?" Jace said, while Mixy's robe suffused with ebony.

"Don't be angry with him," Silver chided. "Listen to what he has to say."

"We're hired as crew aboard a freighter." Mixy bobbed his head. "Best to keep moving, milord. You're attracting curious glances from those soldiers."

"But we've changed our disguises."

"They're interested in anyone who talks to me. Those vegetables will come in handy," Mixy remarked as they followed him toward a cigar-shaped Class II Foxhorne with blast damage on its hull and old-style round portholes. "I've signed on as cook."

"I have things aboard the Avenger," Silver protested. "I can't just leave them there."

Jace agreed with Mixy's assessment. "We have no choice. Exposing your identity as the station's benefactor won't help us, either. You'd still have to answer to security same as me for those two bodies below. I doubt you want to be outlawed."

She whirled to face him. "I could take you into custody as a S.I.N. agent and blame you for their deaths."

"Don't threaten me."

Mixy's robe mixed green with hot pink swirls. "Oh, dear. This is so upsetting." He raised a hand to his forehead. "Will you two please express this tension you feel in each other's presence in another manner?"

Silver didn't have a chance to reply because a woman stepped forward to greet them as soon as they boarded the freighter and the hatch sealed. She wore soiled fatigues, a weary expression, and scraggly bangs above a bony forehead that proclaimed her Findale origins. So did the unusual shimmer to her hair.

"Welcome to the Sawbone. I am Eynice. Come, I will show you to your duty stations."

"Can we meet the captain?" Silver asked, anxious to confirm their destination. The deck vibrated underfoot. A series of thumps indicated the docking clamps being detached.

"Later. Captain Keelo is occupied on the bridge."

"Where should we deposit this food?" Jace swung the vegetable-laden basket.

Mixy raised his wispy brown eyebrows. "My companions are hungry," he told Eynice. "Might I be allowed to fix them a meal before they begin work? They will toil more efficiently if their culinary needs are met first."

Silver gritted her teeth. She didn't care for this delay in their plans and liked it even less that she didn't know exactly where they were heading. From the frown on his face, and the emerald tint to Mixy's robe, Jace seemed unhappy as well.

The mess hall revealed several crew members taking their late shift meal. Their disinterested glances reassured her. Likely they had more to hide than she or Jace.

They murmured greetings, expressing gratitude to Mixy that they wouldn't have to eat ration packs anymore. Fortunately, he'd been able to transfer their fresh stores to this ship's galley. The men were a motley lot, which increased Silver's resolve to keep to herself.

Fate had other plans, however. Once they finished a quick repast, their guide Eynice indicated on a schematic the deck where their cabin was located.

"Cook will stay with us in the crew quarters, but your credits rate better accommodations. Our second mate cashed out on our last haul, so his cabin is yours. Don't think it merits special treatment, though. You're expected to pull your weight same as everyone else, otherwise we'll drop you at our next stop."

"Where is that?" Jace drawled.

"Remnant Two."

Silver fixated on what Eynice had said first. "Wait a minute. Did Mixy already pay for our cabin? Because if not, we'd rather stay with the crew."

No way was she going to room with Jace. If anything, his valet should share his space.

"The arrangements are complete." Eynice moved off to join a group of chattering females in a corner. They flicked glances her way, making her uncomfortable.

"Do not be concerned." Mixy spoke to Jace in an undertone which her auditory sensors picked up. "I used our open line of credit from Falkner's World."

So, now she knew where Jace the outlaw had stashed his reserves. If he had sufficient funds, he could obtain a new credit chip at any depot. Why hadn't he said something earlier? Moreover, this crew knew he wasn't destitute. Hard pressed for cash, some of them might be tempted to thievery.

She noticed Mixy's robe lightening to a happy orange. "What's so amusing?" she snapped at Jace, aware the valet merely reflected Jace's emotions.

Her companion slapped a hand on her shoulder. "You're more concerned with our sleeping arrangements than where we're going."

"I am not." She remembered what Eynice had said. "Remnant Two is close to Stacktown. It's an easy jumping off point."

"Who said anything about Stacktown? We'll be only twelve days from Earth at top speed. Maybe we can convince Captain Keelo there's good business in that direction."

Silver shut her mouth, remembering Jace hadn't heard her conversation with Bluth's thugs. Somehow she'd have to get another ship, so she could follow the hot tip about Stacktown before the Marauder's trail went cold again.

Eynice rejoined them. "Come, I will take you to your duty stations."

Silver and Jace, with Mixy shuffling behind, followed her through a maze of corridors.

"What's that noise?" Silver winced, twisting her earring to lower the sudden din. It came from behind a pair of double doors blocking the passage ahead.

Mixy halted, his robe swishing. "If you do not require my services any further, milord, I shall return to the galley. I can check in with you later regarding your toilette."

"Never mind." Jace patted his shoulder. "You'll have your hands full feeding this lot."

Mixy hurried off, while Jace's nose wrinkled. Silver guessed he smelled the same odor she did. No doubt that's why Mixy had been so eager to leave.

Eynice pushed open the doors and indicated they should enter. Silver could never have guessed what lay beyond. Dozens of wounded civilians, groaning and twisting in agony, rested on makeshift gurneys while a paucity of staff tended to their intravenous lines and monitors.

Silver gazed around in dismay. "Is this a hospital ship? I thought you carried cargo."

A predatory gleam entered the crew member's eyes. "So it says on our manifest."

"But these are people."

Beside her, Jace stiffened. "I gather these unfortunates are their cargo. Explain," he ordered Eynice.

Eynice's gaze turned cold. "It's relatively simple. We move

in at the aftermath of a battle, pick up the wounded, and care for them."

"And then?" Jace encouraged while Silver surveyed the scene with horror. She'd seen enough outcomes of brutal attacks to never want to be a witness again.

"Then we deliver them to the Crockers."

"T-those reptilians? Whatever for?" Silver sputtered.

"I get it." Jace glowered at Eynice. "That's why the Raptor star system is off-limits for my people. The Crockers feed on other species."

Eynice led them inside toward a central post. "They pay well for each live human. We nurse the unfortunates back to relative health and boost their nutrients."

"So they can be eaten?" Silver's skin crawled.

"They'd be dead anyway if left alone."

"Why did you stop at the space station?" She hoped no one there was in cahoots with these degenerates.

"We needed to make some repairs and took in a fresh supply of branna leaf for our medical stores. We use the herb in a poultice that makes wounds heal faster. Everyone knows their hydroponics labs produce the best greens in this sector. Wait here. I'll tell Sublieutenant Mos'ot you are starting your shift."

Jace thrust his fingers through his decidedly darker hair. The dye was fading fast after their water bath. If the crew recognized him, they were doomed.

"I'm going to kill him," Jace growled, facing her.

"Who?"

"Mixy. He must have known what he was getting us into."

"I doubt he had many other choices. We'll have to jump ship at the first opportunity."

"And leave these people?"

Silver planted a hand on her hip. "Much as I'd like to save everyone, it's impossible. May I remind you that our goal is to locate Tyrone Bluth? If we get sidetracked, we risk failure."

"You'd mentioned Stacktown earlier. What is so interesting about it?"

She glanced away. "I heard rumors that Bluth hangs there sometimes." Her auditory sensors picked up the sound of his teeth gnashing.

"Just when were you going to share this information? After you deserted Mixy and me to follow your target? Bluth is there, isn't he?"

She gave a reluctant nod. "The goons who attacked me said the Razor plans to visit Stacktown for an auction of carolla nuts." At this rate, she'd never catch the scum.

"We have to go to Earth first," Jace insisted. "You've got a mole in your organization. How else could Bluth have traced your ship's registry so fast? Plus we can obtain a new vessel at the yard where your cousin works."

"I'd only planned to stop at Gravicom Wells to get the Avenger fixed. That detour is unnecessary now."

"Do you know when this auction will take place?"

"I have no idea. But even if we missed it, we might gain information about Bluth's next target."

"Stacktown is a sinkhole. People go there and never return. It's said to be haunted."

"Nonsense, they hold the auctions, don't they? Who would go planetside if it was so dangerous?"

His icy glare revealed his opinion. "We'll stick to our original plan. S.I.N. has resources we can use to track him."

"I'm more worried about getting off this ship without becoming a piece of cargo."

He grasped her arm. "We need to watch each other's backs. Can I count on you?"

Her gaze hardened, even as her heart quickened at his touch. "As long as we keep following the Razor's trail, you're my man."

Chapter Seven

While Jace tended an injured child as instructed by the medical supervisor, he considered Silver's words. Single-minded in her goal of assassinating Tyrone Bluth, she couldn't be swayed from her purpose. Not even if it meant saving dozens of innocents destined for a meal platter. He could no more leave them to their horrendous fate than he could tear his own heart out.

What if his sister had been sold to the Crockers? Pain dug deep into his soul, pricking him with needle points of guilt. Maybe he'd failed his family, but he might be able to do some good here. That is, if Silver didn't betray him.

The child, a blond-haired girl about six years old, stared up at him with misery-glazed eyes. He'd been irrigating her leg wound with a saline solution, astounded by the lack of analgesics. From their pitiful moaning, most of these people would be better off dead. He wondered if he could steal some pain medicine from the crew's sickbay.

"Where's my mommy?" the girl asked in a plaintive tone.

"I'm sorry, I don't know. What's your name, honey?"

"Liselle. I want to go home," she sniffed. "Ow, that hurts."

"Hold still, please." Using an abrasor, he scraped away some necrotic tissue, while relating a childhood tale to distract her. She could use an antibiotic, too. Wishing his medical skills went past basic training, he applied a clean dressing. At least he'd gained some first-hand trauma experience during his combat tour.

How was Silver doing? She worked over a woman's

draped form, fiddling with some tubing. Her pasty complexion nearly matched the color of her glorious hair. Jace wouldn't have taken her for the squeamish sort, but live and learn. You'd think seeing these people's anguish would make her want to help them, but only a miracle could melt her icy core.

He completed care on three more patients, consulted his assignment sheet, and moved on to a shriveled old man crying for someone named Angie. The poor guy had his foot blown off and wore a bloody dressing that needed to be changed. Jace swore under his breath, wishing for an ounce of delium. How could he inflict this kind of torment without the proper medication?

Putting down the patient's chart on a mobile table, he stalked to their supervisor, a burly fellow wearing a red-splattered apron. Sublieutenant Mos'ot was resetting someone's broken forearm. Fortunately, the victim remained unconscious, but Jace still wondered why the guy bothered. Perhaps the bounty was higher if bodies were in better condition.

"What is it?" Mos'ot demanded without glancing up. His thick yellowish hide came from a race unfamiliar to Jace.

"Are any other medications available?" Jace pointed to the little girl. "She needs analgesics and an antibiotic."

Mos'ot snorted with laughter. "We don't waste resources on property. Get back to work. You've been given all you'll need."

"These people must have something for their pain. It's inhumane to make them suffer."

The supervisor straightened to his full height, a good head above Jace. "They ain't people. They're fodder. Our only job is to keep them alive. If you have a problem with that, I'll be happy to set you straight."

Mos'ot snatched a scalpel with a two-inch blade and brandished it in the air. A dribble of spit formed at the corner of his mouth.

Maintaining eye contact, Jace tensed his muscles. Before the conflict escalated, the doors behind them burst open.

"You!" An armed crewman aimed a disruptor at Jace. "The captain wants to see you. Now."

****

"Why have you disguised yourself?" Captain Keelo asked Jace when he arrived on the bridge. "You've changed your hair color. You and your woman wear clothing like station maintenance crew, yet you are not on our recruitment roster."

"Mixy said you were taking us on without asking questions."

"I'm asking them now." The captain's cobalt eyes bored into him. From his commanding presence, close-cropped hair, and tailored uniform—insignias missing—Jace surmised the stocky man had military training.

Folding his arms across his chest, Jace assumed a cocky expression. "I've done a few things to make me steer clear of the law. I'm sure you understand."

"Normally I don't question my crew, but your Elusian companion didn't sign on for our regular payroll. You and your lady friend are transient crew. I gotta make sure you won't relate what you've seen. So who are you?"

Jace considered his response. It appeared Keelo was more concerned with saving his own skin than turning Jace in. "If I tell you, how do I know you won't sell me out?"

The captain grinned, exposing a row of yellowed teeth. Evidently, his grooming didn't include visits to the dentist.

"For the same reason you don't care to share your identity. If I surrender you, the patrols will look into my logs. Standard freighter cargo is listed on our manifest. We're not prepared for an official inspection."

Jace spread his hands in a magnanimous gesture. "Don't you bribe people? I assume that's how you continue your trade."

"We're good at dodging patrols. I ask again, who are you?"

"My name is Jace Vernon."

Keelo's face registered stunned recognition. "The

Kurashki criminal? The Elusian said you needed passage to the Terran system. Why there?"

"I have to buy another ship. Mine got confiscated on the space station."

The captain's gaze chilled. "We almost didn't make it out because someone murdered two men on delta level. Station security threatened to close all traffic." He tightened his lips, and Jace guessed Keelo was calculating the odds of turning him in for the bounty versus the risk of exposure. Perhaps he could sweeten the pot.

"How much do you get for each of your, uh, bodies?" He swallowed the distaste on his tongue.

"Five hundred high grade turanium bars."

"I'll pay you three thousand above what Mixy offered if you deliver us to the nearest starbase with a transport hub."

A wily look crossed the captain's face. "You're dangerous to have aboard."

"Very well. Five thousand."

"Ten."

"I understand you're heading for Remnant Two."

The captain scratched his bristled jaw. "First we're set to rendezvous with the Crockers to unload our cargo."

"When is that?"

"In about ten hours."

Remnant Two might be a short stop on the way to Earth, but Jace didn't want to debark there. "You'll get your ten thousand, but only if you take us closer in."

"You still have to earn your keep during transit."

"No problem."

"Who's the woman you brought along? I heard she's a looker."

Jace didn't like the gleam in his eyes. "Just a companion I picked up along the way."

"Give her to me, and I'll call us even."

"She's not available." Jace folded his arms across his chest, making it clear he wouldn't budge on the offer.

"I'll reassign your status from crew to guest. You could enjoy the voyage."

"Not without her. She's mine, even if she doesn't know it yet."

Keelo's voice roughened. "Go back to work. After we make our drop to the Crockers, I'll consider your offer. Until then, think about your choices."

What choices? Jace wondered as he strode through the corridors under armed escort. Keelo might believe Jace wouldn't reveal their illicit cargo, but it would be just as easy to space his passengers, or Jace alone, out the nearest airlock.

The captain would be right to remain suspicious, because Jace didn't intend to allow him to deliver the goods. Conscience dictated that he do something to save the poor souls trapped on board, although that same conscience argued that rescuing his sister should be his first priority.

"Absolutely not," Silver said when he told her his plan later in their cabin. "It isn't that I don't care about saving innocent lives. Quite the contrary. Our goal is to eliminate the bigger threat."

He faced her squarely, trying to ignore the way her hair streamed down her back after she'd untwisted her braid. "This human cargo is destined for food to the beastly Crockers. How can you ignore their plight?"

"They're just dozens, or hundreds if you count the runs Keelo has already made. Tyrone Bluth kills thousands in his raids, enslaves women and children, and destroys entire colonies. We can't risk our mission for the few as opposed to the many."

"I like how you call it our mission," Jace sneered, "when you won't listen to anything I say."

"You're obsessed because you couldn't save your parents, so now you think you can rescue these people instead. If you don't maintain your focus, you'll accomplish nothing." She paused, thoughtful. "Or maybe you want to get caught and that's what this is really about."

"Excuse me?"

"You feel you deserve punishment. No wonder you sympathize with those people below. Your misplaced sense of guilt says it should be you who's delivered to the Crockers, not them."

"You're insane. My goal is to see justice done. Stopping the trade in human cargo is just as important as clearing my name and ridding the galaxy of Bluth's tyranny."

"I don't see it that way, and you'd better not do anything to endanger my job."

Despite his irritation, he enjoyed the way her eyes blazed and her lips pursed with challenge. Their verbal sparring made her come alive. Parts of him jumped to life, too, as his gaze raked over her. She'd be angrier when she realized their heading took them closer to Earth instead of Stacktown. They could go there afterward, when they'd obtained another ship. Likely Bluth had already come and gone from the place.

"What do you say we make peace?" He sidled closer, breathing in her scent. "It might be difficult to share a berth otherwise."

Her glance shifted to the single bunk and back to him. "You'll sleep on the floor."

"I don't think so. My funds paid for these accommodations. That being the case, I get to take a shower first." His brows furrowed. "I wonder if Mixy transferred our luggage."

"Great Cosmos, is your wardrobe all that concerns you?" Unfastening her jumpsuit, she jiggled out of it, oblivious to the effect her motions had on him. "You can consult with your valet while I use the facilities." And she strode, naked as a babe, into the lavatory.

****

Pulsating streams of hot water soothed her anger but didn't ease the tension that poured through her veins. Being too close to Jace had that effect on her. As she soaped her hair, she realized she'd left behind her only item of clothing, and sonic dryers obliterated the need for towels. Maybe she'd been too hasty in dismissing Mixy's usefulness.

Since there didn't appear to be any water restrictions, she took her time. It required several scrubs for her to feel cleansed from the blood and grime of her patients. She shuddered from the horror of it. Despite what Jace had said, she wasn't immune to the sufferings of those poor captives, but maintaining priorities necessitated a certain level of emotional detachment.

She'd had enough practice in that regard to ensure she wouldn't get off track. If you cared too much about people, you just got hurt. Silver didn't allow herself to care too deeply about anyone, except for Tyrone Bluth. She hated him enough to black out anything else in her peripheral vision.

Jace got sidetracked too easily because he viewed himself as a sword of justice. Maybe it stemmed from his guilt or maybe he'd always been that way. Being around him proved a distraction she couldn't ignore, making her lose sight of her target like she'd done in the woods at Al'ron. But even if she wanted to get away on her own, how to go about it?

Somehow Keelo transferred his cargo to the Crockers. She should ask Jace if he knew how this would be done. If there were shuttle bays, she could steal a ship. Unless the Crockers docked here, which would be a different story. She didn't want to be aboard when that happened.

How in the world did Jace plan to free those people without having a means of transportation? She could see only one obvious route without shuttles being available—take over the ship. So the first piece of business would be to scout the other decks.

She turned off the water and pushed the button for the drying vents. When the sonic vibrations began, she considered their other options. They could always jump ship, but the captain didn't plan to dock until after his rendezvous with the beasts.

According to Jace, Captain Keelo knew his identity. She didn't for one minute believe the captain would pass up the opportunity to make more credits. He'd probably already notified the bounty hunters, which made their departure all the more imperative. This four-hour break would be their only chance. They should try to communicate with Mixy, who had the run of the ship more easily than she or Jace. A plan budded in her mind.

Excited to tell Jace, she opened the door and strode into their cabin. He lay on the single bunk, arms folded behind his head, staring at the ceiling. He'd stripped off his outer clothing but still wore his briefs.

At her entry, he jerked to a sitting position, eyes wide open as his gaze shifted her way. His male body part leapt to attention. Warmth suffused her cheeks. Stars above, she hadn't meant for him to get the wrong impression. Didn't he realize time was short? They couldn't waste it fooling around.

"You know, Silver, if you keep coming on to me like this, we'll accomplish nothing." He jumped to his feet, a sexy smile curving his lips.

"We need to talk." She stared at his hair-sprinkled chest as he sauntered over. "Have you contacted Mixy? I need something clean to wear."

"You don't need to wear anything at all." He halted in front of her, so close she smelled his manly scent.

Languor enveloped her when his gaze leisurely roamed her body. "Stop right there and listen to me. I have a plan to get us off this vessel."

"I'm sure you do. Wait until I take a shower. I'll be quick."

"Not until…" Her protest dissipated as he shut the lavatory door.

Danged if I'm going to hang around. She yanked the sheet off the bed and wrapped it around herself in a makeshift sarong. Then she figured out how to use the intercom to summon Mixy.

"Madam, why are you calling me now?" The Elusian spoke from the galley amidst the clang of pots and pans. "Oh, I do hope he gets some relief. I can't stand this tension."

"What are you talking about?"

"Master Jace. He's very aroused. It's most peculiar, but I'm also getting a sense of your interest. You're making it very difficult for me to concentrate."

"Dingbat's tail, Mixy, get out of our heads and bring me some clothes."

"I wouldn't think of interrupting. I'll come when I know you're done." He disconnected, making Silver mutter several curses in different tongues.

"Was that Mixy I heard?"

Silver whirled at Jace's voice. He advanced toward her with an arrogant stride and halted directly in front of her sheet-wrapped body. Water glistened in his dark hair, returned to its natural color. Damp strands plastered his forehead, inviting her to straighten them.

Her gaze dropped to the stubble dotting his jaw, reminding her they needed toiletries in addition to outfits. Speaking of need, his equipment stood at full salute, demanding attention. She swallowed, tamping her own surge of desire.

"Mixy said he'd come by shortly." Her voice sounded hoarse.

"He won't bother us." Without further preamble, Jace unwound her sheet. Cool air hit her skin when he dropped the material to the floor.

"We don't have time for this. I said I wanted to talk."

"About that horror below? Or about your plan of action? Let it wait. Right now, I just want to lose myself in you."

A groan escaped her lips when he tickled the inner surface of her upper arms. As her nerves sang in delight, he pressed his hips against her belly. Oh my, she hoped Mixy didn't share these sensations, but she feared the valet could sense them both. That wicked notion heightened her excitement.

She considered pushing Jace away to discuss her escape plan, but his magical hands dissuaded her. It had been too long since she'd succumbed to desire, and she needed release.

Besides, they both could use a break from the pressure that plagued them.

Maybe it was Mixy's confluence that made her lean into Jace's hard form and wrap her arms around him, or maybe she just wanted to forget what they'd seen in the cargo hold. It didn't matter. She tilted her face, darting her tongue out to tease the contours of his mouth. Her feminine pride swelled when he sucked in a sharp breath before capturing her lips in a hungry kiss.

His hands slithering over her skin, he nudged her toward the bunk. Her knees yielded, and they tumbled together onto the narrow berth. She unfolded her legs as he explored her body, finding her pleasure zones, teasing her into a state of coiled tension.

She reached for his erection, but he swatted her hand away. Her thighs opened involuntarily, and he accepted her offering, closing his stroking fingers upon her swollen folds. While she writhed in passionate abandon, he rolled atop her, readying himself for entry.

"Silver, is this what you want?" His intense gaze snagged hers as he dragged his mouth away. She saw uncertainty cross his expression. "I didn't mean to—"

"Yes," she whispered.

"You're so beautiful." He smoothed her hair off her face. "I'd love to see you dressed in rich finery and sparkling jewels, but I like you this way even better. You make me forget who I am and what I've done."

She kissed him lightly. "Don't go there. Go here instead, inside me." She thrust her hips upward to grind against him.

A primal growl issued from his throat. He prodded her waiting wetness, and then inserted himself in a quick thrust. Their breaths intermingled as they danced in a rhythm ages old. Her inner flame ignited, churned into lava, and rushed toward an explosive climax. When the eruption came, a faint hint of another consciousness pinged her awareness. It compounded the waves of ecstasy rocking her. Jace's exultant cry when he let loose his seed reverberated in her as though they were one.

Exhaustion followed, seeping her strength as she lay with Jace sprawled partially on top, his heavy form covering her like a blanket. His labored breathing eventually slowed, and she drifted into a state of semi-conscious bliss with the sound of his light snores acting as a lullaby.

It was the first time in years she fell asleep without missing her parents, regretting her lost future with Burrell, and condemning Tyrone Bluth.

****

"I brought your valise." Mixy handed the case to Jace. "They searched through it first. Thankfully, nothing got wrinkled."

"I'm glad you were able to salvage our stuff." Jace flung the case on the foot of the bed, careful to avoid jarring Silver.

She shifted on the bunk, her eyes fluttering open. Confusion turned to clarity as she glanced at the valet, down at her naked body, and back to Mixy. Her face turned scarlet.

"Madam, I packed some of your items as well."

"Do you always show up unannounced?" She drew the sheet to chin level.

"You were sleeping. Master Jace let me in." A beatific smile lit the Elusian's delicate features.

Jace chuckled, patting her arm. "Get used to it, deermin."

Silver glared at him while he shrugged into a clean pair of briefs. "It's a good thing I'm still sleepy, or I'd knock the two of you to the floor right now."

Lying on the floor brought other connotations to Jace's mind. From the corner of his eye, he noted Mixy's robe deepening into a sensuous hot pink. He couldn't hide anything from his atrani. Even as he pulled on the pressed trousers handed to him, Jace's arousal stirred again. Mixy's wispy brows elevated but the valet remained wordless, offering Silver a lacy black bra and thong.

"Milord, your shirt."

Jace blinked, realizing he'd been staring at Silver as she stretched her long naked body and rose to dress. He snatched the shirt from his valet's elongated fingers with an embarrassed cough. His sexual energy seemed to have acquired an additional component. It emanated from Silver's awareness of him, plus another presence, as though Mixy acted as a link compounding their responses. The effect stimulated him even further.

He'd hoped having sex with Silver would satisfy his need for her, but not so. He wanted her more than ever and had trouble clearing his brain for any other thought.

"Did Captain Keelo tell you how long it would be until he made contact with the Crockers?" Silver asked. Her hair streamed down her back as she belted a black tunic over a pair of stretch pants.

"Ten hours." Glancing at his chronometer, he grimaced. "Only six hours left, and we've used up three hours of our break." Finished tucking his shirt into his waistband, he submitted to Mixy's hairstyling. No time to shave. "We have to come up with a plan."

"It is unsafe for you here, milord," Mixy said. "I heard talk in the crew's mess. When the Crockers come, Keelo will space you out the airlock and keep the lady for entertainment. As for myself, I believe he likes my cooking."

"Jolly for you, friend. So the Crockers are docking with Keelo's ship. Does that mean there aren't any shuttles aboard?"

Silver, who'd been braiding her hair, turned to face him. "We need to see a schematic. As I view it, we have two choices: steal a vessel from the shuttle bay, if one exists, or take command of this ship before the Crockers get here."

"Oh sure." Jace regarded her with a sardonic lift of his eyebrow. "Has it escaped your notice that we're outnumbered?"

"I can make a knockout gas from chemicals in sickbay." Silver's eyes shone with purpose. "When it takes out the crew, we can alter our heading from the bridge. Did Keelo tell you our course?"

"Not for the rendezvous. Besides, you're forgetting something." Jace folded his arms across his chest. "I'm not leaving our human cargo behind to be eaten alive."

She gave him a withering glare. "If we're forced to option number two, the knockout gas will render the wounded unconscious as well as the crew. You won't be able to move them, even if we find somewhere to land or another way off this bucket."

An idea dawned, one that posed less difficulty than the other alternatives but just as much risk to himself. He wouldn't share his plan with Silver. He only hoped she didn't notice the lavender infusing his valet's garment. Had she figured out what the different hues meant yet? They would clue her in to his feelings as though he wore a sign on his forehead.

He surmised Mixy remained purposefully quiet, hovering in the background, so he wouldn't betray Jace's deceit.

"Let's split up," he told Silver. "You can investigate the environmental systems. Mixy will look for a launch bay. I'll start collecting those chemicals you need from the sick ward."

"Fine." Silver pointed to the ceiling. "I could squeeze through that vent with your help, and then you can leave. Inform the guard that I'm still resting. Mixy, pack some food when you get back to the galley. We'll need to keep up our energy."

The time passed quickly, and Jace managed to distract his security escort long enough to locate a central com hub. He'd piggybacked a signal pattern onto the conduser platform before the guy returned with the captain as requested.

"What is it?" Captain Keelo snarled, clearly not pleased about being summoned.

Jace gave him an ingratiating smile. "Forgive me for taking you from the bridge, Captain, but I didn't want your command staff to hear us."

"Go on. This better be worth my time."

"I'm willing to cut you a deal."

"You already made an offer."

"Well, I've been thinking about it. I'd rather trade you the woman instead of the credits. It's obvious you fancy her, and I can get another female anywhere. So what do you say? Let me and my valet off at the nearest port, before the Crockers get here. I'd like to be long gone by then."

"I'll bet you would." The captain scratched his jaw. "How about this? You transfer the credits to me right now, and I keep the woman. In exchange, you can remain with the crew instead of becoming space debris."

"You lying son of a—"

Keelo swung his fist, clipping Jace on the jaw. "You're not in any position to bargain." The captain's blow to his stomach emphasized the point. "Understand?"

What Jace understood was that if he fought back, he wouldn't get very far. Armed crewmen stood ready to restrain him. He had to pretend compliance until his plan carried through. "Yes, sir," he mumbled though clenched teeth. The guards marched him back to the hospital ward where he resumed his duties.

"How did you make out?" he whispered when he and Silver found a moment alone, several hours later. They'd been too closely observed to talk earlier.

He handed her a blood-pressure calibrator, gesturing to a thin-faced woman lying on a pallet as though they conferred over a patient.

"Mixy said there aren't any smaller ships onboard," she advised him, keeping her head bent. "This ward was the shuttle bay, but they converted it into an expanded cargo hold and sold the ships." Shifting her feet, she gave him a scrutinizing glance. "What happened to you? Your face is bruised."

She touched her own jaw which sported a yellowish tinge from her encounter on Bartlett Station.

"Keelo and I had a disagreement."

Her mouth curved downward. "Can't you stay out of trouble without me?"

"What else did you learn?" he snapped in return.

"I can access life support within five minutes through the ventilation system. Did you find those components I need for the knockout gas?"

"Got them. They're in a bowl under that sink. Found some masks, too, in case we need them."

She kept her voice low. "Good. When I signal you, bring me the stuff. It'll work fast once I mix the components, so hold your breath."

Lifting his chin, he announced in a louder tone, "I mixed up a healing salve for your patient. You can use it on her wound."

Jace strode away with a surge of pride for her expertise. His training included flight ops and combat tactics, while hers deviated toward more subtle arts of intrigue. Together, they made a good team.

He needed someone like her on his side, especially when nearly everyone else stood against him. But their relationship remained tenuous, based on survival instincts, and certainly not on a sense of trust.

Chapter Eight

Inside the makeshift medical facility, Silver examined the items in her hands. A grunt of surprise escaped her lips. Jace indeed had managed to acquire all the goods on her list. They worked well together, she realized. Too bad their association had to be temporary. Soon she'd shed his company to track Tyrone Bluth on her own.

Once they commandeered Keelo's ship, she'd gain the upper hand, drop her companions off at the nearest base, then head for Stacktown. Jace's difficulties with the law were his problem. As for the bounty, she'd readily give up the credits to catch her quarry. Nothing mattered beyond that goal, although it annoyed her how she had to keep strengthening her resolve since Jace had crashed into her life.

Even more distracting was her unseemly lust for the man. She remembered with sweet satisfaction how it had felt to lie with him, to feel his hands on her body and his rigid sex between her legs. It wouldn't be easy to leave him behind.

Regret swept through her, as though Jace filled a hole within her soul she hadn't known existed. Mixy, too, if truth be told. Stars above, she hoped the Elusian didn't sense her plans to betray his master.

Something jarred the ship, making her drop the atomizer she held. Another impact rocked the vessel and set off a shrieking siren. Alarm blossomed in her chest when the guards raised their weapons.

"What's going on?" she called.

"A naval patrol is firing off our port side," Sublieutenant Mos'ot said after a brief exchange on his comm unit. "They received a distress call from our ship and are demanding to board. You must be secured. Come."

Silver acted quickly, scooping up the atomizer and spritzing him with the solution. The compound, upon contacting air, transformed into a gas. Silver held her breath and sprayed the armed team by the door. Meanwhile, Jace grabbed a mask and put it on. She stretched one over her face as the gas affected their patients and the ward quieted.

"We won't be able to diffuse the gas to the rest of the crew," she said in an urgent tone. "I didn't have time to load the solution into the canister you gave me."

Jace's eyes darkened to malachite. "Never mind. Navy personnel are boarding the ship. We don't want to be mistaken for Keelo's people." He thumbed his comm device. "Mixy, get to the med center on the double. Did you obtain our bags?"

Mixy's haughty voice replied. "Do you think I would leave our belongings behind, milord, after I went to so much trouble to bring them? Of course I have our things, stowed and ready to go at your command."

****

Jace suppressed a grin when he noticed Silver staring at him, her eyes large above the mask that covered her mouth and nose. "You warned Mixy ahead of time?" she said. "How did you—?"

"I sent the distress call. When can we remove these masks?"

She checked her chronometer. "Probably now. It should be neutralized." Ripping her mask off, she sniffed the air. "All clear. We'll wait until the troops arrive, then I'll tell their commander who I am. As a S.I.N. operative, my authority is beyond question."

"Like on the space station? If I recall, those scientists knew your identity, but they couldn't keep security off our tail."

She flipped a strand of hair over her shoulder. "They know me as Silver Malloy, a major investor in the Hoatch Foundation. I never told them I'm a covert operative. Security may have let me go, but they would have tossed you in confinement."

He grimaced. "How long until these people wake up?"

"They'll be out for hours. I have to admit, sending a distress call was a clever ploy. I wouldn't have thought of it. We're fortunate a patrol happened to be in the area."

"It was a gamble, but mainly for me."

Jace grabbed the atomizer and sprayed her full in the face. As she went down, he caught her limp form and lowered her onto an empty pallet, covering her with a sheet.

By the time Mixy burst through the double doors, the gas had dissipated. Jace threw his mask aside.

"Master Jace, soldiers have invaded the bridge. What shall we do?" Dropping his bags, the valet wrung his hands and moaned.

"Use the cosmetics in Silver's case to lighten my skin. If our plan works, we'll be transferred to a real hospital."

Mixy's soft wailing reflected his doubts. Nonetheless, the Elusian slathered stage paint on his face while Jace squeezed his eyes shut.

"Someone's coming," Jace whispered upon hearing footsteps outside. "Put that stuff away."

Mixy shoved their supplies out of sight, then they flopped onto empty cots seconds before the door crashed open.

"By the suns," a man's voice said. "Stryker to Captain Fenster. We have dozens of injured people in here, sir, either dead or unconscious. This doesn't jive with the cargo manifest. And armed crew are lying on the floor, out cold like everyone else."

A pause before he spoke again. "Affirmative, sir. We'll impound the vessel and tow it back to Earth Base Alpha. I'll notify Medical we have incoming. May I respectfully suggest we install our surplus hyperdrive module? Then I can buy you that drink I owe you within eight hours at the most, sir."

Eight hours, instead of days. Jace couldn't believe their luck. But even as he relaxed his limbs, pretending to be a drugged victim, he realized what that meant.

When Silver awakened, she'd be home. He'd given her every reason to turn him in. Instead of achieving his freedom, the only thing he'd managed to accomplish was to jump from the volcanic rim into the fiery crater.

****

Blood rushed to Silver's head as the cobwebs of unconsciousness ebbed away. She appeared to be hanging upside down while her face bounced against a man's back. His arm gripped her legs, steadying her. Was it one of Captain Keelo's men?

His scent seemed familiar, a hint of musk mixed with tincture of iodine. Images haunted her mind of adhesive, syringes, bandages, and intravenous tubing. She'd been in sickbay. Wait a minute. Jace had grabbed the atomizer and sprayed her. He must be carting her somewhere.

A door creaked open. He flipped her upright and then down. She landed on her rump on a hard surface. Dust rose in a cloud, tickling her nostrils. A quick visual survey showed they were in some sort of closet with Mixy crowding in behind them.

She backed against the wall, banging into a broom that teetered ominously. Jace's hand shot out to straighten it while his concerned green eyes raked over her.

"Are you all right? How do you feel?" He crouched beside her while Mixy shut the door, sealing them inside.

"You knocked me out, you slimy piece of rothgut bait. Get away from me," she rasped past a dry throat. She needed water. Her tongue seemed to have grown a layer of fuzz.

"We're on Earth. I need your help."

Her jaw dropped. "How did we get here?"

"My distress call summoned a Consortium naval patrol.

They impounded Keelo's ship and outfitted it with an accelerated hyperdrive to cut transport time. We landed at a base on the Terran home world, where the wounded—including the three of us—were transferred to a real hospital."

She gave him a shrewd glance. "So why did you put me out of action? Afraid I'd turn you in?" Her gaze shifted to the door. After calculating the odds against combating both Jace and Mixy, she decided to hear him out.

"You'd planned to reveal yourself as a S.I.N. agent. What better time to denounce me, collect the bounty, and file for mining rights on Al'ron?"

"Good points, but if I may remind you, you're the one who called in the cavalry."

"That's correct. So why can't you trust me? If I'd wanted you dead, I would have done it already. Then I could go after Bluth on my own. I've never harmed you, have I? And that episode on the space station came out of my fear for you. I may react to circumstance, but I'm not innately a violent person. At least, I don't think I am."

She saw the flicker of self-doubt before he continued. "You originally said you would help me with a disguise when we reached Earth. We can find another ship to resume our hunt for Bluth and his Marauders. You want to go to Stacktown? I'd suggest you check on the possible mole in your organization first."

Hating to admit he was right, she glanced away from his earnest expression. What was the alternative? Expose him as a criminal, claim her reward, and watch him get sent to his death on Kurash? That would be akin to murdering him. He could have harmed her when he'd had the chance, but he hadn't. Undoubtedly, self-preservation was partially his motive besides utilizing her resources, but she believed Jace's claim that he wasn't violent by nature.

Think how much your support would mean to him. He has no one else.

Isolated on an alien planet, how would he survive when his

tall frame and bronze complexion were dead giveaways to his origins? He must have used her bag of tricks to disguise himself, judging from the smeared makeup on his face. She could do a better job if she meant to introduce him to her cousins. In return, she could use his analytical skills to pinpoint the traitor who had sold information about the Avenger to Tyrone Bluth.

She surveyed the haggard lines on his face and the taut angle of his jaw while he waited for her response. Mixy's whimper swung her attention to his valet. The Elusian's robe, a dismal shade of amber, swirled about his ankles as he rocked back and forth.

"Woe is me. We are trapped, and your sister will be lost if we do not save her. It means disaster for Kurash, should you be imprisoned. Who else will stop Garth from influencing Ruler Hurat? Who will sway him toward peace instead of war? Milord, you must not let such a fate overtake you." Tears dribbled down Mixy's pallid cheeks. Turning toward Silver, he raised his hands in supplication.

Great Cosmos, was this terrible despair truly what Jace felt inside? He'd turned his head, leaving his face in shadows. But she could tell from his slumped shoulders that these burdens challenged him. Her heart softened, despite her resolve to complete her mission.

"Very well, but you must agree to one thing if I continue to work with you," she said. "When we catch Bluth, after you learn your sister's whereabouts, you'll allow me to take him out."

Jace met her gaze, his eyes glistening in the faint light coming from the door cracks.

"I still need him to act as a witness in my defense."

"We'll figure out a way to make it happen." Silver's own eyes stung when Mixy's robe took on a tangerine hue.

"I knew it," Mixy cried, raising his arms. "You care for Master Jace. You won't let him down."

"Don't be absurd. It's the logical path to take, that's all." Silver rose unsteadily to her feet and brushed down her tunic.

Jace stretched to his full height. He took her hands in his and grinned, looking like a little boy who'd just been invited to a carnival.

"You won't regret your decision, deermin. Believe me when I say there's more at stake than what we want for ourselves. In time, I hope you'll come to see that, because it'll give you a reason to keep going."

Discomforted by the emotions he stirred in her, Silver withdrew her hands. She hadn't considered her existence after killing Bluth, because she hadn't expected to survive the assault from his men in retaliation. Was this what Jace meant? That it wasn't worth sacrificing herself in exchange for Bluth's life? That she had more to live for, and it was selfish of her to think otherwise? Right now, she couldn't think beyond her target. She'd been given an assignment. It was her task to finish the job.

She grabbed her sack from the floor and slung it over her shoulder. "Let's find a restroom. If you didn't totally mess up my makeup kit, we'll fix you to look like an Orelian. They can be tall and brawny with tanned skin. No arguments, but you're going to have to go with contact lenses and red hair. We'll say you're an armsman from the Menagua System, and Mixy is a linguistics expert. Elusians are fluent in several languages, aren't they?"

"Yes, madam, we—"

Silver cut him off. "I hired you as my escort after I lost my ship. In case we're asked about the space station, you weren't there. I met you on Keelo's vessel where we both took passage. Unfortunately, the hunted criminal Jace Vernon escaped in the confusion when the vessel was boarded."

Jace's brilliant smile took her breath away. "Let's go," he said before opening the door. He peered outside, and then signaled for the others to follow.

****

When they emerged outside the hospital walls, no one would have recognized Jace as a Kurashki. Not only had his appearance been altered, thanks to Silver's makeup and a new khaki outfit, but his bearing differed. As an armsman, he should always be on his guard, she'd told him. Lower his aristocratic nose and hunch his shoulders in a more aggressive stance.

What she hadn't counted on was his reaction to the bustling metropolis. They'd no sooner stepped onto the pedway when he gawked in disbelief. Aircars whizzed past, jostling up and down in traffic as they competed with landrovers. Horns blasted, mingling with people chatter and blaring loudspeakers advertising the latest specials in the shopping dromes. The resultant cacophony existed as mere background noise to the natives, but Mixy covered his ears and howled. Jace craned his neck, staring upward at the sliver of sky visible through a collage of skyscrapers.

"What's wrong?" She nudged Jace to move on. "Mixy, will you shut up? People are looking at us."

"We don't have cities like this on my world." Jace scowled at his valet who fell mute under his glare. "Our landholders rule their districts, with towns surrounding each lord's manor. Even our capital where Hurat resides isn't this grand."

"You're kidding, right?"

He shook his head. "It's not that we aren't capable of constructing these wonders. We'd decided to keep the old ways after sending delegations abroad and seeing how too much machinery softens a civilization."

"I'd heard Kurash was feudal but not that bad."

"Our space fleet uses the latest technology." His brows drew together like a gathering storm. "That's one area where Hurat won't skimp. Victories in battle still bring glory to the crown."

He stepped aside to avoid being run down by a woman with a baby carriage. A man in a suit bumped into him. As he backed up, two teenage girls, their arms weighted with shopping bags, collided at his rear.

"Numbuster!" one of them cried. "You can't just stop here. Get a move on it."

"Oh dear, oh dear." Mixy whirled in confusion. His hand gripped Jace's valise as though it were a lifeline. In his jade-tinged robe—reflecting their jitters, Silver supposed—and with his ascending hairstyle, he drew curious looks from passersby.

"Where are we going?" Jace asked, while Silver became aware of a crawling sensation at her nape. Were they being watched?

She spun around, wondering if any of Bluth's men had picked up their trail. When she realized the uneasiness emanated from Mixy, it was her turn to stare at him in confusion. How could she feel the valet's terror, the tumult to his senses? Or was it Jace's reaction magnified by the Elusian? How had their emotions filtered into her consciousness?

"We're in New Virginia City," she explained, attempting to regain her composure. "After Washington D.C. was destroyed at the start of World War III, we moved things here. This is where the Terran Consortium first formed, so it seemed appropriate. S.I.N. headquarters is located on the west side, but we'll visit my apartment first so I can contact my uncle. It's better if I notify him ahead of time that we're coming. Then you won't have to go through security protocols."

Jace indicated her wrist. "Can't you just call him on your comm unit?"

She brushed a couple of stray hairs off her face. "If we have operatives working for Bluth within our system, I don't care to alert them. I have a private channel at home that goes directly to Uncle Manny's office. You might know him as Mans Lyonus."

Jace's eyes widened. "Not Mans Lyonus, of Lyonus Metals?"

"Yep, that's him."

"But he's a ranking council member for the Terran Consortium."

"Actually, he's been elected Maxima Chancellor."

"And you're taking me to see him?"

"Oh no, oh no, we'll surely be exposed." Horror twisting his delicate features, Mixy stumbled off the curb and into the street.

"Look out!" Silver shrieked when an aircar swooped in from behind. Mixy didn't even see it coming. An ominous thump resounded. The tall Elusian flew through the air before hitting the ground several feet away.

"Stars above." She sprinted to his side among a bevy of onlookers. With a numbing sense of dread, she stared down at the valet's still form.

Jace knelt to feel for a pulse. "Someone get help! He's hurt but still alive." His fingers gently probed Mixy's bloodied face. "You'll make it, my friend. I'll see to it."

His voice cracked, and Silver glanced at him. She didn't need a sixth sense to discern his fear. Jace's pinched face said it all. So did the color of Mixy's robe, a neutral blue. Their link had been broken.

Silver placed her hand on Jace's shoulder in commiseration. She hadn't realized how fond she'd become of the lanky Elusian. An inexplicable loss gripped her that felt like a gap in her heart.

And so they ended up back at the hospital. Silver paced in the waiting room, sharing Jace's anguish as he sat slumped in a chair, hands covering his face. Her stomach churned as she considered all the possible outcomes. She smoothed sweaty palms over her tunic as though that action would solve their problems.

At last, a woman in scrubs arrived and called Jace's name. They followed her through a door, down a long corridor, and to the nurses' station.

"Since neither of you is next of kin, we need a responsible party," the charge nurse said. "The Elusian has gone to surgery. His spleen has ruptured, and he has internal bleeding. We can repair him, but he needs a blood transfusion… Elusian blood."

Jace gasped in dismay. Silver stood by his side, shivering in the air-conditioned climate.

A doctor in a white coat joined them. "You're with the alien, right? Ordinarily, we could use a synthetic infusion, but it doesn't work with his species. It'll maintain him for a certain amount of time until it breaks down, causing more harm than good. We'll have to use molecular transport to obtain his blood type from the nearest depot."

"That will cost a fortune," Silver protested, aware their socialized medicine didn't cover extras for offworlders.

"Which one of you is his bond-mate?" the doctor asked, making Silver realize he must be a specialist in xenobiology.

"He's my responsibility. I'll cover it." Jace reached into his pants pocket. A few futile gropes, and his worried glance met Silver's. "Oops, I forgot. My credit chip was stolen."

"So was mine. Let me make a call," Silver implored the doctor. "I'll clear it with my repository."

"Sorry. We don't accept transfers without authorization."

"But using a credit disk is the same thing. It would transfer funds from my account to the hospital."

The doctor shook his head. "Our administrative department has to clear deposits from repositories. That can take time that we don't have in this case."

"Wait, Mixy has a card, and I'm a signatory on his account," Jace inserted. "Can we get his clothes?"

"Of course. Wait here." The doctor left, returning a few moments later with a clear bag encasing Mixy's possessions. "You might as well keep these in the event he doesn't respond to treatment."

Silver didn't like the implication. Hoping they could aid the valet, she helped Jace sift through Mixy's possessions. His shoes, socks, undergarments, and robes were as clean and starched as their wearer.

His blood-splattered robe was bagged separately. Silver held it pinched between her fingers while Jace inserted his hand into one pocket after another. A grimace distorted his face at the unpleasant duty.

"Here's the disk. I found it." He raised the small round card, his voice exultant.

Silver's eyes misted, and she blinked away her tears. This reminded her of the time she'd had to sort through the wreckage on Altuis Three, searching for the remains of her parents' lives. And then later, when she'd sent Burrell's mother his wallet, data pad, and red stylus for scribbling in the margins of his research notes. She had kept the pocket knife with his initials, wanting to cherish something he'd owned.

It's amazing how your life boils down to a few data disks and fewer trinkets. Hopefully, this wouldn't be the case with Mixy. But when the doctor returned, holding the credit chip out to Jace, her mood dampened.

"I'm afraid this doesn't work in our processor without the patient's access code," the physician said. "Do you know his personal identifier?"

A muscle twitched in Jace's jaw. "It's Mixy's account. If he ever told me, I don't remember."

"I'm sorry, but I have to get someone else ready for surgery." The doctor tugged on his lab coat. "You'll have to take this up with administration."

Silver raised a hand. "We can't wait that long. My uncle is Mans Lyonus. Surely my credit is good."

Respect flared in his eyes. "Yes, ma'am, but our policy stands, especially for services rendered to aliens without a home account. Either you have a credit disk, or you'll have to affect the transfer from your repository through administration. I know it involves useless red tape, but that's the way it goes. Unfortunately, your friend may not have the time to wait."

He started to turn away, but Jace grabbed his sleeve. "Hold on. I have another credit disk." Lifting his foot, he twisted the heel of his boot. From a small cavity, out fell a circular card. "Here you go, this should work."

Silver's body heated like quick fire. Anger mixed with astonishment as she watched the doctor take the disk, ask for Jace's personal code, and stride away.

"Where did you get that? And why didn't you tell me about it sooner?" she demanded.

Jace's mouth thinned into a grim line. "I set up this account for emergencies. It would take too much time for your funds to transfer, and I'm not willing to risk Mixy's life when I have the means to save him."

He placed his hands on her shoulders and drew her close. "You've been a comfort to me, deermin. Now I have to ask for a favor. In the event you catch up to Bluth, find out where he sent my sister Shanna. If she still lives, help her get to freedom."

"But you'll be with me." She gazed at him, wondering at the desperation in his voice.

"I have my own path to follow." He gripped her tighter. "Promise me."

"All right, but I don't understand." Her auditory sensors picked up a commotion coming from around the corner. At the same time, Jace stepped away from her. The doctor charged into view followed by six armed security officers.

The physician wagged a finger. "That's him. Jace Vernon, the Kurashki criminal."

"Oh, no. Jace, what did you do?" Silver hadn't realized what it meant for him to present his credit chip.

He didn't budge, lifting his jaw resolutely. The security team surrounded him, one of them thrusting Jace's hands behind his back to attach manacles.

As her blood chilled, she realized why Jace had spoken the words he did. He'd known that giving the access code to his account would reveal his identity, but he'd purposefully sacrificed himself so Mixy could get the treatment he needed.

Seeing him restrained made her throat close. There was only one way to save him now. She didn't question her decision, even though it violated protocol.

A steely-eyed fellow in a beret approached her. "Are you his associate?"

"I'm a S.I.N. operative, and this man is under my custody. I'm taking him to Defense Command for interrogation." To prove her identity, she spread her right hand to show him the symbol branded between her index and middle fingers. "Now you've blown my cover. We're only here because his Elusian manservant got injured in an accident."

She turned and pointed to the doctor. "You'd better make sure Mixy survives, or I'll hold you responsible for obstruction of justice. Are Jace's credits any good?"

A frown creased the doctor's face. "Falkner's World doesn't recognize the authority of the Terran Consortium regarding confiscation of criminal property. His account is valid."

"Good, then use his funds to pay for Mixy's care. And if you need more, let me know." Returning her attention to the team leader, she ordered, "Give Vernon to me."

The man stiffened. "I'm sorry, ma'am, but you'll have to take up your claim with Internal Affairs. We're taking him in."

"Don't fight it, Silver," Jace told her in a resigned tone. He had never looked so magnificent, she thought, even with that ridiculous red spiked hair and those blue contacts. With his proud carriage, no one could deny his noble lineage. Yet he didn't protest being treated like a common criminal.

"You gave yourself up deliberately," she said in a low tone while the officers confirmed their orders.

"It was necessary to help Mixy."

"I'll talk to my uncle to see what he can do. We'll make sure Mixy recovers. Trust me, Jace. I won't let them send you back to Kurash."

"That won't happen anyway. Bluth's agents will have targeted me by now."

"You think they'd attempt something here?" Maybe he'd experienced the same eerie sensation of being watched as she did on the street.

Before he could reply, the soldier in charge gave a command, and they marched him away. Staring at his retreating back, Silver bit her lower lip. If she were smart, she'd let go and focus on her own mission. Jace was simply another criminal who'd been removed as a threat to the public.

She could still request the bounty, since she'd been with him when he was caught. At the same time, she could file a claim for the rubilite formations on Al'ron. That would leave her free to pursue Tyrone Bluth without encumbrances, and she'd have plenty of funds to purchase another ship. But her conscience nagged at her. Bluth had a reputation for eliminating his enemies. He'd already figured Silver was tracking him, and now he knew Jace Vernon was also on his tail. Being imprisoned might actually provide Jace with more security, but that left his valet in peril.

"Doctor," she said, approaching the physician studying another patient's chart. "Please call me when Mixy awakens. My superiors will have some questions to ask him. Here's a number where you can reach me." She scribbled it on a nearby datapad. "May I suggest you post guards for Mixy's protection?"

"Very well." He gave her a sympathetic glance as though he weren't wholly heartless.

Concerned more than ever about a mole at Security Integrated Network, she left the hospital to do what needed to be done.

Chapter Nine

Silver decided to forego stopping at her apartment. Instead she caught a public airbus directly to the Terran Consortium central complex. After getting off in front of the gate, she passed through an elaborate security protocol before gaining admittance. Here she paused, scanning the directional signs.

Her cousin Dash worked at Earth Centrum headquarters, but she'd see him later. Colonies Division was off to the right, while the S.I.N. bureau could be accessed from a small structure in the rear. She chose none of those, heading down the path toward the massive capitol building.

Approaching the glittery white facade always filled her with awe. This building housed the Assembly Hall, Consular Chamber, administrative offices and numerous supportive departments. She'd been coming here for over ten years, ever since Uncle Manny's election to the Council. As CEO of Lyonus Metals, he'd held an influential position as long as she'd been part of his household.

Her pulse accelerated as she cleared another security checkpoint and entered the hallowed halls of the Directorial Wing. Despite her preferred detachment from her family, her heart swelled with a sense of homecoming.

She glanced up as her auditory sensors picked up men's laughter from around the next corner. It didn't surprise her to see a group of prominent councilmen strolling her way. They wore slate gray suits distinguished by Great Seal gold medallions.

"Silver, my dear, what brings you here?" Fester Niles

boomed when he spotted her. Owner of Solvent Minerals, he produced the largest supply of trona for the shipyards.

She observed his receding gray hair, trimmed beard, and perennial squint with an amused eye. He'd been her uncle's favorite Takeover Bids game partner for ages.

"I need to see Uncle Manny. Is he in his office?"

"You know Silver Malloy, don't you?" Niles asked his companions.

"Of course." Angus MacIntyre winked at her. A man of large girth, he smelled like apples and cinnamon, reminding Silver it had been a while since her last meal.

She greeted the other three, also heads of important corporations. It took her a moment to realize they all belonged to the Expansionist Party. That's why she didn't note any women among them. The lady diplomats mostly supported the Conservatives.

"I'm afraid Lyonus wasn't feeling well, so he elected to go home early," Niles told her in a solemn voice.

"It's nothing serious, I hope."

"No, no. Something he ate at our breakfast meeting didn't agree with him."

"More likely, he partied too hard last night at the Ratcliff's fundraiser," Litmus Carroll said with a chuckle.

Silver fell into step beside them, veering down another corridor that featured plasma screens depicting infomercials. One of the travelogues showed snow-peaked mountains advertising Carroll's entertainment and tourism conglomerate. She sniffed a mixture of pine-scented air and wild heather as they passed by.

Niles gave her a curious glance. "Where have you been? We haven't seen you around in a while, and you look somewhat discombobulated."

"I've been traveling."

"Is that so? Maybe you can take your cousin Evelina with you the next time. She's driving your uncle crazy. What with the Yamens pressing for more concessions and the Kurashkis threatening war, he doesn't have time for frivolities."

"What do you mean about the Kurashkis?" She held her breath, waiting for his answer.

"Ask Lyonus. He'll be glad if you take an interest."

His tone implied what he didn't say. After the way she'd rudely cut them off, her aunt and uncle would still welcome her home.

"I'll do that. Thanks, Chairman. Peace be with you."

Silver left to report in at S.I.N. central. She'd better do that before visiting her cousin, Dash, a vice president in the Department of Science and Technology. Her compatriots must know by now she was on the grounds.

Inside the nondescript bureau building, she strode past a receptionist, giving a nod of acknowledgment. The booth at the far end was similar to the one in Bartlett Station giving access to the science node, except this time she knew the correct sequences. When she finished with the retinal scan, a steel door slid shut, and the entire cage descended. She emerged into a bustling control room several levels below the surface.

"Silver!" Her boss, Major Wendy Dean, greeted her with a crisp smile that didn't quite extend to her glacial blue eyes. "I didn't expect you back… so soon."

Or at all? Silver pondered the implications as she surveyed the roomful of technicians.

"I had a delay in accomplishing my mission," she replied. "Shall we discuss it in your office? I have a request to make."

The idea had come to her as she'd reminded herself to stop at the Criminal Justice Court to file for Jace's bounty, and at Mining in Colonies to stake her claim.

Her stomach growled, altering her plans. If she didn't get something to eat, she wouldn't have the energy to accomplish much else. A hot shower and new clothes would also be welcome, but those were low on her priority list. Who knew what indignities Jace was suffering? She pictured him alone in his cell, despair as his company. Her own needs could wait.

Major Dean regarded her from across a spacious

mahogany desk. She didn't ask Silver to take a seat, which reinforced her feeling of being reprimanded. "Intelligence reports that Tyrone's Marauders hit the Comax system, leaving fifty thousand dead. He succeeded in raiding their ore stations and putting them back ten years in satellite repairs."

The Major folded her hands on the desk near one of her expensive monogrammed pens. "Explain to me why you failed to carry out your assignment."

Silver shifted her feet, clasping sweaty palms behind her back. "A Kurashki criminal known as Jace Vernon interfered with my mission. He was fleeing pursuit when I ran into him. I took him into custody."

"Where did this happen?"

Her gaze drifted to an empty candy wrapper in the wastebasket. "On Al'ron. I was just about to fire on Bluth when a man knocked into me. I got off a shot, but Bluth ran away."

"This man was Jace Vernon?"

"Yes, that's right. Jace said he had to capture the Marauder alive in order to prove his innocence."

The Major's lips tightened, and Silver realized the use of Jace's first name might have sounded overly familiar.

"So why didn't you eliminate Vernon and chase after your target?"

"Bluth's henchmen were searching for us in the woods."

"Us? You mean, you and the Kurashki?"

Silver fiddled with her fingers. "I didn't know Jace's identity at that point—we were too intent on escape. I'd hoped to reach the spaceport before Bluth lifted off, but Jace and I had to hide in a cave."

Should she tell her superior about the rubilite lode? Probably. It would be better coming from her than for Major Dean to find out from other sources.

"We discovered a cavern riddled with streaks of rubilite. If you have no objections, I'd like to stake a claim."

The major stiffened. "Let me get this straight. You were

about to fire on Bluth, but that Kurashki fellow prevented you. Together, the two of you fled from Bluth's men. You ended up in a cave loaded with rich gemstones."

She swallowed, aware of how weak her story sounded. "We made it to the spaceport, and that's when Jace told me his name. I arrested him, confined him to my ship, and towed his vessel while searching for Bluth's ion trail. We came under fire by Bluth's rear guard."

The look in Dean's eyes matched the darkness of her hair. "Are you expecting me to believe that a wanted criminal willingly gave you his name when you hadn't recognized him up to that point?"

"He told me he'd been framed and tried to convince me to help him." She straightened her spine. How she presented her case would make all the difference. "Of course, I didn't believe his lies. My ship got damaged, and we put in for repairs at Bartlett Station. I meant to play along with him until my vessel was fixed, but things happened and we ended up as crew on a slave trader's ship."

Her superior's silence cut the air like a fine-edged blade. Silver babbled on, sweat pricking her brow.

"I was afraid Jace—I mean Vernon—would get away, so I engineered a distress call to summon the fleet. When we arrived on Earth, I took him into custody again. We were on our way here when his Elusian friend had an accident."

Silver fidgeted under Major Dean's impervious glare. Would lying ever come easily to her? What made her think she could succeed at this job? Hadn't Uncle Manny told her she was better suited for the biodromes?

"What do you plan to do now?" The major's icy tone wafted her way like a winter chill.

"I've got a lead on Bluth. I'll follow it through and complete my mission, but I am hoping I can take Jace Vernon to Kurash on the way. He's caused me enough trouble that I deserve payback."

"Emotional involvement is dangerous in our game." Dean hunched forward, creasing her black jacket. She always wore black, which suited her somber mood. "You, of all people, should know this. Or maybe it's why you failed."

"I didn't fail. As I said, I'm not finished where Bluth is concerned. Next time he won't get away." *As long as you let me keep my job.*

"I'm sure you are aware of the Chancellor's reservations that you're not cut out for this role. I, on the other hand, fear it might prove too suitable a job for someone with your sentiments." The major studied Silver, as though weighing her options. "I'm not sure yet which one of us is right, so I'll give you another chance. But be warned, if Bluth survives, that's the end of your career."

"And Jace Vernon?" An ember of hope kindled in her chest.

"He has no bearing on your mission, but I'll mention it to Justice. That's their department." Major Dean paused a moment to punch a button on her console. "Off the record, talk to your cousin Dash, and you didn't hear this from me. He's been transferred to Internal Affairs."

Moisture filled her eyes at the unexpected kindness. "Thank you. It's just that I'm the logical person to transfer Jace, since I'll be going in that direction anyway. Oh, I'll need a new ship. The Avenger got impounded on Bartlett Station."

The major lifted a skeptical eyebrow. "You'll put all this in your report, I presume."

Sure, with a few omissions. Silver pursed her lips. "A man on the station linked the Avenger to me. He worked for Tyrone Bluth. How do you suppose they nailed me so quickly?"

Dean's gaze veiled, shuttering her emotions. "I wonder. Vernon snuffed a couple of men on the station, didn't he? I heard the broadcast."

"They were Bluth's men who meant to bring me to him by force. Jace helped me escape, when he could have used the diversion for his own getaway. I'm more concerned about how Bluth traced my identity so fast."

"As you should be. Let me worry about that." Rising, the major gave Silver a weary smile. "You just concentrate on catching your target."

****

Three days later, Jace paced the confines of his cell. A vague sensation of unease made his temples throb. It didn't stem from his predicament but reeked of another consciousness. Not Mixy's familiar presence. Could it be Silver?

He halted, staring morosely at the shimmering energy shield that barred entrance to his concrete block. Yes, the essence in his mind bore her faint signature. That meant Mixy must be alive, if the Elusian facilitated their link. But it worried Jace that he couldn't gain reassurance beyond that point. Mixy's mental absence remained an ominous sign.

Comet dust, if only he knew his friend would survive.

While that wouldn't mitigate his failure, at least he would not claim responsibility for another death. As for his sister, he'd tried his best. Her destiny rested in Silver's hands now. Regarding the Kurashki Alliance, his influence had dissolved to the trace elements to which he would soon return.

Scratching his scruffy beard, Jace resumed pacing, his legs restless. The cell stank of sweat and urine, and no doubt, he did too. A metal toilet and sink were the only furnishings.

His muscles ached, not so much from the exercises he performed as from the interrogation sessions. Over and over, he'd been questioned about Silver's involvement, but he'd stuck to his story. As soon as he had revealed his identity, she arrested him. They'd have reached base sooner had it not been for Bluth's men. She had been betrayed by someone back home who had access to secure S.I.N. files.

Things had turned uglier after he'd made that accusation.

106

They'd used drugs, from which his arms still wore purplish bruises. Fortunately, his combat training had included anti-interrogation techniques. He hadn't swayed from his account, but that only increased their determination to crack him.

More painful methods left him weak and gasping, but he didn't fold. Perhaps the Terrans wouldn't send him to Kurash so fast if they considered him useful. In particular, the Internal Affairs officer in charge of his case seemed intent on learning what he'd done to Silver. This man claimed Jace must have brainwashed her. Visualizing her wide violet eyes and flowing silken hair helped him maintain his sanity. For all he knew, she'd abandoned him to his fate. He wouldn't put it beyond her to claim the bounty, either.

His mouth curved down in irony. Here he was trying to defend the woman, when she probably hadn't given him another thought. The uneasiness she broadcast must stem from some other source. It gnawed at him with tendrils of dread.

Somewhere a door clanged, and his stomach heaved. They were coming for him again.

He backed away, hating how his gut turned to ice, and how his body reacted with the scent of fear. Their methods might be unpleasant, but it was nothing compared to what his own people had done to him to force a confession. By now his reactions were automatic. While his mind remained strong, he couldn't help the way his nerves responded to imminent pain.

Two guards stood on duty outside the containment field. They snapped to attention when a squad rounded the corner. A choked cry escaped his dry throat when he spotted Silver in their midst. Had they arrested her for complicity, despite his protests that he hadn't compromised her? Was she being led into an adjacent cell?

He stood stock-still, aware his confusion must be evident when the officer from Internal Affairs disengaged the energy shield. The lean, dark-haired man hadn't been his interrogator, but he'd ordered the sessions focusing on Jace's corruptive influence over Silver. So his deference toward her was all the more puzzling.

"Vernon is all yours," the stern man said to Silver, whose reaction to his haggard appearance didn't show on her impassive face.

Regardless of her seeming disinterest, a sense of dismay emanated from her through their empathic bond. So she did care about what happened to him. When the officer gave him a keen glance, Jace washed his face of any emotion.

Silver raised a hand when the officer drew out a pair of manacles. "That won't be necessary. Vernon is fond of his manservant. If I promise him news, he'll cooperate."

"Mixy? Is he all right?" Jace's heart leapt in hope.

"Just barely. Behave, and I'll tell you more. Come with me."

"Where?" An armed escort formed around him.

She lifted her chin, while his gaze focused on the wisps of silvery hair fanning her face. "I'm taking you to Kurash by the fastest route possible. I've acquired another ship. We're leaving as soon as I receive clearance from your government."

His lips compressed. Maybe he'd been wrong about her. She could be disturbed by the thought of traveling with such a grungy companion. Hopefully she'd let him clean up before his execution.

He marched along dutifully, wondering at the possibility of escape. What would happen to Mixy if he evaded captivity? Great Cosmos, he'd never considered that anyone could use the Elusian as leverage against him. But he hadn't realized how much affection he held for his friend, nor how Mixy's emotional outbursts reflected his own need for release. Now that the immediate threat of physical torment was past, tension coiled through him like a bunger snake.

An aircar waited for them outside the grounds of the detention complex.

"Why is he coming with us?" Jace froze when the Internal Affairs officer climbed into the front seat beside the driver.

“Get in. It’s okay, Jace.”

Puzzling over Silver’s reassuring tone, he strapped down in a rear seat next to her and eased back against the leather cushion.

“Am I in your custody or the government’s?” He glanced pointedly at the rigid shoulders of the man in front of them.

“You’ll see.” Once they’d lifted off, Silver sagged visibly. Lines of fatigue etched her face. “We’re going to my uncle’s house. They wouldn’t let me take you to my apartment. Dash is my cousin.”

Jace’s mouth dropped open when she pointed to the officer. “Him?”

She inclined her head, her silvery hair spilling over her shoulders. Her gaze held a hint of sadness as she patted his hand.

“I’m sorry for what’s happened to you.” She spoke quietly but he doubted they’d be heard over the engine noise. “I can’t explain everything now, but just play along. Things aren’t right here.”

“What do you mean?”

He glanced out the window where the sun’s brightness made him squint. They’d entered a traffic lane and soared upward at an angle. A smell like burnt electrical wiring stung his nostrils. An air cooling system kicked in with a low hiss, dissipating the odor. If he recalled properly, this month was called July here, and heat pervaded the region.

As they dodged skyscrapers, he peered below at the people scurrying among the city streets like a bunch of crawlers.

Silver leaned toward him, giving off a vanilla scent that tightened his loins.

“I told Major Dean, my superior, about someone obtaining classified information from S.I.N. files. She said she’d look into it, but I got the impression she’d already known. Then I talked to Dash. My cousin thought you were sent here as a spy.”

His eyebrows arched. “How is that possible? I never intended to come to Earth.”

"No? Dash proposed that our encounter didn't happen by chance. He said your entire story could have been concocted by the Kurashki Assembly to plant you here. Or you could be in league with Tyrone's Marauders, setting his goons on me when we arrived at Bartlett Station. Either way, you have conveniently arrived on Earth just when Kurashki forces threaten our borders."

He winced. "You don't believe him, do you?"

"Of course not. I'm just repeating Dash's theories."

"Thanks… I think. I don't like what you're saying about our forces aligning on the border, though. Garth must have gotten enough votes for a declaration of war. It is doubtful Hurat will oppose him. Our ruler likes to keep his treasury full, and Garth's lands provide revenue."

"What about your estates?"

"Once Garth is sworn in as Parsater at the Incantation Ceremony four weeks from now, he'll gain my political seat along with my votes. He's already taken title to my property."

He fell silent, his thoughts turning inward. While it was imperative for him to return to Kurash to prevent Hurat from falling prey to Garth's schemes, he couldn't arrive there overtly. Enlisting Silver's help was the only way he'd make it back undercover, but he wouldn't jeopardize Mixy's situation. How could he obtain information on his valet's condition?

Ten minutes later, they descended onto a wide lawn fronting a gated property. He caught a glimpse of a palatial structure that he assumed was her uncle's dwelling. It looked like one of his king's summer palaces. Mica embedded in the sandstone exterior sparkled in the sun's brilliant rays. While the domed roof and wings that spun off the multi-story main house gave an impression of formality, columns in front supported a portico with lounge chairs and lazily rotating ceiling fans. This softened the impact, making a statement that this was a home, not an official government address.

As they emerged from the aircar, uniformed security agents rushed to form an escort.

"Be careful," Silver warned before they climbed the few steps to the veranda. "Other than my family, I'm not sure who to trust. Someone is watching my apartment. It could be my own people, or it might be Bluth's men. I'm not even sure Mixy's accident happened by chance."

His blood chilled at her words, but he didn't have time to contemplate them. Inside the house, he glimpsed classic works of art decorating silk-paneled walls, gold leaf trim, and antique furniture smelling from citrus oil polish.

His guards veered off as did Silver, leaving him in the care of a somber-faced manservant. The gray-haired man led him upstairs to a chamber where he received a shower, shave, and fresh set of clothing. He'd barely expressed his appreciation for the fine suede fabric of his shirt when the footman ushered him downstairs to a lavish dining room.

Jace paused outside the doors, catching sight of at least ten people laughing and chatting around an elegantly set table. A silver-haired man occupied the head position, his patrician features and confident posture marking his position of authority. His deep-hued violet eyes were flanked by worn creases that showed he smiled often. Instead of being formally attired like his compatriots, he wore an open-collared knit shirt and belted trousers.

Jace swallowed as everyone's attention swung toward him. Without conscious thought, he sought Mixy's reassuring mental essence. It wasn't there, but he sensed Silver's warm presence in its place. Her awareness filled him with a feeling of completion he hadn't known he'd been missing.

Had Silver heard anything about Mixy's condition? Where in Zolifer was she? He presumed those two empty seats were reserved for them, but he couldn't conceive of why he'd been invited to dinner. True, armed guards stood at posts around the house, but he felt more like a welcomed visitor than a prisoner.

"Lord Vernon, please enter." Their host rose and swept his arm in a commanding gesture. "While you're in my house, consider yourself a guest. I trust my niece will keep you in line."

So, this was the great Mans Obrigard Lyonus. Jace advanced a few paces and bowed. "Maxima Chancellor, it is an honor, sir."

It would have been more of an honor if he were here in his diplomatic status. Resisting the urge to curl his fingers, Jace assumed the mask of a charming country gentleman. Good thing Mixy wasn't there, or the Elusian would be crawling the walls.

Lyonus extended his hand, and Jace remembered the Earth custom. He accepted the handshake.

"Let me introduce you to my family. This is my dear wife, Marguerite. I believe you already know Dash, and these are my other children—Remy and Evelina."

Jace bowed to the attractive older woman seated at the opposite end of the table. With her raven hair fixed into an upsweep, laughing dark eyes, and open friendly smile, Marguerite exuded warmth. She didn't stand on ceremony, either. The lady of the house wore a racy red blouse with trim gray pants.

Jace washed his face of any reaction. On his world, the landholder's wife wouldn't be seen in such indecent attire.

Dash, the Internal Affairs man, sat on their host's right. In his family's embrace, he seemed an entirely different person than the stiff officer he'd appeared in their earlier encounters. Upon Jace's guarded greeting, he broke into a grin. Dimples totally transformed his handsome face into an almost likable demeanor. Almost. Jace couldn't quite trust him yet.

He liked the other two on sight. Evelina, a stunning young woman with a mane of curly black hair and her mother's dancing eyes, fluttered her lashes at him. He wondered if she'd caught something in her eye, especially when his offhand acknowledgment caused her to pout. Remy was the text book meaning of antithesis, his head of blond hair and towering height seemingly incongruous with the other family traits. When Jace addressed him in turn, Remy stood and stuck out his hand. His handshake was effusive but firm.

Mans Lyonus introduced the other distinguished guests at the table. These included Wendell Reiss, Earth Centrum leader;

Hildegard Palomar, president of the Colonies; Fester Niles, chairman of the board and owner of Solvent Minerals; Angus MacIntyre, CEO of Morse Cybertronics; Litmus Carroll, entertainment and tourism mogul; and High Admiral Sam Canter, Defense Command. They were all members of the Consortium ruling council, Jace realized with a sense of awe.

He'd studied the Consortium government system. Based upon galactic trade, with its merchant ships protected by a navy, the Terran federation's heads of state were mostly owners of multi-world business conglomerates. Nothing could be farther from his own coalition government, an alliance with other worlds based on conquest and hereditary rule.

Progressives such as Jace recognized that their current problems, like the blight on their crops, needed outside help. It was time to widen Kurash's trade prospects, both in goods and technology. But the warmongers preferred to gain their spoils through aggression, otherwise the merchant class might threaten their power base.

Perhaps the situation on his home world wasn't so distant from the division of political parties here on Earth, after all. They both needed people like him, willing to find common ground, in order to co-exist in peaceful harmony. Who among this group was likely to share his sentiments?

"We're gathered together because of the grave situation confronting us," Lyonus said when they were seated again. "The Kurashki fleet is amassing forces on the border. Lord Vernon, what can you tell us about their intentions?"

Ah, they brought me here for another round of questioning. So much for the possibility of finding allies. Then again, the man addressed me by my proper title. What does that mean?

"My ruler prepares for battle. I am not in agreement with him, nor are certain other factions within our inner circle, but we have little influence." He twirled his water glass, reflecting the sparkle from a crystal chandelier. "If I were able to execute my vote, it would make a difference."

"You expect us to believe this, when you're conspiring

with the Marauders?" Across the table, Fester Niles stroked his beard.

Jace shot the sharp-tongued fellow a level glance. "Tyrone Bluth destroyed my family. I seek him for justice."

"The Marauders would love to see our peoples go to war," the female president remarked. With her walnut hair swept into a severe bun, minimal makeup, and a tailored suit, she gave a no-nonsense impression. "They swoop in on weakened worlds, plunder their cities, and enslave their populace. I've heard how Bluth disembowels heads of state without mercy." Everyone shuddered at her words.

"We think Bluth is acting as a spark to set our war machines aflame," the portly chairman of Morse Cybertronics said.

MacIntyre spoke with an accent that made understanding him difficult. Jace needed Mixy's proficiency in linguistics. He'd never missed his atrani more than now.

"You interfered with Silver's mission to terminate Bluth," cut in the Admiral, lowering his brows. "Some people might believe you work for him."

Jace fought an urge to punch his accuser's complacent face. No wonder Silver wasn't here. They'd wanted to corner him in her absence.

"If that's what you think, you're wrong," he said quietly. "My aim is to see justice done."

"Justice will be done at your execution," sneered Niles.

Half-rising from his chair, Jace clenched his fist. He'd have been better off left in a detention cell. This humiliation burned him. He would never be treated this way if he'd taken his rightful position in the Parsate.

"Gentleman, this is a dinner party, not a courtroom," Mans Lyonus admonished them. "I invited you here to meet our guest, not to make him uncomfortable. Remy, tell him what you've accomplished."

The blond man aimed a sympathetic glance his way. Jace

sank back into his seat, hoping glumly that Silver would make an appearance soon. Perhaps she was even now inquiring into Mixy's condition. Tightening his mouth, he resolved not to leave without his valet if the Elusian's status permitted moving him.

"I managed to get your ship released from Bartlett Station." Remy's drawling tone matched his lazy posture. "Silver's, too. Our pilots are flying them in as we speak."

Jace's expression brightened. "I'll get the Stinger back?"

Remy shook his head. "According to maintenance, both of your vessels need further repairs. Silver has been issued a new ship, a Kelvin Class IV Corvette. It's one of our smaller models, but it has six double turboboost lasers." He beamed like a proud father. "I'm to fly you to the shipyards in the morning."

For what, my extradition to Kurash? "How about my valet? Is he all right? Will he come with us?"

"Mixy is much better," Silver called from the doorway. "He's being kept under sedation while his body heals."

As she strode into the room, all eyes turned toward her. She wore a navy jumpsuit with a utility belt, as though dressed for a mission rather than a genteel dinner. Her platinum hair shone like brightly polished silver, spilling over her midnight-clad shoulders like snow on asphalt. The only touch of color came from her vibrant eyes and reddened cheeks. Jace suspected the latter came more from self-consciousness than cosmetics.

Scooting to his feet, he glanced around in surprise when the rest of the party remained seated. Did they not rise when ladies entered, even though their women dressed in manly attire?

With a hint of a smile, Jace pulled out the chair next to his and offered her the seat. After she'd plopped herself down with an irreverent grunt, he reclaimed his place.

A bevy of servants paraded into the room carrying a load of steaming tureens. The aroma of potato leek soup wafted into his nostrils.

Silver scanned the company. "Why didn't you tell me to

come down earlier?" At her uncle's silent response, she nodded. "Oh, I see. You wanted to question Jace without me. Learn anything new?"

Lyonus winced at her cynical tone. "He is prepared to leave with you in the morning. Remy will provide transport."

"Is Mixy well enough to go?" Jace hated the eagerness in his voice. The Elusian had turned into his Achilles heel, if that was the proper Earth reference.

"He's stable but not cleared yet."

Silver's unspoken words hung in the air. Mixy's welfare depended upon Jace's cooperation. Even if he went along with his captors docilely, Jace feared the Terrans might not release his friend. If they suspected him of collusion with their enemy, Mixy might even be incarcerated at a later date… unless Bluth's operatives got to him first.

One way or another, Jace vowed to smuggle Mixy out on that ship with them tomorrow.

Chapter Ten

Conversation during dinner focused on politics, which puzzled Silver. Uncle Manny should be more circumspect considering the company, but maybe he had his reasons for discussing the readiness of Terran forces to meet the threat posed by the Kurashki Alliance.

"It's not our wish to go to war," MacIntyre claimed in his booming voice, addressing his colleagues. "By God, our troops are prepared to defend our lands, but we'd like to avoid bloodshed."

"Perhaps an alternative will present itself." President Hildegard offered a hopeful smile with her conciliatory tone.

Silver glanced at Jace. He'd downed the soup like a starving man, keeping his head bowed as though food were the only thing on his mind. However, she knew he was listening from the way the cords stood out on his forearms. His tension electrified the air between them.

"What is this?" Jace asked, pointing to the mud-colored mound on his plate after the servants delivered the next course.

"Chopped liver." Silver admired his dashing figure. He sat at the table as though born to nobility, which she supposed fit his former status on Kurash. His resolute jaw, keen eyes, and confident pose resonated through her. "Spread it on a cracker, and try a bite. It goes good with the sweetbreads."

"That is bread?" He looked askance at the dish.

"Sweetbreads are made from the thymus or pancreas of a calf," Festor Niles pronounced in a loud voice. "It's quite a delicacy."

Jace's complexion turned a sickly hue. "Liver that looks like mashed dung, and other organs from the bodies of dead animals? I didn't read anything about this in my cultural studies."

"Really?" Niles sneered at him. "What did you learn, that we'd be an easy race to conquer? Or as easy to kill as those two men you beat to a pulp on the space station?"

Silver gave Niles a sharp glance. She hadn't discussed that incident with anyone except Major Dean.

"I learned your women are beautiful." Jace sipped his wine. "And your politicians can lie as well as our own."

Niles snickered. "You have personal experience in that arena. Ruler Hurat listens to what your cousin Garth tells him. Too bad you're not there to lend your influence, but then again, you've lost your position of power."

Jace's knuckles went white. Before he could make a retort he might regret, Silver placed her hand over his.

"Current political tensions aren't our only concern," she said, glancing from person to person. "After I took Jace into custody, a squad of Marauders attacked us. We got away, but they'd damaged our ships. We stopped at Bartlett Station for repairs. You know that's part of my investments through the Hoatch Foundation?"

At everyone's nod, she plunged on. "What surprised me was the ripple of discontent in the labor force. Workers say pirates have disrupted their supply lines, and maintenance is missing critical parts. The resultant drop in income from lost business has filtered down to all levels. Didn't the Rymerian Outpost cede to Dorius two years ago?"

"What's your point?" Uncle Manny hunched forward with an intent expression.

"We got a berth on Captain Keelo's ship on our way home. His manifest says he delivers medical supplies, but in actuality, he picks up survivors of raids and ferries them to the Crockers for sale as food. My point is, why are we allowing scoundrels like Keelo and terrorists like Bluth to run rampant? Can't our military step up their patrols?"

"That Rymerian Outpost was near the Dorian border," President Hildegard remarked, sitting rigidly. "We are stretched thin as it is. Now with war preparations underway, it's even more difficult to bolster defenses of our settlements."

"Perhaps the Dorians are trying to do economically what they couldn't accomplish with their military," Silver suggested. "These pirates may be getting funded by someone who has an ulterior purpose in mind."

"Or maybe it's a subplot by the Kurashkis to weaken our supply lines and subvert our repair bases," High Admiral Sam Canter rumbled in his deep tone.

"My people have no need to resort to such tactics," Jace replied. "We won the war with the Dorians. Although the casualties were high, our military ranks have swelled. We expect nothing less from our opponents than defeat. This is why it's imperative to sway Ruler Hurat from his dangerous path."

The Admiral's jaw clenched. "That sounds like a threat to me, sonny. Maybe this extradition treaty is just a trick to send you home. We should execute you here for being a spy."

Silver half-rose in alarm when a murmur of consensus swept through the room. "Jace supports a peace treaty between the Kurashki Alliance and the Terran Consortium. He opposes military action. That's why he thinks his cousin Garth framed him."

"Maybe the reasons are closer to home," suggested Niles with a sly grin. "With Vernon's family out of the way, Garth stands to gain their adjacent estate. Isn't that how your hereditary laws work? Then again, if you get pardoned, you assume your father's title and all privileges therein. Was that your plan, to kill your parents and blame the Marauders?"

Jace's hand slapped to his side, then he seemed to remember he lacked a weapon. "If this were my world, I would challenge you for that slur to my honor. I grieve my parents' loss."

"How did you escape confinement on Kurash? You must have had help." Festor's eyes narrowed to slits. "Who were they?"

Jace clamped his mouth shut in the aura of suspicion that followed, while Silver sensed his anguish. The man claimed to want peace between their peoples, yet no one credited his motives. Alone and condemned, he'd even lost his one true companion to an accident that Silver suspected had malicious origins.

"Remy, why don't you tell us about those new upgrades to our Tag 120 Star Cruisers you're working on at Gravicom Wells?" the Admiral broke in, cutting the heavy silence.

Remy's blond eyebrows raised. "You want me to—?" He stopped, clearing his throat. "Oh, right. We're refitting them with our hyperdrive upgrade, a chameleon device, and redesigned antiflux missles. The first division will be receiving delivery shortly."

"It's already passed simulations with fantastic results." A proud gleam in his eyes, the admiral puffed out his chest. "We project this will increase our strength by at least twenty-five percent, especially with the reinforced repellant shields."

Beside her, Jace stiffened. She understood why the Admiral wanted him to know about their updated equipment. It only added to his humiliation. She felt his frustration at not being able to avert a war, and his despair of ever restoring his name.

Not that it's any business of mine, she reminded herself.

Tyrone Bluth would take advantage of any war that erupted, contributing to the deaths of civilians left vulnerable by enemy attacks. For certain, he'd undermine Terran forces by raiding their supply lines. He had to be stopped, by any means possible.

As for dropping Jace off at Kurash, she'd only requested permission to take him home in order to use him for her own ends. She was heading to Stacktown, and she needed him to watch her back. With the two of them tracking Bluth together, they had a better chance of reaching him. If she were still alive after her mission, she'd worry about the consequences then.

She gave a sigh a relief when their guests left for the

evening. Turning away from the entry where her family had said their farewells, she veered toward the grand staircase. Time to recite her memorial prayers and retire.

Even though she'd moved into her own apartment, Marguerite kept her room here available. While she felt grateful, Silver still preferred to keep her distance.

Having been torn from the bosom of her parents after the disaster on Altuis Three, she'd been thrust into this home in the midst of culture shock, coming from a relatively backward agricultural colony to the high-speed city, and a gregarious and close-knit family all at once. She'd fought to remain emotionally isolated. It had been a wise decision, considering what happened when she lowered her barriers—more grief and pain to bury along with her memories.

She put her foot on the first carpeted step but paused when Uncle Manny spoke.

"It's a good thing they didn't bring their spouses," the elder statesman said with a chuckle. "We had enough dirt flying through the air tonight to plant a cornfield."

"I'm glad you didn't invite the S.I.N. chief," Dash said with his usual somber inflection. "It's no secret about her and Niles. She would have distracted him, and he might not have talked so readily. Did you get what you wanted, Father?"

"Come on, guys," Evelina urged in her frothy voice, "lighten up. We haven't been very welcoming to our guest. I don't believe that hogwash about him." Sidling up to Jace who stood awkwardly off to the side, she stroked his arm. "My brother said you used to be a combat pilot. I'll bet you looked smashing in your uniform."

Silver spun around, intending to stop Evelina from making a fool of herself. She stopped at the look of exasperation on her older cousin's face.

"For God's sake, he's an enemy officer," Dash said, ploughing a hand through his hair.

"Evelina wouldn't care if he was shooting at her, as long as he looked good," Remy drawled with a grin.

Jace's face broke into a slow smile, and Silver felt his mood shift.

"Your eyes are so hypnotic," he told the girl, "they could charm a snake into submission. No one could hurt a jiggerfly in your presence."

"Puh-lease," Silver said, rolling her eyes.

"Let's go into the parlor," Aunt Marguerite suggested. She'd been conferring with the kitchen staff and had returned to join them. "Remy promised to play that new piece he learned. Tell me, Mr. Vernon, have you ever heard our music before?"

"Lord Vernon is your proper title, isn't it?" Dash said. "I understand you're from one of the noble families on Kurash."

Jace gave a nod of acknowledgement. "That is correct, although I've been stripped of my rank along with my property. I hope to reinstate them both when I get evidence proving my innocence." He spoke in a formal manner, as though he knew they wouldn't believe him.

They took seats inside a brightly lit room with hydroponic plants and cushioned furniture that molded to their forms. Silver claimed the chaise lounge she'd always favored, setting the aromatherapy sphere to produce an orange blossom scent.

Warmth settled into her bones as Remy began playing his guitar, that being his one concession to entertainment besides his collection of holoflicks. Normally, he read technical manuals in his spare time. Evelina was constantly inviting him to parties, but he didn't care for crowds.

Unlike his mechanical-minded brother and frivolous sister, Dash aimed for a political career following in his father's footsteps. Evelina's efforts to get him to crack a smile seemed fruitless. He took his responsibilities seriously, making Silver wonder how much he knew about her mission.

"That was great," Evelina gushed after Remy finished his brief recital to their enthusiastic applause. "Why don't you play something catchier so we can dance? I'll bet Lord Vernon can teach us some new steps."

"We should go to bed," Silver cut in, tapping Jace's arm. "I'd like to get an early start tomorrow." She caught her uncle's speculative glance and jerked her hand away.

Jace glanced wistfully at the antique piano that had been part of her great aunt's legacy. "Do you mind if I have a go at this first?" Before anyone could protest, he plunked himself on the bench. "We have something like it on my world." He splayed his fingers lovingly on the keys and played a haunting melody that enthralled his listeners.

"You play better than a rec-bot model six," Remy said in admiration as Jace's nimble hands poured fluid notes from the instrument. "We should get a group together. Evelina sings. All we'd need would be a bass and another guitar."

"If I'm spared my execution, I might take you up on the offer." Jace spoke in a breezy tone which didn't fool Silver. His voice held a note of desperation only she could detect.

After finishing his remarkable concert, he leapt to his feet and bowed with a courtly flourish.

"I can't believe you're a killer," Aunt Marguerite inserted, tucking a stray black hair into her upsweep. "You play so magnificently. Silver, you'll help him clear his name, won't you?"

"I'll do my job." Rising, she rubbed her neck.

"That girl has always been very goal directed." Her aunt's eyes twinkled as she addressed Jace. "I've tried to convince her to ease up on herself, but she resists. Part of her is still in that hellhole back on Altuis Three."

"I know what you mean," Jace said with a wink at Marguerite. "She's erected barriers that are tough to pull down, but when she does relax, it's worth the effort."

Silver ignored him and addressed her cousin. "Remy, what time should we be downstairs for breakfast?"

The blond man shrugged. "You tell me, cuz. You're the one in a hurry."

"Why don't we meet you at the spaceport?" Jace suggested.

"You can go earlier and prep the shuttle. Then there won't be any delays for our launch."

Silver resented his commanding tone of voice. He wasn't in any position to issue orders. And why the haste in getting to Gravicom Wells? Did he have an interest in seeing the military vessels under construction there? Were his accusers right, that he'd been sent here to spy on Earth's preparations for war? The idiot should be more careful about what he said. Dash was likely to report their conversation to Major Dean.

"Come on, Jace." Tugging on his arm, she grated her teeth.

He seemed perfectly at home with her cousins, as though he'd lived here for years. Even Aunt Marguerite had taken a liking to him. What lady wouldn't? His disarming grin, combined with his aristocratic bearing, made him undeniably attractive. No wonder Evelina succumbed so easily to his charm. Why, the girl's eyes were eating him up as though he were dessert.

Fortunately, Silver was immune to his magnetism. His mocking gaze told her he believed otherwise.

"Thank you for your hospitality," he said in an earnest tone to her aunt and uncle. "I hope my presence here hasn't been too disruptive."

"Not at all," Uncle Manny said. "It's been most illuminating." Silver could almost swear she noted a twinkle in his eye as he glanced her way.

"Go on and get some rest," Aunt Marguerite told them both. She urged them upstairs with a sweep of her arm.

After saying goodnight, Silver preceded Jace up the staircase. What was the matter with her relatives? They had a possible murderer in their midst, yet they treated him like a family friend. Did they know something she didn't? No matter, tomorrow would see a new path on their journey.

****

Jace lay awake in bed, waiting for the house to quiet before he made his move. If only the hospital personnel hadn't taken Mixy's possessions, he'd try to contact the Elusian via his comm unit. He couldn't credit reports that Mixy was recovering until he heard the valet's voice for himself. The only way to know for sure would be to see him in person.

At any rate, Jace didn't intend to leave Mixy behind. With guards posted outside in the hallway, he couldn't use that route. However, he could attempt an escape via the balcony. Security personnel patrolled the grounds, but he'd timed their movements and determined how to elude them.

His soft pillow tried to dissuade him from his plan. Shutting his eyes, he relaxed on the plump mattress while a vision of Silver in her slinky dark blue outfit rose in his mind.

Something else lifted at the same time, and his attempt to tamp down his response failed. She'd alternately delighted and dismayed him with her reactions tonight. Her jealousy over Evelina had been evident but so had her mistrust. Seething emotions ran deep beneath her surface, buried where they couldn't hurt her. He'd rather bury something else inside to unleash her hidden passion.

Twisting to his side, he forced himself to forget the way her clothing molded to her sensuous form, her long-legged stride, and the flash of defiance in her jeweled eyes.

Action was better than this hopeless longing. He swung his legs over the edge of the bed and reached for his shirt.

His motion stopped when a scratching noise sounded at the window. What was that? He dropped the clothing, strode over and swept aside one of the drapes.

Silver's luminous eyes glared back at him, her long hair lashing in the wind. His gaze dropped to the lawn. No one was visible. He unhooked the latch and flung open the window wide enough for her to come inside. Her vanilla-scented perfume wafted into the air as she entered, carrying a sack and wearing nothing but a filmy nightdress.

"I was in a hurry," she explained when she caught him staring at her. "We won't wait for morning. We'll leave now."

"Is that an order, ma'am?" he asked with an upward tilt to his mouth.

Her lips compressed, their sensual curves making him want to taste them. "I've been in touch with Mixy's doctor. Your valet is healed, but he's being kept under sedation because of an added complication. The doctor said it's nothing serious." She paused, frowning. "I'm concerned for his safety. If his condition is stable, we'll take him with us."

Jace gaped at her in disbelief. His own plan had been to rescue Mixy from the hospital, forcing Silver to compliance if necessary. Yet here she'd proposed the same thing.

"Won't Mixy's presence hinder your mission to track Bluth?"

"Worrying about your valet would distract me more."

He scrutinized her face, surprised to see genuine concern etched on her features. Perhaps the assassin had a weak spot in her armor after all. Warmth trickled through him. Despite her appearance as a hardened government agent, Silver nourished a kernel of compassion. More than that, she hadn't given him up on the space station, nor had she abandoned him to his fate here on Earth. She'd involved herself in his case for reasons even she probably didn't understand. Nor could her rationale provide the answer for why she had appeared in his chamber dressed in a transparent gown that highlighted every curve of her body. As his gaze roamed south, her rosy nipples peaked.

"What are you doing?" he rasped when Silver stepped forward and spread her hand on his bare chest.

"Do all Kurashkis have this much hair?" she crooned in an uncharacteristically seductive tone. Her slender fingers stroked his skin, causing him to draw in a sharp intake of air.

"Comet dust, woman, you tempt me beyond reason." Grasping her behind the head, he brought her face closer. Her lips parted, and he groaned with need. His mouth descended, and he wasn't surprised when she responded by clutching her arms around his neck.

Tasting her wine-drenched depths, he lost himself in heady sensations of lust. Her tongue teased him, challenging his explorations with her own. Touring the contours of her mouth, he sought to discover secreted pleasure in its hot, moist interior.

When her breasts pressed against his heated skin, flames spiraled through him. He nudged her toward the bed, unable to control his erection. They tumbled together onto the mattress where she writhed under him like a wild woman. His briefs and her gown quickly became discards on the floor. Their legs entwined, and he stroked and caressed her silken flesh until she panted in delight. Before she surged over the crest, he prodded her thighs apart and thrust into her.

A storm slammed into him, blazing in its intensity, battering his awareness. Mixy… the Elusian had awakened, jolted from his somnolence by their lovemaking. Silver jerked under him as though she, too, felt the added presence.

Their sensations mingled, until he couldn't tell which was hers and which belonged to him. Another thrust, and more, faster, until a crescendo swelled and burst. He spurted into her, suppressing his cry of triumph and release. Her cascading response prolonged his discharge until he collapsed, satiated and sweaty, on top of her. Their ragged breathing punctuated the silence as deep satisfaction filled him.

He'd never wanted anyone like he needed Silver, nor had Mixy's response ever been so intense. It was almost as though the Elusian approved and sought to unite them. Jace didn't understand. The woman was stubborn, fixated on her murderous goal, and determined to challenge every word he said. Yet deep inside, she hid the vulnerability of a child. His protective instincts threatened to overpower his reason. No one could soothe her hurtful memories, but he could give her a reason to live.

She already felt a sense of responsibility toward the people on the space station. Given a purpose, she devoted herself to a cause with unerring aim. If only he could make her see that her current path would lead nowhere except to perdition. Killing Bluth wouldn't assuage her demons. Only by opening herself to her full range of passion could she dismiss the past. Sleeping with him wasn't the answer, either. She merely used him to satisfy her lust. To prove she cared, she'd have to denounce her mission, but with revenge blackening her heart, that would not happen soon enough.

****

Silver lay motionless under Jace, sensing the emotions roiling within him. Doubt mingled with disappointment. Did he regret their incredible experience? She'd rushed here with the intent of leaving to salvage Mixy and smuggle him aboard their shuttle, but her state of undress suggested otherwise.

What had gotten into her that she became such a wanton in Jace's presence? Had she wanted to prove he was attracted to her, and not to her cousin? Did she feel his appeal so strongly that while she pretended he didn't affect her, she succumbed like any other female?

Her skin heated, and her feet shifted restlessly. She couldn't afford to be weak, because it made her lose sight of her goals. Or maybe that had been his plan all along, to create a pliant ally whom he could control. She'd complete his scheme perfectly by rescuing Mixy and aiding his escape. His doubts could merely be an attack of conscience.

"Somehow you always make me forget my intentions. This won't happen again." She rolled off the bed and grabbed her sack from the floor.

"Excuse me?" He stood and faced her squarely. His dark hair tumbled in disarray across his forehead, its reddish tint gone along with his blue contacts. "You're the one who appeared in my room wearing a see-through nightie."

"My mistake. Get ready, we're moving out." She pulled on

a hooded black top, tight pants, utility belt, and canvas shoes. Fortunately, she still kept some of her clothes here.

"How do you propose to get past the guards outside?"

"We can follow the balconies around the corner, then we'll have access to the roof. Our biggest problem is getting to the hospital without being tracked."

While he got dressed, she used the bathroom.

Ten minutes later, they stood at the open window waiting for the security detail to pass below their checkpoint. When the shadowy figures moved from sight, they edged outside. After drawing the hood over her braided hair, Silver proceeded to the left edge where she grasped the painted aluminum railing.

"Oh, I forgot to mention something," she said, swinging her leg over and straddling the space between rails. "I have to stop by my apartment to pick up my spare equipment."

"That'll waste time." He followed suit when she jumped to the next balcony.

"Quiet. We don't want to wake anyone inside." She motioned to the opened glass doors, a curtain fluttering in the breeze.

As they proceeded to the next ledge, their way lit by moonlight, a heavy scent of night jasmine filled the air. Her nerves energized, and she zoomed in on the slightest nuance of movement below. Halting, she tuned in her auditory sensors to a faint rustling sound. Damn, someone stood right under where they needed to cross. Her quick signal stopped Jace in his tracks.

"Is someone there?" Marguerite's crystal clear voice called. When no one responded, she moved away and silence reigned once again.

Silver had planned to maneuver from the second story to ground level. But after her aunt moved off, she changed her mind. She gestured toward the ivy covering a sturdy trellis against the wall. The trellis rose four stories high, nearly meeting the roof. Climbing up seemed a better option.

She stretched for a handhold on the trellis. It should hold their weight, if they went one at a time. Their slow pace would increase the risk of discovery, but it was a chance they'd have to take.

Swallowing hard, she stepped off the balcony, clinging with one hand to the trellis and cursing her lack of grappling equipment. Her hood fell back as she struggled to gain a grip with her other hand. Once secured, she found notches for her feet, adhering like a spider to a sticky web. The night air brought her Jace's heavy breathing along with an occasional bird cry. Crickets sang in the distance in a monotonous chorus.

Moving cautiously so as not to make any noise, she inched her way upward, careful to avoid splinters. The roof's edge loomed nearer until she grasped its tiled rim. Heaving herself onto the top proved difficult when her sweaty hands kept sliding.

A jarring impact on her butt shoved her over the edge. Jace had caught up and given her the boost she needed—just in time. An ominous cracking sounded just before he scrambled after her. Panting, they lay prone for a few moments gathering their breath. Silver didn't dare move in case the noise had alerted security. Keeping still, she probed with her auditory sensors for marching feet. When no further sounds issued from the night, she let out a breath of relief. A warm breeze lifted the hairs on her nape, and she spared a moment to breathe in the moist earth-scented air.

Jace pointed to her right. "What if we go that way? Won't we end up in the same spot you intended?" The whites of his eyes shone in the moonlight.

"That's what I planned," she retorted. "You go first."

His cocky grin raised her hackles. "Afraid I'll push you off the roof? You know, you have some bad control issues. I'd work on them if I were you."

"Move it." She swatted at him, but the motion dislodged her precarious position, and she slid downward. Her fingers scraped the slick surface, but she lost her grip.

Jace grabbed her wrist. Her pulse thundered in her ears, while her feet dangled more than four stories off the ground.

Now look where your outburst has gotten you. Hadn't she learned during training to detach herself emotionally when on a case? That had been the easiest part up until now. Jace continually wormed his way past her defenses, making her lose control and challenging her to assert authority. If she'd listen to her head instead of her body, she wouldn't be so inept at the job.

This job will be over if he lets go.

Craning her neck, she strained to discern his expression. A grim smile twisted his face as he allowed her arm to slip from his grasp.

Chapter Eleven

"You may survive the fall, but I wouldn't count on it," Jace said, grabbing her hand. "If you want me to save you, quit ordering me around." His eyes glinted in the moonlight. "In case you haven't noticed, we work better as a team. You're more afraid of your feelings for me than you are of failing your mission. We can help each other, but only if you believe in me."

"Look, I haven't turned you in, have I?"

"No, you've kept your word." With a grunt, he hauled her onto the roof. "Now consider this. If I really were a vicious criminal, you'd be dead several times over by now. You're using me to get to Tyrone Bluth, but what happens after that? You've promised to help rescue my sister. Will you follow through to see justice is done?"

"Justice is carrying out Bluth's sentence of execution. Anything less will be a dereliction of duty."

"Your duty should be to seek the truth."

"So if Bluth is found guilty of framing you, what then? Won't he be executed on Kurash?"

"That's for our courts to decide. I deserve that chance."

She gave him a hard look, discerning his motives. Nothing but honesty reflected in his eyes. Yearning swept over her, and it took her a moment to realize the emotion wasn't coming from her end. Jace longed for someone to have faith in him. He felt Mixy's absence acutely and reached out to her on a level she couldn't fathom. Emptiness yawned before her, but it wasn't the chasm below the roof's edge. It came from within her own heart, where a black hole of hatred sucked her into a vacuum sparked by single-minded purpose. Without that purpose, she had nothing. Except now, a tiny pinprick of light portended a better future, if only she'd allow it to expand.

"Come on," she said in a gentle tone. "Let's get Mixy."

Rather than pressing her for more promises, he shrugged and turned away. They scrambled over the roof to the other side where the wind hit her full in the face. Warm, moist summer air would give them good lift. Her spirits rose, and she signaled for Jace to follow her down to the flat roof at the second-story level behind the higher southeast wing. This location afforded them a view of the expansive grounds while they remained in the shadow of the taller structure.

"Don't we have to get to the garage?" Jace asked with a puzzled frown.

"We're not taking an aircar. That would be too easy to track." Crouching, she pulled back a tarpaulin and showed him her find. "We used to play with turbo scooters when we were kids. These are the newest R-25 models by Royce. I checked the fuel levels earlier, and we should have enough to get to the hospital. We'll blend in with ground cover if we fly low."

He gave her an admiring glance. "Resourceful. How about the noise?"

"Dampeners take care of that problem. Are you okay with driving your own?" She grabbed hold of one device and uprighted it.

"I'll manage." Following her example, he placed one foot in front of the other on the single board, fastened a safety strap around his torso, and gripped the handle bars.

"It can get bumpy when you hit an air current, but we'll go faster with a tailwind. Stay on my tack." Silver pushed the start button, and a familiar vibration rumbled underfoot. She punched the anti-grav flow valve, suppressing a whoop of exhilaration when her scooter lifted. Hoping she could maintain her balance with her rusty skills, she jabbed the turbo boost.

Her pulse raced as she shot over the edge of the roof, tilted sideways, centered her rider, and soared forward. *Uh oh, security detail below at two o'clock.*

Veering left, she avoided the estate's main entrance and surged toward a clump of trees leading to a major thoroughfare. That would take them into the city. Loose hairs whipped her cheeks and stung her eyes as she spun into the air lane.

Glancing backward, she grinned at Jace who proved his mettle by waving. Gods, this was fun. It had been eons since she'd done something so sinfully playful. A flush warmed her skin as she remembered their lovemaking. Well, maybe not so long.

As they neared her apartment complex, she slipped into a stream of other night owls prowling the streets. The rush of wind in her ears died, replaced by roaring engines and nonstop loudspeaker advertisements. She plunged her scooter up and down geometrically designed avenues and looped around skyscrapers.

Intent on checking over her shoulder for signs of pursuit, she narrowly missed a dive-bombing aircar. Her stomach catapulted into her throat as she careened sideways and flipped upside-down. With a lurch, she righted herself and swooped north just in time to avoid hitting a flyby night train.

Sweat beading her brow, Silver cursed the urban congestion. Never let it be said she preferred the glamour of the city over the bucolic peacefulness of the countryside. Maybe she'd been brought up on a backwater world, but she appreciated the green, open spaces much more than these crowded byways.

Her apartment building loomed into sight. She glided in for a landing at the rooftop pool. Hydroponic plants spilled from containers on the ledge, and she took care not to nick any stems before easing her scooter down. She settled in an aisle between lounge chairs on the concrete deck and shut off her engine.

"That was great." Jace brought his scooter in for a smooth landing beside hers.

His exuberant tone made her laugh. "My cousins and I loved to ride these things. It gave me a sense of freedom."

"I can see why. Are we using them to get to the hospital?"

She grunted affirmatively. "Hopefully anyone watching from the street won't have noticed our descent. Why don't you wait here? I'll just be a few minutes."

His expression turned serious. "If Bluth really does have agents in the city, he may have posted someone by your door. I'll accompany you. Do we need to secure our transport?"

"No one comes up here at this hour. Let's go."

Jace carried his meager possessions bundled in a roll along with Mixy's items, while Silver strode ahead unencumbered. She'd pick up any necessary supplies in her apartment.

After descending an interior stairway, she paused at the landing to her floor and cracked open the door. Recirculated air with a chemical tinge pervaded the hallway, which appeared empty. She motioned for Jace to follow as she crept forward.

A quick check around the perimeter of her apartment indicated no disturbances. Good. She stuck her hand into the identifier and offered her eye for the retinal scan. The latch unlocked, and her door opened. "Welcome home, Silver," intoned a sexy male voice.

****

"Don't go in there," Jace ordered upon hearing the intruder.

He reached for a weapon, but his hand found a flattened pocket. Instead, he thrust Silver aside and stalked into the block of space she called home.

His quick glance told him no one posed an immediate threat, but the man might be hiding in another room. He scanned the chrome and glass shelves, sleek modern furniture, and holovid entertainment center.

Silver's laughter rang from behind. She didn't show mirth very often, and he liked the way it softened her face when he whirled around to regard her.

"That's just Tom, my AI. Tom, raise the lights, please."

"You speak to your artificial intelligence program on such familiar terms?"

She nodded, while he studied her hair that had loosened from its braid and tumbled over her shoulders. He'd had a glimpse of the woman she might become when they rode their airborne scooters. She'd grinned with unleashed passion as the wind battered them, her eyes shining. He'd never felt so captivated.

If only he could free her from the bonds of grief, then she'd realize what she had been missing. Jace was no stranger to the pain of loss, but it filled him with a need to serve others instead of emptying him like a used jug.

"You have several messages," the AI's disembodied voice stated. "And while you were out, we had a—"

"Save it." Silver strode toward an open doorway. "I keep emergency supplies hidden in my bedroom," she told Jace. "Wait here."

"This software program, what does it do for you?"

She paused. "It makes my life easier. Don't you have smart networks where you live?"

"We have no use for cybernetic intrusion into our private space."

She glanced back at him. "I didn't think I would like it either, but I've gotten quite used to Tom."

"Hmm. I cannot imagine an artificial construct supplying the same satisfaction as a real man." Jace gave a smug grin in response to her heightened color.

Pursing her lips, she scurried into the next room. Jace lingered to scan her shelves, noting the lack of personal items and family portraits. Did she hesitate to invest emotional energy in mementos because whenever she cared too much, someone died?

"Jace!" she hollered, her voice laced with distress.

"What's wrong?" He raced to her side and skidded to a stop.

Inside her bedroom, opened drawers spilled clothing onto the carpet. Info chips splattered among torn papers and broken glass. Paintings tilted askew on the walls, while a wooden chair lay broken on the floor next to a smashed mirror.

Silver pointed to a still form beside her circular bed. A woman lay on the floor, vacant eyes staring at the ceiling, dark hair spread in a congealed pool of blood.

"Major Wendy Dean, Chief of S.I.N." Silver's voice came out a choked mumble. "She's dead."

"I can see that." Alarms clanged in his head. "Silver, it's a setup. We have to get out of here."

Her dazed eyes regarded him. "How could this happen? I just spoke to the major in her office earlier."

He felt her mingled guilt and horror, amplified by Mixy's bond between them. "Likely the killer lured her here. This place is probably being watched. The authorities may already be on their way." Panic seized him. He'd been in this situation before.

"But they'll know we didn't do it. Witnesses will confirm our presence at my uncle's house."

"Evidence can be planted." His mouth set in a grim line, he shoved the body with the toe of his boot. "Bluth's agents could be responsible, or else the traitor in your government might use this as an excuse to incarcerate us. Any leads in that regard?"

"Major Dean said she'd look into it. She might have found more than she'd bargained for. Oh, stars."

"We've got to move. Now."

"I'll get my stuff."

Her forlorn expression tugged at his heart. "I'm sorry for your loss, but you can grieve for her later. We have to make it to the spaceport."

"Just give me a minute." She approached a large round clock hanging on the wall.

"Hurry. I'm worried about Mixy. He could be their next target."

Silver removed the glass cover on the clock. She twisted the hour hand counter-clockwise to read eight o'clock, then forward to four. After a click sounded, she slid the entire clock aside, exposing a hidden cubbyhole. Her hand stretched inside and she withdrew a bulging backpack.

Loud voices sounded from somewhere near the front door. Jace glanced at her in alarm. How would they get out now?

"Follow me." Silver yanked a pen-like device from her sack. She headed for the window, slipping her arms into the backpack straps. "Tom," she told the artificial intelligence, "activate evasion plan alpha one."

With a grunt, she opened the window and leaned outside. She pressed a trigger on the device, causing a tensile line to shoot toward the roof.

"Let's go," she cried, scrambling onto their tether after giving it a tug.

As soon as he leaped after her, the window slid shut, but not before he heard the hiss of gas from inside the apartment.

"Let's hope they haven't discovered our scooters," he called, his heart pounding.

Their second climb of the night proved easy, and they scored an unchallenged approach to the rooftop. Shortly thereafter, they soared into the sky.

"What about your cousin? Will he still be able to meet us?" He aligned his rider parallel to hers.

"I'll notify him as soon as we touch down." Leaving her hood off, she let her hair fly free.

Long silvery strands lashed her face. She flashed him a tentative smile, making hope surge within him that her icy heart had begun to melt. Fear of loss still held her back, but she was wrong to be afraid to love again.

Oh, like you should talk. He understood the pain of losing a loved one but also knew his heart would never be healed by revenge, only by giving. So many people, like the workers at the space station, could benefit from Silver's attention. Why couldn't she see that life was a gift, despite its heartbreaks?

He didn't have time for further thought because they'd landed at the hospital's rooftop site.

"Let's get Mixy," he said, after she spoke to her cousin via her private comm channel.

Inside the building, Jace waylaid two attendants and stole their scrubs. Leaving the unconscious men inside a storage closet, he commandeered a stretcher. While he and Silver wheeled it down the hallway at a reckless pace, they kept their faces lowered. Jace halted when they reached a levelator.

"Do you know where to go?" he asked, punching the down button.

"Third-floor, xenobiology east." She grabbed a chip from her backpack that she'd stashed under the gurney. "I've forged a release using my S.I.N. authorization."

A doctor was examining the patient when they entered Mixy's room. The Elusian's normally pale complexion looked worse, almost translucent. He gazed at them in surprise.

"We've come to transfer you," Jace said, a note of warning in his tone.

"Transfer? On whose authority?" the doctor snapped.

Silver thrust her faked disk at him. While she regaled the physician with circuitous arguments, Jace detached Mixy's intravenous lines and bioprobes.

"How are you feeling?" he asked in an undertone, wanting to secure Mixy's safety without compromising his condition.

"I am doing well, milord, except for your anxiety which is making my two stomachs churn. May I politely request you refrain from emotional extremes? It taxes my growing one."

"Your what?" He assisted Mixy to scoot onto the stretcher and covered him with a blanket.

The doctor turned to Jace. "We thought it odd how the fellow required so many nutritional supplements after his transfusion, until we ran a few tests. Then it all became clear. He's budding."

Silver crinkled her face in confusion. "What's that? He's recovered from his head injuries, hasn't he?"

"Oh, yes. It was either his time, or the trauma induced his

expectancy. Given the accelerated rate of reproduction among Elusians, he should be producing a little one within the next few months. I find it quite fascinating, don't you?" the doctor said with a proud grin.

Silver stared at him. "You can't mean what I think you do. Mixy is *pregnant*?"

****

Mixy must have sensed her dismay, because he became agitated. "Oh, forgive me," he cried, wringing his hands in the air. "You don't need another complication. I'll be a burden to you. I'll hinder your mission. I'll—"

"You'll shut up," Jace commanded, his expression grim.

Silver met his eyes in silent understanding. They would never abandon their friend, but this added circumstance increased their risk. Plus, the longer they remained there, the higher their chances of being apprehended.

"We have to go," she told the doctor. "Thank you for your help."

With Jace acting as point man, she maneuvered the stretcher out the door and down the corridor.

"Wait," the doctor called, his footfalls sounding behind them. "I've received an alert. You can't—"

"Bye," she replied, shoving Mixy inside the empty levelator when it arrived. She punched the rooftop button.

While they zipped to their destination, Jace handed Mixy a robe and assisted him in dressing. Before the doors opened again, Silver had retrieved her backpack, yanked it open, and pulled out a cache of weapons.

Jace caught the Zed CX 920 laser pistol she tossed him.

"Thanks," he said in a surprised tone. When she glared at him, he smiled. "I guess this means you trust me."

He looked devilishly handsome when his eyes twinkled. She tampered her reaction with a sharp retort. "No, it means we may need the firepower if a reception committee is waiting for us."

She aimed her TechVix KL-24 when the levelator jerked to a halt. Her model had a longer lasting power pack.

Mixy half-rose, leaning on his elbows, but Jace pushed him down. "Stay put," he ordered, readying his weapon to fire.

Personnel swarmed the rooftop where a team had secured their scooters. One of the soldiers spotted them and pointed. "There they are! Stop those people."

Blue laser fire erupted as Silver jabbed at the controls. The levelator door shut, and they descended at a rapid pace.

She pushed another button, and they careened into a horizontal plane.

"We can't go to the ground floor. They'll be waiting for us. I have another plan," Silver said in a rushed voice.

It would take bravado, but they could do it. Thumbing her comm unit, she contacted her cousin, Remy, and rattled off a series of new instructions. He'd agreed to meet them not at the spaceport, but at another rendezvous. Now she had to switch their strategy.

They emerged into a surgical suite, where green-gowned nurses shuffled among patients in a prep ward. No one paid them any attention, which was what she'd been hoping. Their appearance spoke of just another entry on the day's schedule.

"Mixy, are you very weak or can you stand?" Their success depended upon his stamina. She didn't want to think about what it might do to his budding offspring.

"Your adrenaline rush is quite stimulating," the Elusian replied in a lilting tone. "It's giving me a delightful boost of energy, almost akin to your sexual excitement."

"Comet dust, Mixy, can you get up or not?" Jace said.

Mixy bounced to his feet, fixed his robe around his ankles, then steadied himself with a hand on the gurney. "Lead on, madam." A hank of mahogany hair tumbled onto his slim shoulder. "Oh dear, I'll have to fix my hair. It's quite improper to wear it this way when one is reproducing, you know."

She glanced at the swirls atop his head. "No, I don't know,

but that doesn't matter right now. See that little door in the wall? It's a waste disposal unit, leading directly down to a photon incinerator. The chute is wide enough to accommodate those large bags." She pointed to a tall lined can in a corner.

"What do you propose?" Jace asked. "That we go down the chute as trash?"

"Very good, you're catching on."

"How did you know this would be here?"

"My school went on a tour of the hospital once." She hesitated. "There's only one problem. I don't know what lies at the bottom of the slide."

"That's great." Jace didn't sound too enthusiastic. "Assuming we're not immediately vaporized, what then?"

"We'll be on the lower maintenance level that leads outside. I'm thinking we can steal one of the trucks from the loading platform."

She grabbed a portable oxygen cylinder from a wall unit, hooked up face masks to its ports, and tossed them to her companions. "Put these on."

After covering her own mouth and nose, she snapped open a pouch on her utility belt and withdrew a rod-shaped object. She cracked it at the center and tossed the item into the room. A plume of smoke erupted. The occupants began coughing and choking, then they slumped to the ground.

"It's nothing dangerous, just sleeping gas." Silver ripped off her mask after the requisite time had passed. "The air is clear. Let's go."

Feet first, she jumped into the chute. She shifted her backpack forward and folded her arms across her chest as the decline steepened. Confining blackness surrounded her. She squeezed her eyes shut as she careened down the metal tube into the bowels of the building.

Air escaped her lungs when she landed on a lumpy pile of filled plastic trash bags. She'd barely rolled over when Jace crashed beside her, followed by Mixy's lighter form.

A rancid smell entered her nostrils while her auditory sensors picked up an ominous rumbling noise. She opened her eyes and saw a shadowy arm sucking one of the bags into its wide maw. A brief flash of light blinded her, then the arm reached for more.

"Stay away from that thing," she yelled, rolling. The walls of the receptacle were too high for them to easily climb out. She'd have to use her tensile device again but didn't know if Mixy would have the strength. While contemplating the best approach, she forgot her own warning.

"Look out," Jace hollered.

A strong suction slammed her backward. She grappled for a hold as the incinerator tube swallowed her feet. Pinpoints of light flickered in its interior. She kicked futilely against the drag. Wrenched inward, her torso followed. At any moment, a photon discharge would ignite. Desperation made her unsnap a quantum grenade from her belt while she struggled against the force yanking her inward. Without a moment's hesitation, she activated the grenade and tossed it into the maw. Her sensors registered a tremendous roar before her body was flung outward. A concussive blast hit her, and all went black.

****

Jace watched with horror as the massive disposal device devoured Silver's slim form. Only her crown of hair remained in view. As he wrestled to gain his footing, a blinding flash brightened the room.

The device swallowing Silver disintegrated, the resultant force propelling them toward a newly created gap in the wall. Mixy howled as they tumbled amongst the laden bags onto an asphalt surface.

"Hey, what's going on?" a man shouted.

Jace, glancing quickly at his fallen companion, dragged himself to his feet. Silver had been correct in one regard. They'd landed in a trucking depot. Beyond the loading ramps, he spied an exit to the street. He looked for her and was relieved to see her stirring on the ground.

A heavyset fellow approached. He wore thick work gloves and a scowling expression. "You're in surgical scrubs, but you ain't no doctor. What did you guys do to the incinerator?"

"Maintenance," Jace mumbled, signaling for him to come closer. "We had a bit of a problem. I'll show you." A few moves later, and the guy lay motionless on the asphalt.

Mixy sat up, rubbing his eyes. "Thank you, milord. That was quite invigorating. I'd like to punch out a few more of these people. Or rather, you would. Is Mistress Silver hurt?"

"No, I'm just winded, and my brain is rattled," she said in a shaky voice. "I figured most of the blast would go backward, and I'd be thrown out. Guess it worked." She staggered to her feet. "Did my backpack survive?"

"Here it is." Jace found her bag in the rubble and handed it over. "Are you both able to walk?"

"I'll be fine." She pointed. "Look, there's an empty truck. I can drive." She noted his questionable glance. "Really, I'm regaining my strength as we speak."

"If you say so." Concerned for Mixy's well-being, Jace assisted the Elusian into the vehicle's cab.

Scrunched together in the front seat, the trio crouched low as Silver pressed the accelerator and sped from the loading dock.

"Brilliant plan," he concluded once they were free of the medical compound. "Now what?"

Silver, keeping her attention on the road, thumbed her comm unit. "Remy, are you tracking us?"

"Got ya, cuz," Remy drawled. "I'm on it."

Jace steadied Mixy as they wound through city streets. Silver had no trouble handling the large vehicle, although her frown of concentration made him bite back his remarks on her speed.

When they raced at an oncoming bus at a breakneck pace, Mixy clutched him and shrieked.

"We're almost there." Silver twisted the wheel at the last minute. Her wicked grin affirmed his growing conviction that she relished a sense of danger. That might be essential for an undercover operative, but not for a diplomat.

Assuming Jace ever regained his title, he meant to pursue diplomacy rather than war. Kurash could further its aims through trade rather than conquest, if only he could quell the combative elements within Hurat's regime.

Outside the city, Silver drove off the road onto a meadow. The cab rocked over bumpy terrain.

"We're in a preserve," she explained. "As overpopulation extended to cities around the globe, we set aside land for wildlife preservation. These parks are the only places where you can escape the crowds. It's one of the reasons why I emigrated to Roth Colony."

"You'd like Kurash," he said, relieved to leave the urban congestion behind. Mixy quivered in the seat beside him. "My estate consists of five hundred thousand hectares, most of which is dedicated to agricultural use. We grow crops and breed cattle. Villagers sell handicrafts in the larger towns. We've been self-sustaining until the recent blight affected our fields."

"Don't you use technology at all?" she asked in a tone of disbelief. Although she appreciated wide, open spaces, Jace suspected she valued her conveniences even more.

"Our mechanized industries are mostly relegated to orbiting stations to reduce pollution. We do use technology, but in a manner that's less intrusive than your society. You'll see when you visit my home world."

"Oh my," Mixy murmured, leaning heavily against him, "how I miss the scent of fresh alfalfa kissed by the morning dew, not to mention the sweet crescents baked by Cook when we take breakfast outside. Will we ever see our home again?" His robe segued into a sad amber color.

"You're homesick." Silver made it a statement, not a question, correctly surmising Mixy was expressing Jace's feelings. Sympathy filled her violet eyes as she glanced at him.

Jace gave a curt nod, swallowing his nostalgia when he spotted a shuttle ahead. "Look. Is that Remy's vessel?"

"He's right on target." Silver hit the brakes, and Jace threw out an arm to prevent Mixy from crashing forward.

Remy, who'd been waiting at the boarding ramp, greeted them with a broad smile. His blond hair gleamed in a ray of morning sunshine.

"You sure give a fellow a good chase," he chastised his cousin before glancing curiously at Mixy. "So this is your alien friend."

Silver introduced them. "Have you encountered any problems before we lift off?"

"Oh, just one, not that it would stop me. You and Jace are wanted for murder."

Chapter Twelve

"The police must have found Major Dean's body in my apartment," Silver explained, strapping herself into the copilot's seat in preparation for launch.

Jace and Mixy secured themselves in the row of seats behind. Her cousin had purloined a small transport, presumably one scheduled for maintenance. Smart guy to claim he wanted to ferry it to the shipyards himself.

"You mean, you're not responsible?" Remy drawled. The smile on his mouth took the sting from his words. "I thought maybe the major had been about to scratch your mission." He bent his head to start the preflight, the low ceiling infringing on his tall frame.

"Silver didn't kill the S.I.N. chief," a strong male voice proclaimed from the open door. Dash hopped into the cabin along with Evelina.

"What are you two doing here?" Silver demanded, her pulse quickening. "If you're here to take us in—"

"We have issues to discuss." Dash's firm tone brooked no argument.

She swivelled to face him as her two cousins belted themselves into the row behind Jace and Mixy. Evelina cast a worshipful glance at Jace, whose posture had gone rigid with their arrival.

"Don't be a dolt." Evelina dragged her gaze to Silver. "We came to help."

"We know you didn't kill anyone," Dash told her. Did he use the plural pronoun for the family, or in his official capacity?

"Surely you don't think Jace is guilty?" she said when he gave the Kurashki an oblique glance. "We were together nearly the entire time after dinner."

"Is that so?" Evelina tossed back her curly black hair. "Doing what?"

Silver had the grace to blush. "Escaping from our house and stopping by my apartment to get my things. We found the major when we arrived."

"You were set up. We put out a bulletin to throw the bad guys off track." Dash wagged a finger. "Father knows someone on the Council is leaking classified information. We've also been dealing with sabotage at Lyonus Metals. I believe our troubles are connected."

Jace twisted to regard him. "If I ever regain my post, I'd want to improve relations between our peoples. But that won't happen if I'm detained here. What are your intentions toward me?" He spoke in a stiff tone that hid his uncertainty.

I know Evelina's intent. She'd rather devour you than see you arrested, Silver thought.

She waved an arm at her cousin. "Dash, explain how our system works since you plan to follow in Uncle's illustrious footsteps." She turned to address Jace. "Don't mind my cousin. He's all work and no play. I'm hoping he'll meet a woman who will loosen him up."

"Better you than me, bro," Remy quipped, just before launch. He worked the controls with a feather-light touch.

The engine whined from the strain until the anti-grav drive kicked in. They rose straight up like a helicopter, then Remy punched the thrust and they shot toward the sky at a steep angle. Silver gripped her armrests, feeling the pressure weighting her down.

"Remy is our resident nerd," Evelina teased. "Do you know he reads technical manuals for fun, when he isn't jamming with his band or chasing women? How sick can you get?"

"Hey, don't knock my talents. I didn't become chief of

mechanical engineering at Gravicom Wells from being an airhead, unlike someone else I know."

"I'm a public relations director, jerkoff. Just because I care about what I wear doesn't mean I lack smarts."

Silver rolled her eyes. Getting away from this constant bickering was another reason why she'd moved into her own apartment. While fond of her cousins, she found it easier to maintain her focus when she distanced herself from them. Nor did they understand her evening prayer ritual. They criticized her for being too morbid and prolonging her grief.

Although welcomed into their home, she still felt alienated. They'd never experienced life in the colonies, nor did they know what it meant to be orphaned. No one else could ever understand the depth of her loss. Well, except for Jace, who'd lost his parents in an equally abrupt disaster.

"I sense your morale sinking along with your blood sugar level," Mixy's voice said in her ear. "Shall I fix you something to eat?"

Leave it to their valet to levitate her mood. *Their* valet? Silver gave him an appraising glance over her shoulder. Since when had he become such an essential part of her? She realized that being cut off from Mixy had been like losing a limb. Now that the three of them were together again, she felt whole.

We're almost like the old world Holy Trinity, she thought with amusement. Me and Jace, empathically connected through our Elusian friend. Soon there would be a fourth among them, she realized with a start.

"You probably need to eat more yourself now that you're, um…" She hesitated, her glance flickering uncertainly between Jace and Mixy. She didn't know if Elusians considered expectancy a delicate topic or not.

"He's pregnant," Jace announced with a proud grin.

"No!" Evelina, gripping her armrests, stared at Mixy.

Mixy beat his chest and grinned. "The proper term is budding. A form of asexual reproduction, it provides for consistency among our population. There is one matter that may prove troublesome." He addressed his master. "The young one must be raised on Elusia. It will go into a sustenance pod until fully mature."

"You mean, you don't raise your own kind?" Silver gaped at him.

"Not personally, no. It needs more than mere physical nourishment. This will necessitate a stopover on my home world when the budding process is nearly complete."

"Oh, great." Jace tightened his mouth, and Silver could read his dismay. Delays were something they couldn't afford, not with his sister's safety at stake.

Worry transformed Mixy's delicate features. "Do not be concerned, milord. I would not jeopardize your chances."

At Remy's nod, the valet unbuckled his restraint and headed for a tiny galley in the rear. Silver had managed to retrieve some of the food stocks he'd acquired on the space station. They'd been among his belongings that she'd salvaged after his accident, and Remy had offered to sneak them aboard.

"Hey, I'm hungry too," Remy called out. "Do you have enough for the rest of us?"

"I believe so," Mixy replied from their rear. Banging noises ensued from the galley. "Oh dear, remind me to make another requisition list, Master Jace. We're missing my favorite spice."

"Do we have enough time for a debriefing?" Dash asked his brother.

"ETA is ninety minutes." Once they reached orbit, Remy changed course for Gravicom Wells Shipyards.

"Evelina, would you sit still?" Dash's tone held a hint of reproval. "Your constant fidgeting drives me nuts."

"Stuffy prig," she retorted. Ignoring his stern glare, she reached into her bag and withdrew a nail file and a bottle of magenta polish. "At least I can do my nails during this interminable ride. Silver, how about you? Your hands are a mess. You could use a decent manicure."

Their recent physical exertions came to mind. "It's not important to me, and besides, where we're going, I don't care to attract attention."

"Where's that?" Dash demanded.

"Stacktown." Silver clapped a hand to her mouth. She didn't mean to give away their destination.

Remy whistled. "Bad place. Why do you want to go there?"

"It's a lead to Tyrone Bluth. We need to pick up his trail again. That reminds me, his men traced my ship and were waiting for me at Bartlett Station. Ownership files on the Avenger were supposed to be classified after I joined S.I.N." Her cousins knew about her job. "What were you saying about a leak, Dash?"

His voice rose to a louder pitch as the engine whine increased. "Someone on our Council hopes to reap rewards if war erupts between us and the Kurashki Alliance. This traitor has been feeding information to Tyrone Bluth, who is acting as intermediary to a contact on the Kurashki home world."

Jace's eyes widened. "How do you know this?"

"Bluth has an informant among his brigade. That's how we got the tip about Al'ron."

"Does Uncle Manny know who's responsible?" Silver asked.

"He believes the traitor is a member of the Expansionist Party. They're pressing for more colonization. Since we were neutral in the war between Dorius and the Kurashkis, we couldn't provoke the Dorians by assimilating any of their border territories. That leaves the unchartered western sector, which would require longer, more dangerous expeditions, or the unclaimed worlds between us and Kurash. Those contain valuable minerals, but Kurash covets our Earth resources as well. The Conservatives are pushing for a trade-off, meaning we would have to offer concessions. If we go to war instead, we can grab what we want."

"What is your chancellor's position?" Jace inquired.

He must realize he's getting privileged information, Silver thought, but it also meant her cousins trusted him. Or perhaps Uncle Manny had sent them along. If Jace regained his status, his understanding of Earth's viewpoint would add a voice of reason to Hurat's Assembly. Each side needed to accept that peaceful trade was preferable to violence.

"My father's aim is to avoid war, without lessening our position of strength," Dash replied.

Silver frowned in puzzlement. "But the traitor in our government is paying Bluth, and not the other way around?"

"Yes, that's our understanding of the situation. We are still trying to identify this vermin and get proof of his treachery."

Dash's name suited his striking appearance, Silver decided. Despite the hours he toiled in an office, he maintained his athletic prowess. Combined with his arresting features and commanding presence, it made him a prime catch. She wondered if society matrons still pushed their daughters at him. Yet he was too involved in his job to pursue a serious relationship. As for the rest of her relations, Remy had too good a time playing the field, and Evelina was overly selective when it came to men.

Aunt Marguerite must be crawling the walls in despair of ever having grandchildren. Thank goodness Silver was under no obligation to produce offspring.

Awareness of the possibility crept into her mind, and she glanced at Jace. He flipped her a quick, sensual smile as though he knew the direction of her thoughts. Forcing her gaze away, she refocused her attention on what her cousin Dash was saying.

"Fester Niles, owner of Solvent Minerals, produces the largest supply of trona for the shipyards. If war erupts, government contracts would give his company a windfall. Niles plays Takeover Bids with Father. My guess is he's passing along information he gleans during these games. Angus MacIntyre, chairman of Morse Cybertronics, has no desire to go to war. And

Hildegard condones exploration rather than conquest. So it's unlikely either of those two are the source of the leak."

"Fester Niles mentioned that Ruler Hurat listens to my cousin Garth," Jace contributed, his brow folded in thought. "How would he know this unless he's conversant with Kurashki politics? Niles also seems familiar with our hereditary laws. Has he taken to studying our culture? Or does he have intimate knowledge through some other means?"

"Another thing," Silver said, excited by this thread of conversation. "Remember my theory that someone is funding pirates who are disrupting supply lines? Who stands to benefit if extra parts are needed for ship repairs?"

Dash's gaze ignited. "Here's something else you should know. Fester Niles and Major Dean were having an affair."

"That clinches it. Either he killed her because their relationship soured, or she discovered he's the mole." She gripped her armrests as the side thrusters fired and their craft banked into a steep turn.

Jace poked her shoulder from behind. "That's what the dinner conversation was all about? The Chancellor appeared suspicious of me, but he was really hoping Niles would slip up?"

"You got it," Evelina told him. "Father trusts Silver's judgement. He believes your story."

"Until Father gets evidence against Niles, you two should maintain a low profile," Dash advised them. "Now that you've stolen the Elusian, it'll look even worse. Give us time to straighten things out at home. Sorry for the rough treatment you received in detention, by the way. Everyone knew a Kurashki had been detained, and we had to follow protocol. Plus, I needed to make sure Silver hadn't been turned."

"I understand. Don't worry about it."

"You're not without friends on Kurash either," Silver reminded him. "You wouldn't have escaped otherwise."

"That's true, but no one in power—such as your uncle— was on my side. I still have to prove my innocence, and the only way I can do it is to capture Tyrone Bluth alive so he can act as a witness on my behalf."

"What about Niles?" Evelina piped in. "If he's collaborating with the Kurashki warmongers, he could provide testimony, especially if he was involved in the plot to entrap you using Bluth."

All eyes turned toward the dark-haired beauty.

"You may be right," Dash said with a note of admiration. "In the meantime, if you guys catch up to Bluth, see if you can get him to confess his role as middleman between Niles and Garth Vernon. That would nail things for both of us."

"Hey, man, we're a team," Remy drawled. He switched on some music and rocked to the rhythm. Once he had the coordinates set, there wasn't much else for him to do on such a short flight.

Outside, the stars crawled by. Silver sniffed an aroma reminiscent of onions and soy sauce. Mixy chose that moment to shuffle in from the galley.

"Luncheon is served. The provisions are lacking, but I did my best. Those vegetables from Bartlett Station came in handy. Perhaps the procurement officer at Gravicom Wells would open his stores to me?"

Dash grinned broadly. "I'm sure it can be arranged." His expression sobered. "Stacktown isn't a place I'd want to go. You'll need every advantage if you plan to come out of there alive. Take these," he offered, handing Jace and Silver each a credit chip.

"Thanks," Silver replied, grateful to her family for their show of faith. Responsibility weighed heavily on her to succeed. "I have accounts in the Reserve. Uncle didn't have to—"

"Your funds were frozen as soon as the alert went out. Consider it part of your S.I.N. expense account."

"Who'll take over now that Major Dean is gone?"

"The Maxima Chancellor will appoint a new chief. Father hasn't said who he favors," Dash added in a softer tone.

"It's wise of him to keep close counsel until he learns who to trust."

"Same goes for you. I've heard strange things about your next destination. Tales about ghosts, for example. Some say the place conceals a crossing to the Other Side. Few people who go there ever make it home. Stay on guard, and don't trust anyone. That planet sucks something from you, and you're lucky if it spits you out alive."

"Sounds like fun," Evelina chimed in, her gypsy eyes sparkling. "Can I go, too?"

Chapter Thirteen

Their Corvette-class ship spiraled through the atmosphere on its way to a landing at Stacktown. Jace concentrated on the controls, manipulating the craft to avoid turbulence while aiming for the coordinates given by starport command. In the co-pilot's seat, Silver squinted at the haze-enshrouded surface.

"Those look like mountains in the distance. Can you see their peaks?"

Jace detected the anxiety in her tone. "Well enough," he said, adjusting their angle, "but I wish we had better visibility. You can't tell what's directly below."

"I don't see any signs of a city."

"That fog blocks our view. Weird stuff, isn't it? How is it possible, when there aren't any clouds at this level? Moisture can't be causing that vapor."

"Are you sure we're heading in the right direction?" Her brows knitted. "If the inhabitants dislike visitors, maybe they lure them off course on purpose."

"Unlikely. Despite the risks, bidders still come for the auctions."

Silver clung to her seat as he spun the ship into a tight banking decline once they'd cleared the mountain range. "Carolla nuts are a rare commodity," she said. "I can understand why Bluth would want them."

"He may be acting as an agent for his employer. Besides, it's the oil that's important. Pure grade carollium can boost realspeed engines by thirty percent. It acts like a catalyst to the reactor."

She cast him a wry glance. "Would Bluth's employer in this case be the traitor in my government, or the warlord in yours?"

He shrugged. "Either one would gain an advantage by acquiring the oil for their fleet. Or Bluth could mean to keep it for himself."

"I can't imagine him doing anything less." Silver's gaze focused out the viewscreen. "On Roth Colony, I'd discovered a substance with both plant and mineral properties. When I heated it in my lab, it reacted in an unexpected way. Further tests showed this compound might become a fuel even more potent than carollium."

"And then your settlement was attacked by Tyrone's Marauders." Jace understood the implications.

"Someone didn't want my research to succeed." She clasped her hands in her lap, her expression pained. "The raid destroyed my notes, and I received a warning that if I resumed my work, all the rest I held dear would be eliminated."

Meaning her cousins, he assumed. No wonder she wanted Bluth dead. He'd enjoyed his stay with her family despite the tension at dinner. If he regained his title, he'd like to return their hospitality and kindness.

He gave Silver a dark glance. "You and I have a lot in common, you know. We've both been betrayed. But in my view, the path to peace is justice, not revenge."

"We'll see."

Damn woman. She was just as set on her goals as she'd been when they first met. He tightened his jaw and focused on his display readouts. Their altitude dropped sharply. The landing pad should be coming into view soon.

"We're lucky the auction hasn't taken place yet," Silver said, breaking the tense silence that had sprung up between them.

"No kidding. We'd have to wait another five years until the next one. I can't imagine raising a crop that harvests so infrequently."

"That only increases its value," Silver pointed out. "Let's hope our ruse works, and we look rich enough to afford a high stake in the game."

"I don't anticipate any problems in entering our bid. Our greater difficulty will be to locate and capture Bluth."

"He may have brought an entourage," she warned. "We have no idea how this auction works, but I suppose we'll find out soon enough."

Hopefully, their false identities would work. Silver had dressed for her role in a belted tan tunic over black leggings, with her standard utility belt and her favored TechVix KL-24 laser pistol strapped to one thigh. She'd rinsed a color wash through her glorious hair, altering its platinum waves into stark raven, but he'd drawn the line at shearing her locks.

He didn't know where his possessiveness originated, but he'd insisted his woman should keep her long hair.

His woman. He didn't know when the notion had entered his mind, but he thought of Silver that way. A prick of guilt stuck him when he remembered his social obligations at home, but he squashed it down. Wait until Shanna and Yvette were safe. Then he'd worry about his growing feelings for Silver.

They'd inserted contact lenses in a neutral brown, and he'd grown a beard during the voyage. If the Razor were here, Bluth shouldn't recognize either one of them. Mixy was another matter. The Elusian, asleep in one of the cabins, would guard their ship at the spaceport until their safe return.

"Better wake Mixy. We're almost there," he ordered Silver.

On their final approach, the haze dissipated to reveal an industrial complex that counted as the main city on this godforsaken world. Belching pockets of smoke forced him to veer sharply around a refinery, steer between towering precipices of metal, and dip over a vat of bubbling molten liquid before cutting the thrusters. In a sudden rush, they dropped onto the designated landing site with a resounding thump.

****

Without waiting for clearance, Silver unbuckled her safety harness and leapt from her chair. Mixy, stumbling onto the pilot's deck, gazed at them with sleep-dazed eyes.

"Your eagerness to begin the hunt is so palpable, it woke me," the Elusian complained.

He'd rearranged his hair into a coil that fell onto his left shoulder, a sign of expectancy. Glancing between her and Jace, Mixy curved his lips, while his robe turned from cobalt blue to bubblegum pink.

"I cannot believe you are thinking of sex even now, especially after all the couplings you have done during our voyage." Streaks of scarlet bled into the pink. "Master Jace, curb your appetite. This improper, and yet highly stimulating, relationship will hinder your success."

Silver swatted him, careful not to touch the gestational sac growing from his torso. Mini-Mixy, as she called his budding off-spring, seemed to enlarge by the day. "You old farlett, you're enjoying our, uh, relations as much as we are. Why do you keep chastising us, especially Jace? Do not the women on his world practice free choice? Or is it the men who must follow social constraints?"

Jace unstrapped his constraints and cleared his throat. "I have mentioned that our system of government is feudal compared to yours."

"So? You travel among the stars, like others of your kind. The pilots who fought in the Dorian war must have seen things that exposed them to progressive ideas. So don't tell me your culture is prudish and expects people to get married before sex."

"No, it isn't that." Jace strode forward to grab his gear, his mouth sealed.

Mixy swished by, but not before she saw the purple tinge to his robe. Didn't that mean Jace was fudging the truth?

"We need to have a talk," she said to him, planting her hands on her hips.

He looked fierce in his disguise, suitable for the leader of a third world planet. Most of the other entrants had probably lied about their identity, too, but Silver hadn't expected Jace to dissemble to her. What was he hiding? From his sudden sullenness to Mixy's avoidance, she knew she'd hit the mark. If she'd been able to dampen her lust during their voyage, she might have realized something was amiss before now.

During their lovemaking, she'd pushed aside any soul-searching about their future together. When she completed her assignment by killing Tyrone Bluth, she might not be around to consider another tomorrow. So she'd enjoyed the sex without wondering what their relationship meant.

For months, even years, she'd become a shell devoid of any emotion except the thirst for revenge. Death loomed in front of her like a welcoming glove, beckoning her to enter the comfort of oblivion. But now it appeared the icicles surrounding her heart had begun to melt. Her cousins seemed more entertaining, her aunt and uncle more generous, her apartment more empty than ever before. She'd been lacking human companionship, love and laughter, for too long. It had taken a notorious fugitive and his volatile valet to restore her senses.

Controlling her burgeoning feelings took force of will. She couldn't let anything deter her from this assignment, especially now that interstellar politics played a role. No longer just an issue between her and Bluth, the pirate's actions connected traitors on both her world and Jace's, while destroying innocent lives and settlements in between.

The scope had grown too large for her to deal with on her own. Taking out Bluth was only part of the equation. They still had to uncover the tentacles of his organization, where his funding originated, and who'd hired him.

Jace, with his political connections on Kurash, his combat experience, and his criminal reputation, turned out to be the perfect partner. Never mind Mixy and his mental link, although that could prove useful if they ran into trouble. Her irrational yearning to run her hands over Jace's broad chest, curl her fingers in his hair, and mesh her body with his would have to wait.

Dingbat's tail. It drove her crazy to know Jace and Mixy concealed something important from her, but she'd press them about it later. First they had to pass the checkpoints, present their credentials to the Chief Auctioneer, and locate Tyrone Bluth.

An armed escort waited outside in the smoky haze to march them toward a waiting tram. Mixy, remaining behind, welcomed the customs inspector on board. The stern-faced individual shouldn't find anything out of the ordinary, especially when Mixy distracted him with his prattle about budding. The Elusian had been overly talkative during the voyage, as though he were talking with two heads instead of one. It annoyed Silver, who had become used to solitude, but Jace found him amusing.

"Follow me. I'll take you to registration," said their guide, a scaly-faced Monduran in a military uniform. He spoke in a guttural growl, the norm for his species.

Four additional troops accompanied them into the private transport, where she and Jace took seats. As soon as the door swished shut, the car released its anti-grav brakes and lifted into the air. With a lurch, they sped off on a predetermined route.

"What's the procedure for the auction?" Silver asked in a friendly voice. "It's our first time here." Jostled back and forth with the tram's movement, she gripped the seat cushion. Their escorts remained standing, balanced on their sturdy legs.

The Monduran's slitted eyes regarded her with disinterest. "You will be read the rules upon registration."

"Okay." She peered out the window at a jumbled array of smoke stacks, multi-leveled structures, and enormous pipes running every which way. "Somehow because of the harvest, I figured this would be an agricultural world. I didn't expect to see so many factories. Can anyone decide to stay and apply for a work permit?"

Their guide snorted with laughter. "Stay, yes. Work? Opportunities are limited."

"Are your materials available for export?" she persisted, hoping to get an idea of what they produced. People knew so little about Stacktown. Perhaps they manufactured a commodity useful for trade.

The hulking Monduran wiped a dribble of spit from his mouth. "The only material produced here is carolla nuts. These buildings interconnect; the entire complex is a carollium oil refinery."

"But the harvest is once every five years, and doesn't the winner have the option of taking the nuts elsewhere to be processed?" She gave a loopy grin to convince him she was nothing but a ditz. When their escort didn't respond, she considered what other purpose the industrial plant might serve.

Maybe they made weapons. An active arms trade would explain the silence surrounding the place. Considering the rumor that most people who visited Stacktown didn't return home, she wondered if it could be a falsehood to keep folks away.

Then again, maybe what they produced in this dismal place was even more sinister. Her thoughts took a dark turn as she remembered the Crockers. What if the residents abducted stray visitors, sent them to a chop shop, and sold their body parts to the carnivorous beasts?

A shudder rippled through her. Grasping her sack in her lap, she determined to remain alert at all times. That meant letting Mixy's presence filter into her mind, because through him, she could always reach Jace.

Right now, Jace bristled with wariness as though expecting something bad to happen. On that note, she agreed, even more so when they checked in at the Visitor Welcome Center. Ushered into a drab, concrete building, they passed through a security device that sent bells clanging. Her auditory sensors augmented the sound to painful levels so that she had to resist clamping her hands to her ears.

A thin-faced fellow ushered her and Jace toward a high counter, behind which lounged a rotund individual. A desk sign gave his name as Registrar Dunmore Applestone. He wore an impatient scowl, an open-necked shirt, dark pants, and a suntan.

Suntan? Silver squinted at the window, beyond which smog clouded the sky. Perhaps the fellow's skin color was native to his species, like Jace's bronze tinge.

The heavy-set man straightened, folded his hands on the counter, and peered at them from his perch. "Kindly remove your armaments and place them in the receptacle." He spoke in a nasal twang as though he had cotton up his nose.

They complied under the watchful eye of the Monduran officer, depositing their personal firearms into the bin provided. She didn't like it and neither did Jace by his tight-lipped expression.

"State your name and business," Applestone commanded.

Jace faced him and thrust out his jaw in a pompous manner. "I am Jack Zin, Supreme Controller of Nathius Prime. This is my Vice Actuator, Saris. We have entered our application for the auction."

"Very well. Step up to the scanner for an identity sweep."

Silver studiously kept her gaze averted from her companion. If these people had his profile in their files, their game would be finished before it started.

Either the government's technology lacked sophistication or their communication with the outside world didn't include felons, because she and Jace passed inspection. Judging from the workmen they'd sped by in the tram, it didn't appear these folks were too particular where their labor force originated.

"Are you prepared to deposit your credits?" the Registrar demanded. At Jace's nod, he indicated a slot for Jace to insert his chip.

Silver hastened over and swiped the card she'd gotten from her uncle. She'd suggested playing Jace's assistant. The high rollers were likely to ignore her that way, meaning she could eavesdrop more readily. Twisting one of her auditory sensors out of habit, she wondered who to ask about a place to stay.

"All hail the Chief Auctioneer." Applestone shoved his chair back and stood.

A door at the rear slid open, and a broad-shouldered fellow strode inside. The Chief Auctioneer examined them over his hook-like nose, firm chin, and disapproving mouth. Silver's gaze strayed south. Beneath his billowing robe of office, he wore sandals. Were those actual granules of sand between his toes?

They hadn't seen any evidence of seas on their long-range sensors, but a source of water had to exist somewhere.

"Welcome to Stacktown," the auctioneer boomed in a baritone voice. "Our Articles decree that I must read you the rules, so listen carefully. I will only say these once."

His penetrating gaze held them captive. "You will be assigned a suite in our guest hostelry. You will not fraternize with the other bidders. You will enter your bid from the parlor console and will not leave the premises. Decorum is to be observed at all times. If you disregard any of these rules, your account will be disqualified and you will be escorted to your ship for departure."

Silver and Jace exchanged a glance. "Excuse me," she said in a sweet tone. "Aren't we allowed to talk to anyone else? I was hoping to meet our competitors, or at the very least, get a tour of your city."

The auctioneer pursed his lips. "You're already late. We have received most of the starting bids by now. Your turn will come when you hear the buzzer in your room. You may raise your bid in increments of five thousand jinars. If you do not respond within ten minutes, you will forfeit your chance."

That would keep them confined to the premises, all right. At least one of them.

"Where do we eat?" Jace asked, his expression neutral.

"You may order what you wish from the autorama," the Chief Auctioneer said, as though they should know what he meant. "Bidding will conclude when a final offer receives no counterbid. The winner may choose the option of using our processing facilities, or he may take the nuts off-world, but then departure must occur immediately. Remaining guests will then be escorted on a tour and given a consolation prize."

"Oh really?" Jace drawled. "What kind of prize?"

A small smile lit the man's face. "You'll see."

His ominous tone made Silver wonder if this tour was compulsory. Maybe the losers ended up in that vat of molten glop she'd seen on their descent.

"One more thing before you go." The Chief Auctioneer nodded to the Monduran officer, who produced a penlight-sized device from his pocket and pressed its tip to each of their wrists in turn.

Silver gasped at the sharp sting. "Ow, what is that thing?"

"A warning device." The Chief Auctioneer's lips curled in a devious smile. "It emits an audible alarm should you come into close proximity with another bidder. We will remove it once the auction concludes."

"Comet dust," Jace muttered under his breath, while Silver hoped it didn't transmit physiological data. She still worried about Jace being exposed, plus herself as well, now that she stood accused of Major Dean's murder back on Earth.

Marched outside after the Chief Auctioneer dismissed them, she and Jace had no choice but to follow the hulking Monduran troops on foot to the hostelry for alien guests. Each breath brought a miasma of sulfur-scented air that clogged her nostrils. A steady grinding noise set her nerves on edge, while a dismal mist shrouded the streets. Even the buildings leaned inward with despair. Concrete walls, metal catwalks, and belching chimneys crisscrossed their path. And the heat… sweat broke on her brow and between her breasts.

What did these folks manufacture under such depressing conditions? And why did the few workers she saw scurry quickly out of sight? They wore shapeless robes and faces grubby with grease paint, like the kind she kept in her disguise kit. What was really going on in this place?

Maybe the true treasure wasn't carolla nuts. Maybe it was the consolation prize. She'd have to hope Bluth lost his bid so they could meet up with him on the tour. Otherwise, their chances of running into him were slim to none.

****

Their accommodations turned out to be spartan but adequate. After a speedy shower, Jace pulled on a bathrobe provided by their hosts. His stomach rumbled as he entered the sitting room in their suite. The autorama was located in an alcove. He approached the meal-ordering device and studied the panel.

He was still figuring out how to access the menu when Silver strode into the parlor. Freshly showered, she'd also donned one of the soft white robes. Damp strands of hair hung past her shoulders, curling into natural waves in the air-cooled interior.

"Hey, come over here." He hooked his forefinger. "I need help."

"In a minute." She held a scanning device and proceeded to check the room for surveillance bugs. Her derrière tightened delectably as she crouched to pass the scanner under the sofa. Her belt loosened, giving Jace a tantalizing glimpse of shapely long legs and generous cleavage when she turned in his direction. His blood surged, but he wasn't alone. Someone else experienced a cascade of awareness. Mixy, maybe? Or Silver?

It had become difficult to tell the difference. Their reactions blended, compounding their sensations. He grew hard at the thought of taking her to bed and running his hands over her soft body. Great Cosmos, his rational thought fled in her presence. His loins responded, swelling with need.

Silver regarded him with a sly smile. Another presence egged him on with the same conflict of duty and desire that allowed him to satisfy his lust but withhold his heart. Maybe he couldn't give her his soul, but he could offer comfort and satisfaction.

"We have time to kill," he said in a suggestive tone.

"So we do. We could go down to the bar."

"What's the point, when we can't talk to anyone else?"

"There's always the bartender."

"I have a better idea." He sauntered closer, halting mere inches away. Silver's eyes reflected his desperate want, and her lips parted.

He leaned forward, smelling her soapy scent. Unable to stop himself, he opened her robe and slid his hand inside. Ah, she felt so sweet. He caressed her flesh, savoring its softness. As his hand skirted the mound of her breast, she gave a sharp intake of breath. He circled around, longing to trail his hand downward but not too soon.

Her arousal impinged on his senses. When he stroked his thumb across her nipple, he felt the shockwave as though it had gone straight to his own groin. Groaning, he grabbed her close and ground his body against hers.

Their minds melded into one animalistic stupor. He kissed her, aware of nothing else but his mouth clamped to hers, his tongue exploring her mint-flavored depths. When she sucked on his lower lip and then captured his tongue, he thought he'd explode. Supporting her head at the nape, he changed his slant and devoured her.

Their robes came between them. He paused to rip off his garment while she did the same. Seeing her naked, Jace let out a grunt of admiration. Her ripe curves and toned muscles offered the perfect combination. He perused her body, assimilating Mixy's excited response. He could almost hear the Elusian's panting breaths, see his valet's eyes closed in rapture. Holding himself back, Jace fought his impatience while Silver explored him, her eyes heavy-lidded, her chest rising and falling as she ran her hands over his skin.

His gaze skimmed her breasts and their peaked response, rolled past her flat stomach, and targeted the triangular mound at her feminine junction. He couldn't resist clamping his hand there, stroking her sensitive folds. She moaned into his mouth as he nudged her toward the bedroom.

They tumbled onto the bed together, a tangled mass of arms and legs, firm skin against soft, pliant flesh. He rolled her beneath him and watched her gaze deepen with desire. He yearned to see the wildness enter them, when she lost control and gave herself to him without reservations. She so rarely lost focus otherwise, he thought as he pressed his mouth to hers.

Her lips yielded as she willingly allowed his tongue to plunder her sweetness. His breath came in short, hard pants. With a third consciousness egging him on, he held tough rein on his erection.

Silver's legs parted, and he prodded at her juncture, but he wouldn't comply to her silent request. No, he wanted her to beg him, to realize her need. Only then could he pierce her armor and appeal to the woman inside. He didn't know how or why it had happened, but she meant more to him than just a partner in crime. She needed healing and the will to live, and he could give them to her.

Squirming beneath him, she demonstrated what she would offer in return—a passion so intense that she wasn't afraid to break the rules. Whatever she set her mind to do, she would accomplish. He admired that trait, since he'd been raised in a place where laws were meant to be absolute. Ever since he'd met Silver, he realized shades of gray suited him more.

****

As Silver succumbed under the weight of Jace's body, she sensed the mental grip preventing his release. Wishing to stimulate him beyond reason, she reached down and stroked his shaft. She closed her eyes, relishing the feel of her own touch, as Mixy's link compounded the sensations. Drifting into a zone of pleasure, she experienced the sublime delight of her fingers on her lover's sensitive skin.

He shuddered but wrestled control by inserting a finger into her moist center.

Her eyes flew open. "Stars above."

In response, he rubbed her pulsating nub with the heel of his hand while drawing his finger slowly in and out. It drove her crazy. She rotated her hips, unable to help herself as the circular movement of his hand increased its pace. Her thighs opened involuntarily, and she lost her grasp on reality.

When she gave in to the coiling tension, she felt Jace's conscious barrier break. Removing his hand, he shifted his position and plunged into her. Through their shared link, she felt her own tautness sheathing him, and his impatience to climax. As their rhythm accelerated, Jace's thrusts pierced farther inside while she lifted her hips in a frenzy to join him. Mixy rode along with them, and the Elusian's wild excitement drove her to the brink. Their explosion came as a mutual cataclysm that clenched her muscles in paroxysms of joy. She floated on a surreal plane of existence until the last ripples faded. Only then did reality filter into her brain.

An intermittent buzzing sound emanated from the adjacent room.

"Silver," Jace said, nuzzling her neck, "we have to talk about this… about us. There's something I have to tell you."

Mixy's mental withdrawal left her bereft. Did the Elusian depart their consciousness on purpose, because he knew she wouldn't like what Jace had to say?

"It'll have to wait." Reluctance coated her tongue. "Our console is buzzing."

"You're right." Stark naked, Jace leapt off the bed. He grabbed his pile of clothes and loped toward the parlor. "It must be our turn to enter an opening bid."

"You think? We've only just arrived," she called after him.

"The auction has already started, remember? Comet dust, I'm starving. I'd hoped we could get something to eat first."

"I'll go downstairs and talk to the bartender about

scrounging for a meal. Fresh food is bound to be better than the autorama choices."

Maybe she could slip outside unnoticed. Did the rules apply to her as Jace's assistant, or just to him?

While Jace worked at the comm console, she considered the wardrobe Mixy had hastily packed for her. Which look would be more appropriate, the tough chick or the seductive siren?

Judging from this world's scruffy inhabitants, she'd do better to appear formidable. Without visible firepower, she could still intimidate with black leather, ample cleavage, and heeled boots. If those didn't disarm the populace, she needn't worry. An assassin possessed other means to accomplish her goals.

You haven't done too great so far.

That wasn't her doing. If Jace hadn't interrupted her first assault on Bluth, the terrorist leader would be dead by now.

Reaffirming her resolve, she trotted down the stairs in a dimly lit stairwell that smelled like stale urine and joyfa weed smoke.

At the ground level, she pushed open the door and entered the lobby. Besides a reception desk, it held a dingy lounge plus a small bistro offering counter service for takeout orders. Clearly the inhabitants didn't invite outsiders to linger. The bidders who came for the auction stayed just long enough for the competition. So where did all the folks go who never left the planet?

Voices sounded from inside the lounge. She headed in that direction and stopped by the bistro to order a veggie burger for Jace. She'd see if the bar had anything else to offer. Not that she was hungry. The scent of the hunt drew her over.

Ignoring the blatant stares from the lobby clerks, she strode inside the lounge rife with ale fumes and spiced vapor from a matue pot. The pungent scent invaded her nostrils and made her eyes burn. Taking a moment to scan the interior, she noted the laborers who sat in a corner nursing their mugs, the veiled woman all in black sitting alone, and the men in rich robes laughing over bowls of fresh cut Pava melon.

Pava melon? That prized fruit grew in the tropics, nor had it been on the menu in the bistro. Had these men brought along their private stock, or did they know something she didn't?

"Whaddya want, sela?" the bartender growled. His bristly jaw barely hid his overbite, but more pronounced were his bulbous nose and bloodshot eyes.

"A bottle of Stentorian wine and some information."

His gaze narrowed. "The first will cost ya ten jinars and the second ain't available."

She swiped her credit chip through the slot. "Now that's unfortunate," she murmured, bending over the bar so he got a good look at her chest. "I'm merely curious about what your factories produce. My employer might be interested in a trade agreement."

His guffaw elicited dark looks from the other occupants. "Sela, ain't no way we can trade what we got. Ya see," he said, staring her in the eye, "once ya get a taste, ya don't want nothin' else."

"Your commodity must be valuable, like that Pava melon over there." *Or addictive, maybe. Could they be operating a black market in illicit drugs?* "Is that fruit on your bar menu?"

He snorted. "Depends on who ya are, where ya going, and where ya been."

Was he deliberately being obtuse? Silver watched carefully as the bartender uncorked her bottle of wine and poured the crimson liquid into a filmy glass. Resisting the urge to wipe its rim, she brought the glass to her mouth and took a sip. Smooth. Grub Face stared at her impassively while the other men resumed their discussions.

All except for the lady in black. Balancing her drink, an extra glass and the wine bottle, Silver approached the loner's table while skirting the gaudily dressed patrons downing their second round. They could be partners in town for the bidding, meaning she couldn't talk to them. Fearful her implant might sound an alert, she relaxed when nothing happened. Not bidders, then. That was logical—they'd need to be upstairs by their consoles if they had entered the competition. So who were they, and what about the female?

"Mind if I join you?" she asked the veiled woman, plopping into a chair. "This place is so incredibly boring. Are you here for the auction? I wouldn't want to break the rules."

The lady stared at her from behind her dark gauze. Silver couldn't quite discern her features, but she appeared young and attractive. She was also well groomed, with recently polished nails.

"Neither would I." The woman's low tone would have been difficult to hear if not for Silver's auditory sensors.

"Care for some wine? Your glass is nearly empty." When the woman shook her head, Silver plowed on. "Are you here as an assistant like me? My boss is upstairs. I've ordered him a meal from the bistro."

"And I should care because…?"

"You want company. Isn't that why you're sitting in the bar? Or are you here to escape your companion?"

"The room makes me feel claustrophobic."

Silver nodded. "I understand this auction could go on for days. I'll go bonkers if we have to stay indoors the whole time. The city is pretty dismal, but I sure could use some exercise."

"It would be unwise to venture outside. Then your team would be disqualified."

"Yes, it would be a waste to come all this way for nothing. Why do you suppose they don't want us to explore?"

The lady glanced at the entrance. "I do not know, nor do I mind. We are here solely for the auction."

"We're here for many reasons, and that's just one of them. If we don't win the carolla nuts, my employer will have some heavy debts to pay off. We'll have to sell our ship and find new berths."

"How unfortunate for you."

"You wouldn't know of any folks looking to pick up new crew, would you?" Silver asked in the odd chance she knew Tyrone Bluth.

"I am not acquainted with the other bidders." The woman shifted her feet, as though getting restless. "But do not worry about falling behind in the bids. You may not win the carolla crop, but that is not the only prize."

"So I've heard. Rumors say the planet is haunted. Maybe you get to meet with your ancestors," she said in jest.

The woman leaned forward, and Silver glimpsed her intelligent expression. "There is only one way to find out."

"And what's that?"

"Tell your boss to underbid on purpose and lose the auction."

Chapter Fourteen

At the edge of Stacktown, the mist lifted, and the hiking party spied a mountain range ahead. All twelve members of the expedition halted as one. Jace gawked at the trail, a winding path that snaked through a verdant jungle toward granite cliffs ahead. A jungle? Where had this rainforest sprung from? In orbit, the planet had appeared to be mostly desert terrain, what they could see of it through that mysterious haze.

Then again, ever since they'd set foot here, he and Silver had been regaled with surprises.

A twinge of anticipation surfaced along with Mixy's mental presence, but Jace also sensed an element of concern from his valet. Concern for their safety, or anxiety that the Elusian wouldn't make it to his home world in time for his birthing?

If only they'd been allowed to leave right after the bidding concluded, but no, all the losers had been herded outside at dawn, where their proximity transmitters had been removed. As they received marching orders, they were told the unidentified winner had lifted off with his cargo hold full of carolla nuts.

"Those of you who are pure of heart shall pass through the veil," said their guide, a craggy-faced fellow who wore a safari outfit and carried a staff. He spoke with the solemn tone of a priest but appeared remarkably fit for a clergyman. Clearly he was a man of action, not of monastic studies.

"We're hiking into the mountains?" Jace asked. "Without food or equipment?"

"Provisions won't be a problem. We shall find what we need as our journey progresses."

"Impossible. I don't have time to waste," cried the portly fellow who called himself Primus Pilus Augustus.

During their brief round of introductions, he'd claimed to be the highest ranking centurion serving Emperor Nerod of the Xerxes Imperialate. Their empire bordered Consortium space on the side opposite from Kurash and the Dorians. Thus they'd remained out of the recent conflict, although Jace had heard rumors they were bolstering their fleet.

"The longer you delay, the longer will be your return home," their guide intoned. "There will be three challenges ahead. Let us see how far we can get today."

"What is this, another contest?" A man with a stubby beard, glass eye, and bald head scuttled behind the guide, who started ahead at a quick pace. "I hate contests. So much tension, so much suspicion. What challenges? Are they dangerous? And what does passing beyond the veil mean?"

"Will you shut up?" the short, fat Nacosian named Y'ort huffed. He waddled along the dirt path, his eyes twisting on flexible stalks.

Tripping over a root, Y'ort shoved away a steadying hand from his partner. Scummer was a tattooed guy with a ridged forehead, beak-like nose, and feathery things on his skin.

"I'm curious, too," Jace told the bearded man, matching his stride. "Did you get a look at the city before we left? My partner checked out some buildings yesterday, and she didn't see a soul operating any of the machinery. By the way, I'm Jack Zin."

"Gruber here. This place gives me the creeps. My boss should have taken me with him, but no-no. The Razor couldn't pass up the chance to get his hands on another prize."

"You work for Tyrone Bluth?" Too late, Jace realized his error. He shouldn't have mentioned the terrorist's name.

Fortunately, Gruber didn't pick up on it. Instead, the fellow stabbed a pudgy finger in the air. "Oops, forget I said that, will ya? The boss would have my hide if he knew I'd blabbed about him."

Would he? Or had Gruber dropped that information on purpose? Great Cosmos, no wonder Bluth wasn't among them. He must have won the bid.

Jace turned to tell Silver, but she was chatting with General Liu Chi, a dark-haired woman in military garb. The prim female's companion snarled in response as Silver spoke. The tall, rangy warrior with speckled skin kept slapping his side as though reaching for an absent firearm.

Jace's hands curled into fists as he regarded the Dorian. What was a soldier from their realm doing here? Perhaps he should use this trek as an opportunity to gain intelligence.

He exchanged a glance with Silver, who arched her eyebrows. Good idea, her expression read. Or did he hear that through their mental connection?

Instantly, his desire swelled, magnified by Mixy's resonance. Silver's face flushed as though her mind strayed in the same direction. His urge to bed her right then and there overwhelmed him. If he didn't control his impulses, he'd disrupt their plans. They made a good team, but only if they focused on their jobs.

With much effort, he returned his attention to the pirate.

"My partner and I are experienced Spacers," he told Gruber. "We're looking for a berth if your employer has any openings. How are you getting home if he took your transport?"

"No worries," the man said with a dismissive shrug.

Likely he'd arranged a signal for pickup, but maybe Jace could offer the guy a lift. The possibility of coming face-to-face with the leader of Tyrone's Marauders cooled his lust. Now they just had to make it alive to the end point.

"How high does this trail go? Will we get our promised bonus at the summit?" Dagitha said in a whiny voice.

Electricity crackled from the blue-skinned woman's fingertips, but more impressive was her charge of sexual energy. Jace's gaze roamed to her large breasts that swelled above a skimpy dress, her slender legs, and her absurdly impractical high heels. Staggering forward, she showed her lack of athletic prowess on the trail, although he had no doubt she could boast another kind of prowess in the bedroom. Why had she entered the auction? Sarcoids were usually known for their generosity.

"The reward will be worth your effort," their guide responded, without breaking pace.

"Seein' is believin', buddy." Y'ort scratched his armpit.

"Believing is quite the thing," the guide said, flashing them a beatific grin from over his shoulder. "You'll do well to remember that in the near future."

Jace glanced at the only two who hadn't spoken. Silver had told him about Analise, the woman dressed in black whom she'd met in the lounge. The lady's companion was a mustached man with soulless dark eyes and a jagged scar across his cheek. He stomped along with boots that had metal tips.

Silver, departing the lady general, strode toward the path ahead. She'd twisted her dark tinted hair into a braid and wore leggings with a loose cotton top. He watched her taut bottom, unable to curb his need as his loins tightened. To get his mind off his annoying reaction, he observed their surroundings. His nose sniffed a rich, earthy scent rife with moisture. His feet crunched dead leaves as he dodged roots and fallen branches. His ears heard strange chittering noises and raucous bird cries.

A flock of tiger gnats fluttered into the air, their orange and black spotted wings flapping to the heartbeat of the woods. Sunlight dappled through the tree canopy, glistening on the morning dew and illuminating cobwebs.

"I've never liked the woods," Dagitha said, swatting at an insect. "Are there snakes? By the fires of Zor, is that a spider? I hate crawly things."

"At least it's warm," Analise told her with a measure of sympathy, "and you're not wearing a hot robe like I am."

"Quiet, you forget your place," the mustache man ordered. "You are not to speak unless Fargus gives permission."

It appeared he spoke about himself in the third person, because Analise bowed her head, shuffling ahead in her slippered feet. Jace saw Silver's jaw clench but she didn't say a word. Instead, she twisted her earring and tilted her head slightly as though listening to the wind.

He caught up to her, taking her elbow. Ignoring her disapproving frown, he whispered in her ear what he'd learned from Gruber.

"I spoke to General Liu Chi," she replied in an undertone. "I'm not sure why she's here, but did you see her talking to Y'ort? I was catching their conversation when you interrupted. I'm not familiar with his race."

His brow furrowed. "Y'ort is a Nacosian. They're mercenaries who we suspect work for the Weavers."

"The Weavers?" She regarded him with her large, violet eyes. They'd discarded their brown contacts before joining the group that morning. "I thought those were children's tales meant to scare us."

"It's said their realm lies beyond the Wolf's Tail Nebula. We've sent patrols there. The ships returned on auto pilots, their crews dead. My father, when he was Parsater, theorized the Weavers were hiring Nacosians to acquire supplies."

"For what purpose?"

He shrugged. "We've been unable to gather sufficient intelligence."

"Does the Dorian work for the general, or vice versa? I hope the Dorians aren't trying to forge an alliance with the Weavers through Y'ort."

"If Dorius and the Weavers join together…" Jace's voice trailed off. That would be bad indeed. He should bring word of this potential threat to his ruler, but he dare not show his face on Kurash yet. Damn his impotence.

He noticed curious glances cast their way. "Remember, you're supposed to be my assistant. Smile and act more flirtatious."

"You're the one who looks like he swallowed a lemon pit."

Primus Augustus bumped into them. Had he been listening?

The stout man huffed and puffed. "I can't go any farther. I'm hungry and sweating like a yurb. There's no point to this ridiculous exercise." Whipping around, he scuttled back toward their point of origin.

"The trail is closed," their guide shouted. "The only way home is to move forward."

"Do you think I'm stupid? Our vessels sit idle at the spaceport. I don't care what game you're playing, but I'm out."

Was he being truthful, or did he just want to reach his ship and report what he'd overheard?

"It's too dangerous," the guide insisted, banging his staff on the ground. "I'm the only one who can lead you to safety."

"Farewell, suckers." Primus Augustus rounded a curve on the winding trail and disappeared from view.

The rest of the party milled around, indecisive. Jace stumbled when vibrations shook the ground. An ominous cracking noise sounded, followed by a crashing rumble. Silver clapped her hands over her ears, while Jace rushed back along the trail the centurion had taken.

"What the—?" He skidded to a stop, the others at his heels.

Rocks had broken off a nearby peak, creating an avalanche that swept away the section of path where they'd just walked. The path dropped off to a ravine on the other side. No sign remained of Primus Pilus Augustus.

"He's gone?" Dagitha screeched, tottering in her shoes. Electricity crackled around her as the group backed away.

Their guide steepled his hands together and bowed. "May his soul find peace and the everlasting beneficence of our Creator."

"That's it?" Y'ort spat. His eye stalks stretched, peered over the cliff, then retracted. "We leave the poor slug and move on?"

Jace studied the gap across to the next slope. "We don't have any choice." He doubted the centurion had survived, and anyway, he had no desire to waste time to find out.

Consternation pressed upon him. He could almost hear Mixy's wailing in his head.

"You knew this was going to happen." Dagitha jabbed a finger at the guide. "We're all going to meet our end. It's a one-way trip."

The mustached man beside Analise stepped forward. "You took our money to enter the auction. Fargus does not like to be taken for a fool. Tell us your scam, now." His jaw clenched, giving his face an even meaner look with its jagged scar.

Their guide spread his arms with priestly patience. "This is no hoax. If you are worthy and truly wish to receive the reward that awaits you, you'll follow me to the gate."

"What gate? You talk in riddles, old man." Fargus pushed him aside and took the lead.

Vegetation grew sparse as they climbed higher, out of the forested lowlands and into the mountain range where the terrain consisted of large boulders, sheer drops, and narrow ledges. The heat intensified, making them deplete their water reserves and energy bars.

Jace squinted in the sunlight, sweat dripping from his forehead. Glancing behind, he saw Dagitha had long since given up on her high heels, removing her shoes and cursing as she stumbled along, pebbles digging into her feet.

In contrast, Silver didn't issue one word of complaint. He reached out to assist her across the next rocky ridge when Fargus emitted a grunt of surprise.

A mountain lion stood in their path, twitching its long tail and glaring at them with impassive eyes. Flanked by a cliff on one side and a sheer drop on the other, the animal effectively held reign. Its fierce amber gaze and proudly lifted head proclaimed its mastery.

"Only the stalwart shall prevail," their guide remarked. Backing against the cliff face, he closed his eyes and bowed his head, folding his hands together in prayer.

"Move, you dumb animal," Fargus yelled. The lion snorted and raised its haunches.

"Maybe if you tried reasoning with it," Gruber suggested, stroking his beard.

"It doesn't understand Basic, idiot. Fargus has to provide a distraction." Stooping, he lifted a rock and tossed it to a spot behind the creature where it bounced off a boulder.

His adversary's nostrils flared and its teeth bared, but it didn't lose eye contact.

"Stupid beast. All wonkbys on my world are like that. They look fierce but are slow to attack. If we make enough noise, we'll scare it off," Fargus reassured the others.

He demonstrated his advice by hollering at the top of his lungs and racing past the animal.

The lion flicked its tail and swung around. With a low growl, it leapt forward. Fargus screamed, while a creeping mist swept in from a nearby crevice. The swirling haze swallowed them both.

Silence permeated the cluster of travelers. No one spoke. Jace listened to the wind whistling through the hollows.

"Patience and kindness would have served him better," their guide commented. Shaking his head, he regarded them sadly. "There's always one in every bunch. Let's go, then. Sustenance and rest are just ahead."

****

Silver spied the log hut in the distance and rushed forward. At last. This may only be a way station, but she hoped for food and drink and a place to recoup her strength.

Through their empathic link, she sensed Jace's spirits flagging as he caught up. Taking his hand, she squeezed it gently. They should discuss their situation, but weariness stole her words. She followed in a numb state while the guide gathered his flock and dictated the parameters for their rest stop.

A table laden with fruits, cheese, nuts, and bread waited for them inside the structure, along with cool water piped-in from a mountain stream. They'd remain here overnight, as the sun had already begun its descent, but their guide promised they'd reach their destination tomorrow.

How many of them would be left by then? One by one, they were being weeded out, the criteria unknown and the purpose a mystery. Silver understood they needed to complete this odd trek in order to attain their freedom. All she wanted was to reunite with Mixy, escape the planet, and locate Bluth.

"I'm sorry for your loss," she said to Analise who sat on a wooden bench by an open window. The others steered clear, as though communicating with her would condemn them to the same fate as her employer.

Analise adjusted her robe. "Do not fret for me. I am better off alone. Unlike your man, Fargus was not a kind master."

Silver didn't bother to correct her. Casting an appreciative glance at Jace, she admitted there was more to admire about the Kurashki than his physique. In all her dealings with him, he'd acted with honor and integrity. That he reacted with violence at times didn't escape her, but he wasn't cruel by nature. Quite the opposite when they made love.

Warmth stole into her veins as she recalled his tender words and gentle strokes. Stars above, he must sense her mood. His malachite eyes swung toward her with that look. Her lower region tightened with wanting and her breasts ached. Someone else's spiraling excitement magnified her response. She had to clasp her hands in her lap to avoid jumping Jace's bones right then.

Dingbat's tail. Get out of my head, Mixy.

"That lion came out of nowhere," she said to Analise. "Fargus might have been okay if he'd waited, like our guide advised. The creature would probably have left once it saw we weren't a threat."

"Lion? That was a wonkby. Couldn't you tell by its horns? Or is a lion what you call it on your world?"

"I didn't see any horns. It looked like a big cat, with a mane, a long tufted tail, and a powerful body. That thing must have weighed several hundred pounds."

Analise looked at her like she were daft, so Silver dropped the subject. Strange. Did everyone have a different perception of how the animal appeared?

"Look, if you need a ride to get home, Jace and I could give you a tow to the nearest transit point," she offered.

Analise's face softened. "Thanks, but I am trained to pilot our ship. I'll be glad to get rid of Fargus's stash in the cargo hold. His antiflux missiles and blaster bombs took up too much space." She paused. "His customers won't be happy to hear the news about him."

"Fargus sold weapons?" She'd seen him in conversation with Gruber. Had he been making a deal to sell arms to Tyrone Bluth?

"Aye, he did." Giving a furtive glance about the room, Analise leaned closer. "In confidence, my friend, I work for the Pamoria Merchant Marine Agency. My job was to track Fargus's clients."

"Really?" Silver regarded her with new respect. So Analise wasn't solely a paid companion.

Wishing she could blurt out her own identity, Silver held her tongue. She still had a lot to learn in her role as Jace's assistant. "Did he come to Stacktown for the auction or to meet with one of his customers?"

The woman's eyes narrowed. "He made contact with someone. I can't decide if it was Gruber or Dagitha. He had words with them both. Now I'll never find out."

Interesting, Silver thought as Analise rose and walked away. Gruber had blurted out who he worked for, but Dagitha hadn't said what she was doing at the auction. Why would the blue-skinned sexpot have joined the bidding?

This group represented a microcosm of political players. Was it any coincidence they'd all gathered here?

Consider the lady general and her Dorian friend, whose name was Cur. General Liu Chi had spoken to Y'ort, the Nacosian who might have a connection to the Weavers. Jace had proposed the frightening notion that Liu Chi's role might be to forge a link between Dorius and the Weavers.

Did Cur represent his people's military arm? Or could there be a rebellious faction within Dorius itself? In that case, had the rebels hired Liu Chi and any forces she commanded to attack their own government?

If only she and Jace had more time to snoop out everyone's secrets, but completing their mission took priority. And yet, killing Tyrone Bluth suddenly didn't seem as important as figuring out the ties between these people.

Jace's influence must be affecting her. He'd mentioned how matters of galactic politics had wider repercussions than her goal of revenge. Think how much more useful she'd be to S.I.N. if she gathered intelligence on such a comprehensive scale.

But that wasn't her job. Her assignment was to terminate Bluth's reign of terror. And that could only end one way.

Fatigue clouded her mind, but she sought Jace's company. They needed to exchange information, determine their next plan of action, and soothe this restless urge afflicting her. Only his touch searing her skin would relieve it.

From across the room, he broke off his conversation and strode toward her, his expression purposeful. Through Mixy's link, she shared his arousal and his valet's unrequited tension. So when he took her arm and steered her outside, she didn't protest.

Their guide, hovering by the doorway, gave a knowing grin. "If you seek repose in the fresh air, there is a grassy knoll by the stream downhill. But be forewarned." He waved a hand. "The air promises rain, and we are close to a gorge. You will need to come inside the hut to be protected when the rain starts."

"Any creatures we should worry about, or rock slides?" Silver asked, lifting her eyebrows.

"You need not be concerned. The pure of heart shall pass through the veil," the guide repeated, gazing upon a distant granite peak.

"Just what is this veil or gate you keep mentioning?" she shot back, hoping he didn't mean the veil of life or the gates of Zolifer. Maybe none of the losers returned home because they were dead. But why kill them off? To keep anyone from telling tales?

There wasn't much to tell. When she'd scouted the town, she had seen no evidence of a working oil refinery, weapons manufacturing plant, or illicit drug lab. Machinery spouted smoke and gears grinded and wheels turned, but to what purpose? Everything had been automated; there hadn't been any laborers in sight, not even the few evident on their arrival.

"Patience and kindness will serve you along your path," the guide droned, maintaining his stance.

Justice, too. Those words popped into her head. Puzzled, Silver glanced questioningly between Jace and their guide. That sounded like something Jace would say, but had it come from him? The guide leaned upon his staff like an old man, but she bet he could switch hands to use the long stick for defense if necessary. As she regarded him, the corners of his mouth quivered. Was he toying with her?

Creeped out by the guy, she turned away. This whole planet deserved its reputation. Strange things happened here and people disappeared. She'd just as soon be facing those thugs from Bartlett Station than continue their trek into the unknown.

"We need to get back to our ship," Jace said as they half-stumbled and half-slid down a gravelly slope toward the copse below.

"Don't I know," she agreed. "Following this stupid tour to its end seems like the only way to get there. That guide holds all the cards."

"He speaks in riddles. I don't trust him."

"Me neither." The only people they could trust were each other, but she didn't want to admit it. Depending on other people only led to pain and despair down the road. Already she cared too much for Jace and his valet. If anything happened to them… well, she'd make sure it never did.

Evergreen trees flanked a small brook that bubbled its way through outcrops of rock. A soft roar hinted at a waterfall beyond. The fresh scent of pine mingled with crisp mountain air. They headed for the grassy knoll sprinkled with tiny purple wild-flowers.

"It's lovely here," she commented.

Wind whistled through the trees, the sound magnified by her auditory sensors. Listening a moment, Silver relaxed when she heard nothing to alarm them.

"It's been a long day." Jace's hot breath seared her neck as he massaged her shoulders from behind.

Silver closed her eyes and lowered her mental armor, wanting nothing more than to savor the pressure of his thumbs digging into her stiff muscles. Her body melted into putty, and a moan of pure pleasure escaped her lips. She focused solely on his skilled touch, willing to promise anything if he kept kneading her knots of tension and soothing her worries.

"That feels so good. Don't stop," she said when his hands lifted away.

"You'll feel better with your hair loose." He untwisted her braid, then spread her strands and massaged her scalp.

"Ahhh..." Words failed her as she yielded to the pleasurable sensations emanating from his magic fingers.

"Your hair feels like filaments of silk. It gives me joy to touch it," he said in a husky voice. His circular movements edged to her temples which he rubbed ever so gently.

Tears moistened her eyes. When had she met a man before who ministered to her so tenderly? Not even her dead fiancé had zeroed in on her desires like Jace. But then their reactions synched in a way she wouldn't have thought possible.

Part of her pleasure came from his arousal. His bulge pressed against her buttocks, his organ swelling with need. Stars above, she couldn't think of anything except him. Correction— she couldn't think at all.

Her clothing scraped her body like sandpaper. "Let me take

off my shirt. I want to feel your hands on my bare skin," she said, wriggling free.

"Not yet, deermin." He pulled her back into his length, rubbing himself against her while gutteral sounds issued from his throat. "I want you to know my touch, now and forever."

His arms circled her waist and his hands sought her breasts. Over the fabric of her shirt, he cupped her, teased her nipples, and stroked her until she felt a responsive wetness between her thighs. "Jace… I can't wait much longer."

Weak with passion, she sagged against him. Such sweet torture would unravel her. But he held her in place, not allowing her to move from his grasp.

She heard his erratic breathing, felt his heart pounding in his rib cage as though it were her own. Maybe it was. She couldn't tell the difference anymore, including that voice screaming for release inside her head. Mixy? The Elusian's voyeurism added to the fog of lust consuming her.

Her breath hitched when his hand roamed lower, scratching at the itch below her belly where her leggings split. He knew exactly the right movement to stimulate her.

"You're killing me," she said, aware he could do just that with a single motion. She didn't care. She was going to die anyway from sheer delight in his arms.

"Oh… oh."

When he dipped his fingers inside her waistband and found her naked folds of flesh, a shudder rose through her. What was he doing? He coddled her nether lips, spreading and tweaking her sensitive regions until she could bear no more.

Her release came with violent fury, spasms rocking her body.

How could he so easily demolish her defenses? And how could he be so giving without asking for anything in return? She knew Jace had derived pleasure from her response. Still, that he could care for her with such tenderness made her wonder about her purpose in life. Truly, she didn't deserve a man like him after what she'd become.

Was it so wrong to honor her dead parents and want to avenge their murders? According to his opinion, her single-minded goal stank of selfishness. He believed she should work for the greater good, like him, to save the galaxy. Could she be as magnanimous, given the chance?

Wanting to please him, to demonstrate that she could think of someone else besides herself, she tried to stroke him. But keeping the upper hand, he wouldn't let her. And for once in her lifetime, she didn't mind yielding control.

Did she really trust him that much? Did she want to pleasure him not only to offer physical release but also because he meant more to her than she could admit? Thoughts of him already filled her waking hours and dissolved her reason. Which path should she follow—his to justice, or hers to revenge?

"You're thinking too much," he murmured, turning her into his embrace.

His mouth descended, and he took her in a hot, passionate kiss that left her breathless. Coming up for air, she grasped him by the head to draw him close again, while his hands roamed to her breasts and brought her nipples to peaks. Desperate wanting made her wet and wild. She grasped at him as he conquered her with steamy kisses.

Nearly at the boiling point a second time, she gasped when his hands probed inside her pants again. His nimble fingers invaded the crease between her thighs while she writhed in desire.

"I want to explore all of you," he murmured, sliding his finger inside the portal to her womb.

"Ah… ah." She moaned an incoherent reply.

"Do you like this?" He flicked her sensitive spot, making her jerk in response.

Her clothes got in the way. She stepped back, shed her garments, and spread them on the ground. Then she lay down and gestured for Jace to join her. He stretched his long body beside her but swatted her hand away when she tugged on his shirt.

"Not yet, let me play with you first." He proceeded to lavish attention on her by gently stroking her cheek while she gazed up into his beautiful green eyes. Kissing her mouth, he moved his hands lower, teasing her nipples to taut points while she moaned against his lips for release.

She spread her legs, giving him easy access. Finally, his roaming hand touched her there. She bit back a cry as he glided one finger in and out of her while his thumb did the rest. Her tension mounted, rushed to the surface, and erupted.

Her spasms took forever to subside, and then she went limp with exhaustion, her face covered in sweat.

"You're the most responsive woman I've ever met." Jace brushed a stray strand of hair from her face. "And the most beautiful."

She smiled at his handsome visage. "Only because you make me feel that way. Even now, I can't get enough of you."

She should be satisfied, but she still felt an aching need for him. Her glance lowered to the bulge in his pants. Or maybe it was his thirst that needed to be quenched.

"Your turn," she said, sitting upright.

****

Jace had controlled himself as long as possible, but now his need surmounted his will. He tugged off his boots then divested himself of his clothing.

Silver watched him with passion-glazed eyes and swollen lips, bruised from his kissing, especially with his days-old growth of beard. He wanted more. He wanted to plunder her mouth and steal her breath and seduce her mind.

He prided himself on his conquest of a fascinating woman whose tough exterior hid a vulnerable core.

It hadn't been easy. Through their adventures together, he'd broken her barriers, but did she understand the point? Could he sway her from her quest for revenge and enlist her aid in toppling Garth, the cousin who'd betrayed him? Did she care enough to share his hopes for peace?

He wanted her to know how much he needed her. Lying at her side, he drew an intake of breath when she caressed his shaft.

His blood pounded when she scraped her fingernail along his slit, tickled her way downward, and gently squeezed him. Consumed with lust, he let his head loll back so she could have her way with him.

Rolling on top, she thrust her knee between his legs and pressed her breasts against his chest. He didn't wait for her mouth to close on his. Lifting his head, he met her lips, claiming possession. And then he lost himself to her heated caresses, her lathing tongue, and her strokes of fire.

When he could stand no more, he flipped her on her back, pushed open her legs with his knees, and thrust inside her in one quick motion. Here he paused, relishing her tightness and her moist warmth. Hearing her sigh of content accelerated his ardor. He began pumping, his hips rocking as madness overwhelmed him.

Mixy's essence filtered into his passion-dazed mind. He sensed Silver's glory at sheathing him while she experienced his frenzy. Knowing how he satisfied her drove him wild.

His hips rotated faster and faster until he exploded in a maelstrom of ecstasy. The aftershocks kept him in a state of bliss until he finally collapsed.

Spent and sweaty, he drifted into a half-sleep, partly aware that he lay naked to the burgeoning night. Silver's steady breathing told him she had succumbed as well. And so they stayed, until rain drops splattered his face.

He awoke to the warning shout of their guide.

Chapter Fifteen

Jace must have slept for hours because dawn was just breaking when he roused from his sleep-induced stupor. Leaping to his feet at the guard's bellowing voice, he tossed on his clothes while Silver awoke and did the same. Rain swept in from the mountain heights, laden clouds blanketing the sky.

"Hurry, we'd better get back to the hut." He hastened up the trail as the light rain intensified.

Silver's tousled hair and rumpled clothing didn't escape their guide's notice. He stood in the doorway, his brows arching at the sight of them.

"It's about time. At least you have more sense than those fools." He pointed to a path on a ledge rimming the gorge. "I warned them of the danger, but they're too impatient. They insisted on going ahead."

"Who are you talking about?" Jace asked as he and Silver huddled next to him beneath the roof's overhang. Water dripped from the eaves, a steady pitter-patter, while the scent of fresh earth entered his nose.

"The two called Y'ort and Scummer." The guide's disdainful tone said what he thought about them.

"That's the Nacosian and his tattooed friend," Silver told Jace. "I'd hoped to discover... to get to know them better. Maybe if we hurry, we can catch up to them."

The wise man barred the way with his staff. "Get inside and remain there. The storm will move fast with torrential downpours and flash floods. That doesn't bode well for anyone caught in the mountain pass."

Jace and Silver exchanged glances. They'd already learned how disobeying the guide could be fatal.

Jace stepped across the threshold, cheered by the warmth inside and the aroma of Dorian tea. That had been the only good thing to come from the recent war. Their enemy cultivated tea plants that gave off a fragrance unmatched on any other world.

The mouth-watering scent of baked bread drew him to the center table, where a selection of foods tempted him. He'd missed dinner last night in his lust-filled state, and now his gut growled as a reminder.

Silver rolled her eyes. "Just like a man to think of his stomach before anything else. I'm going to wash up before I eat. Don't wait for me." She headed toward the rear.

After greeting the others, Jace grabbed a plate and piled on a selection of melon slices, juicy bangleberries, nuts, cheese, and a hunk of soft bread. He took a seat, reaching for the teapot and pouring a cup. Steam wafted into the air.

"Where have you been?" General Liu Chi demanded. "We thought you'd left us and moved on."

Cur, the Dorian warrior, bristled. He reached for his nonexistent weapon but his hand came up empty.

"We needed some fresh air," Jace said quickly. "You know what I mean. Not much privacy in this place."

"You're telling me." Gruber, sitting opposite Jace and stuffing grapes into his mouth, regarded him with his good eye. "Especially when some of these people snore. This freakin' prize had better be worth it, or I'm gonna break some bones."

Electricity crackled from Dagitha's fingertips. "I agree. Every day we spend on this miserable planet is costing me jinars. I need to add money to my accounts, not deplete them. And these accommodations are disgraceful."

She indicated the bare pallets around the room's perimeter. "We might as well have been sleeping in tents for all the rest I got. Is this any way to treat guests of our caliber? What do you think, Analise?"

"You are correct." Analise pressed her lips together. Her eyes appeared bleary, as though she hadn't slept well.

Jace's instincts told him Silver had emerged from the lavatory. Just then, he heard an ominous rumbling noise that sounded above the raindrops pelting the roof.

His fingers dripped with berry juice. He wiped them on a paper napkin and leapt to his feet. Along with the others, he rushed to the doorway, where the guide spread his arms to block their path.

"You must not go outside."

The Dorian's speckled skin darkened. His beefy arm pushed the guide aside. "Move, vermin."

"What is it?" Silver tapped Jace's shoulder. She'd braided her hair and washed her face.

Devoid of makeup, she appeared even more kissable. Jace pushed aside his longing to sweep her into his arms and peered outdoors.

A torrent of water rode down the gorge like an avenging angel. He watched the enormous wave with horror, realizing what would have happened if their party had started along the trail.

"Y'ort and Scummer," Silver cried, her thoughts on the same page.

A collective gasp arose from their group as one. They huddled back inside the shelter.

"It was their destiny, but it is not yours," their guide said, facing the assemblage. "Eat and drink, for we move off as soon as the flood subsides. Usually it is gone as quickly as it comes, so prepare for departure."

"Do you suppose they have a flash flood like this every five years after the auction?" Jace mused, plopping himself down at the table to finish his meal. "Mighty convenient, if you ask me."

"Now only seven of us are left." Silver, sitting by his side, reached for the fruit and cheese platter. "Let's hope the rest of our group makes it."

"At least we're not lacking for provisions and shelter. Where did this food come from?" he queried Analise, who sat with her hands folded as though meditating. Dagitha, meanwhile, simpered at Cur, as though she hoped to convince the warrior to protect her.

"The meal was here when we woke up." Analise's gaze flickered to their guide. "This journey is most peculiar."

"No kidding." Jace gulped down his tea. "Why do I get the feeling we're not going to like what's at the end?"

****

Fortunately, nothing bad happened when they resumed their trek after the rain stopped. The flood receded just as rapidly as their host had predicted. Weak sunlight sliced through the dissipating clouds, highlighting the mountain peaks above like rays from heaven.

Silver watched her footing on the slippery ledge that wound through the gorge. On her right rose a sheer cliff, while on the left the terrain dropped precipitously to the river rapids below. The air grew thinner and cooler the higher they climbed. Hours passed while they hiked until her muscles ached and her mind numbed.

A cloud bank loomed beyond the next rise, and soon a swirling white mist surrounded them. She couldn't see in front, having to advance single-file by putting a hand on Jace's shoulder ahead.

When their guide halted, they all stumbled to a stop. Not one of them complained, afraid to incur his wrath. They had to believe he was leading them to the promised elixir and not to their deaths.

"Congratulations. You have passed through the veil. Beyond is the gate to Selia Dar."

"What's that?" General Liu Chi demanded.

"It's not a thing. It's a place." Their guide held a twinkle in his eye as he regarded each of them in turn.

"Is that where we get our prize?" Gruber said, rubbing his hands with glee.

"I just want to take it and leave." Dagitha shrugged off the wrap Analise had loaned her along with a pair of sensible shoes. "I've only got two more days until my appointment."

"For what?" Silver asked curiously.

"My rejuv treatment."

The woman general's lip curled with scorn. "Is that why you wanted to win the carolla crop, to finance your cosmetic enhancements?" Her glance slid meaningfully to Dagitha's generous bosom.

Dagitha stiffened. "*Non'k meteur op'Kur,*" she snapped in her native tongue. "I've opened a welfare center for needy women on my world. We need the credits for operating capital."

"Please, you must shed your earthly concerns to proceed." The guide indicated a crevice in the solid rock face.

Silver blinked. Had that opening been there before?

"What does that mean, shed our earthly concerns?" Cur snarled to their leader.

"If you wish to obtain the full benefit of your reward, you'll act beyond your own self-interest."

"That sounds good enough for me." Silver stepped forward, unable to wait any longer. Mixy's vibes felt increasingly agitated, although she didn't know if that reflected Jace's impatience or the valet's own anxiety.

Turning sideways, she squeezed through the narrow confines that reminded her of the rubilite cavern on Al'ron. It would help if her claim came through, but she had no way to check on it now. Whispers of the past fell away as she emerged on the other side of the short passage. She crossed the threshold into the light, shivering at a tingling sensation on her skin. The mist lifted, and she gawked at the view.

Stars above. What was this place?

"Incredible," Jace said, reaching her side.

Lush greenery cascaded down the mountainside to a valley

where a village nestled, its white tiled roofs and gleaming buildings visible even from the mountaintop. Silver spied trees weighted with fruit and palms bulging with coconuts. In the far distance, an ocean stretched into infinity.

"You gaze upon the sacred city of Selia Dar," their guide said in a hushed tone. "That is where you will receive your prizes."

Two of the questions she'd had about the residents of Stacktown became clear—why they'd worn sandals with sand between their toes and where they'd gotten suntans.

"I don't get it," she said. "Do you mean we've won a vacation at the beach?"

The longer they delayed, the worse her chances for tracking Tyrone Bluth. She couldn't believe they still had farther to go. Was this all a trick? Perhaps their guide never intended for them to leave this place. Her spirits sank to a new low at the thought of being trapped here forever.

"Continue into the valley, and then all will be revealed," the guide told them, his face impassive.

It didn't take as long to climb down the mountain as it had to gain elevation. They followed an easy path from the timberline down through the tropical forest and into the seaside town.

Friendly citizens greeted them. The people favored brightly colored clothing. Women had on long dresses and men wore belted tunics with trousers. Their hair appeared a uniform shoulder length, styled as though they all went to the same salon.

"Peace and harmony, sister," a woman said to Silver with a smile. She clung to the arm of a man whose face seemed vaguely familiar, but Silver couldn't place him.

It didn't seem to matter, so she let it go. The residents seemed happy, strolling through sculpted gardens, painting on easels by the street front, eating at outdoor cafés. Her mood lifted, soaring on a cinnamon-scented breeze. She heard the eternal rhythm of the ocean gently whooshing in the background.

The guide halted in front of a structure that stood separate at the end of an alley. It looked like a former stable. The long building held a row of closed doors.

"You're welcome to explore our city and stay as long as you wish, but when you're ready, your prize can be found behind one of those doors. Choose wisely. Inside could be your biggest blessing or your worst nightmare."

"How do we get back? To our ships, I mean?" Silver asked.

The guide regarded her with an enigmatic expression. "The path will open at the right time. You won't be needing my services any longer. Oh, and there's one more thing," he added, wagging a finger. "You must enter the portal alone, or your gift will be unable to materialize. The source comes from within. You may have passed through the veil, but now it must be lifted from your eyes. This is your final test."

"Damn fellow speaks in riddles," Jace muttered after the guide left.

"I don't want to stay here a minute longer than necessary." Silver's mouth watered from the cinnamon aroma. They could try the cuisine before they left, couldn't they? A decent meal would fuel them for the return trip.

The sun's warmth heated her cheeks, and she raised her face. She hadn't been to the beach in so long. Would it hurt to kick off their shoes and spend an hour or two absorbing the rays? Something within impinged her consciousness at the idea, but she ignored it, excited by the possibility of exploration.

"I'm going in this one," she said, twisting the doorknob to the second door on the left before Jace could stop her.

Gruber had already gone inside another entry, while Analise, Dagitha, and the woman general gazed at the remaining doors in confusion. Cur yanked one open with a growl and stalked in. They heard his exclamation of surprise before the door slammed shut.

Silver flung her own door wide and stepped inside the darkened interior. While her eyes adjusted to the lack of light, she heard the door swing shut from behind. And then her auditory sensors went dead. She heard nothing, saw nothing.

A spicy incense-like scent swirled into her nostrils. *Open your eyes*, said a voice in her head.

Mixy? No, not his essence. How come she couldn't sense the Elusian in here?

My eyes are open, she replied in silence, staring into the black depths. All parameters shrunk and vanished as though she'd entered a void of time and space. Her balance felt off, as though she no longer stood upright, and yet she didn't fall.

Examine your heart.

"Who are you? Where are you? Why don't you turn on the lights?"

You don't need light to see us. We are always with you.

A feeling of love and caring enveloped her along with a faint sparkle that showered her like glitter. Goosebumps rose on her skin. Her hair lifted, as though an electric current charged the air.

Feel us, need us, bring us forth.

"Who are you?" she asked again as she shivered.

Who do you want?

"What?"

Who do you want? the voice repeated.

Alone in the dark, she wrapped her arms around herself. It felt as though the vestiges of time had slipped away.

Once again, she was a child hiding from Tyrone's Marauders during their raid upon her farming community. Squeezed inside a narrow underground conduit, she crouched, covering her ears and praying. The pounding explosions, the sweat-filled terror, the fear for her parents returned with such force that her throat swelled, and she couldn't swallow.

"Mama! Papa!" she cried, tears flooding her eyes.

We're here, bellamia, her mother's voice said, using her favorite endearment.

Sparkles of light infused the darkness, swirled, and took shape. A woman and a man appeared before her, their dear faces familiar in her dreams, their arms outstretched. Silver ran toward them, not knowing if they were illusory and not caring. If this was some sort of hallucination, she welcomed it.

Their forms seemed corporeal enough as they embraced her, her father's beard scraping her skin, her mother's soft hair touching her cheek.

"I've missed you so much," Silver sobbed, shattered by her grief. She'd suppressed it for so long, she'd forgotten she had a heart.

We never got to say goodbye, her father said in his kindly tone, patting her. *We want you to know that we love you, and that you must move on.*

"No, I can't, at least not until I kill the man who murdered you. Then I'll rest, maybe I'll even join you."

That's not the way.

Silver spun at the sound of Burrell's manly voice. His shade distinguished itself from the gloom. Her fiancé was present, too?

"I'm hallucinating," she concluded aloud. "You're not really here. The incense must be fogging my brain."

We are here. Burrell stroked her lips with his thumb and gazed into her eyes with tender affection. *This valley holds a rift between dimensions,* he explained.

Ah, how she'd missed his gentleness and quiet wit, his keen scientific mind. Her pulse throbbed in her temples. Could this be the veil their guide spoke about?

We are permitted to visit, Silver's mother said, her eyes adoring as she regarded her daughter. *However, certain rules apply. Only those who will eventually pass through the heavenly gates may contact us. We are still here because you haven't let us go.*

"How can I? You were taken from me too soon."

You're not a child any longer. Besides, you are in danger if you continue along the path you've chosen.

"I know that. I'm prepared to confront Tyrone Bluth."

That's not what I meant. This revenge you seek... it blurs your purpose and blackens your soul. Let it go. Let us go, bellamia. Or you'll forever lose your chance to be with us again.

Her father nodded. *The man who accompanies you, listen to him. Go to him. He needs you.*

"No, I need you more." As she spoke, they seemed to grow more transparent. She clutched at them, terrified they'd leave her alone.

Our time is up, her mother said, sad-faced.

"Wait, will I see you again?"

If you remain in the village, you may visit us as often as you wish, but only once per cycle.

"What does that mean?" Once a day, or once a month? She didn't want them to go, having so much more to say. Chills raced up her spine as she watched their forms get dimmer. "I love you. I love you. Don't leave me."

She reached out, touched her mother's fingers, then felt nothing but empty air.

****

Jace staggered past the doorway into the bright sunlight, his mind jumbled with images of his dead parents. He couldn't assimilate what had just happened. It was too raw, too painful. How could they have been there without the horrific wounds that had caused their deaths? What did they mean when they said it had been their destiny to die for the greater good?

"I'm sorry. I'm so sorry," he croaked, same as he'd told them.

At first he thought they'd come back to haunt him because he had murdered them in a drunken fit and didn't remember. But they'd said he wasn't responsible and shouldn't blame himself. As Mixy claimed, a drug had been put into his wine that night. While he slept, terrorists had done the deed. Jace must free himself of the past and pursue a higher purpose.

Clearing his throat, he noticed Silver standing in a corner. Her hair hung loose across her face, shadowing her expression.

"Are you all right?" he said when he reached her side.

Someone gave a loud sniffle behind them. Spinning, he regarded Cur with astonishment. The Dorian had emerged from his chamber, tears running down his speckled face. Could the fierce warrior be crying?

"What did you see?" he felt compelled to ask, but Cur brushed past him without a word.

The other doors had already opened where his companions had gone in. Perhaps their interludes were preset to a certain time limit. If so, then where had the others gone?

"I need a drink," Silver said in a quiet voice.

He swiveled his attention back to her and studied her pale face and stricken eyes. "Me, too."

They wound through the picturesque streets until they came to a town square. Jace pointed to a café with outdoor tables filled with happy, chatting customers.

"Let's sit here. I wasn't hungry, but that smell in the air is making my mouth water." He could almost taste the cinnamon flavor on his tongue.

Silver fell into a chair as though requiring its support. He felt oddly languid as well, as though his experience had sapped his energy and stolen his will. With the sun beating down upon his neck and the lap of ocean waves in the near distance, he didn't feel inclined to budge any time soon.

A waiter approached carrying two mugs of a frothy liquid which he placed before them on the cloth-covered table. "Try this. It's our best ale."

"Do you have a menu?" Jace drew his mug close.

The bald-headed man smiled merrily. "We don't need menus, sirrah. Whatever you desire is yours."

"How much for a krellian steak with roasted peratoes and root greens?"

"As I said, whatever you desire is yours. You don't need credits here. Just relax, and enjoy yourselves."

Silver perked up. "Really? In that case, I'd like some grilled mantay fish with wild rice and asparagus. I'm suddenly hungry, too."

Once the waiter left, she raised her mug too fast and some of the golden liquid sloshed onto the table. Taking no heed, she drank a long swallow.

"So what happened to you in there?" Jace jerked his thumb toward the stable, for lack of a better word.

"I'd rather not talk about it."

"Suit yourself." He didn't pursue the topic, his cares drifting away on the gentle sea breeze. Sipping his ale, he listened to the banter of a couple flirting at the next table.

"Hey, listen, where can we find a place to stay?" he asked the waiter who delivered their meals within an astonishing fifteen minutes of their orders. Steam rose from his dish along with the aroma of charbroiled meat. A knife and fork were in Jace's hands before he realized he'd picked them up.

"You must have missed orientation," the server said. "All new residents are assigned quarters."

"Oh yeah?" Silver glanced around. "No one told us."

"I'll find out where you're supposed to go." The guy bustled away before they could question him further.

"Everyone seems so friendly." Silver dug into her fish. She closed her eyes, rolling the food on her tongue. "Umm, this is good. It tastes just like home."

"No kidding. I haven't had peratoes since the blight wiped out half our crop."

Her eyes slitted open. "I remember you'd mentioned some sort of plant disease on your home world. With my agronomy background, I might be able to help you find a cure."

"You're going after Bluth, remember?"

"Oh, right. I forgot."

Why didn't their mission seem important anymore? Jace's thoughts retreated to the past. "My parents used to serve peratoes when they treated the servants to our annual barbecue."

Chewing on his steak, he visualized the long tables set out in their garden, the platters of food, the bowls of fruits and nuts, the bottles of wine. Like the wine he'd drunk the night they died, except their servants had the night off. It had just been him, his folks, and Shanna and Yvette at home.

"The girls must be alive," he blurted.

"Who?" Busy eating, Silver shot him a puzzled glance.

"My sister and my betrothed. They weren't in the vision with my parents."

Silver choked, coughing. She grabbed for her drink. "W-what are you talking about?" A stray hair caught in her mouth, and she tucked it behind her ear. Her dangly gold earrings sparkled in the sunlight.

"My parents spoke to me inside that room." Putting his fork down, he bowed his head. "They said this place allows them to cross into our plane for brief moments. I didn't think… if Shanna and Yvette were dead, they'd have been there, too."

"What did you mean by your *betrothed*?" Her eyes narrowed as she regarded him across the table.

"Yvette and I aren't officially engaged, but Ruler Hurat expects me to offer for her. Or rather, he'd expected it of me before I was accused of murder and thrown into prison. I didn't know if we'd find the girls alive, so what was the point of mentioning it?"

A frown crossed her face but then the crease lines erased, replaced by a look of serenity. "You're right. What's the point? It's better not to think about these things, especially in such beautiful surroundings."

He gazed at her lush lips, and a more carnal type of beauty came to mind. "I'd love to find a secluded stretch of beach, spread a blanket on the sand, and strip you naked."

"Would you now?" Her teasing tone implied she'd forgiven him his omission.

Jace's cares evaporated on the wind. The sea breeze and a full stomach lulled him into a state of tranquility.

"Peace and harmony, brother." The waiter steepled his hands and bowed when they got up to leave.

"Are you sure you won't accept a gratuity?" Jace offered a second time, holding out a few jinars.

"Payment is unnecessary. We all take turns doing the chores. You'll be assigned a rotation once you're acclimated."

The server had given them an address where they could stay. It proved to be a small cottage on the outskirts of town, with a grove of banana plants in the rear yard and a bed of pretty flowers in the front. No one came to greet them, but they found a note tacked onto the whitewashed door.

Welcome to your new home, citizens. If you need anything, please use the communicor. Whatever you desire is yours.

"Shall we see what's inside?" Jace pushed open the front door that lacked a keyhole and lock. It swung wide, squeaking on its hinges. "This place must not have any crime. Then again, if you can get whatever you want, who needs to steal anything?"

"Good point." Silver moved off to explore.

Wondering how far the 'your wish is my command' thing would go, he turned on the communicor located in their fully stocked kitchen.

"Yes?" a robotic voice answered. "How may I assist you?"

"This house is too small. Would something bigger be available?"

"How big?"

"Say, a mansion." He described the dimensions of his palatial birthplace. "I'd also like a full wardrobe of clothing for both of us, plus servants to cook and clean."

"It shall be done. Whatever—"

"… you desire is yours," Jace completed.

He switched off the unit, rolling his shoulders. It had been a long day, although he couldn't remember why. They'd come here from… where? His mind blanked, the thread slipping away.

No matter. His woman waited for him. Deciding to find Silver, he whipped around. What the—?

The kitchen had expanded, encompassing a vast space with an industrial range, paneled refrigeration unit, gleaming maple cabinets, a stainless steel sink, and a center island. A stocky woman wearing an apron chopped vegetables at a counter beside an open pantry.

"You'd better get your hide upstairs, milord," she said in an accent reminiscent of Kurash. "Mistress Silver needs your help in choosing her gown. You'll both want to look your best for the court ball."

Giddy as a teenager, Jace sprinted for the grand staircase at the heart of his ancestral home.

Chapter Sixteen

Silver whirled when she heard Jace's voice from the doorway. "Do you like this?" She held up her new sun-protective jumpsuit. "Its embedded sensors will absorb ultraviolet rays in the danger zone, so I can work in the fields longer."

"That's great."

As Jace entered the master bedroom, Silver marveled at their good fortune. They'd rated the largest quarters of the entire base settlement. She breathed in the sweet scent of orange blossoms, figuring she deserved the luxury. After all, as Chief of Research and Development for the colony, she ran the show. And so far she'd done a bang-up job, just like her parents.

She couldn't wait to get back to her research project. While her lab assistants ran the standardized tests, she intended to break down the unique material she'd discovered to its molecular level. Then she could manipulate its properties for new and exciting technologies.

Yes, you're being manipulated, said a familiar voice in her head. *Shake out of it.*

She glanced at Jace, but his green eyes merely gazed back at her in confusion. They'd had such an idyllic time since he joined her here—making love, cooking together in the small country kitchen, heading to the fields to sift the rich soil between their fingers. She'd never have thought such bliss was possible.

It's not real. Come back to me. I need you.

A sharp pain gutted her side. She pressed a hand there, wincing. Oh, no. Mixy.

Her world shimmered, and the room's boundaries shifted. She blinked while reality took form. This wasn't a colonial housing module. She and Jace were in that same small cottage as when they'd arrived.

"What's going on?" Silver whispered, wary of surveillance.

She hadn't even thought to check for bugs, but surely someone must be keeping watch on them. They'd been here how many hours already, lost in their fantasies?

Jace grabbed her arm. "I don't know, but we have to return to the ship. Mixy's budding time is near. Thank the stars for our mental link. His presence cleared my mind."

Silver couldn't agree more. Hastily, she rummaged through the closet, glad to find her backpack untouched. She wore the same outfit as when they'd started on their trek, although it had been freshly laundered and pressed.

"I had the strangest dreams," she began, setting the straps from her bag over her shoulders.

"Later. We may run into trouble when we try to leave."

"Didn't the guide say the way would be open if we wanted it to be? This place seems big on granting wishes. Maybe we can wish ourselves back at the spaceport."

When that didn't work, they went outside. People bustled about the town as usual, offering friendly greetings and cheerful smiles. They headed toward the foothills at the opposite end.

Silver tugged on his arm. "Look, there's Dagitha coming out of that emporium. She may want to come with us."

"We can't afford any delays." His voice sounded terse.

He must be anxious to leave for Mixy's sake, same as her. "Just let me ask. She'll want to get back to her work, I imagine. Wasn't Dagitha planning to establish a center for disadvantaged women? That makes it worth a try."

Dagitha shook her head soundly when Silver made the offer. "I am happy here. Why would I want to leave?" She clutched several packages against her chest, small arcs of electricity bouncing between her fingers.

"Your fantasies aren't real," Silver said. "This place puts a spell on you. Aren't you forgetting why you came?"

"I don't care. There is no ugliness here, no division among the people. Everyone shares the work and the bounty. And I can be with Jonee."

"Who's that?"

Dagitha bent her head. "My son," she said in a low voice. "He caught a fever… I thought I'd never see him again."

Jace jabbed his finger in the air. "Are you talking about what you saw inside that chamber? Those ghosts from our past need to be put to rest. We're meant to move on."

His pointed gaze aimed at Silver. She averted her eyes, unwilling to put her haunts to rest just yet.

Dagitha firmed her lips. "Please step aside. You can have the outside world. I wish to remain here." Her eyes sparked, as though she would shoot lightning bolts at them if they continued to block her way.

Regretfully, Silver let her go, wondering what Dagitha's people would think when their delegate failed to return home. If possible, she'd send a message to Sarcoidonia that Dagitha chose to remain at Stacktown.

The Sarcoid wasn't the only member of their party who resisted Silver's summons. General Liu Chi, who they found sunbathing at the beach, refused to budge.

Her second-in-command, however, shook himself loose from his torpor and joined them. Silver wondered how Cur had made it this far. What goodness resided within the warrior's heart that he had passed the barriers?

She could say the same for Gruber. Tyrone Bluth's money-grubbing lackey fell in with their gang and happily, so did Analise. Five of them, from their original party of eleven.

"How do you propose we get through the mountain pass?" Analise asked. She had discarded her black garb and wore a bright tangerine sundress.

Silver gazed at the woman's curly raven locks, painted lips, and dangling bracelets. Was this her true nature revealed?

Jace took the lead. "We'll retreat the same way we came. We can spend the night in that traveler's hut."

Easier said than done. Despite a complete revolution around the city's perimeter, they found no hint of a trail. If an opening existed to the dense jungle, its markings had vanished.

"I won't stand for this." Jace regarded them with a taut expression. "Follow me. We need some answers."

Hoping they wouldn't have to hack their way through the tropical forest, Silver trudged beside him back into town. Sweat pooled between her breasts. The afternoon heat tempted her to head to the beach for a dip in the ocean. It would feel so good to languish in the current, letting the waves caress her skin… and the salty breeze clear her brain.

Wait… what?

That's right. Clear your brain.

She shook her head, feeling the insidious cobwebs of the place trying to ensnare her. Mixy's link forced open a door in her mind, a door back to reality.

"Look, it's our former guide." Coming to an abrupt halt, Jace pointed to a citizen crouching by a flower bed in the town square, part of a work crew yanking weeds. "You, there. We want out of here, now."

With a perplexed expression, the man stretched to his feet and scratched his forehead under a wide-brimmed hat. "Peace and harmony, brother. I do not understand your request."

"Take us back to the spaceport." The others crowded around him. "All of us."

The guide glanced at the commitment in their eyes, and his shoulders sagged. "You do know what you will be giving up? Whatever you want, it can be yours. Even if you don't wish to fulfill your fantasies, you'll dwell in a place of beauty where you can explore the arts, expand your learning, and establish new friendships. What more can you possibly desire?"

"Spreading your peace and beauty throughout the galaxy? Not turning our backs on our loved ones at home? Fulfilling our destinies?" Silver suggested, to her own surprise.

The man turned the full force of his gaze on her, his eyes intense. "You speak of destiny? You, who believes her path lies one way when in truth it follows another? Either way will bring you pain and strife. Are you sure this is what you want?"

She knew one thing. The way to go wasn't back in that chamber with her dead parents. Her fate and Jace's were inexorably bound, beyond the link they experienced through Mixy. She wasn't certain where life would lead her, but she wanted the opportunity to find out.

Stunned, she realized what she'd just admitted. She wanted to live, to carry on after her mission ended. Nodding her reply, she clamped her lips tight, unable to voice her thoughts.

The older man heaved a resigned sigh. "Very well. You must reenter your chambers. If you truly want to return to the spaceport, that is the way. Once you reach your destination, you will not remember what has happened here."

Their group headed back toward the stable, dodging townsfolk who bustled about their daily routine. They passed an acting troupe practicing in front of a theater. Sounds of a violin came from inside, while a budding artist set up an easel nearby. On the surface, Selia Dar provided an idyllic lifestyle. But in truth, Silver realized, it merely reflected what burned within its occupants's souls.

"I wish there were another way." Her stomach clenched when they rounded a bend to face the row of closed doors.

Jace regarded her with a grim smile. "I'm afraid we'll come out of there thinking we're at the spaceport, when in reality we're still here."

"I have an idea. If we make it to the other side, we're going to forget everything, according to our guide. Why don't we write notes to each other? They can act as reminders, alerting us to what's real and what isn't."

After a brief discussion over the details, they each scribbled down their names and ship hailing frequency. If nothing else, they might jostle each other's memory.

Analise entered the chamber first, her skirt swishing out of view. The door swung shut behind her with a solid thud.

Her pulse accelerating, Silver watched Cur and Gruber get swallowed into the dark maws of their future.

Two of them left. Her turn. "Can't we go inside together?" she asked Jace, her knees wobbling. She dreaded the enclosed space and what she might find in there.

He stroked her cheek. "I don't think it works that way, deermin. We each have to face our own demons. Try to keep your focus on Mixy. Our friend needs us."

Our friend. Silver liked the sound of that. How long had it been since she really felt close to anyone… could trust anyone? Did she truly trust Jace and his valet?

Yes, she'd already come to that conclusion. She could count on them to watch her back, but more importantly, she cared for them both far more than she'd cared for anyone in recent memory. And yet, soft emotions played no part in an assassin's role.

She moved forward slowly, as though slogging through a dense fog. If this didn't work, if she met her parents again inside that room, Silver knew she'd be stuck here forever.

She couldn't allow that to happen.

Regardless of what choices she made concerning Jace and Mixy, she had to let go of the past. That much was clear. Whether she accomplished it by killing Tyrone Bluth or by aiding Jace in pursuing justice, she had to modify her goals.

She hadn't any reason to live before, but now a multitude of causes blossomed before her eyes. Her head cleared as though a mist lifted, and she stepped across the threshold with a lighter heart.

The door slammed shut from behind, leaving her in the dark. Forcing her eyes to remain open, she repeated a refrain: "Take me to the spaceport. Mixy needs help." Before, she might have said, "I have a job to do." Now the job didn't seem as urgent as getting Mixy to his home planet.

A piece of darkness separated, swirled, grew into a vortex that sucked her into a crack between time and space. Electricity snapped all around, raising goosebumps on her skin and sending pinpricks along her nerves. She couldn't see as her hair whipped about her face.

Suddenly the storm abated. She blinked, and in that instant found herself on the launchpad. Jace stood beside the open hatch to their Corvette. He signaled for her to join him.

She stared at him, confused. Hadn't they just arrived at Stacktown? Why were they leaving so soon?

"Is it time to go already?" she asked, adjusting her bag and climbing the ramp.

"Yes, didn't you see the message from Mixy? He needs us to depart immediately."

She examined his tousled hair and weary expression as he sealed the hatch. Why did she get the distinct impression she'd missed something?

Mixy greeted them on the command deck, his robe brightening from blue to brilliant orange as they relieved him at his duty station.

"Master Jace! Mistress! Oh, I am so ecstatic to see you." Rushing forward, he threw his arms around them, sobbing with joy.

Jace plucked him off gently. "Now, now, we don't want to squish junior. Let's start the pre-flight, shall we?" He dropped into the pilot's seat to warm the engines.

"Thanks for keeping watch," Silver told Mixy. Why did she feel so deeply relieved to see him?

He pointed at her hand. "What's that you're holding?"

Silver hadn't even realized she'd been clutching those scraps of paper. She unfolded them.

"How odd. People scribbled their names and contact info, but I've no recollection of meeting anyone, especially when we were disqualified from the auction so fast."

"Disqualified?" Mixy's wispy eyebrows shot up. "What are you talking about?"

Jace ignored him. "They must have seen through our false IDs." With a disgusted grimace, he punched the launch code at his command post. They lifted off without a hitch.

Silver stuffed the papers into her pocket. She'd dispose of them later. The farther away they got from Stacktown, the better she'd feel. This place held nothing but bad vibes, and while she couldn't put her finger on what bothered her, she wouldn't advise anyone else to go there.

Too bad they hadn't picked up any trace of Tyrone Bluth. Stacktown had been their best lead, but it had turned into a wild goose chase.

"Don't worry, we'll get you home in time," Jace told Mixy, after they'd removed their launch harnesses. "We still have, what, two weeks to get you there?"

"Less than that," Silver said, eyeing the bulge at the valet's side. It seemed to have grown exponentially since they'd seen him last. "Mixy looks like he's about to burst."

Mixy set his mouth in disapproval. "I'm vastly overdue. The auction finished days ago, and when you failed to return, I got alarmed. You didn't respond on your comm units, and ground authorities thwarted my attempts to reach you." He shook his head. "If I weren't your atrani, milord, I would have despaired of ever seeing you again. This terrible stress started my birthing pains."

"What do you mean? We've only been gone a few hours, and we never made it to the auction." Jace's face showed the same confusion that befuddled Silver.

"Your minds have been clouded." Mixy faced them, his robe swirling at his feet. He wore his mahogany tresses piled atop his head except for one long strand coiled over his shoulder. His garment bled with jade.

"I don't understand." Jace scratched his bristled jaw.

"You have been gone a total of six days, twelve hours, and thirty minutes, Master Jace. Have you forgotten your encounters of a spiritual nature? Your pleasure at recreating the home of your youth? Your, uh, interludes with the lady?"

Rose infused the valet's garment while Silver regarded Jace in shock. Now that she thought about it, she did recall his hands exploring her body in a tropical setting. Where had that been?

"I do remember certain moments." Jace spoke slowly, various emotions crossing his face.

Silver wanted to discuss the strange thoughts swirling in her head, but she forgot about them when Mixy clutched a hand to his side.

"Aiyee, it's my little one. I must go and rest." After he departed, Silver decided to take a shower and wash out the dye from her hair. Maybe the force of the water would wash away those cobwebs in her mind, too.

****

Right after Jace broke orbit, the communication console pinged. It wasn't any hailing frequency he recognized.

"Can I help you?" he asked the caller while only offering his ship's ID and not his name.

"Hey, man, Gruber here. I found a piece of paper with your name on it. I've just come from Stacktown. I don't remember much about that blasted place except my employer left me behind. Dunno why, do you? What's our connection?"

His memory jogged. "My pal and I were looking for a new berth. We needed more credits than we're making hauling freight."

Even though Jace had a criminal record, which normally would serve as a good recommendation to Tyrone Bluth, the Razor knew Jace was after him. Taking a gamble, he'd written down a false name for Gruber, different than the one he'd used on Stacktown.

"Meet us at our rendezvous," Gruber offered. "The Razor is always looking for recruits."

"Standing by for coordinates." Jace's pulse raced. At last,

a chance to confront the murderous terrorist. That is, if he and Silver disguised themselves enough to pass muster. Infiltrating the bandit's crew would place them within optimal range to gather intelligence. Before capturing Bluth, he'd attempt to learn his sister's whereabouts.

His exultation deflated. What about Mixy? If they followed Gruber's instructions, the Elusian and his offspring might not survive. Jace had no idea what kind of special treatment Mixy required. Could he risk his valet's life to pursue Tyrone Bluth?

His mouth set in a grim line, Jace watched the nav computer accept Gruber's coordinates. Yet how could he give up the opportunity to rescue Shanna and Yvette and salvage his honor?

"I'm jumping to hyperspeed," Gruber's voice said from the console. "I'll tell the Razor to expect you."

"Wait a minute," Jace replied. "I have to finish this job I'm on. If I miss your rendezvous point, where will you be next?"

Gruber grunted. "Contact me when you're ready, and we'll see. Say, do you know these other folks named Dagitha, Cur, and Analise?"

Jace examined the scraps of paper from his pocket. "I have their names, too, but if we met them, I don't remember. Something happened to us on that planet. I'm hoping the mist in my head will clear soon."

His brow knitted. Mist? Why did that word conjure a hazy image of a rocky cliff?

"You said it. I'm signing off. Better luck in another five years," Gruber said with a snort.

The bald man's ship flickered off the sensor sweep. His ship? If Jace remembered correctly, Bluth had taken their transport. So who had given this guy a ride?

"Son of a guttersnipe." Jace banged his knuckles on the console. He'd just lost their best lead at catching Bluth. But what else could he do? He set the coordinates for Elusia, waited until the autopilot engaged, then rose to his feet.

He headed toward his cabin, debating his choices. He didn't have any other options, not with Mixy's well-being at stake.

One of the doors along the corridor stood partially ajar. Silver's low voice chanted from inside. Without preamble, he pushed the door open. A foul smell entered his nostrils.

He pinched his nose. "What's that awful odor? And how come you're in this cabin? I thought you'd be sharing mine."

Silver stood with her head bowed before a pair of lit tapers emitting incense. Her filmy shift revealed alluring curves that made his breath quicken. So did her platinum tresses flowing down her back. However, while he was pleased to note she'd restored her hair to its natural luster, he wasn't happy to see her resume old habits.

"I'm honoring my parents with a prayer for the dead," she said. "It's been days since I've been able to perform the ceremony."

"Didn't you agree to put your ghosts to rest? Isn't that what we learned on Stacktown? That was the whole point of the place." He rubbed his eyes, remembering. "Those factories were nothing but a front. The real prize was a spiritual journey."

"Oh, like you've given up your search for Bluth?"

"No, because I still need him to find my sister. But I don't blame myself for what happened anymore."

"Jolly for you."

"You weren't immune to the experience. I saw it in your eyes at Selia Dar. You'd begun to realize your path was wrong."

"Ah yes, Selia Dar, where I seem to recall you mentioning an unofficial engagement."

A weight settled in his stomach. "I already told you Ruler Hurat expected an alliance between my family and Yvette's merchant clan. But that was before my fall from grace."

"And now?" She didn't move a muscle.

"Her brother Connor helped me escape from prison. If we rescue his sister and restore my title, he may call in his debt by having me offer for Yvette."

"And being a man of honor, you'd comply."

Jace hated the hurt look in her eyes. If she'd been tempted to fall back on old rituals, he'd just pushed her over the edge.

"You're the only one I care about," he said with a helpless gesture. "I have no romantic feelings toward Yvette, merely brotherly concern and affection."

"Does that matter in a society that arranges marriages based on political agendas? A convenient match is even more important for someone who aspires to a diplomatic post. What choice would you have, especially when your moderate vote might sway your ruler toward peace instead of war?"

Jace sought a tactful reply, because he truly didn't know what he would do when faced with his dilemma at home. "I'll deal with that hurdle when I come to it. Besides, I just gave up a chance to learn the girls' location. Gruber contacted me and offered to introduce us to Bluth as possible recruits."

Her jaw dropped. "You turned him down? Why?"

"We're going to Elusia. My valet's health takes precedence." His tone cooled. "Maybe you don't agree, but that's where my loyalties lie. Mixy has stood by me from the start, and I won't desert him now."

Her mouth curled with disdain. "We had a chance to infiltrate Bluth's gang, and you threw it away? You'll never reach the Razor when you're so soft. First those passengers on the cargo ship, and now this. I care about Mixy too, but you should have consulted me before making a decision that affects us both."

"I did the right thing. Unfortunately, you haven't changed at all. Your words show that you don't care about anyone except yourself. You want to go after Bluth alone? That's fine with me. Once we're done on Elusia, I'll pack my bags and get my own transport offworld."

How could he have been so wrong? Jace thought as he stomped down the corridor. He'd never won her over as an ally. She'd been rigid in her views from the start.

A deep depression settled over him. He sought Mixy for solace, knocking lightly on the Elusian's door. When Mixy called out a morose greeting, Jace pushed inside.

The valet lay on his bunk, his torso swollen, his robe showing a sad shade of amber. His hair had come undone, which alarmed Jace. For Mixy to grow lax in his toilette was a bad sign.

"Are you in pain?" he asked, feeling his dark mood reflected back at him.

A tear leaked from Mixy's eye. "My discomfort is nothing compared to your torment. We gave our heart, and it turned into stone. And yet—"

"What?"

"I sense Mistress Silver is just as heartbroken."

"You are mistaken. Catching Tyrone Bluth is more important to her than either of us."

Mixy's luminous gaze studied him. "Open your mind, milord. You can be too quick to judge after your tragic loss."

Hoping to prove himself wrong, Jace focused on loosening his mental barriers. Mixy's pervading sadness reached him along with a sense of the valet's physical state.

Mixy felt as though his insides were being ripped apart by his added appendage, but he had to reach Elusia to complete the budding process. Jace's own anxiety escalated and then he felt *her* presence. Silver was just as concerned but trying to fight it, denying how much she really cared.

Uncomfortable with this glimpse into her psyche, Jace tightened his resolve. "Her words and her emotions may not match, but I can't stop to analyze her motives whenever we argue. If she cannot accept what she feels, the woman may act counter to her truths and betray me. I thought she was willing to change after our trip to Stacktown, but she needs more time. And time is one commodity we don't have."

Mixy struggled to a sitting position. "You remember what happened during your excursion there?"

Jace nodded, realizing conversation might distract the

Elusian from his discomfort. He described their companions and their sojourn to Selia Dar.

"So according to your guide, only those of you with pure hearts survived the ordeals," Mixy repeated. "How did that work?"

Leaning against the door jam, Jace attempted to relate his own conclusions. "Analise worked undercover for the Pamoria Merchant Marine Agency. Her mission was to pose as Fargus's assistant and get a list of the arms dealer's clients. It appeared Fargus sold weapons to Tyrone Bluth through Gruber, his middleman. Fargus and Gruber consulted with each other on our journey."

"And you say Gruber contacted you once we reached orbit and offered to bring you along on his rendezvous? Could he have recognized you and laid a trap?"

"That's a possibility, but then how would he have passed the trials? If he harbored malice in his heart, he never would have made it to Selia Dar."

Mixy's robe infused with jade. "So you think there may be more to him than meets the eye?" His tone shook with excitement.

"Perhaps. Cur is the one I can't figure out. The Dorian warrior was clearly working for General Liu Chi, a mercenary leader. I saw her speak to the Nacosian. We've heard the Nacosians are employed by the Weavers. So how are the Dorians involved? Are they trying to form an alliance with the Weavers?"

Black spokes darkened the valet's garment. "Goodness, I hope not. That would bode ill for us all."

"There's another option." Jace scratched his head, still trying to figure out the connections. "What if Cur represents a faction within the Dorian army that runs counter to the government? After their war losses, a rebellion wouldn't surprise anyone. In that case, I'd assume Cur's role was to hire the general's mercenaries for the rebel force."

Mixy's eyes rounded. "Oh, my. This is too confusing."

Jace patted his shoulder. "You'll be home soon, my friend. We'll be receiving clearance to land from Elusian Space Command before you know it, and then all will be well."
For you, maybe. Not for the rest of us.

Chapter Seventeen

Silver sat in the medical center's waiting room twisting her hands in her lap while waiting for news of Mixy. She didn't look at Jace, who paced back and forth in front of the check-in desk, his bags dropped in a corner. How could she earn back his regard? Moreover, why did she want to remain with the man after he'd admitted his obligation to Yvette? Jace had made love to her without once mentioning his ties at home, no doubt hoping to seduce her into compliance.

His plan had worked, she thought dismally. Like a fool, she'd believed he actually cared for her. He'd given her a reason to live beyond Bluth's assassination. She had even considered abandoning her mission to help him.

What a gullible lillysnort. Maybe he did possess feelings for her, but they didn't matter in the political arena. He had his duty to perform, and she'd learned that Jace and a sense of honor went together on Kurash like peanut butter and jelly on Earth.

Now she'd have to continue her search for the Marauders alone, but not until she knew Mixy would be all right. Despite Jace's mistaken impression, she cared about his valet. Had the same choice been hers, she likely would have also given Gruber a negative response. What miffed her was that Jace hadn't discussed it with her, because she would have suggested that she transfer to Gruber's ship while Jace continued on with Mixy.

His decision proved he didn't trust her. No way would Jace allow her to gain the advantage in catching their adversary.

Cursing under her breath, she caught his gaze on her. She

stared back, aching for his regard. His green eyes narrowed, then averted to the whitewashed wall. Silence encompassed her, worse than the noise from screaming thrusters. Had their link dissolved? Or had Mixy been rendered unconscious?

She wished there were something to look at other than the blank walls. Buildings on Elusia had little adornment. Mostly a uniform mud color on the exterior, they had wide windows and skylights to let in the weak sunlight, a result of wyndcor particles in the atmosphere. She'd gotten a quick glimpse during their ride in the medivac vehicle.

A door opened, and she half-rose from her seat, hoping it was Mixy's doctor. This wasn't a hospital per se but someplace called the Institute where the budding process came to completion and the young were raised. She didn't understand their cultural practices and probably never would, if she left soon after the birthing. The doctor had promised to check the valet over for any residual effects from his accident as well.

That reminded her to contact Uncle Manny and ask if Major Dean's murder investigation had turned up any suspects. She couldn't return to Earth until her own name was cleared. Dingbat's tail. Didn't Jace see how their personal situations ran parallel? Their best chance of success lay in working together, despite their differences.

Heaviness weighed her soul, but she couldn't tell if it emanated from her or Jace. He should have been truthful with her about Yvette and the offer from Gruber. She would have made the right choice.

Relaxing her mental barriers, she searched for a hint of him. His male presence pervaded her senses. Far from being annoyed with her, the lout was actually randy as a teen.

Her cheeks flushing, she sat upright. If she'd gotten the drift of his lust, that meant Mixy must be awake.

She stood just as the door burst open and the valet's doctor strode inside. The female's robe showed neutral blue.

"Your atrani is resting comfortably," the doctor told Jace.

Her assessing glance took in both of them. "He's a bit weak, no doubt a result of the little one's delayed detachment, but he'll be fine. His other tests are normal. We'd like to keep him overnight for observation."

"Of course." Jace brushed aside a lock of dark hair that had fallen across his forehead, while Silver yearned to touch him to offer comfort. "What about the, uh, you know, the baby?"

"Purt is doing just fine. Mixy will be pleased you asked."

"I don't understand how he can allow his child to be raised by strangers." Silver shook her head, her braid swinging.

"It is our way, Mistress. Now if you'll return in the morning at 0800 hours, your bond-mate should be ready to go."

"What now?" Silver asked Jace after the doctor left.

Jace gave her an inscrutable look. "Why are you asking me? Mixy is out of danger, so you're free to leave."

"I don't want to chase Bluth by myself." Curling her fists at her side, she waited for his response. Despite her training, she couldn't go back to being a lone operative while tracking the Razor. Her experiences at Selia Dar had taught her that much.

"Meaning what?" Jace tilted his head, his reaction unreadable.

"Look, I got angry because you didn't consult me about Gruber's offer, not because I didn't care about your valet. I could have gone with Gruber, while you tended to Mixy. Then the two of you could have caught up to us later. Now we've lost our best lead."

His eyes smoldered. "I didn't think of that option."

"You were concerned for Mixy. Or else you didn't trust me. Which was it, Jace? And how do I know I can trust you, when you purposefully omitted telling me about Yvette?"

Jace took her by the elbow, leaning so close his hot breath could have scorched her skin. "My responsibilities come before my personal feelings. Otherwise, I'd…" His gaze lowered to her mouth. "I'd take you somewhere to bring you mindless pleasure for days on end."

Joy wrapped its tendrils around her heart that she hadn't lost his affection, while her female parts responded to his words and his nearness. "Really? Perhaps we should get a room," she replied in a husky tone. "I hear the local accommodations can be quite comfortable."

"Indeed, we would save time by not going back and forth to the spaceport."

They broke apart as three Elusians entered, chattering in subdued tones. "Greetings of the day, Ulu," one of them told the reception clerk.

"Same to you, Kira. I believe your friend has been discharged. Let me call for him to be brought out."

Kira's robe infused with orange streaks. She nodded, shaking the auburn hair pinned in swirls atop her head.

Silver could only tell her gender by the pitch of her voice and the more refined features on her face. Elusians all had such slight builds that you couldn't tell the difference from their figures. Maybe if she were more familiar with their culture, she could distinguish them better.

The one called Kira turned slowly and regarded Silver with a curious glance. Her companions fell silent, staring at the humans as well. Silver's ears buzzed as though something pricked the edge of her mind. She twisted her earring, but the low hum remained in her head. Maybe her sensors were picking up a sound from outside.

"Excuse me," Jace said to the receptionist. "Would there be any hotels in the vicinity? My atrani has to stay here overnight, so we need a place to stay until morning."

Kira's eyes widened. They were the same dark brown color as Mixy's. "You have bonded with one of us? Forgive me for asking, but how did this occur? We do not have many offworlders visit here."

"Mixy and I met during the Dorian conflict."

"Aiyee, a terrible time." Her robe turned amber with sorrow. "We have rebuilt our city since then but pockets of destruction remain. They act as memorials to those whose lives were lost. But please, go on." Her face lit with interest.

Jace's shoulders stiffened. "There isn't much to tell. I was a combat pilot. We'd strafed the enemy's position and were helping extract some refugees from a bombed encampment. Mixy was among them. He got caught in the crossfire. I… managed to haul him aboard."

"Ah." A sigh escaped Kira's lips. "Long have I wondered what it would be like to experience such a depth of distress, or any strong emotion for that matter."

Silver turned to Jace, wanting more details herself. "Is this how the bonding occurs, during moments of extreme duress?"

Kira's gaze swung to Silver, assessing her. "You are correct. The link fuses when we touch a receptive mind during a period of severe emotional trauma. Since we are not prone to experience this type of reaction often, it is a rare occurrence and a great honor for one of us to become atrani."

One of her companions interrupted. "The visitors are seeking shelter. Mayhap they would accept our hospitality? We can continue our cultural exchange at home."

"An excellent idea, Frok. Would you, please?" she said, addressing Silver. "It would be a boon to our household."

Silver exchanged a glance with Jace. It wouldn't hurt to take advantage of this opportunity to learn more about Mixy's people. Every little bit added to her arsenal of knowledge.

"Are you sure it wouldn't inconvenience your family?" she asked with a hesitant smile.

The natives tittered with laughter.

"We do not understand the concept of family, although we have the definition in our databases." Kira's other friend spoke in a soft voice. "We form groups based on similar interests."

"And you are…?" Silver inquired.

"My name is Sari."

"Pleased to meet you," Jace said after Silver poked him. "We'd be delighted to accept."

The inner door opened, and a willowy Elusian strolled out. His friends greeted him with pats on the shoulder and words of congratulation. His robe tinged with streaks of scarlet.

"I am glad my time is finished. No more visits to this place. We are getting old, eh, Kira?"

"You and me both, Enis." Kira introduced the new arrival to Silver and Jace, who offered their names.

"I have no reason to hide my identity in this place," he told Silver in an undertone after she gave him a questioning glance. "I've been here before so I'm already on their register, plus they don't honor extradition treaties. We're perfectly safe."

Silver nodded, then turned to Kira. "You certainly don't look old." She hoped she wasn't being rude. None of them showed any signs of aging, but maybe their pale skin didn't wrinkle like a human.

"Enis means that we've both donated our allotment. Of offspring," Kira clarified. "We go through budding twice in our life span. Most of us are glad to complete the process."

Silver's cheeks warmed. "Oh."

"Humans do it differently, do they not? Perhaps you would care to describe the procedure?"

Silver's eyes widened, and she glanced at Jace for support. His lips curved up at the edges but he left her in the fray.

"Later," she said in a choked tone.

Jace nudged her, his eyes twinkling. "We can always give them a demonstration."

"Now that's a thought." And a stimulating one, judging from her hot-blooded response. Not wishing to betray her surge of desire, Silver followed their hosts out the main entrance.

She felt someone's gaze burning a hole in her back. Looking around, she caught Kira watching her closely as though fascinated by her human guest. Were those vibes coming from the Elusian, or from somewhere else?

City noises drew her attention. The usual sounds of traffic, construction, and chatter from people going about their daily business, filled the air. On the street, personal vehicles sped along magnetic tracks while an air tram whizzed by overhead.

"We just missed one." Frok's green robe showed his annoyance. "I told you we should have brought our own transport."

"Not when we're trying to save credits to pay for the roof repair," Kira chided.

"There's enough in our account."

"There's never enough. We agreed to keep our personal vehicles garaged for the month."

Frok turned to their guests. "You see what happens when we let a Finance Specialist into our household?"

"You should talk," Sari cut in. "Aren't you the one who purchased that new filtering system and threw our budget off?"

"It will save us money in the long run," Frok retorted.

"Stop arguing." Kira compressed her lips. "Enis is tired. He needs to get home and rest."

Intent on their conversation, Silver didn't react when a passerby bumped into her.

"Sorry," the fellow said. "Is this the tram stop to Ruby District?" He gripped a package under his arm. At Kira's affirmative reply, he stepped into line.

Other residents glanced their way, slowing their steps and staring. Were they looking at the newcomer, whose robe showed black with threads of lavender? Or were Silver and Jace the curiosities?

"Forget about being inconspicuous in this place," she muttered. "We stand out like swans on a lake full of black ducks."

Jace clasped her hand and gave an affectionate squeeze. "On the contrary, they probably regard us as the ugly ducklings. Don't worry. Since we got rid of the Dorian invaders, these people have welcomed humans. Nonetheless, they're careful who they let pass through the planetary defense grid."

She couldn't help feeling self-conscious as they piled onto the next public anti-grav train. The Elusian who'd bumped her arm sped past to gain a seat in the corner. A couple of females, holding shopping bags, dashed in just before the doors closed. She watched the scenery go by as they lifted into the air and soared away on a pre-determined route.

"How many stops?" Jace asked their companions.

The Elusians might be as tall as him, but his broad shoulders seemed to cramp the space in the narrow car where they crowded together. A long bench lined each side of the tram. Silver's stomach lurched with the air train's movements.

"We live in the city outskirts, so it's the fourth stop." Sitting opposite Jace and Silver, Frok picked at his robe. "I would have liked to save on car fare by living closer to work, but no, Kira insisted we'd save more money by commuting."

"It costs us each ten point five jinars less per month than if we had to pay city taxes," Kira replied, "so stop your whining." Her glance switched to Silver. "I suppose you Earthlings have the same concerns."

Silver grinned. "Yep, we're always looking for ways to save a buck."

She gripped her seat as the air tram dived to the first stop. The shoppers struggled through the close quarters before hopping off. That left the stranger in the corner and Silver's posse until a lone male came inside. He looked fairly young, raising Silver's curiosity about their child rearing practices. After he got off at the next station, she leaned forward.

"Tell me, how old are your children when they get released on their own?" she asked Kira, whose gaze barely wavered from her. *Is it my hair?* Perhaps the Elusian had never seen a shade like hers before.

"Our offspring develop in the Institute until they reach twelve annums," Kira answered. "They receive their schooling there, guidance from the older stemlings, food and clothing, plus a government allowance to meet their other needs."

"Does the parent ever visit? And what happens when they reach twelve? They're cast out?"

“We give up our offspring to the collective, so we have no need to follow their progress. They receive enough training. By the time they leave, they are able to find work and function independently.”

“But that’s so… cold.” *To not have parents or any relatives looking after you?* No wonder Elusians lacked strong feelings. They never learned how to love.

Kira’s lips pursed. “Many of us form friendships in the Institute and decide to share housing. Your disapproval is unwarranted and based on ignorance of our customs.” Fingers of jade infused her cobalt blue robe.

“You’re right, and I look forward to learning more about your people.” Silver jostled against Jace when the car slid to another landing. This was number three. Theirs should be the next stop. “It must have been difficult when the Dorians invaded. Have you ever had warfare before in your history?”

The one called Sari regarded Silver with glistening eyes while her robe turned amber. “We are a peaceful race, and most of us prefer not to talk about that dark time. It’s still too recent, and our losses are too raw.”

“I’m sorry.” *Shut up, Silver. You keep sticking your tongue in your cheek.*

The door buzzer sounded, indicating imminent departure. She swallowed, preparing for the gut-wrenching angle of ascent. At the last minute, the man in the black robe jumped from his seat and squeezed out the doors. He’d been so silent, she’d forgotten about him.

She slid over on the bench seat for more space. As the tram tilted into the air and zoomed toward the rooftops, something fell to the floor.

“Oh no, that guy forgot his package.” Silver moved to retrieve it, but she halted at Jace’s sudden intake of breath. She knew at once what he was thinking even before she felt the impact of his fear.

“Stop this thing,” she shouted. The sky tilted outside the windows as they careened to a new heading.

She credited Frok for quick thinking. He leapt up and yanked an overhead pulley. The sudden stop made them crash into each other.

"Quick, open the doors," Jace urged.

With Frok's assistance, he forced them wide enough to squeeze through while the tram hovered above a tall building.

"What's wrong?" Kira asked, glancing at Silver for guidance.

"Bomb." She couldn't get another word past her dry throat. Nor could she explain to their newfound friends how she and Jace knew without a doubt they'd been set up. That Elusian had been waiting for them outside the Institute.

Jace stood aside to let the others pass. "We have to jump. Aim for that roof. We should be able to make it. Hurry."

Silver tapped her utility belt. "I have a tensile line. Let me—" Her words died on her tongue as Jace snatched her and tossed her out the open door.

"Drop and roll," he yelled as air vacuumed from her lungs and wind blinded her eyes.

A tremendous explosion rent the sky. Shattering noise hit her ears, then a concussive blast slammed her onto the roof. Her side impacted, sending shooting pains through her shoulder. Her teeth jarred, and then she lay still, too stunned to move.

Cries for help returned her to full awareness. She lifted her head, scanning the rooftop.

The view didn't look good.

Burning debris sizzled and smoked among a couple of still bodies. Elusians, from the remnants of their robes. Oh God. Where was Jace? Dragging herself along the surface and realizing its artificial turf had softened her fall, she reached for him mentally. A consciousness touched her, but not his.

Was he dead? No, not possible.

"Help me, please!" Kira's cry ended on a whimper.

Silver couldn't see anything beyond the edge of the roof. Ignoring the agony in her shoulder, she crawled toward the bodies. A quick check told her Sari and Frok couldn't be saved.

Bile rose in her throat. Jace might be used to death from trauma, but she'd never grow accustomed to it. Poor sods. Guilt assailed her. If she and Jace hadn't come along… *Don't think about it.*

Scrambling to the far end, she knelt and peered over the side of the high-rise structure.

Kira clung to a flagpole. No sign of Jace… or Enis, for that matter.

What now?

She still had her utility belt, but even if she tossed a tensile line and Kira grabbed it, would the Elusian have the strength to climb? Blood sprinkled Kira's robe. She might have internal injuries that weren't readily apparent.

One thing was certain, Silver couldn't do much without a painkiller. She took an injectable from her pack and shot herself full of Attocaine. A pleasant numbness took residence along her throbbing nerves.

Sirens wailed in the distance. Her auditory sensors must have reset after the blast.

She unsnapped the pouch holding her line and searched the roof for an anchor. That vent duct might do. Wincing from the effort, she pulled the line out and wrapped one end around the slats, tying a nautical knot as she'd been taught. The cord felt solid when she yanked on it using her good arm. She laid out the line as she moved toward the edge of the roof, freed the other end and tossed it toward the flagpole.

Blinking, she tried to clear her vision as smoke from the burning debris blew her way. Its pungent odor stung her eyes. Had Kira caught the lifeline? Stretching herself flat on the roof top, she peered over, reeling as a wave of dizziness caught her by surprise.

Take it easy. You're injured, and you won't be able to help her unless you go slow.

Vaguely noting the flashing lights of emergency vehicles below, she wondered if Jace's remains lay splattered on the ground.

Focus on getting Kira to safety.

Kira's hands slipped on the flagpole. "I can't hold on," the Elusian cried.

"Grab the rope."

"If I let go, I'll fall." Terror gave the female's voice a desperate edge.

"Hang on. I'm coming."

Her fingers fumbled with another pouch. She withdrew a safety buckle, wrapped it around her thighs, drew it tight, and snapped it to the tensile line. Then she carefully lowered herself over the edge, feet first.

Inch by inch, she descended to Kira's perch, where she plucked the free end of the tensile line from the air and hooked it to another device on her belt.

Kira's raspy breath reached her ears. The Elusian's robe billowed beneath her flailing legs. Her pupils dilated with fear, she held on to the slender pole by the barest margin of her fingertips that slipped another notch toward death.

As Silver snagged Kira by the waist, an electric current jumped between them. Her mind flooded with the female's panic, with her sorrow for things left undone, and for people left behind.

Silver clenched her jaw against the barrage of emotions. Freeing her other hand, she hauled Kira closer. Her leg muscles strained to maintain a grip on the tensile line. "It's all right. Let go, I've got you."

She pushed the button on her belt, and they shot upward like a rocket. Just under the roof's rim, they jerked to a stop.

Bracing herself, Silver shoved Kira's slim body over the edge. Her turn next.

Exhaustion battered her. Her shoulder throbbed and her limbs trembled. With a final effort, she thrust herself after Kira and collapsed in a shuddering heap on the rooftop's surface.

A cool palm slid into her hand. "Mistress?"

Face to face with the Elusian, Silver's puzzled gaze stared

into Kira's clear brown eyes then lowered to her robe, no longer darkened by fear but now gleaming with an affectionate tangerine.

Silver sat, yanking back her hand. Where did that tingling sensation come from? At least her brain had cleared. She no longer noticed that strange humming at the back of her mind.

These odd perceptions must be due to Jace's absence. A lump formed in her throat. The explosion must have killed him.

Stumbling to her feet, she disregarded the ache in her shoulder. Meanwhile, Kira struggled to rise. Her garment changed to amber as she confronted Silver.

"We shall grieve deeply for him, Mistress." She startled Silver by embracing her.

"We?" Silver detached herself, shaking her head. That Attocaine must have numbed more than her nerves.

"Do you not feel the link? We experienced the *mok tay* when you rescued me."

"The what?"

"The bonding. You have fulfilled my dream. I am thrilled to be your atrani."

"Impossible. I am not bonded to you."

Streaks of green entered Kira's robe. "I understand your dismay, but you'll grow accustomed to the change. Forgive my excitement. I have always wanted to travel to the stars and explore new places, and now I can share your adventures."

"I don't think so." Silver cradled her bad arm, its hurt intensifying. "We'll talk about this later. See if you can unknot my line so I can put it back in my pouch."

While the Elusian scrambled to do her bidding, she picked up the sound of shouting male voices.

"Hello, we're up here," she yelled.

A roof door banged open and rescue personnel charged onto the scene… along with a bruised and battered Jace.

She ran toward his outstretched arms and folded into his embrace. "Where were you? I thought you'd blown up."

Stuffing her face against his shirt, she smelled a mixture of smoke and sweat. Under the circumstances, it was as heady as perfume.

"Enis and I grabbed the bench cushion just as the car exploded. It protected us from the impact and acted like a glider, allowing us to make a soft landing. I was worried sick about you."

At that moment, Silver didn't care about his obligations at home to Yvette or even if he included her in his future. She just wanted to bask in the comfort of his presence.

"How peculiar," Kira said in a mild tone. "I've never experienced anything like this before. Tell me, Mistress, why does close contact with this human male affect you so strongly?"

Silver stepped away from Jace and glared menacingly at the female's pink-tinged robe. "Oh no, you're not exposing my feelings. Don't you dare."

Kira smiled, and Silver swore she saw a hint of mischief in her eyes. "I am unable to change what has happened. If you can spare a moment, that medic is waiting to examine you. I'd like to make certain you are all right, since your well-being is now entangled with mine."

Jace glanced between the two of them. "Am I missing something?"

Kira beamed proudly. "My mind touched hers when I felt terror for the first time in my life. I'd sensed we were compatible at the Institute. I am blessed to become Mistress Silver's atrani."

His jaw dropped. "She's joking, right?"

"I'm afraid not." Silver grimaced. Her shoulder felt like a hot iron had touched it. When she let the medic take a look, he pronounced her diagnosis as a dislocation. He remedied it without warning. Silver shrieked, nearly passing out from the pain.

"Sit down," Jace ordered. "They'll air-lift you to a medical facility for a complete examination."

"No way," Silver said, shaking her head.

She remained standing as the medic probed Kira's body for hidden injuries. Kira had a gash on her leg that needed tissue repair, which he provided on the spot. Otherwise, he gave her a clean bill of health. Silver felt relieved, telling herself it was only because she cared about their newfound friends. Speaking of which, where was Enis?

"He went to the transportation center to view the security recordings," Jace said when she inquired after the new parent. "He thought the bomber looked familiar. If he's right, we might have just gained another lead to Tyrone Bluth."

Chapter Eighteen

"I thought I recognized the person on the tram," Enis said when they gathered for the evening meal together. "Parl is atrani to a bad person. It cannot be helped. When the bonding occurs, it is irreversible. We cannot predict when or where it will happen, nor can we control the outcome."

Jace's heart pounded. "Does this bad guy work for the Razor, by any chance?"

Enis nodded, his piled high hair-do quivering atop his head. "Parl's bond-mate travels with Tyrone's Marauders. We can only assume Parl followed his atrani's orders."

They sat around a low table, leaning against cushions on the floor. Kira and Enis had offered a selection of fruits, cheeses, and bread, but Jace's appetite had fled. Sari and Frok were dead; security on Elusia had been compromised; and the serenity of their world had been shattered. This was the first time one of their citizens had acted against their own kind. An alert had been issued and the spaceport closed, but the fellow still eluded custody.

Jace's mood matched the muted earth tones of Enis's multi-room dwelling. Wide windows opened to the outdoors, capturing the twilight and letting in the cool, fresh air. A chill wracked his shoulders. No wonder the Elusians were so thin. Their metabolism had to work faster to compensate for the climate.

Or maybe he felt chilled because the bomber could still pose a threat. He broke off a piece of bread and stuffed a chunk in his mouth. It tasted a bit doughy, but its texture melted like butter on his tongue.

Across the table, Kira's robe infused with fingers of teal.

"Don't you understand what this means?" Silver said, glancing at each of them. "No one knew Mixy's condition except the doctors on Earth and my relatives. The traitor in our government must have farther-reaching connections than we thought."

Admiring her flowing hair, Jace's thoughts turned traitorously in another direction. He'd like to sink into her soft body, forget himself in the throes of passion, and blank out their problems for the night.

She caught him watching and her cheeks flushed.

Interestingly, Kira's robe streaked with tendrils of rose. When Jace noticed, her lips curved in a knowing smile.

"Stop that," Silver ordered, glaring at the Elusian.

"My reactions reflect yours, Mistress. I am unable to control them. Perhaps in time, I can learn how to filter their potency. Meanwhile, may I suggest you rein in your strong desire for the handsome Kurashki? Although I find these feelings most stimulating, they disrupt my thought processes. Nonetheless, be assured that I will enjoy being your bond-mate."

"Shut up, flyboy," Silver told Jace when he opened his mouth. "I won't hear it. I refuse to be one of these atrani people."

Enis's eyes sparkled. "Congratulations, Kira. You have long wanted to travel offworld. Now you'll have your chance."

"She is not coming with us," Silver said, her voice edged with steel.

Jace hadn't realized the consequences. Great Cosmos, how would his valet feel about having another Elusian on board? Where would they put her? Although they had a bigger ship with more firepower, the Corvette had similar accommodations to the Avenger.

"We'll deal with it later." Jace piled some food onto his plate. Better eat now, before another disaster befell them.

"When do you propose to leave? I must pack my things." Kira gave them a smug smile. "Do not worry. I shall act as unobtrusive as an abigail to a great lady."

"We already have a valet," Silver interjected. "Mixy serves our needs in that regard." A frown creased her brow, as though she were reconsidering her decision about bringing Kira onboard. "What am I saying? You can't come with us. It's too dangerous. In case you haven't noticed, Jace and I are targets. If that's not enough to scare you off, we're both wanted for murder."

Kira clapped her hands together. "How delightful. I cannot wait to see where this journey takes me."

"You nearly lost your life and your two friends were killed," Jace reminded her, his tone grim. "Consider your options very carefully, Kira." He and Silver didn't need any more blood on their hands.

The Elusian lowered her eyes. "It isn't my choice. I must go where my atrani goes."

"She is correct," Enis agreed. "Once the bonding has taken place, the two cannot be separated for long."

Jace regarded him in surprise. "Mixy and I have been apart before. We didn't suffer any ill effects."

"Did you not? Mayhap Mixy's birthing time would not have come up for a few more annums if he had not been confined in your Terran institute for his injuries."

"More likely, the hit-and-run accident initiated the budding process, not my absence." Jace stuffed a hunk of cheese into his mouth and chewed. Its tangy flavor lingered on his tongue.

"Can you be certain?"

Jace didn't answer, the concept being revolutionary. He didn't care to delve too deeply into this bonding business. He'd accepted Mixy as a casual consequence of the Dorian war. Subsequently he had realized Mixy understood him better than most of his friends, and the Elusian's loyalty would be steadfast no matter what.

"We don't have space for an extra crew member," Silver mentioned in an obvious last-ditch attempt to get rid of Kira.

The Elusian rose, her movements graceful. Jace noticed

she hadn't touched her meal. "I require little in the way of accommodations. I shall prepare my things, and then I must notify my bureau that I am leaving."

"She is a very good finance specialist." Enis nibbled at a leafy green vegetable. "You would be wise to employ her in that capacity."

Kira straightened her slim shoulders. "Ships need supplies, yes? I could take charge of procurement and relieve you of that duty."

"Mixy does our shopping." Jace imagined how the valet would feel if Kira took over his job. Now that could be interesting. Did Elusians experience rivalry?

Kira fixed him a stern glare. "Then I shall examine your records and put them in order."

Jace didn't like bookkeeping anyway. "Sounds good to me," he said with a shrug.

Ultimately, Kira's duties would be Silver's call. When they finished with Tyrone Bluth, the assassin had her own choices to make. He might have to stop thinking of them as a team at that point, although the notion left him with a bitter taste.

Pushing away those thoughts, he attacked his meal.

As soon as Enis left them alone, Silver jabbed her finger at him. "You weren't much help. Thanks for nothing."

He wanted to grab her and kiss that pout off her luscious lips. "Like I could make a difference? I couldn't prevent Mixy from coming with me."

"I can't have anyone following me around, not with my job." She put a hand on her hip, looking glorious with her cascading hair and angry violet eyes. "I'm an agent for S.I.N., or have you forgotten? Once we've taken out our target, I'll be assigned another mission."

"You won't get another assignment until you're cleared of Major Dean's murder. That won't happen unless we can ID the traitor on your world and get evidence you were framed. Sound familiar?" His mouth twisted in wry humor.

"Tell me about it. Once we meet our goals, though, we'll split up. We each have our own battles to fight, and they're in separate parts of the galaxy."

So she meant to leave him, regardless of their feelings for each other. Despite the lessons she'd learned at Selia Dar, Silver still found it easier to retreat than to acknowledge her need for him. Not that he could offer the woman anything permanent when duty required him to wed Yvette. Perhaps knowing that was what pushed her away.

Theirs was a sad state of affairs, both of them wanting what they couldn't have.

Aching to touch her as she got up to clear the dishes, he strode to the comm unit instead and rang the Institute.

"Master Jace," Mixy said when Jace reached his ward. "I shall be prepared to depart in the morning."

"That's good to hear. We've had some new developments."

"Aiyee, I heard about the attack. Has the person responsible been apprehended?"

"No, he got away, but Enis says the guy has links to Tyrone Bluth."

"Who is Enis?"

Jace waited until Silver departed for the kitchen, a stack of plates in her hands. "One of our new friends. So is his roommate, Kira. There were four of them." He explained how they'd met. "Now Frok and Sari are dead. I'd stay for the memorial service, but it's better if we leave as soon as possible."

"Do not concern yourself about proprieties, milord. The Mourning Guild will chant their song for the departed ones."

"You don't have funerals for the dead?"

"Not in the sense you mean." Mixy paused. "Mistress Silver is sending out unusually high vibrations, milord. I realize our link extends to her somehow, but this is different. Her emotions almost seem to be augmented. It is most odd."

"We'll talk about that later," Jace said quickly. "Look, the bomber was waiting for us outside the Institute. I'm concerned for your safety."

"I shall be fine. Security is tight inside this facility. May I suggest, Master Jace, that you untangle your confused feelings for the lady before our launch? You need to focus and find a lead to your quarry."

He opened his mouth to say he still had Gruber's frequency, but a clicking sound on the line indicated another call. Jace said goodbye to Mixy and answered.

"Enis?" crooned a soft female voice.

"Sorry, I'm just a houseguest. Hold on while I get him." Jace stood by when Enis took over the console.

"Is that so?" Enis said to the caller after switching to his private comm unit. "This is good news. We'll be right over." After signing off, he turned to Jace. "The Home Guard has found Parl."

"What?" Kira swept into the room. "They have caught the traitor? Let us hope justice is swift."

Silver joined them, her hair neatly braided and her manner brisk. She'd changed into a borrowed blouse made for someone smaller. It pulled tightly across her bosom, making two nicely defined tents that Jace couldn't help admire.

Thank goodness Mixy wasn't there to reveal his hot-blooded response. But Kira's robe infused with scarlet streaks as Silver noticed his blatant stare. The Elusian's face took on a smirk as she regarded them both.

"Parl slipped into his apartment under the security net," Enis said. "He's there now. Home Guard forces have surrounded the place."

"We'll take my personal aircar," Kira said. "Let's go."

****

Silver ground her teeth during the ride to the criminal's abode. So far, stopping off on Elusia was getting her nowhere. If Jace had consulted her about Gruber's offer, she could be in the midst of Bluth's lair by now. Instead, another one of his lackeys almost got to them.

Maybe this Parl person would provide intelligence on the informant back home. It might pay to stick around for his interrogation. Then she'd contact Uncle Manny. Her only hope of erasing the murder charge against her was to get proof against Fester Niles, if indeed he was the mole in their government.

"Oh, dear." Kira steered the vehicle in for a landing.

"What's wrong?" Silver craned her neck for a look. Emergency vehicles had skewed to a stop near their destination.

"That's a medical evac." Enis pointed to a white truck. "Someone must be hurt." He waited for Kira to park then sprang from his seat. "I'll find out what's going on. Wait here."

Silver bit her lip and kept her worries to herself. Following Jace's lead, she got out of the car and stood by the curb among a milling crowd. Kira trailed after them, restlessly stepping from foot to foot and fidgeting with her robe.

"Parl is dead," Enis announced upon his return. "The fool jumped from his twenty-fourth story balcony."

Silver cursed. "Now we'll never get him to talk. What a waste."

"We might still learn something if we can we get inside his apartment," Jace suggested. His brow furrowed as though he didn't like this delay any more than she did.

"I'll get us in." Kira tapped his arm. "I recognize that officer over there. His account has just come up for audit at my department. He'll be happy to help if I promise leniency. Follow me."

With a little coaxing, the officer revealed that Parl's death had been ruled a suicide based on a handwritten note, wherein he'd apologized for being loyal to his atrani.

Silver got permission to scan the computer files in his apartment, while Kira and Enis consulted with the security detail by the door.

"I can't find anything unusual except a bunch of numbers," she told Jace, who watched over her shoulder.

"Numbers? Let me see." Kira stalked over and brushed her aside.

Silver would have to teach her bond-mate some respect. Wasn't she supposed to be in charge? Then again, even though Mixy called Jace his master, the two acted as though they were best friends. She still had to get the hang of this bonding thing.

Kira's fingers flew over the panel. "These are bank accounts. I can tap into them using my Finance Bureau authorization."

Silver glanced at Jace, surprised to find his warm gaze regarding her. How could she ever leave him when he looked at her like that? Her face flushing, she averted her eyes. That decision would come later, when she knew where to find Bluth.

"Parl has been receiving credits from offworld, depositing them, and then transferring portions to others. I must get through these layers of encryption." Kira's forehead creased in concentration as she worked the touchscreen.

"Ah, here we go. Parl acted as a middleman between several parties. He received credits from some place in the outer regions, plus from the Balak Province on Kurash."

Jace drew in a breath. "That is Garth's domain. How were you able to acquire information so quickly when I've been unable to gain evidence against him?"

"It is what I do, Master Jace."

Silver raised an eyebrow. It might not be so bad to have someone with Kira's skills on their team. She caught Jace glancing at her. Was he thinking the same thing?

"Can you send a copy of that to my solicitor?" he asked.

"Certainly." Kira pointed to the monitor. "Parl withdrew a percentage of credits for himself first. Then he transferred another portion to a holding company. That company, in turn, feeds into a mining colony on Anriat."

Enis joined their group. "I've heard rumors, stories meant to frighten travelers, that Tyrone's Marauders sells their captives into slavery at the mines."

"Maybe that's where Bluth sent my sister." Jace's face brightened.

A surge of hope fluttered in Silver's chest on his behalf. Could it be that easy to locate the girl?

"Hold on, I'm also seeing transfers to another address." Kira squinted at the screen. "Does a company called Solvent Minerals sound familiar?"

Silver's pulse raced. "Fester Niles owns Solvent Minerals. He's a councilman in our government and a suspected mole. This may be the link we need to nail him. I'll have to pass this information along to my uncle."

"What can your relative do?" Kira looked perplexed.

"He's Maxima Chancellor of the Terran Consortium. Uncle Manny will assign any follow-up to the appropriate people."

She didn't know who'd be appointed her new boss. Not that it mattered, since she couldn't return home yet. At any rate, she still meant to finish her assignment and end Bluth's rampage.

"What about that other transfer from the outer regions?" She thought of the Weavers. "Can you define it better?"

Kira's robe blackened to reflect Silver's dark thoughts. "Sorry, it's buried too deep, but I found something else."

"What's that?" Silver snapped, aware the Elusian disapproved of her hostility toward the obscure race.

Tough for her. If she's stuck with me, she's stuck with my feelings, too. That's what Kira wants, isn't it? So live with it, honey, for better or for worse.

Chagrin swept through her. Was this what Jace put up with all the time? It wasn't easy when someone else wore your emotions on their sleeve… er, robe.

"Parl's last transmission went to a place on the Yagath Perimeter." Kira's eyes shone with the thrill of the hunt. "I believe he intended to rejoin his bond-mate after eliminating you."

"Wouldn't Parl's atrani be aware of his death?" Jace queried.

"The human might be feeling out of sorts, but he may attribute it to their distance from each other," Enis said, peering over Kira's shoulder. "The man could not have predicted Parl's reaction to betraying his homeland."

Silver's brow wrinkled in puzzlement. "Couldn't Parl have refused the order? Elusians who are bonded don't have to obey. Not that I have much experience at this business." Dingbat's tail, she'd never get used to having someone trail her around.

Jace tapped Kira on the shoulder. "Can you read the reply?"

"Parl's atrani, whose code name is the Blade, says his gang is stopping off at Al'ron to pick up supplies and some new recruits. Parl is to meet him there."

"Al'ron!" Silver stiffened. Could she possibly have been given a second chance to complete what she couldn't finish the first time around?

"No, Silver." Jace's expression brooked no argument. "We have to find out what happened to my sister and Yvette. Possibly Bluth sold them to that mining colony on Anriat."

She gritted her teeth. "Fine, we'll gather intelligence, and then I'll end the Razor's reign of terror."

Kira sent the message she wrote out for Uncle Manny and another from Jace to his solicitor. Then she copied the data onto a cube to take along with them. After shutting down the system, Kira rose to confer with Enis.

"You said you'd help me save Shanna." Jace's gaze scoured Silver when the others had moved away.

"And I will. You can follow through on the information once we know the girls' locale, and I'll stay behind to carry out my orders."

She didn't voice her inner doubts, that if they saved the kidnapped women, Jace would be lost to her forever. He'd return to Kurash, oust his cousin Garth, and marry Yvette from the merchant clan. Silver didn't belong in their society. What other path did she have? He'd cast her away later rather than sooner, but the outcome would be the same.

"You still refuse to see the light." Jace shook his head, a rueful smile on his face, while a sense of his pain swept her. "Bluth must stand trial on Kurash. My crime will be absolved only if he vindicates me in public and confesses his link to Garth. And pray don't forget his connection to the traitor on Earth. We can learn much from him, deermin."

"I'm a trained assassin. My job is—"

He grasped her arm. "You have no job until you're cleared of murder charges like me. That means you can make your own choices. Open your heart. Listen to the voices you heard in Selia Dar."

Painful memories swept her. *Let it go,* her mother had said. *You must move on. Jace needs you. Go to him.*

Should she? Could she give up everything she'd strived for, to aid a man who would toss her aside in the end?

She'd shriveled into herself for so long that she had forgotten how to enjoy life until he showed her. She hadn't noticed the love from her cousins until he'd pointed it out to her. Did she really want to turn her back on the hope he offered when there was another way to extract revenge?

"All right," she conceded. "I'll stick to your plan for now. But if it appears that our success is at risk, I won't hesitate to fulfill my directive."

He gave a curt nod. "Agreed." And even if he didn't acknowledge it aloud, she sensed his pleased response.

Stars above, how she'd like to pleasure him in bed, to run her hands over his sculpted muscles and cradle his manroot in her hot embrace.

Her body felt bereft of his caresses, and now the opportunities for sex would be limited. Would Kira always reside in her awareness as a voyeur? It would be the Elusian's first such experience, she realized. Hmm, that could be entertaining.

She looked up to see Jace's sexy grin as though his thoughts swung in the same direction. But then his expression sobered as he turned to the Elusians.

"I'd like to launch immediately and set a course for Al'ron."

"How do you plan to gain access to Bluth in that hellhole?" Silver asked.

"I'll contact Gruber and tell him we're coming."

"I have another idea. The Blade is expecting his Elusian to return, right? Why not comply? We can make Mixy look like Parl. It's difficult to tell their people apart."

Jace lifted an eyebrow. "When you're as close to them as I am, you get the nuances."

"The Blade might not notice the distinctions. It's the psychic link that will be the clincher. We'll have to think up a reason why he doesn't feel Parl's mental presence."

"It's too risky." With an adamant shake of his head, Jace folded his arms across his chest.

"Don't you want to learn what happened to Shanna?"

"We could accomplish the same thing if we join Bluth's band as recruits." His lips firmed. "I won't put Mixy in jeopardy. He'll stay on the ship."

"Gruber will want to know how we located them."

"That's easy. We met Parl on Elusia, and he gave away the game."

"All right. Let's hope they buy our story."

Her throat clogged. She didn't like the idea of entering the lion's den. She'd rather take out Bluth on her own terms. But she didn't want to jeopardize Mixy either. This was their battle, not the Elusian's. She had only offered that idea from a sense of desperation.

"Kira, can you notify the Institute we'll be picking up Mixy?" Jace said. "I don't think he'll mind our early departure."

The female nodded, tilting her mile-high auburn locks. She and Enis had been chatting off to the side. "I'm looking forward to meeting your bond-mate in person. He can show me your accounts."

"Mixy will be happy to have your assistance." Jace's mirth-filled eyes told Silver another story.

When had they become a crew? Suddenly Kira was managing communications and accounting. Mixy had taken charge of procurement, meals, and more. Imagine what they could do with a full complement and weaponry. Jace had military training. He'd take command while Silver… what? Led clandestine missions?

Not a bad idea for someone who'd started out alone.

However, if she carried out her assignment as ordered, working alone was crucial. She didn't need the distraction of having her feelings engaged elsewhere. Caring for others just led to pain and loss down the road.

Pushing those demons into the dark recesses of her mind, she accompanied the others into their transport and gazed at the view during their uneventful ride to the health institute.

Mixy was waiting when they arrived to check him out. While Kira and Enis waited outside to guard their vehicle, Silver and Jace supported Mixy through the discharge process. Beaming proudly, he stopped by the nursery to show them his child, a hairless little thing curled inside a pod. It was one of many in a hall that stretched a city-block long. Attendants moved among them, tending to feeding lines and adjusting temperatures.

"He's adorable," Silver said, thinking all babies looked like aliens until they grew.

"Purt will be fortunate to have so many playmates." Mixy turned to his human friends. "Please feel no distress on our account. This is our way. We build units from friendship, not blood relations.".

"Lucky for you," Jace drawled. "We're stuck with our relatives. I like my friends better, what few of them are left."

Mixy shuffled along beside them toward the lobby entrance, his robe an affectionate tangerine. "I care about you too, milord. And you, Mistress Silver." He halted, his expression hurt. "You are displeased?"

She stopped to face him. "Of course not. You aren't… it

isn't me. I mean, I'm sensing that Kira is jealous. Dingbat's tail, this is confusing."

"Kira is an Elusian?"

"Yes, she was in the air tram accident with us." Silver hesitated. "You know how Jace saved your life during the Dorian war, and that trauma precipitated your bond? The same thing happened to me and Kira."

"No!" Mixy stared at her, aghast.

"You'll like her, my friend." Jace slapped his shoulder. "And now you'll have company aboard ship."

"I have all the company I need already." Mixy's stiff tone matched his posture.

Outside, Jace performed introductions. Mixy and Kira sized each other up like two prizefighters.

"I hope you know these are not ordinary humans," Mixy said, sniffing. "They're at each other's throats more often than their enemies."

Kira looked down her nose at him. "Fascinating. I'll look forward to these new experiences. Did Silver tell you I'm doing the bookkeeping from now on?"

"Mistress Silver to you. Do we have to teach you proper forms of address?"

"Is he always so snippety?" Kira asked Silver.

Silver rolled her eyes. "Let's go, people. Enis is waiting for us."

Their Elusian buddy dropped them off at the spaceport.

"I am sorry to leave you so soon after our loss." Kira faced Enis on the launchpad to say her farewells.

"I'll move to smaller quarters." Enis's voice held no trace of emotion. "It will not be comfortable to occupy such a large space by myself, nor is it fair to others who wait for lodgings."

"Do what you must, my friend. I will contact you when I can."

"Enjoy your good fortune. May the wind be at your back."

They bowed, touching foreheads. Then Kira grabbed her bags and strode with the others toward the boarding ramp.

"What's all this stuff?" Jace gestured at the crates stacked by their assigned parking space.

"I had the foresight to order some things for our journey," Mixy said with a smug smile.

"From the hospital?" Silver gaped at him. Neither she nor Jace had even thought of restocking the ship's stores. Leave it to Mixy to remember his shopping list.

"It was nothing." Mixy gave a dismissive wave. "I merely called some of my former associates and provided your measurements, milord."

"Where we're going, I won't need any suits." Jace regarded his valet with a mixture of amusement and exasperation. "Mixy used to work in a clothing establishment," he explained to the rest of them.

"You sold robes?" Kira's tone dripped with scorn.

"Madam, there are ordinary robes, and then there are equisitely-made robes for citizens with discerning tastes," Mixy retorted. "Fortunately, my former shop also keeps cloth for offworld designs. Master Jace's wardrobe needs particular attention to detail."

"You didn't get us any fresh fruit or vegetables?" Silver couldn't believe he would neglect to replenish their larder.

"Of course I ordered a supply of food. However, I think you will like my textile choices better. I included a variety of garments and accessories. For your disguise kit, mistress," Mixy clarified.

"Excellent!" She clapped her hands, getting perverse pleasure when Kira's robe tinged with warm peach.

"Where are the perishables?" Jace entered the access code to their spacecraft. With a loud hiss, the main hatch slid open.

"In those vented crates marked with orange stripes." Mixy pointed to a stash on their right.

"Good, because I'm starving. Are you cooking, or should we use MUM?" That was their molecular unit matrix.

"I obtained some brookworms, so I can make you our famous mog soup. It's quite a delicacy."

Kira arched her wispy eyebrows. "Don't tell me you cook, too? What a paragon."

Mixy switched on the anti-grav trolley under the nearest crate. "The soup will give us strength. May I remind you, milord, the Incantation Ceremony on Kurash rapidly approaches? You must unseat your cousin Garth before this event, or he'll cement his place as warlord at Hurat's side."

"Thanks for the reminder." Jace's lip curled. "Now get this stuff loaded so we can be on our way."

"Do you always have free rein with the budget?" Kira asked Mixy then clucked her tongue. "Four people cannot possibly require so many provisions. I hope you kept receipts."

"We're on a life and death mission, madam. Under such dire circumstances, I don't do receipts."

"You'll be changing your ways with me handling finances. Get used to it."

Silver accompanied Jace up the ramp to begin pre-launch procedures. If they had to put up with this bickering the entire voyage, it would be a long trip indeed.

Chapter Nineteen

Jace pushed open the double swinging doors to the saloon, his throat dry from the arid air in the ramshackle port town. Smoke from hakah pipes reached him along with a noisy din and the smell of ale. Spacers crowded the dimly lit interior, fellows with bristled jaws, muscled torsos, and loaded bandoliers.

At his side, Silver touched his arm. "Do you see Gruber?"

"I can barely see my own hand. Let's go to the bar. He'll find us."

He hoped their disguises worked. It didn't matter whether or not Gruber remembered what they'd looked like on Stacktown. When they'd contacted him, Bluth's henchman had acknowledged his offer to introduce them as potential recruits. Jace worried more that Bluth might see past their altered appearances.

"I'll have a Talusican ale," he told the scruffy bartender whose hair resembled a snarl of wires. "Raven, what about you?" he asked Silver, who'd chosen the name after her freshly tinted hair.

She wore her wavy black tresses hanging loose down her back. If that wasn't enough to draw male attention, her creamy flesh spilled out of a leather bustier that only enhanced her assets. He noticed more than one roving glance aimed in her direction.

"The same," she said in a curt voice, sliding onto an empty stool and adjusting the TechVix LD-6 rifle slung across her back.

She posed as a sharpshooter, and it wasn't an idle boast.

Jace remembered how she'd been aiming to shoot Tyrone Bluth from atop a hill when they first met.

"Hey, sister," said a large fellow on the next stool over. "Looking for some action?"

"Get lost." Silver chugged her ale, turning her back on the guy. "I already got a man."

"Don't look too manly to me. Bet his dick is the size of my little finger." He wheezed with laughter while others joined in.

Jace stood straight. "Is that an insult?"

"Mebbe. Wanna do somethin' about it?" A knife appeared in the thug's hand as he stretched to his full height.

Jace acted before he could think. In one swirling movement, he tossed his drink at the man's eyes while whipping out his slicer disk. He serrated the guy's throat in the next instant. Blood splashed onto the floor, followed by the heavy thud of a body. Complete silence ensued.

Jace glanced at the watching faces, shrugged, and retrieved his weapon, wiping it on the dead man's tunic.

"Anyone else?" he offered with a menacing scowl.

"You've had your fun for the day, Slicer." Silver curled her forefinger. "Come back to Mama."

He'd no sooner hopped onto his stool and thrown out a few extra jinars to make up for the mess than someone tapped on his elbow.

"Jake Lubin?" said a familiar voice.

"Who's looking for him?" Jace slowly swiveled around.

Gruber scratched his bald head while his good eye looked them over. "I've been expecting you. The Razor will see you now. He was impressed by your reaction."

"He's watching?" That challenge must have been a test.

Silver's sharp inhalation drew Gruber's attention, while Jace winced inwardly. Could she steel herself against the thirst for revenge enough to gain the information they needed? Would she blow their cover by letting her hatred show when they finally confronted Tyrone Bluth?

He needn't have worried; she stuck to her role. "We can prove ourselves in better ways," Silver said to Gruber in an oiled tone. "We have so much more to offer if the Razor hires us." She stroked the laser pistol strapped to her thigh, her double meaning clear.

"Don't piss him off, because it's my head on a platter if you do." Gruber lowered his voice. "Take my advice, and use a bit of flattery. The boss likes people who fawn over him. This way." Bluth's underling led them to a table in a dark corner.

And there he sat, the vicious leader of Tyrone's Marauders, wearing his trademark wide-brimmed black hat and military garb. His glacial blue eyes narrowed as they approached. He'd grown a beard since the photo in the dossier Jace had seen. Particles of hard cooked eggs stuck to his coarse hairs.

"So you're the pilot and the woman that Gruber brought in," Bluth growled. "Tell me why I should add you to my troops."

Silver raised her chin. "Let's be honest—we need the credits."

"That's only one reason," Jace hastened to add, noting Bluth's nostrils flare. "We've heard of your daring raids and believe our skills will benefit your operation."

"You use mighty big words for a space jockey." The Marauder's mouth turned down.

This wasn't going well. Comet dust, his training included combat tactics, not undercover ops. Maybe he should let Silver take the lead. Wishing he could wipe the sweat from his brow, he sent her a mental message.

"He likes to pretend he's better educated," Silver said with a sexy smile aimed at the Razor. "Pay no attention to his blather. He's good in a fight and knows how to fly, and that's what counts. Me, I can shoot straight or I can play other games, if you know what I mean."

Propping herself on the edge of the table, she leaned low on one elbow while Bluth's gaze fixed on her bosom. Then his face lifted and his hard-core eyes examined her closely.

"We're heading to our home base," he said. "You'll both

come along. We'll see how far you're willing to go to prove your worth."

"Sure, sugar," Silver replied. "Just give us the location, and we'll meet you there."

"You think I'm stupid? You'll come with me, woman. Your boyfriend can fly your ship to the coordinates Gruber gives him. He shows up alone, or you die."

Jace's jaw twitched. He couldn't leave Silver in the villain's clutches. No telling what Bluth might do to her. Even knowing she'd been trained for this exact situation, he feared the outcome. She may not want to live after completing her task, but he couldn't live without her.

When had she come to mean so much to him? She'd invaded his dreams with her soft violet eyes and flowing platinum hair. His waking moments with her womanly scent and her sharp wit. His warrior self with her lessons on subtlety and her penchant for disguise.

Being separated from her now would tear him apart… much like he had felt after Mixy's accident. Gods, was the link between them really that strong, augmented by the Elusians? Or had his feelings for Silver deepened beyond lust into something more permanent?

"She goes with me," he insisted. "We work as a pair."

Silver flicked a warning glance his way and imperceptibly shook her head.

A couple of toughs sidled up, flanking him. Bluth stamped his fist on the table. "When I give orders, I expect them to be obeyed. That's the first lesson you're gonna learn. Boys, show him what I mean."

The first jab from a shock stick took Jace by surprise. Hit from behind in the lower back, he doubled over as a sharp pain shot through his kidneys. The second jolt forced him to his knees. When agony shredded his nerves to the point where he couldn't move, the two bruisers hauled him outside. His face met the dirt while loud guffaws sounded from within.

"It don't pay to cross the Razor," said Gruber's voice, close to his ear. "Get up. I'll send the coordinates to your ship. Be at the base within forty-eight hours, or your woman becomes Bluth's property."

As Jace staggered to his feet, he felt waves of concern that must be emanating from Silver. He tried to send back a reassuring response but sensed a blockade. Mixy? His valet's essence seemed muddled, unlike his usual distinct presence.

Jace hobbled toward the launchpad at his best pace. Perhaps the obstruction came from Kira, bombarded with unfamiliar emotions and separated from her atrani at a vulnerable time. The female Elusian would have to manage the best she could.

Great Cosmos, could things get any worse?

Yes, they could. Given the opportunity, Silver might decide to take Bluth out and complete her assignment. Then where would that leave him? Back to stage one, with no witness to prove his innocence and alone in his quest once more.

****

Silver, one eye shut, focused through the targeting sight of her TechVix LD-6 Sharpshooter Special. Blocking all thoughts from her mind, including what was taking Jace so long to arrive at the gang's headquarters, she concentrated on her target.

Bluth had ordered his second in command to assess her skill on the shooting range. Hitting the moving silhouettes was easy compared to the holographic scenarios at S.I.N. training camp. Her lips tightening, she pressed the trigger and was pleased to see her perfect mark light up the score board.

The tension eased from her shoulders. She swept off her safety goggles and headset, and shook out her hair.

"Now what?" she asked the man watching her with new respect. Nonetheless, he'd just as soon bed her as work with her. *Get in line with the rest of your friends, mister.*

Hopefully, Jace would show up soon, not that she needed him to showcase her talents. She felt more secure with him around, as though he completed her. She hadn't even known she'd been missing this sense of wholeness before meeting him.

What was keeping the guy? A small pilot vessel waited at the perimeter of the minefield to guide him in. She had to admit Bluth had been clever to pick a base of operations in a region decimated by the Dorian conflict. His people had deactivated enough explosive devices to forge a path through to a small moon at the far side. Three moons in all circled Kelius Two, but none were known to be inhabited and certainly nobody cared after the Dorians had seeded the surrounding space with mines.

It also meant that anyone who reached Bluth's hideout couldn't depart without the proper sequence. But she'd worry about that problem later. First she had to ditch this fellow so she could do her job.

"Now that you've proven your skill on the range, the Razor has another test for you," said the brawny fellow with a neck as thick as a small tree trunk. His grin widened, and she got a glimpse of a pierced stud on his tongue. "Come with me." He signaled with his tattooed forearm.

Silver hefted her rifle and followed, wishing she'd tied her hair into a ponytail. Wearing it loose complemented her femme fatale image, but projecting an aura of toughness became increasingly difficult. Jace had changed her, taken away her edge. Now she had to maintain even tighter control or risk exposure. That could prove to be fatal.

A dribble of sweat ran down her spine, and she shifted her weapon. She hadn't done a very good job as an assassin so far. Her failure must be rectified.

Hoping to catch Bluth alone, she swallowed her disappointment when her escort led the way through a series of utility corridors. They entered a section where the mingled smells of sweat and stale urine ran rampant. She wrinkled her nose.

Up ahead, a force field held back a gaggle of people. Armed troops stood in front of the energy shield. The entire moon complex, built inside a biosphere with recycled air and artificial gravity, allowed for freedom of movement, but not for these folks. They looked like cattle feed for the Crockers.

Tyrone Bluth stood in the hallway consulting with one of his lieutenants. Silver's hands curled into fists at the sight of him, her face assuming a cool mask of indifference. He wore olive green fatigues but no hat over his fuzz of dark hair. His face was as mean as the one emblazoned in her memory.

Bluth glanced up at their arrival. "Ah, here's our new recruit. How'd she do, Gus?"

"Right on the mark, Razor. She's got a good grip."

"We'll see. Takes more than a tight trigger finger to make the list, eh boys?" His face sobered and he pointed. "Grab that one."

A guard deactivated the shield and snatched a small child. The boy's mother screamed, "My baby," while other prisoners cursed and wailed.

"Put him over there by that column, and we'll teach this rabble to obey their master. This is what'll happen to the rest of them if they get out of order."

The guard shoved the crying child as directed. In front of the post, he flipped the boy around to face them.

"Tie him," Bluth ordered, an eager light in his eyes.

Silver squashed the urge to smash his ugly nose into his brain. What kind of cruel game was this?

When the boy was reasonably secured, the guard stepped away.

"Shoot him," Tyrone ordered, his gaze fixed on Silver.

"What?"

"You heard me. Kill the brat."

Silver didn't need her auditory sensors to pick up the anguished howls of the child's mother. Her gut clenched, and she felt the blood drain from her face. Steeling her expression, she raised her rifle to shoulder height and took aim. As she appeared to assess her target, a plan formed in her mind.

"I'll do better than that." She shifted her weapon upward a notch. She had to be really accurate for this idea to work.

Swing the barrel around. Shoot Bluth. Who cares what happens afterward?

No. She hadn't found out the information they needed to rescue Jace's sister. The time wasn't ripe. If she played her cards straight, she'd have another chance.

Her jaw clenched. *Get him now, while those guards deal with crowd control.* They'd raised the force field's strength, and she heard the cries from men who flung themselves against the energy flux in a futile attempt to break free. The sizzle and pop of the shield added to the decibels in the small space.

"What are you waiting for?" Bluth demanded.

Silver's gaze didn't divert when he stepped closer. He smelled like soap. She was surprised personal hygiene meant something to him. Too bad his fastidiousness didn't extend to his sense of moral decency.

"Accuracy is more important than speed." She kept her attention on the kid. "Watch this. I'll get him by a mere hairbreadth." She focused on the targeting site's parameters.

Bluth grunted his excitement, while her palms grew slick with sweat.

Do it.

She fired.

"You missed, imbecile."

"No sir, I didn't. I said I would get him by a hairbreadth. If you will examine the post just above the center of his head, you will see that I split his hair in two."

"She's right," said the nearest guard after taking a look. His pudgy face held grudging respect mixed with confusion, as though he couldn't decide if she'd altered her aim on purpose.

"You didn't kill him." Bluth's voice held an ominous undertone.

She shrugged, slinging her rifle over her shoulder. "Seems a waste of good flesh. What do you do with these people?"

"The men and children go to the mines on Anriat. The women serve the colony's overlords."

And you get rich on the profits, she thought. This brute had too many sources of funding. If she wanted to disrupt his organization, she'd have to cut it off at the financial roots. Kira would be good at that job.

Silver resisted the urge to scrub a hand over her face. Getting rid of Bluth might cut off the head, but then they'd have to deal with the tentacles. Maybe Jace was right; the stakes were bigger than her need for personal revenge.

Meanwhile, she had to save this child.

She faced Bluth and spread her hands. "Why lose a young, supple body? Let the kid dig his worth in ore before he dies. He can fit into small spaces where others can't go."

Bluth's brow furrowed. "You have a point. Okay then, put the brat back in the coop. But keep in mind, rabble, we'll take the children for target practice if you don't shut up, and next time, they'll all end up dead."

Silver planted a hand on her hip, hoping she presented the tough image of a warrior woman when what she wanted to do was lose her lunch. That had been too close. She would have blown her cover rather than murder a helpless hostage.

"You're a wise leader," she crooned to Bluth with a seductive smile. "These mines you mentioned, I suppose they're different than the mines seeding the space around this moon?"

Bluth guffawed. "The Anriat lode produces trona for our ships and weapons. It's a profitable operation."

"Trona? But don't you get that from—" Stopping herself, she bit her lip.

"From where, beautiful one?"

"I'd heard rumors, that's all." His hard stare made her quake inside. Would he see the telltale outlines of her contact lenses? The lighter roots of her hair? "Where's my partner?" she said, hoping to distract him. "He's overdue to join us."

"The lucky man has already arrived." Pressing his thick lips together, Bluth gestured. "I'll take you to him."

"We haven't been assigned quarters yet."

"You will be. I like to get a feel for how my new people will fit in first."

"You're certainly a hands-on type of leader," she said in a syrupy tone, thrusting her bosom forward.

As she'd hoped, his gaze shifted. Her bustier, albeit uncomfortable to wear, served its purpose admirably. Bluth moistened his mouth. "You catch on quickly, Raven. If you have more questions, I can entertain them in my quarters."

She allowed herself a small smirk of triumph. At last! After she forced the truth from him about Jace's family and obtained proof of his connection between Fester Niles and Garth Vernon, she could finally rid the galaxy of this blight on humanity.

"Water," one of the prisoners croaked. "Can we have some water? My wife is with child. She is growing weak."

Oh no. Her stomach sank as Bluth's nostrils flared.

"I told you not to speak in my presence." A murderous look on his face, Bluth clomped toward the jail. "What did I say the punishment would be?"

Inside the penned area, the captives recoiled with gasps of horror. "Not our children!" a woman among them screeched.

"Sir," Silver said, hastening to the Marauder's side and resisting the urge to plead. "With due respect, the children can yet benefit you in the mines. It wouldn't be profitable to waste them over such a pathetic being."

The fellow who'd spoken cowered in a corner. With his thin frame, he wouldn't last long as a laborer anyway. If a choice had to be made… Silver swallowed hard.

At Tyrone's indication, the guard lowered the force field while another brute yanked out the man and his pregnant wife.

Before the energy shield had even been reactivated, the Marauder leader slashed open the woman's belly with his curved dagger. While her husband screamed, she crumpled to the floor in a pool of blood.

The man sank to his knees, sobbing.

"There's your punishment. Live with it for the rest of your short days. Or not." Tyrone kicked the guy with his steel-toed boot, cursing at him, until the prisoner lay still on the ground. Speechless, Silver watched in mute horror.

"Clean up this mess," Bluth told his guards, grasping Silver's elbow and yanking her away. "Come with me. I need to wash this filth off, and then we'll talk. You can get changed in the meantime."

"I really should check in with J-Jake." She remembered to say his false name just in time. Although she couldn't wait to get Bluth alone, she wanted to make sure Jace was all right.

Bluth glowered at her. "Where does your loyalty lie, pretty one? With him or with me? Because I can't have anyone in my camp whose favor is in question."

"Not a problem, sir. I trust Jake as my pilot, that's all. He's highly skilled at the controls. He gets me where I need to go so I can do my job."

"And what was that before you joined us?" Bluth asked with a snarl.

"Gun for hire. Jake was a fugitive from Kurash when I met him."

"Ah, Kurash. Good source of jinars for me, there."

She'd have liked to ask more but felt it prudent to keep her mouth shut. Various military-garbed personnel patrolled the corridors. Gruber passed by, nodding absently as he headed in the opposite direction. Silver tried to take note of their route, but too many twists and turns confused her. She'd have to get a schematic of the place, but first she had to locate Jace.

And why was Tyrone Bluth taking such a personal interest in her, when the other recruits went through processing with his subordinates? Did he hope to add her to his harem, or had she aroused his suspicions?

She kept on track, uncertain if they were heading to Bluth's private quarters or to another site. Then a sudden mental jolt almost made her stumble.

Jace! She hadn't gotten a sense of him before, but suddenly he came through loud and clear. The man was in pain.

Oh, no. What trap had he fallen into now?

Chapter Twenty

Jace cringed as his tormentor approached, shock stick in hand. Each jolt seemed more magnified than the last. No longer able to bite back his cries, he screamed at the next jab to his gut. Shackled by his wrists to a cell wall, he sagged against the cold concrete. His body, covered in sweat, trembled from fatigue and after-shocks of pain.

What had given him away? His lie that Parl had talked but decided not to return to his atrani? Gruber's resurgent memory of their time on Selia Dar? Or had it been the retinal scan during recruit processing?

Not that it mattered. Bluth had ordered his henchman to find out what Jace knew about their operations.

"I'll ask you again." The thug nicknamed the Blade pushed his scruffy face in front of Jace's. "How did you learn Gruber worked for the Razor?"

"We met at Stacktown. I don't remember exactly what happened down there. Ask Gruber, he'll tell you the same."

"So Gruber has no idea who you really are? He doesn't know you're the convicted murderer, Jace Vernon?"

"That's right." Jace drew in a raspy breath between dry lips. "Some water might help loosen my tongue."

The mercenary scratched his crotch. His skin flaked, so he probably itched all over. That's what happened when you never bathed, Jace thought.

"Why did you come here?" The man narrowed ferret-like eyes that sat over a broad nose and snarling mouth.

"Where else could I go? I thought I might join Bluth's band, for lack of other options. I couldn't give my real name, or he might turn me in to the bounty hunters."

Bending back his arm holding the stick, the Blade sneered. "It's more likely you've been sent as a spy."

"No way." A surge of concern reached him from Mixy, but he maintained his stoic expression. The Elusians were their only hope of escape, as long as they remained undetected.

A reassuring finger touched his mind like a warm caress. Silver. She must be all right if he could sense her emotions. Thank the stars.

Swallowing, he wondered how to convince this guy that he merely sought employment. His enemies would only buy that story if they believed Jace to be so desperate that he had no other recourse. He may have voiced his suspicions on Kurash about Bluth's involvement in his parents' murder, but only during closed testimony not accessible to his cousin Garth.

On Earth, however, the traitor in league with Bluth must have linked him to Silver. The Razor already knew Silver was on his tail. It followed that she and Jace were working together. Thus Bluth had set the trap for them on Elusia. Or… maybe Bluth hadn't been the one to order the bombing?

Either way, his identity had been compromised. Bluth must have seen past Silver's cover as well. She should terminate her target now, while she had the chance, and forget about him.

Pain obliterated his thoughts as the shock stick jabbed his stomach. His body twitched in agony.

"How did you avoid the mines on the route in?" the Blade demanded.

"You sent a pilot to guide us… me… through a clear path," Jace said between clenched teeth.

"Gruber vouched for you. Were you playing him, or has he been in your pocket from the start?"

"That porcupine? He's only interested in himself." Jace almost laughed but a strangled cough came out of his mouth instead. "If he'd realized my true identity, he would have claimed the reward for my capture."

"You risked much to come here. Why?"

"I told you, I need a job. My funds are frozen; I'm nearly out of credits. I have nowhere else to go."

"Liar."

The stick got him lower this time. Needles of pain bit through his clothing. He jerked in reaction, his muscles quivering.

Then warm encouragement enveloped him, buoyed him. Its feminine imprint provided comfort and strength.

Footsteps sounded from outside the corridor. Tyrone Bluth marched into view beyond the open cell door.

"What have you learned?" Bluth asked his henchman in a gravelly tone.

The Blade stood aside in deference. "Vernon insists he came here looking to get hired."

"And Gruber?"

"Hard to tell. Vernon claims they met at Stacktown by chance."

"You expect me to believe you're here for a job?" the Marauder sneered. "I know who the woman is and why she's come. She plans to kill me." He snorted with laughter. "I let her believe she's fooled me with her disguise. As we speak, she prepares to seduce me."

"Bastard. Let her go."

"I'll deal with her later. Tell me why you're really here. Did you think I'd point the finger at your cousin Garth?"

So he admits the connection. Jace licked his parched lips. "I need to be cleared of murder charges so I can regain my lands. Testify against my cousin, and I'll make it worth your while."

"Our plans go way beyond your family feud, Lord Vernon. You're just a cog in a big wheel, and you're wrong if you think you can stop its motion. Things are moving at a rate that not even the Consortium suspects."

His blood chilled. Were his fears about the Weavers correct? Could there be larger stakes involved, a conspiracy broader than anyone realized? He kept silent, hoping the lout would reveal more.

"He wasted my Elusian slave." The Blade swung his stick with an evil grin. "Let me kill him. He ain't told us nothing useful."

"You've got it wrong," Jace retorted. "Parl ended his own life. He couldn't stand betraying his own people."

"Shut up." The thug jabbed Jace again, until a moan of anguish escaped his lips.

"You can thank your fearless leader for giving the order that led to your atrani's death," he gritted between gasping breaths. "He's to blame, not me."

The Blade raised his arm to deliver another blow, but he hesitated, glancing at his superior.

"Idiot, don't listen to him. He lies," Bluth responded.

"Then let me end this."

"You're not sending me to Anriat to work the trona mines?" Jace ignored the agony in his shoulders as he sought more answers. He wished his voice didn't sound so hoarse. "Is that where you sent my sister?"

Bluth bared his teeth. "The girl will be lucky if she's still alive. She would have been assigned as concubine to one of the overlords. They can be forceful when taking their pleasure."

At least I know Shanna is there, Jace told himself. Fury strengthened him, and he straightened as best he could with his wrists restrained. "If she's dead, you'll pay for it," he warned the Razor.

"You're not in any position to make threats." Bluth grabbed the stick from his lieutenant and jabbed Jace repeatedly until he slumped against the wall, unable to raise his head. "Prepare him for the games," he told the Blade, before tossing the punishment device to the floor.

"What's that?" Jace rasped.

"It's how we amuse ourselves with prisoners. A fight to the

death." Bluth turned away as though he'd already dismissed Jace. "It should be quite entertaining to have Silver Malloy watch your slaughter."

****

Silver primped for the leader of Tyrone's Marauders in a spacious chamber while a stocky female warden watched over her. She bathed and dressed in a low-cut gown the woman provided and chatted the entire time. Cousin Evelina would be proud. Silver could prattle about clothes and makeup like any ditz.

After brushing out her hair, she made a show of folding her worn clothing into a neat pile. The warden didn't even notice her prying off one of the studs on her belt.

A minute later, the woman lay unconscious on the floor. Silver smirked above her. Those gas pellets had come in handy more than once.

Wishing her firearms hadn't been confiscated, she stuffed her personal belongings into a pillow case before scurrying to the door. She opened it a mere crack and peeked out. Thank the stars no one patrolled this sector. Bluth must have felt secure with the warden watching over her.

Item number one was to free Jace. From the pressure grazing her temples, Silver knew he was alive but suffered greatly.

On the other hand, she should complete her directive and terminate Tyrone Bluth.

One action ran contrary to the other. The latter would be better served if she waited to be brought to Bluth, maintaining her pretense of being a recruit. But if Bluth knew her true mission, she'd be wise to create her own opportunity to take him out.

She spared a moment to rummage in her sack and retrieve the comm unit she'd stashed in her utility belt.

"Kira?" she whispered after snapping it on her wrist. "Can you hear me?"

Hopefully, Bluth's personnel wouldn't be able to triangulate her position from the broadcast, but she had to risk it.

"I am here, mistress. Are you well?"

Dead ahead, she faced an intersection. Upon hearing voices approach, she pressed into the recess of a doorway. When the sound receded, she pushed the call button again.

"Yes, I'm fine. Can you tap into the base's mainframe for a schematic? I need to find Jace but don't know where the detention block is located."

"That's impossible without upgrades to your ship's systems. One moment, please."

Silver heard muttering in the background. "Keep silent," Kira snapped. "Sorry, I do not address you, mistress. Mixy suggests you look for proof of Tyrone Bluth's connection to Garth Vernon. After you free Master Jace, of course. That is not the course of action I would advise."

"Oh no? What would you have me do, then?" Silver smiled inwardly. Was she actually asking the Elusian for her trusted opinion?

"Attempt to gain access to the organization's financial records," Kira said. "Copy as much as you can, and I'll analyze it later."

"Really? I'd just been thinking how we could curtail the Marauders's activities by snipping their sources of income."

"What is your Earth expression? Great minds think alike? I've been studying your culture." A blast of agony penetrated their link. "*Kurkmak dos!*"

"What's wrong?" Silver heard Mixy moaning in the background. Jace couldn't have been mortally injured. She'd have felt his absence.

"Mixy's atrani is experiencing much pain. I am sharing their distress. How can this be possible?"

Silver sought an explanation. "Mixy's link to Jace extends to me, and through me, to you."

Sounds of a shuffle ensued on the other end. "Madam, I must tell you," Mixy said in a breathless rush. He must have grabbed the comm unit from Kira. "Master Jace despairs that his cause is lost. He wants you to complete your mission. Terminate Tyrone Bluth."

"Give me that." Kira's snide tone came back. "You must decide which path is right, mistress. I will support your decision."

"What, don't tell me you're resisting the urge to offer advice?" Mixy's muted voice said. "I am shocked, truly shocked."

Silver gritted her teeth. "Look, I need you both to focus. Jace and I require your help if we're to get out of here alive."

Oh yeah? What happened to the kick-ass woman who worked alone? Does she no longer exist? And is that a good thing, or is it a weakness that could get her killed?

"Create a diversion," she ordered. "I've got to go."

Silver's heart leapt when she heard voices coming from around the bend. Flattening herself against the wall, she tuned in her auditory sensors.

"The signal's coming from that direction," a man's guttural voice said.

"Who could be communicating with the surface?" another male replied.

"We know it's not Vernon, since he's in the stockade on level ten."

Level Ten! Thanks, guys.

"Better check out this signal. The Razor will be roaring mad if Vernon's woman got loose."

Her hands sweaty, Silver changed the function on her comm unit and deactivated the nearest door lock. Her skirt swished as she entered what looked like upscale quarters.

A quick glance told her the suite consisted of a sitting area, bedroom, and lavatory. The citrus-scented air made her wonder who rated such luxury. Maybe one of Bluth's higher ranking officers?

She plopped down her pillow case and quietly shut the outer door. Sounds came from inside the washroom. *Damn. Nowhere to hide.*

The bathroom door opened, and a dark-haired man emerged, an oversized towel wrapped around his torso. His eyes widened when he spotted her. "Who are you? How did you get in here?"

Aware the dress she wore flattered her figure, Silver thrust out her bosom and simpered. "I'm a gift, sent here to please you." She swirled her skirt for emphasis.

He sauntered closer. "What's that sack by the door?"

"Some of my toys. You'll like what I have to offer." She twisted her ring, another handy gadget with multiple functions.

"Who sent you?"

"One of your close friends."

He swept his dispassionate gaze over her. "You lie, woman. My friends know I favor my own persuasion."

Grabbing her hair, he yanked her head back. Tears sprang to her eyes but she didn't resist. "Why are you really here? Did you think to steal my files?"

"I-I don't know what you mean." Perhaps she could gain some information before she took him down.

With a grunt of disgust, he pushed her away. "I know why you've come. You want a cut of the action."

"All right, I'll confess," she said slowly. "I'm a new recruit, and I've heard about you. I figure you're probably skimming the pot, so to speak, and I could get a piece of the pie."

"Too bad, because I don't cheat. Did the Razor send you? I'll bet this is one of his stupid tests."

"Everyone cheats, pal. Look, you can trust me. I'm good with numbers." Smiling, she touched his arm. A tiny needle sprang from her ring and pricked his flesh. "I'm good at this, too." She watched dispassionately as he slumped to the ground.

Satisfied he wouldn't get up for several hours, she scanned the suite for his personal reader. Maybe he'd secured it in his desk before taking a shower.

Sure enough, she found the device inside the center drawer and flicked on the power button. Now if only accessing his files proved as easy.

Unfortunately, she couldn't pass beyond the first layer. Even though her training had included data retrieval skills, his encryption lockouts stymied her. She'd have to make a ghost copy. That would have to do until Kira broke the codes.

She'd lucked out in one way. This guy appeared to be the payroll manager for Bluth's organization. No wonder he rated such cushy quarters.

While the material downloaded onto a clean crystal, she brought up a schematic of the lunar complex. The detention cells were there on level ten. How could she get below without using the main shaft?

Utility conduits. It would be grueling, but she could make it. Not in this gown, though. Glad she'd brought her own clothes, she retrieved her stuffed pillow case and dumped the contents on the carpet. By the time her crystal flashed its readiness for removal, she'd changed back into her belted trousers but balked at exposing herself in the bustier again.

She put it on anyway, but covered herself with a man's shirt from her host's closet. With silent thanks to the unconscious fellow for loaning it to her, she fastened her hair into a ponytail. Then she grabbed the crystal, stuck it inside an empty pouch on her belt, and headed for the door.

Her passage through the service tunnels failed to trigger any alarms, either because they hadn't thought to put sensors in there, or because something else grabbed people's attention. Likely they were searching for her, but she reached level ten without incident.

Locating and freeing Jace was another matter. She peeked her head out from the maintenance room where she'd landed and recoiled quickly. Guards milled about in the corridor, viewing a monitor mounted on the wall. Some sort of crisis had erupted in the hangar bay.

Through her auditory sensors, she caught snatches of dialogue about "reactor overload" and "ammo dump".

All right, Mixy and Kira. Those two had to be responsible.

A familiar form slunk by her slightly ajar door. Gruber.

What was that lowlife doing down here? Moreover, how should she use this opportunity? Grab the guy as a hostage? Swagger out and pretend she'd gotten lost?

Gruber halted before a guard wearing a beret. He presented a document, and they proceeded to have a heated argument. A moment later, the guard marched away, a disapproving scowl on his face.

Silver waited for Gruber to disappear, but the bald man with the glass eye and stubby beard stood his ground. The guard reappeared with Jace in tow, his hands and ankles shackled. A brawny man with a scarred face and peeling skin accompanied them. He held some kind of stick pointed at Jace's back.

Silver bit back a cry at Jace's appearance. His shoulders slouched. His eyelids drooped, and his feet shuffled like an old man's. Bruises marred his haggard, unshaven face. What had they done to him?

"You can't be taking him to the arena yet. He hasn't been fed," the gruff guard said to Gruber.

"I have my orders, Blade." Gruber jutted his chin.

"Maybe I should call the Razor."

"Bad idea." Gruber whipped out a disruptor and shot all the guards, including the one called Blade.

Silver's jaw dropped. Did he plan to kill Jace, too?

"Stand by, I'm on your side," Gruber told an astonished Jace. He riffled through his victims's pockets until he found a set of key cards. With a grunt of triumph, he deactivated the manacles.

Jace, freed from his restraints, tottered on his feet, looking stunned.

Silver didn't question Gruber's actions. She rushed forward to embrace Jace in a careful hug so as not to hurt him.

"I'm so glad to see you. Are you okay?" Her arms fell away, and she stepped back to assess him.

He gave her a jaunty grin. "Now that we're together again, I'm fine. You?" His gaze deepened as he raked her over. It melted her heart that his prime concern was for her welfare.

"I'm good, thanks to some help from our Elusian friends."

He spun to Gruber. "Is this a setup? Will we be killed as we escape?"

Gruber jerked his thumb toward Silver. "Hell, no. I didn't know she would be here. I'd planned to get her out later."

"Can we reach the launch bay?" Aware they had to avoid the levelators, Silver was loath to use the utility tunnels again. Jace wasn't in any shape for a climb.

"The Razor will expect us to head for the surface." Gruber scratched his beard in thought.

"Speaking of Bluth, I need to finish my mission." Silver eyed Gruber's weapon.

"No, you don't." Jace gripped her arm. "Bluth paid me a visit. He admitted sending Shanna to the mines at Anriat. We have to go there to confirm he told the truth."

She jerked out of his grasp. "This is my best chance to take him out. You go on ahead. Mixy and Kira can assist you. Besides, what happened to getting proof linking your cousin Garth to the Marauder leader? If I stay behind, I can search for evidence."

He grimaced, as though the reminder of his cousin's treachery pained him. "Rescuing my sister takes priority. I can't do it without you. Please, don't argue with me. We'll go after Bluth together once Shanna is safe."

If Jace could put aside his personal needs to rescue the girl, shouldn't she be willing to subjugate her goals as well? Wasn't this what she'd learned on Selia Dar?

"All right. I'll go along with your plan for now." She considered mentioning the data recording but kept silent in front of Gruber, who bounced on his feet impatiently and kept glancing down the hall.

"Will you two get the lead out?" Gruber gestured for them to follow as he proceeded ahead at a fast clip.

"We should get in touch with Mixy to see what's happening." Jace jogged down the corridor alongside Silver. "Unfortunately, the Blade confiscated my comm unit."

"Use mine," she offered.

"Master!" Mixy cried after Jace checked in. "Are you well? Aiyee, such pain! Such rage! Such a terrible need to shove my fist into Bluth's ugly face." Mixy railed in a voice loud enough for them all to hear.

"Quiet," Jace said. "We need a way out of here. We can't take the levelator."

"The false reactor meltdown in one of their shuttles was my idea." Kira retorted as she came online. "They've released the docking clamps on all vessels as a precaution. Our spacecraft is cleared for immediate departure."

"As soon as they detect your launch, Bluth's men will aim their laser batteries," Jace warned. "They'll blast you into bits once you're clear of the complex."

"With those mines planted out there?" Kira scoffed. "One wrong hit, and they'll blow up their defense grid. It's my guess they'll assume we can't get too far, and they'll let us go."

"How were you planning to pass through the minefield?"

"Kira recorded the coordinate changes coming in," Mixy interrupted. Silver could just picture them jostling at the controls. "She says all we have to do is reverse the route."

"That seems too simple." Jace scratched his jaw. "We still have the problem of reaching the surface."

Gruber's expression lit. "I have an idea."

"Who's that?" Mixy asked, his tone puzzled.

"Our friend Gruber from Stacktown. He'll tell us why he's helping us once we're on our way." Jace slapped their one-eyed comrade on the back. "Looks like you're coming along, my friend."

Despite his haggard appearance, Silver knew Jace would enforce that order if necessary.

Gruber compressed his lips. "Listen, tell your friends to pretend as though they're heading into orbit but then switch to vector one-five-seven. Wait for us there."

Jace muttered instructions while they hurried along in the direction Gruber indicated.

Conscious of security monitors, Silver felt better when Gruber nonchalantly mentioned that he'd neutralized them.

Why did he assist them? Still afraid this might be a trap, she gazed at the double metal doors in front of them.

Gruber pointed forward. "We have to go in there. Don't let the smell bother you." With a chuckle, he pushed open the doors and swaggered inside.

A foul odor hit her nostrils as she trailed after him. She stopped short to survey a metal table surrounded by troughs and a set of gleaming instruments arrayed on a nearby tray. Several small square doors fitted into one entire wall. On another side, she saw some sort of trap door. However, what captured her morbid fascination was the massive device centered above the rust-stained table.

Not rust. Old blood.

Bile rose in her throat as she realized the purpose of the room. "Why did you bring us to the morgue?" she asked Gruber. Jace's nostrils flared as he stood by her side.

"Because there's a direct route to the surface from here, but you're not gonna like it."

Visions of their laundry chute adventure came to mind. Her heart sank. Was this a devious attempt by Tyrone Bluth to incapacitate them through some sort of faux escape plan? Or should they trust Gruber's sincerity?

"Hurry, before Bluth orders a sensor sweep of this entire level," Jace urged. "He's waiting for me at the arena, so he'll know something is up when I don't show, if the alarm hasn't sounded already."

Gruber motioned for Jace to get on the table. "We're probably minutes away from getting knockout gas through the vent system. First the Razor will seal off this entire level, but nobody thought to include the crossing here in the security parameters."

"What do you mean?" Jace stared him down and didn't budge.

"You'll lie on the table, one at a time. This hood will slide down and seal your body in a cocoon. See how the table fits on a track? It'll move you to that hatch. It opens automatically. Then you're propelled through the system to the depot at the other end. There should be just enough air for each ride. I'll go last."

"Where do we end up?" Silver asked in a choked voice, not liking this idea one bit.

"Above ground, in an unmanned storage depot. It's still under the atmospheric bubble."

"Are you telling me bodies are stored there, rather than being cremated?" Jace looked at him askance.

Gruber nodded. "Once every lunar cycle, the pods are launched and used for target practice. We don't get many of them. People get sick, or prisoners die. There ain't no need for supervision up top. Just prayers." He laughed at his own joke.

Jace glanced at Silver as though he sensed her reticence to be enclosed in another small, dark space.

Panic fluttered in her breast. *You can do this, for his sake if not for yours.*

"I'll go first," she volunteered with a bravado she didn't feel.

Jace helped her stretch out on the cold metal surface. "It'll be okay. Think of something pleasant," he said, tucking her stray hair behind her ears.

It didn't help. Ice filled her veins when he stepped away, leaving her alone, arms folded across her chest.

Gulping in short, erratic breaths, she listened as a clicking noise sounded. The overhead machinery began its descent, looking like a giant suction cup about to swallow her.

She couldn't breathe. Her vision tunneled.

The last sound she heard before darkness closed in was the pounding of her heart.

Chapter Twenty-One

"I don't want us to get separated again." Seated in their ship's tiny galley, Jace folded his hands on the tabletop. "We have to come up with a better plan."

Jammed into the small space along with him were Silver, Kira, and Gruber, who'd been assigned bunk space in the cargo hold. Mixy piloted the ship. They'd already escaped the minefield using Kira's reverse strategy. Now their heading took them toward the mining colony on Anriat.

Gruber snorted. "Our best bet is for you and Silver to pretend you're my prisoners. The Razor won't have broadcast my defection yet. I can get you inside."

Jace still couldn't get used to his fixed glass eye. "And then what? You said attractive women become property of the overlords. I'd go into the mines, assuming we're not executed outright, and Silver would end up in some brute's harem."

"True, but consider this. While the two women you're hunting may live among the concubines, they could have been assigned to any village. We can't search the entire world. Silver could gain access to a database from inside a warlord's mansion."

"Kira," Silver spoke softly, "did you have a chance to look at the material I copied? Maybe it contains information we can use."

"I am sorry, mistress. I briefly examined the data. It is mostly financial transactions and holds nothing specific about personnel on Anriat."

The Elusian's robe darkened, reflecting Silver's somber

mood. Jace worried about her. She'd said little since they had surfaced on the moon, appearing pale and shaken from their brief sojourn in the pod. She'd lifted her face toward the weak sunlight filtering through the domed ceiling in the storage depot as though another tomorrow might never come.

Gruber had led them to an airlock, from which the Elusians scooped them up in a fast maneuver that left Bluth's men scrambling. Once aboard, Jace put Mixy in charge of the command deck so the rest of them could hold a war council and grab a bite to eat at the same time. Dying of thirst, he gulped a glass of water before offering his opinion.

Silver's eyes blazed. "I have a better idea. Jace and I will disguise ourselves as Mynorans again. This time, Kira will join us. Bluth doesn't know about her, so she'll enhance our cover."

Gruber nodded thoughtfully. "Wealthy prisoners are often held for ransom. That could work."

"Once we're near a comm center, Kira can access the global database. I don't see how we can do it otherwise." Silver glanced at her atrani. "That is, if you agree. It'll be dangerous."

"I couldn't be more pleased." Kira's robe infused with tinges of gold.

Gruber clapped his hands. "Brilliant. As rich merchants, you'll be taken to the Chief Overlord. Most of the colony's official records are kept at his palace compound."

"Good work," Jace said, delighted to see Silver's violet eyes warm with pleasure.

She tilted her head, swinging her ponytail. He wanted to smooth away the worry creases on her brow. Kiss her pursed lips. Ease the tension from her shoulders. Comet dust, all he could think about was how he yearned to relieve his tension and drive into her. Deliberately looking away, he focused on the wall. But not before he saw an answering flush on Silver's cheeks and Kira's robe tinge with pink.

Remembering how he could make her burn with passion, he shifted in his chair. Never mind the aches and pains that still throbbed from his recent encounter with a shock stick. Spending a night in her bed would cure him.

Kira's lips tightened. "Can we focus, people? You've omitted one potential problem. Won't Bluth be expecting us to show up on Anriat? He'll have forewarned them."

Gruber regarded her with his good eye. "I don't think so. It's more likely he'll think Vernon is heading directly home with the intelligence he's gained. He may alert Garth to begin damage control."

Jace glowered at them. "Gruber is right. I should be heading home to confront my traitorous cousin. Only by regaining my title can I influence the Parsate's vote, but I still need proof of Garth's treason. And I won't return without my sister."

Silver's glance slid away, while Kira's robe imbued with ribbons of amber. He could almost hear Silver's thoughts. *If you're able to postpone dealing with political issues and make your sister a priority, why not me?*

He winced inwardly, knowing the situation with Yvette upset her. It hadn't helped that she'd found out through a slip of his tongue. If he wasn't indebted to Yvette's brother, Jace would disregard convention and ask Silver to… what? Become his bride? He'd lived by a creed of honor his entire life. How could he thrust aside his duty to wed a woman from another world?

And did she really want him to offer for her, or was she so bent on revenge that she'd desert him once they rescued Shanna? Despite their intimacy, the lady assassin had given no indication she expected anything further from their relationship.

Yet her actions proved otherwise. She'd had the opportunity to betray him many times over, and still she remained by his side. Likely she didn't even know what motivated her.

They'd have to sort out these problems later. For now, his path was clear—save Shanna, collect the evidence he needed, and then head home to face the consequences.

****

"Are you sure there is nothing more you require?" Kira asked Silver in her cabin.

Silver nodded. She'd prepare their disguises in the morning. Fatigue weighed her down, and she could think of nothing she'd like better than to sleep for hours.

A rustling noise sounded from the open doorway, where she glimpsed Mixy's disapproving frown and green-tinged robe.

"It is my place to serve the lady," he informed Kira. "What are you doing here?"

"I am making sure my atrani is comfortable. I thought you were piloting the ship."

"Master Jace relieved me."

"Very well. I shall resume my studies of the copied data files while you act as maid."

"I am a valet, not a maid, madam. And by relieving our bond mates of their mundane tasks, I allow them to concentrate on graver matters."

"Indeed? Then it's a good thing you brought me aboard. In addition to my superior computer skills, my financial training is desperately needed. Expect to account for your spending habits. Your budget is totally out of balance. Soon we'll have no more credits to buy fuel, and where will that get us?"

"Uh, guys." Silver rubbed her aching temples. "Can you take this outside? I'm tired, and I need to rest." *Does no one remember this is MY ship? Let me worry about buying fuel.*

Left alone, she took out a set of kewl sticks to begin her nightly prayers, but then she paused. At Selia Dar, hadn't her parents advised her to focus her energy outward? Retaining painful memories only held her back and kept her from moving on. She should have done this sooner, if she'd been thinking straight, but now was as good a time as any to put the past to rest.

She snapped the candles in half just as a knock sounded on the door.

"Come in." She tossed the broken pieces onto a counter.

Jace sauntered in. He'd showered, shaved, and changed into a linen shirt and pressed trousers. "I came to see how you're doing." His eyebrows lifted when he spotted the broken tapers.

"Aren't you supposed to be driving the ship?" she countered. "Mixy was just here. He said you'd taken the night shift."

"We're on autopilot. I wanted to talk."

"Oh, yeah? That's a new one for a man."

"You're not happy."

"Why do you say that?"

His eyes narrowed, and he stepped closer. "Something is bothering you. What's wrong?"

Like you don't know. "After our trip to Anriat, what then?"

"We'll split up if that's what you want. It seems our relationship means nothing more to you than great sex."

"So you're admitting we have a relationship?"

Behind him, he kicked the door shut. "Do we? I'm not really sure where I stand in your view."

"You're nearly engaged to Yvette. *We* don't stand a chance. You should have told me about her from the start. All of your rambling about bringing peace to the universe, and you really just mean to rescue your sister and fiancé."

"Not true. There's much more at stake here."

"What's at stake is your political clout at home. You dare to accuse me of being selfish? I should have shot Bluth when I had the chance."

"His men would have pounced on you. You know what they would do before killing you."

"Is it any different from what you're doing, bringing parts of me to life that were dormant and then stealing my hope?"

She bowed her head. Just when she'd finally cast aside the darkness of her past to grasp the light, he snatched it from her. By the stars, she didn't want him to know how much she cared. Evidently, duty meant more to him than she did, or he'd renounce his obligations in favor of staying with her. She should have realized happiness was merely an illusion.

"I bring you to life, huh?" Jace repeated, stepping closer. "Like this?"

Pressing a hand to the small of her back, he dragged her against him. With his other hand, he tilted her face upward. She lifted her gaze to his resolute jaw and contoured lips.

His mouth crushed down on hers, sending signals to her nerves to wake up and smell his clean soap scent, to taste his mint-scented breath. At first, she refused to respond, but his relentless kiss weakened her defense.

She parted her lips, letting his tongue swirl inside her mouth. He explored her crevices, leaving nothing untouched, while she grew languorous in his embrace. Switching his angle, he scoured her mouth until her teeth hurt.

You want to play with fire? I can handle the game. She knew he wasn't immune to her charms. Maybe he had to marry Yvette, but the proper Kurashki lady could never give him what Silver could. She'd make him remember her for all eternity.

She sucked on his tongue while thrusting her knee between his legs and rubbing it against his thigh. A low growl rent from his throat. He kissed her harder, forcing her neck back. His hands roamed to her breasts, kneading them as though the beast in him had come unleashed.

Silver's breath came in short, ragged bursts while a sweet lethargy swept her. As his thumbs brushed her nipples, she moaned from sheer pleasure, unable to stop the embers within her from igniting.

Her sound of passion spurred him on. Sweeping his foot behind her ankles, he tripped her onto the bed. Within minutes, they'd both shed their clothing. He hovered over her, his hard body touching hers, his powerful biceps bulging. His admiring gaze roamed her body.

"Gods, you're so beautiful." Then his hands were everywhere, as he showered kisses over her bare skin.

"Do it," she rasped, unable to wait any longer, especially when he closed his mouth on her nipple and suckled. She felt a responding chain reaction in her lower regions speeding toward a conclusion. Spreading her legs, she grasped his shaft. "Now."

He stretched his body, his glazed eyes staring into hers.

Then he found her entrance and thrust inside, pounding to the rhythm of his own grunts. A conflagration erupted, consuming her in waves of pleasure that cascaded outward, touching Jace who cried out his own release. Then he collapsed on her, while she lay satiated and sweaty with her eyes closed.

I want to do this every day, she realized, relishing the warmth of his weight and the security of his arms. *But it's not to be. This is all I will ever have.*

A terrible sadness filled her. Her life would have meaning if she could give herself to this man, but he'd never promised her a future.

****

Jace slid to his side to get his weight off Silver, but he didn't let go. He held her in his arms, feeling her soft breasts pressed against his chest and entwining his legs with hers. Being with her was like coming home. She made him forget his losses, believe in himself, and feel valued.

Nuzzling his face in her citrus-scented hair, he fumbled for the right words to let her know he cared. He couldn't allow her to go her own way once Shanna and Yvette were safe. Silver might do something foolish, like confront Tyrone Bluth alone and get herself killed.

He couldn't bear the thought of never seeing her again. Her intelligent eyes and platinum hair would haunt him forever. So would her desperate need to find a purpose. He could give her that reason to live. Somehow, they'd work things out so she wouldn't have to leave.

Even she'd admitted they made a good team. Maybe they

had started out as reluctant partners, but now he couldn't imagine his life without her.

"Silver, deermin," he said, intending to tell her how he felt. Her eyelids fluttered open, and he noticed moisture tipping her lashes. "You must know that I—"

The door chime sounded.

"I'm terribly sorry to interrupt," Mixy announced, "but you said to notify you when we reached Anriat. We are here."

****

Surrounded by an armed escort, Silver strode beside Jace through the streets of Central One, the capital of Anriat. They wore the rich garments of Mynoran traders and the faces of a couple in their sixties. Kira, shuffling behind them, posed as a servant, while Gruber claimed the bounty for bringing in wealthy hostages. He'd insisted on an audience with Wagun, the Chief Overlord.

"Watch where we're going," Silver remarked from between her teeth to Jace. "We'll need to know how to get out of here when the time comes."

Gruber claimed to own their ship, guarded by Mixy on the launchpad. He'd even ordered trona-enhanced armor plating for the hull and the computer upgrades Kira had requested, pledging as payment the reward money he expected to receive for his prisoners.

A sense of disquiet touched her. No doubt Jace wondered how they would find his sister when she might have been assigned to any minor administrator around the world. But deep down, Silver knew what he really feared—Shanna was dead.

She took hold of his hand and squeezed it. He gave her a grateful glance in return which warmed her heart. What had he been about to say before Mixy interrupted them?

Not that it mattered in the long run. What did matter was how to get word to her uncle about this source of trona. The mines supplied the raw materials that were shipped for refining to Solvent Minerals. Fester Niles didn't own the mines as everyone thought. He bought the ore from Tyrone Bluth. Tracing the convoluted financial trails was Kira's job, thank goodness. Silver had her own directive to fulfill.

According to what she'd learned from Gruber, the mines were below ground, whereas the slave laborers lived on the surface in rat-infested camps. They depended entirely on imports for sustenance.

Bluth's overlords, former slaves themselves, were happy with a small measure of power and a supply of women. Each overlord established a village for his support staff, in effect ruling their district like a king.

By buying trona from Solvent Minerals, the Consortium supported this system and allowed Bluth to buy more weapons. War would raise the price of trona even further.

If she got the chance, she would document this operation. In the meantime, she'd focus on their prime objectives—get Kira to a data terminal, find the captive women, and then hightail it out of there.

A stone structure stood at the far end of a street lined with craftsmen's shops. The building's columned facade proclaimed its importance. Dust clogged her nostrils as she strode forward. She missed the sweet pine scent from the woods they'd passed beyond the launchpad. She'd seen one of the labor camps along the way, clusters of log huts at the foot of a mountain.

At the mountain's base was an arched entrance supported by wood beams. Since it appeared to be carved into the rock, it must lead to the mines. Workers dressed in rags transferred chunks of ore outside from wheeled carts into shipping crates.

As Silver's party passed through the mansion's heavy wood front door, guards wearing crisp uniforms and carrying spear-like weapons replaced their escort. Modern comforts prevailed for the lucky inhabitants, as evidenced by the electric fixtures designed as wall sconces and by the sanitary facilities she visited while the guards radioed for instructions. She wrinkled her nose at a musty smell, likely from a set of dusty drapes bordering the windows.

Upon receiving orders, the guards marched them through a series of twisting corridors. Finally, her group arrived at a great hall with a raised dais at the far end.

Sitting on a throne-like chair was a middle-aged man who wore a colorful brocade robe over a black tunic and trousers. He had a hook nose, piercing dark eyes, and a scowl on his face—a face that bore the ravages of time and hard labor.

"Kneel before Chief Overlord Wagun." A sentry whacked them behind the knees, and they crumpled into position.

Lined up in a row for inspection, Silver and her friends faced the planet's governor, appointed by Bluth himself.

"Three of you, eh?" Wagun addressed Silver and her mates while ignoring Gruber.

He descended a flight of stone steps to examine each one of them in turn. When he got to Silver, he grasped her chin and turned her head from side to side. Clenching her teeth, she regarded him through slitted eyes. She wasn't a piece of meat he could add to his table. She'd fight if he dared to defile her, but that would blow their cover.

Her headdress swayed, and she reached up to steady it.

Wagun snagged her wrist, halting her. "Let's see what's hiding under that fancy hat." He tore it off, loosening the pins that held her hair in a twist. Long gray-tinted strands tumbled onto her shoulders. "Nice, but you're too old for me."

"Get away from her," Jace snapped, while Silver waggled her eyebrows to remind him of his role. His fierce demeanor didn't match his foppish attire. A guard jammed his spear handle into Jace's back in retribution. Jace grunted and hunched over.

"What's this, an Elusian? We've never had one of them before." Wagon stared at Kira with interest. Her robe darkened, reflecting her atrani's murderous mood. Hopefully, he knew little about their species, Silver thought with a smidgen of alarm.

"Your Eminence, please forgive my presumption," Gruber interrupted. "I'm the one who brought them here. I am under the direct employ of the Razor."

Wagun swung his beady eyes to their companion. "Really? And what do you do for him, fat man?"

"I'm his purchasing agent. I ran across these folks during my last transaction. They're rich merchants, and their people will pay handsomely for their safe return. I'd figured on a sweet bundle of prize money for myself."

"Have we met before?" Wagun studied him more closely.

Sweat glistened on Gruber's bald pate. "As I said, I'm Tyrone's man. I'd like to negotiate on their behalf."

"You won't get any prize money. That only applies to new slaves."

"Then we'll split the ransom fifty-fifty."

Wagun roared with laughter. "No deal. Eighty-twenty."

"Seventy-thirty."

"Deal, but don't tell the Razor." Wagun glanced at Silver, a calculating gleam in his eye. "How long do you think we'll have to keep them?"

"Not too many days, I hope. May I stand? My knees are killing me." At Wagun's nod, Gruber pushed himself off the floor. "You'll want to treat them well. Soiled goods will lower the price."

"You may rise," Wagun told the rest of them. They obeyed.

On her feet, Silver straightened her skirt while surreptitiously glancing at Jace. He looked impressive in those Mynoran clothes, even though he thought them too flamboyant.

When he reached home, Mixy would dress him as befitted his station. She doubted he'd wear anything so fancy, but he'd still have to be well groomed to enter the world of politics. She was no stranger to that environment, being raised in Uncle Manny's household. Too bad she wouldn't see Jace in his true element.

Kira's robe streaked with amber, and Jace glanced at them, raising his brows. Dingbat's tail. It was a damn nuisance to have her feelings so exposed.

"I'll need to send a message to their people. We should

make contact as soon as possible." Gruber jerked his thumb at Kira. "She'll assist me. She's had dealings with their kind before and will know what to say."

"Skinny thing, isn't she?" Wagun peered at Kira with a grimace.

Silver's attention shifted to a couple of uniformed men who strode down a spiral staircase behind the dais. A woman followed who burst into the room like a ray of sunshine. Her silk gown, a bright canary yellow, matched her curly blond hair. She looked as fragile as a porcelain teacup with china blue eyes, delicate features, and creamy, unblemished skin. Her long neck, adorned by diamonds, could have suited a dancer.

Silver heard Jace's sharp intake of breath. So what if this creature was one of the most beautiful women Silver had ever seen? He didn't have to go all goggle-eyed over her.

"We have new guests, Wagun? How exciting." The lady's voice, a musical lilt, would charm any man. Her accent seemed familiar, but Silver couldn't place it.

Wagun began introductions. "Gruber is one of the Razor's lieutenants. He brings us hostages for ransom. I should be able to buy you the rubilite bracelet you wanted with the profits, my dearest." Wagun kissed her hand, his movement fluid, as though he'd performed the gesture before at her whim.

"You're too good to me, my love." She pulled her hand away then turned to them. Her gaze flickered from Kira to Silver and then locked on Jace. "Don't I know you from somewhere?"

Jace lowered his head, shook it, and remained mute.

"Perhaps we should invite this charming couple to dine with us. They can tell us about their beloved family." Wagun gave a harsh laugh. "After all, we'd like to know who will be paying for their swift return."

"That's a wonderful idea." The woman clapped her hands with glee. "But you're being remiss, Wagun. You haven't introduced us."

"Sorry, my sweet." Wagun made an expansive gesture. "Allow me to present to you my lovely consort, Yvette."

Chapter Twenty-Two

Yvette? Jace nearly swallowed his tongue. He thought he'd recognized her. So she'd become Wagun's property? How could she tolerate such a life? Yet she didn't seem forced into submission. If anything, Yvette acted as if she owned the place… and the Chief Overlord.

Fortunately, Gruber stepped into the void and offered their false names.

"Assign our guests comfortable quarters," Wagun told Yvette. "We should show them we're civilized. You," he pointed to Gruber, "come with me. I'll take you to a comm terminal."

Gruber motioned to Kira. "Follow me, female. You will contact the prisoners' family and interpret our demands. We'll give them forty-eight hours to respond."

"I will need my servant afterward." Silver's haughty tone suited a wealthy trader's wife.

"Don't worry, she'll rejoin you shortly," Wagun said with a snicker. "None of my men would be interested in owning her. You, on the other hand, might make some minor overlord happy despite your age. If your people don't comply, you'll be added to our roster."

Jace trailed behind while Silver climbed the staircase after Yvette. He tried to memorize their route as they wound through a maze of corridors. Armsmen stood at every passage. Was Wagun afraid slaves from the labor camps would invade his compound? That was unlikely with the poor saps being so closely watched.

Perhaps Wagun feared defections within his own ranks. How did one become Chief Overlord anyway? Through appointment by Tyrone Bluth, as Gruber indicated? Or by the tried and true royal method—premeditated murder?

"You'll stay here, lady," Yvette told Silver.

They stopped in front of an open door that led to a comfortable bedchamber. Decorated in opulent fabrics, the feminine room held a canopy bed, dressing table, and small entertainment area.

"I'll send my maid to assist you until your servant is free. Dinner is served at eight o'clock. Be prompt."

Yvette activated her personal comm unit and rattled orders, while Jace glanced at his chronometer. Three hours to their agreed upon rendezvous with Mixy. They had to get the information they needed by then and be gone.

Could he trust Yvette? All these months he'd longed to save her… did she want to be rescued? Or would she betray him?

"May I speak to you in private?" he asked when she directed him to another door. Inside were mahogany furnishings befitting a man's tastes.

She glanced at their armed escort. "It is not permitted that I be alone with any of our guests."

"Very well, then let one of them come inside. I mean you no harm. I merely wish to discuss the terms of our ransom."

He gave her an intent gaze, staring into her lovely blue eyes that now seemed more cunning than he remembered. Had he imagined the demure innocent that had been Shanna's and his childhood friend? He watched with satisfaction as her lips parted. Was that a hint of remembrance in her expression?

"Accompany us," she snapped to one of the guards. The man's face remained impassive as he obeyed his overlord's mistress.

As soon as she shut the door, Jace spoke in Kurash. "Pretend that I am speaking in a Mynoran language and pray do not cry out. It's me, Jace. I have come to rescue you."

Her eyes rounded. "Jace, is it really you?" she answered in their native tongue. "I thought you looked familiar, but you'd seemed too old. What are you doing here? How did you find me?"

"Tyrone Bluth." He couldn't keep the hatred from his voice.

"That brute." She shuddered, and he resisted the urge to fold her into his arms.

He couldn't be sure where her loyalties lie. Obviously she had no fondness for the gang leader, but what about Wagun? Had she fallen for him in the classic kidnap victim manner? Or had she been brainwashed into compliance?

"Bluth stole you and Shanna, murdered my parents, and destroyed my honor. He is my enemy. Is he yours?" he demanded.

Her gaze flickered to the guard. "I do not condone his acts of depravity, nor the sorrow he brought you. He dropped me and Shanna off here and cast us onto the platform. I was lucky Wagun selected me."

"What platform? Where is Shanna?" Dread clawed his gut as he waited for her response.

"The platform is where all female captives land. Overlords bid for us, using bonus points they gain from their production quotas. The winning overlord assigns his women to serve either his household or one of his lesser administrators."

"As what? Sex slaves?" Jace clenched his jaw in horror.

"In most cases, yes. Some women become house servants, but they're usually the ones with defects whom the men cast out."

From her pout, Jace surmised those deemed unworthy were distasteful to her, too.

"What kind of defects? Does Bluth maim them?"

She shook her head. "The workers are a superstitious lot. If a woman exhibits the devil's sign, no man will take her. She's relegated to the household staff, grateful for a roof over her head."

"What is this sign?" These women had no hope of ever being reunited with their loved ones. And they should be grateful?

"Just about any type of blemish. Shanna has that little finger with the bone that never grew properly. It's deformed at the tip. At first, I was so jealous. She'd be assigned to scrub floors while I'd have to service the Chief Overlord."

Jace's fists curled. "I'll kill him."

"No." She placed a hand on his arm. "He has been kind to me. Aside from the sentries, I have more freedom here than I would have on Kurash."

"What do you mean? You were born into a life of privilege and should have been a great lady. Don't tell me you prefer this existence?" She might as well have punched him. He couldn't be hearing correctly.

A small smile curved her mouth. "If circumstances had been different, I would have wed you and gladly. But I like my position as Wagun's consort. He honors me by refusing to bed his other concubines. He brings me silks and jewels and delicacies from other worlds. He allows me to visit other districts without censoring my activities."

"So?" He didn't get her point.

"Jace, I've done much to improve the working conditions in the mines. Lives have been saved because of my efforts."

He leaned inward. "Are you insane?" he said, careful to maintain a neutral tone. "This entire planet is a blight on humanity. What happens to children who are captured in Bluth's raids, and old people? Where do they end up? We need to wipe out slavery, not make improvements."

"That won't happen overnight, and you know it."

"There's more at stake. We've had hints the Weavers might be forming an alliance with our enemy. I've heard rumors that the Xerxes Imperialate is amassing hostile forces on its border. A galactic-wide conflict could erupt if we don't intervene now."

He hoped she wouldn't relate this news to Wagun. If word got back to Bluth, the Razor would step up his efforts to eliminate Jace and his friends.

"I'm so sorry, but I will stay. How can I make you understand?"

His eyes burned at the fervor in her voice. "I cannot believe you accept this fate. Captivity must have affected your mind. Once I get you home, you will see reason."

"You're not going anywhere, unless Wagun allows it. Or did you come here with a specific plan of escape?"

"Where's my sister? You said she'd been assigned to a household. Which one? Is she well?" Would Yvette even know? Had she cared enough to concern herself with Shanna's well-being?

Yvette's lips twisted. "I've done you a favor, Jace. Shanna serves as my personal maid. I claimed her when Wagun granted me a boon."

"She's here?" His heart thumped with excitement. They wouldn't have to search the entire world, after all. He had to tell the others. Their timetable could be pushed forward.

"Shanna waits on your companion even as we speak. Who is that woman? I gather she is younger than she appears. Ingenious disguises, by the way."

"She's a friend I picked up during my travels, like the Elusians."

"There's more than one of them?"

Comet dust, he needed to be more careful. "I left my bond-mate behind on his home planet. He's been ill."

"Is that so?" She tilted her head, studying him with a thoughtful frown.

He could almost see the wheels spinning in her head. Would Yvette advise Wagun to search their ship? Was she the one who really wielded power around here?

"I thought to disguise myself and rescue you, but then we encountered Gruber," Jace said to distract her. "He outwitted us and took us hostage." He didn't want to raise their suspicions about Gruber, at least not until the man served his purpose. Was Kira even now sitting at a terminal, learning that Shanna lived in this very same house?

The guard shifted his feet, and Jace realized he and Yvette had been talking in their native language too long. Likely, the fellow would report their conversation to his master.

Yvette realized it, too, and turned toward the door, gesturing for the minion to open it.

"Yvette, even if you don't want to go home, will you help us?" Jace despised the pleading note in his voice.

She flicked a glance his way, but he couldn't read her expression. "I am undecided. I shall think on it."

She swept out the archway, leaving him alone with only his doubts for company.

****

Silver liked the shy maid who'd come to help her dress. The reed-thin girl with limp black hair and sad green eyes barely spoke a word. She kept her head bowed as she fluffed towels, refreshed Silver's gown, and laid out cosmetics on the dressing table.

"Are you sure you do not wish me to wash your hair, madam?" she called as Silver dried herself after a quick shower.

"No, thanks." The last thing Silver needed was to wash the coloring agent out and reveal her distinctive platinum hue. Wondering how to contact Jace and Kira without using their private comm channel, she stepped from the cool tile of the lavatory onto a thick carpet inside the bedchamber.

"Tell me, have you been here long?" she asked while pulling on her underwear.

The girl had offered her new garments, but she'd declined, not knowing if they were spoils from one of Tyrone Bluth's raids.

"A little over a year, but it seems like forever." Giving a quick glance at the door, the maid clamped her lips.

Dingbat's tail, she should check the room for surveillance devices before asking more questions. The maid might be a good source of information, if Silver could convince her to talk.

After pulling on a robe, Silver moved about the room, pretending to admire the furnishings. She passed her bug checker around the four walls, but it didn't light up. All clear.

She dropped into the chair at the dressing table so the girl could style her hair. "Just a simple twist, please. It's better for my headdress." Allowing herself to be pampered like a highborn lady, she waited a few moments before beginning her interview.

"So tell me, is Wagun a good master? Do you get enough to eat and a warm place to sleep? Don't be afraid to speak. No one can hear us." She spoke in a low, coaxing tone, snagging the girl's eyes in the mirror.

"I serve his consort. She treats me well." The maid averted her face, hiding her expression, while her fingers worked their magic on Silver's hair.

"You're awfully thin. Haven't you any appetite? It must be tough to be a prisoner, even if your situation is better than most."

"No, it isn't," the girl murmured. "Yvette thinks she's done me a favor, but she doesn't realize how hard this life is for me, and how much I miss my home."

"She seems to have done well for herself."

The maid fell silent, adding pins to keep Silver's hair in place. Then she lifted her head, her eyes bright with moisture. "May I get you anything else before I go, madam?"

"Tell me your name." The girl's features seemed awfully familiar. Those eyes reminded her of… Could it possibly be this easy?

"I am called Shanna, madam."

"It is you! I should have known." Silver leapt up and embraced her. Poor thing was so bony. "I came with your brother. We're here to rescue you."

Shanna's jaw gaped. "Jace is here?"

Silver's auditory sensors picked up a couple of muted thumps from the hallway. "He's the Mynoran posing as my husband. My name is Silver."

"I can't believe Jace has come for me after all this time." Shanna covered her face with her hands, her shoulders trembling.

"Here's the plan." Silver made it up as she went along. "We lure the guards inside the room, and I take them out. Then we go find Jace and our other friends."

Had Kira already determined their quarry was close? If so, she and Gruber might be heading their way. That would make things easier.

"I… I don't know," Shanna said. "Jace should run and not worry about me. He'll be killed if he's caught."

The door swung open, and Jace stood framed in the archway. Silver glimpsed two limp bodies lying on the ground beyond.

"Did I hear my name?" He shot a glance at Silver, who nodded, a lump in her throat. "Shanna, is it really you?"

Wondering at the vibes of regret she sensed from him, Silver dragged the unconscious guards into the bedchamber while Jace hugged his sister.

"Let's go," she urged. "It's almost eight. They'll be expecting us downstairs for dinner."

Shanna hung back. "It means death if I try to escape. I-I don't know if I can do this."

"You're dead anyway if you stay here much longer," Silver retorted. "Look at you. You're so thin that your bones stick out. We haven't come all this way for nothing."

"Don't argue." Jace gripped his sister's scrawny arm. "You're leaving with us, like it or not."

"Where's Yvette?" Silver peered past him toward the hallway.

"I'm afraid she's turned."

"Turned? What do you mean?"

Shanna answered, fear clouding her eyes. "Yvette has changed. I don't know her anymore. She enjoys her rank and boasts about how much good she's done here, but slaves are slaves, regardless of their conditions. She'll resist if you try to take her."

Jace's brow furrowed. "Yvette gave me the same story. But kidnap victims often fall prey to their captors and adopt their goals. If we get her home, it's possible—"

"No, Jace. She's made her choice." Shanna removed his hand from her arm. "And if she knows who you are, we'd better hurry. She could be reporting to Wagun as we speak."

"Is there a service stairwell?" Silver wished her gown didn't rustle when she walked. Peeking outside the door, she noted the empty corridor. "It's clear."

She led the way while Jace hurried Shanna along. The girl wore a coarse brown shift and sandals, a more serviceable outfit than Silver's elaborate dress. She and Jace stood out like a couple of peacocks. They'd blend into the background better if they could obtain different clothing.

"We have to find Kira," she told them.

"Who's that?" Shanna's voice strengthened, seemed steadier.

"My Elusian bond-mate," Silver explained.

"Reach out with your mind and broadcast our success," Jace advised her. "Kira will understand where to meet us."

I'm already on my way.

Who'd said that? Silver's head jerked up. The others hadn't reacted, so she must be the only one who'd heard it. Or rather, got the drift of the message.

Thank goodness Kira was okay. Silver hadn't even realized she'd been worried about her atrani. In fact, it seemed as though they'd been bonded forever. Like Jace and Mixy, for that matter.

As though he shared her thoughts, Jace clasped her hand as they charged down the servants's staircase. At the bottom level,

Shanna directed them to a wardroom where they exchanged their frivolous garb for brown shifts like she wore.

Reluctant to part with her boots, Silver stuffed her undetected weapons and gizmos inside the stiff leather. Ready to proceed, she disabled the security vids en route with another of her handy gadgets. One thing about those Mynoran headdresses; they held an arsenal befitting an assassin.

Getting beyond the outer village wall would be a challenge. Silver glanced at her chronometer. Ten minutes past eight. Wagun would sound the alarm at any moment.

Or not. An alarm sounded all right, but people ran in the opposite direction, yelling and shouting. Dark smoke billowed into the air. A fire, just the diversion they needed.

One glance at Jace's face, and she knew his theory matched her own. Yvette. Sorrow etched his features, but he stoically hauled his sister out an exit and toward the main gate.

A sergeant-at-arms blocked their path. Shanna shook herself free. Her complexion pale, she approached him.

"Let us pass. I go on business for the master's lady."

"Without an escort? Show me your papers."

"They don't need no papers," a gruff voice said from behind. "I'll vouch for `em."

Silver whipped around. "Gruber, you found us."

"These slaves carry important documents," he told the soldier. "Lady Yvette wishes to secure them from the flames. Let us through before this entire place goes up."

The stone walls might keep the structure from being demolished, but all those heavy draperies and wood furnishings would fuel the fire.

"No one leaves without signed orders." Raising his disruptor, the soldier stood staunchly at his post.

"Send another one of your troops for confirmation," Kira suggested with a sly smile. "In the meantime, I'll serenade you. It is my guess you have never heard an Elusian sing." She opened her mouth, and a screeching sound came forth.

Silver bent, slapping her hands over her ears. By the fires of Zolifar, did Kira's people consider this singing?

Kira stopped, and the relief of silence almost knocked her over. When she straightened, she noticed the guards passed out on the ground.

"I hope you don't mind," Kira told her with a smirk, "but I borrowed some of your knockout spray. You have interesting items among your belongings."

"You searched my stuff?" Silver hopped aside while Jace and Gruber secured the gate.

"Nay, mistress, I simply entered the receipts into our books for the goods requisitioned on Elusia. Then it was merely a matter of taking inventory and storing the surplus."

"Surplus." She regarded her atrani. "I suppose you believe that what's mine is yours."

Kira's robe streaked with tangerine. Stars above, she hated it when the Elusian exhibited affection. Was it Kira's emotion, or hers? Silver couldn't tell the difference anymore.

"Will you two stop gawking at each other and move it?" Jace's question sounded more like a command. "Mixy is impatient to lift off."

They scrambled past the raised gate. The path looked clear toward the wooded encampments and the launchpad beyond.

Suddenly, Gruber pointed to the sky. "Incoming!" he yelled, charging off at a fast clip. Silver glanced up, and her blood ran cold.

A couple of armed drones flew into sight, swooping from the palace heights and aiming straight at them.

Chapter Twenty-Three

"Follow a zigzag pattern," Jace shouted, dodging laser blasts as he sprinted ahead. "Split up. It'll confuse them."

Grabbing his sister's hand, he loped downhill. At the mountain's base, they dashed past the encampment where miners labored to transfer ore rocks into movable crates.

"Jace, wait." Shanna tugged on his arm.

"Not now. We can't help them." He dragged her onward.

A guard spotted their fleeing party and hefted his laser carbine. "Escaped prisoners," the man hollered.

Jace glanced back. Kira was having trouble keeping up. Silver urged her on, while Gruber huffed his way to the lead. For a stocky fellow, he moved fast.

A blast barely missed Jace's ear. He smelled the ozone from superheated air. "Mixy, do you hear me?" he called into his comm unit, letting Shanna run ahead. "We're nearly there. Get ready to emit a pulsed charge."

"Our ship is surrounded by troops, milord. Are you sure it will work?"

"Let's hope so. As soon as the coils reverse polarity, lower the boarding ramp and release the ground clamps at the same time."

He'd used this trick during a desperate moment in the Dorian War. With armed guards blocking their only escape route, they had no other choice.

A wave of emotion cut him like a scythe. His lungs heaved as he forced himself to keep pace. It had to be coming from Kira. Silver's bond-mate hadn't yet learned how to filter her reactions.

He waited for her and Silver to catch up. Rivulets of sweat ran down the Elusian's face. Her robe, lime green ribboned with soot black, reflected mingled anxiety and fear. A trace of citrus twisted through. Great Cosmos, did Silver actually derive pleasure from the chase? Or was that coming from Kira, who'd long sought such depths of feeling?

No matter. Jace gestured toward the women to hurry forward, concerned the soldiers were gaining on them. He angled sideways, yanking Shanna aside just as a blue beam slashed the air where she'd been moments before. One of the drones circled above and then changed angles, diving at them even as he switched direction again. A series of laser bursts barely missed him.

Gruber reached the ship first, weaving between several limp bodies lying on the ground and charging up the waiting ramp. So their gamble had won. Mixy had effectively changed the hull polarity, creating electrical arcs aimed outside the ship.

Now if only the coils had recovered enough for the engines to start.

While the women stumbled past him, Jace paused to gather up the weapons from the fallen soldiers. They might need the extra firepower later. His arms full, he jogged up the ramp and tossed his burden onto the floor. Then he hit the button to seal the hatch.

"Strap in," he ordered, dropping into the pilot's seat while Mixy showed Shanna where to sit. They'd barely fastened their harnesses before he punched the ignition, fired the thrusters, and launched.

After they'd broken orbit, Silver unstrapped her safety belt and rose from the copilot's chair. "Is everyone all right?"

Jace twisted his head to regard his sister. Shanna sat quietly, observing but not speaking.

"We are fine," Kira replied for the rest of them.

"Shanna may want to clean up." Silver gave their guest an appraising glance. "Kira, can you please show her to my cabin and explain how to use the facilities? She can room with me."

"Certainly, mistress. Shall I prepare some refreshments for you afterward?"

"I can do that," Mixy offered, his posture stiff.

"Thanks, but we can get our own." Silver's firm lips forestalled any arguments.

"I'll store these weapons in the arms locker." Mixy stooped to gather the carbine rifles and disruptors Jace had collected.

"I'm gonna hit the galley." Gruber rubbed his belly. "You kids may not be hungry, but I'm starved. Besides, I've got to study the charts to see where you can drop me off. I'll have to steer clear of the Razor's radar for a while."

"Thanks for your help. We owe you," Jace said, still wary of Gruber's agenda, but sincere in his gratitude.

Silver lingered on the bridge deck after the others left. "We should recruit him for S.I.N. His cover might be blown with Tyrone's Marauders, but he could still be useful elsewhere."

Jace swiveled to study her. Wisps of hair had broken loose from her twist and fanned her face. He imagined his fingers there, stroking her smooth skin, circling lower to her luscious mouth. Her lips, a rosy pout, tempted him to leap from his seat and imprint his taste on her. Even that coarse brown shift had shape with her body stretching the fabric.

Something stretched within his pants, making him curse inwardly. He shouldn't be thinking such thoughts until they completed their mission. Thank goodness Mixy wasn't on deck or Silver would sense his mood. As it was, her lips gave a slight upward tilt. His skin heated, and he returned his attention to the console. How had they been so lucky to get two Elusians attached to them?

"Do you think they've replaced your superior officer?" he asked her. "Or found out who killed the woman?"

"I'll have to contact Uncle Manny to see what's going on." Silver's factual tone offered no acknowledgment for his wayward frame of mind. "Kira might be able to uplink us when we're near an amp buoy. Where are we headed?"

"Kurash." He entered the coordinates into the nav computer.

"What? Aren't we going after Bluth?"

He studiously avoided looking at her. "I have the evidence I need of his involvement in my parents' murders. Shanna is my witness, plus we have the financial files you copied at Bluth's hideout as well as the data from Parl. That should be enough to condemn Garth and prove my innocence."

"Shanna was victimized. Your opponents might say she's malleable to any suggestions put to her. They could also claim that you doctored those files. The best evidence would be a recorded confession from Tyrone Bluth."

Hitting the autopilot button, he turned to face her. "You still intend to complete your mission, don't you?"

Her eyes flashed. "I kept my end of the bargain and helped rescue your sister. If we capture Bluth, we'll both get what we want."

"You don't understand. I have to go home. The Incantation Ceremony takes place in less than forty-eight hours. If Ruler Hurat names Garth in my stead, it cannot be undone."

"What's your ETA to Kurash from here?"

He did a quick calculation. "Twelve hours at hyperspeed."

"If Bluth is in the vicinity, you owe it to me to take me there first."

Swallowing hard, he stared at her. *So the lady assassin doesn't care what happens to me on my home world. She only wants to carry out her assignment.*

"I don't have any way to trace him," he replied, his tone flat.

"I do. When I was on his ship on the way to his HQ, I attached a locator beacon. Listen, Jace, you need his confession. I've thought hard about this, and I have a plan."

She told him, and he had to admit that while her scheme held numerous risks, it could work. Part of him itched to confront the terrorist again. He'd have to settle the score between them sooner or later. And while he yearned to stab the point of his ceremonial sword into the brute's chest, he'd be happy to bring him to trial and serve justice that way.

"All right, let's see if we can find him."

Five hours later, he cursed himself for being a fool. Who else would drive his ship straight into Tyrone Bluth's snare? He'd sent the message Silver prepared but didn't believe for a nanosecond the scoundrel would comply.

Face them alone, ship-to-ship? No matter what valuable information they promised to deliver, Bluth wouldn't let down his guard. He'd simply order his patrol to remain hidden.

That's why Silver had chosen their rendezvous point, because it gave them an advantage. Or so he hoped. Her plan was fraught with possibilities for disastrous outcomes, but hadn't that been her expectation all along?

He didn't want to be there when she fulfilled her death wish. It pained him deeply that she didn't care enough for him to renounce her goal. Despite his release from a potential betrothal to Yvette, he still couldn't offer her anything in return, not until he'd restored his lands and title.

Maybe it was just as well. Her fierce independence, bold manner, and liberal views wouldn't fit in with the rigid society on Kurash.

Never mind that he craved her as a thirsty man needed a drink, or that his home world needed the refreshing breeze of progress just as badly. No one would accept her as his wife.

"Really, milord, is this the time to be thinking of your lady love?" Mixy's voice chided from behind.

Jace glanced up, dismayed that he'd been so lost in thought, he hadn't noticed Mixy's arrival on deck. The Elusian's robe was tinted a deep rose. Jace's brow folded. Was that color a reflection of his feelings, and if so, what did it mean?

"I'm merely wondering if Silver's plan will work."

"Nay, master, you wish to ask the mistress to remain at your side, but circumstances restrict you. You fear that even when you are free to ask for her hand in marriage, she will spurn you. Woe be the fickle sentiments of women," Mixy railed, waving his arms above his head.

"Did you come here for a reason?" Jace asked in a terse voice.

"Indeed." Mixy's mood changed abruptly. "I came to see if you'd like to take a short break. You'll need all the rest you can get before we go into battle."

"I'd better stay here. Once we reach our targeted system, I'll have to steer us into position."

He hoped their plan worked. Silver had proposed taking all the disruptors on board and bleeding their energy to create a single shot pulse cannon. It was their best bet for defense, if her other ploy failed.

****

Silver put the finishing touches on the giant reflective matrix they'd rigged in the cargo hold. Their turboboost laser batteries wouldn't be any match for the photon torpedoes and antiflux missiles onboard Bluth's fleet. His lasers seriously outgunned her ship's array, too. Outwitting Bluth brought their only chance to defeat him.

Next time, she'd get a bigger vessel with more living quarters and warclass-rated armaments.

If there was a next time.

"Okay, Gruber, it's ready. Make sure you attach the matrix securely to the robot arm."

She tossed aside her work gloves and strode to a round viewport to watch the delicate maneuver outside the ship.

Gruber sweated and cursed as he manipulated the levers on a control panel inside the hold.

His experience had come in handy. He wasn't merely Bluth's purchasing agent; his knowledge extended to arms dealing and repairs. He'd also revealed himself as the informant in Bluth's organization.

Gruber had dropped the tip that led Silver to Al'ron in the first place. That's why he helped them escape from Bluth's clutches—the raider had caught onto him. Money motivated him, along with an old grudge against his boss.

"I hope this works," the bald man said when he'd completed the operation. He wiped his brow then stretched his arms above his head. They'd spent too much time in a hunched position working on realignments.

"It will." She rubbed her neck, keeping her doubts to herself.

At least Shanna remained out of harm's way. She'd advised the girl to stay inside their cabin. Shanna had merely nodded in response. Silver worried about her, but she'd deal with that problem later.

Feeling guilty because she'd diverted Jace from taking his sister home, she consoled herself with the notion of eliminating Bluth. As long as the Razor roamed the space lanes, Shanna would be afraid of him. End his tyranny, and they could all breathe a sigh of relief.

What then? During her private conversation earlier with Uncle Manny, she'd been happy to learn Internal Security had arrested Fester Niles plus the gunman he'd hired to kill Major Dean. Dash had been instrumental in clearing Silver's name of the murder charge.

In an ironic twist, her cousin had been appointed the new chief of S.I.N. He'd said Silver could have any post she desired, but first her family wanted her to come home.

Jace hadn't once mentioned what might happen between them now that Yvette was no longer an issue. He must regard her as a convenient ally, nothing more. She'd been a quick tumble as well, but she couldn't fault him for that. Her own needs had propelled her into his bed.

What she hadn't counted on was caring so much. Blinking rapidly, she ignored Kira's robe imbued with sad amber and her atrani's downcast face. She'd decide what to do later—if they survived.

Thumbing her comm unit, she asked Jace, "What's our status?"

His deep voice responded. "We're in position waiting for the target to show. Are you about done down there?"

"Yes. Gruber will deploy the reflector when the time comes. Kira will monitor communications from the command console in your cabin. She'll record the conversation as planned." *Assuming Bluth cooperates and doesn't trick us.* "I'll be up there shortly to man the pulse cannon."

"Mixy is here. He can do it."

"You'll need him as copilot, especially if we have to make a quick getaway."

"Okay. Make it fast."

After a final consultation with Gruber and Kira, Silver climbed two levels and scurried toward the bridge deck.

This was it. Her last chance to complete her mission.

She ducked through the hatchway. Her glance took in Jace's tense posture, Mixy's pinched face, and the lone ship heading their way on the viewscreen. Silver assumed a station at the tactical board.

"It's Bluth, he's hailing us," Kira's clear voice rang on the speaker system.

Silver's heart raced, fueled by adrenaline, while energy surged into her brain. Her exhilaration amplified through Kira and reverberated back, augmented by the link between her and Jace and the two Elusians.

Incredible, she thought. But then she tamped down, not wanting to expose her intentions or have anyone anticipate her moves. Having an empath at her side had its pros and cons.

Returning her attention outward, she recognized the Razor's fat Pamorian T-80 Corvette, the largest model of its class fitted with weapons worthy of a destroyer.

As they'd hoped, Bluth took up a position facing them. That left his ship between theirs and the sun. She suspected the rest of the pirate fleet hid behind that small moon, waiting to intercept them upon Bluth's order.

"I'm glad you could make it," Jace drawled after opening a channel.

He turned on the video link, and the terrorist appeared on their monitor. Bluth looked scruffier than usual—one eye twitching, an uneven growth of beard on his face, and a cut on his upper cheek.

"Don't waste my time, you slippery son of a zeeworm. You promised to tell me the secret of Stacktown."

"I said I'd sell it to you, Bluth. I'm learning how to operate at your level. Believe me, you'll be happy to pay the price. No one leaves that place and remembers what they saw."

Bluth snarled. "Why should I believe you, then?"

"Because Gruber remembers, too. He'll corroborate what I tell you."

"That snake is still aboard your ship?"

"Yep. Maybe I'll throw him in as a bonus. So how about it? Do we have a deal?"

"Depends on the price," Bluth countered.

A red light pinged on Silver's station. So far, so good. She hoped Jace could keep him talking long enough for their plan to work.

"Don't push me into a corner," Jace warned, while Silver knew it was an effort for him to speak civilly to the man who'd caused them so much anguish. "We're willing to die without revealing what we know. If you're scanning us, you'll get an increased energy reading. That's a self-destruct device we've planted. At this close range, it'll take you out along with us."

Silver swallowed, her hands hovering above the buttons. That's what they wanted Bluth to believe, so he didn't realize the energy signature really belonged to their pulse cannon. They could only get one shot off. She meant to reserve it for her own deadly purpose.

"What's that thing outside your ship?"

Uh-oh. He'd noticed Gruber's deployment of the reflective matrix on the robot arm.

"It's a makeshift solar panel," Jace lied. "We're using it to boost power to our support systems. We haven't been able to put in for maintenance."

If tilted to just the right angle, the matrix would catch the sun's rays and confine them into a beam of intense power. Aimed at Bluth's ship, it would blow him to smithereens.

Silver was tempted to do just that, but she knew Jace needed Bluth's confession first. That had been her whole point in suggesting this operation. Then she could blast him from space, either with their improvised weapon or with the pulse cannon.

Jace gripped the armrests so tightly his knuckles whitened.

"If you're playing tricks on me, you're dead," Bluth growled. He leaned forward, his face looming larger on the screen, so close Silver could see his clogged pores. "What's your price?"

Her glance flicked to the communications station where the record button flashed. Good, Kira had things under control. She shifted her feet, tired of standing but too anxious to sit.

As though he shared her restlessness, Mixy rose from the copilot's seat and ambled to within a few feet of her. His robe exhibited an unusual mixture of malachite and coal, while his face seethed with emotion.

"I want to know who paid you to murder my parents and abduct my sister and her friend to sell as slaves," Jace said in a tight voice.

Bluth gave a snort of laughter. "Is that all? You already know your cousin, Garth Vernon, claimed your seat of power after usurping you."

"So you admit Garth ordered you to kill my mother and father and steal my sister?"

"You're right on all counts, not that you'll live to spread the word."

"Why did Garth want me out of the way? Was it to influence the Parsate to vote for war? How will he benefit?"

"He's gained your lands and fortune. Meanwhile, his friends are the ones pushing for hostilities. They've been bankrolling Garth and their other agent. Those two, in turn, pay us." He chuckled. "The idiots have acted at cross purposes more than once. It serves our real paymaster well."

"So a third party is involved?" Jace kept his voice even, but Silver's auditory sensors caught the hitch in his breath.

"You got it." Bluth puffed his chest out. "We've increased our profits tenfold. Raids bring in spoils as well as bonuses."

"I suppose by the other agent, you mean Fester Niles? He tried to do the same thing to Silver that Garth did to me, by framing her for Major Dean's murder."

Bluth's glance slid sideways, and Silver could swear he was staring straight at her. "Stupid ass. Niles stepped over the line and got caught. He should have let my people finish the job. We'd already put your alien friend in the hospital."

Mixy stiffened, while Jace cursed. "So you were responsible for his accident?"

"That was too easy, and so was our attempt on Elusia. Once we learned about your bond-mate's condition, we planted our man there in case you showed up. Parl failed, the miserable cur."

"So who's really pulling the strings?" Jace asked, his voice strained.

Silver sympathized. It was difficult to maintain a civil facade when facing the man who'd caused so much destruction and pain. Her finger twitched toward the lever that would tilt their giant space mirror. Just a few more degrees upward and the sun's intensity would focus into a beam capable of... No, not yet.

Wait until Jace finished.

She'd only talked him into this after convincing him they'd use the powerful laser to disable Bluth's ship and tow him back to Kurash. The recorded confession had been necessary in case Bluth resisted. Jace had no idea she planned to terminate their target. Or maybe he did. Her heart bled with the need for revenge as she shared his rage. But he valued honor above all. He would never condone pulling the trigger, not when the court system provided an alternative.

Jace inhaled a deep breath, his eyes fixed on the viewscreen. Mixy's robe swished as he moved nearby to a better vantage point. Silver kept her hand poised above the matrix lever. Her glance fell to the other light blinking on her tactical board. The pulse cannon was fully charged, but only to be used if Bluth fired on them.

"I've told you enough," Bluth snapped. His eyes narrowed, his tic more pronounced. "Now what about Stacktown? What's their big secret? I was there for the auction, and I don't remember nothing except a smoky city and stiff-lipped natives. Did you find where they grow the carolla nuts?"

"There's a village beyond the mountain range called Selia Dar," Jace said. "It holds eternal bliss for those who choose to stay. It also holds a doorway beyond the earthly plane. You can visit the ghosts of your past. Some people find that to be a great comfort. I met my parents, whom you murdered. If you went there, I've no doubt you'd meet the specters of your victims."

Push the lever. Do it now. Blast him to Zolifer. And pray that Jace forgives me.

Silver's hand shifted, but before she touched the control to tilt the matrix, Mixy leapt forward. Shoving her out of the way, he hit the button activating the pulse cannon.

"You villainous beast, you deserve to die," Mixy shouted. "Plunderer of people's lives! Destroyer of dreams! Thief and brigand! We will see you to your doom."

A strong vibration rocked the deck under her feet. Silver regained her balance just in time to see a searing blast of focused particles rip through Bluth's hull. Aimed at a vulnerable seam, the shot hit home.

"Fire the thrusters. Veer off, now!" Silver cried to Jace.

A bright light erupted moments before the enemy vessel exploded. Millions of pieces of debris blew into space, a large chunk flying straight at them.

Chapter Twenty-Four

As Silver stared in shock at the exploding warship, Jace hit the thrusters. Their ship careened away from an oncoming mass of debris.

"What did you do?" she asked Mixy when her voice returned.

Mixy pursed his lips. "Master Jace wanted Tyrone Bluth dead for his crimes as much as you, but pursuit of justice held him back. I acted in his place."

"I don't believe it," Jace said between clenched teeth, while forging a path through dangerous space junk. "You know I meant to bring Bluth to trial. You've lost me the chance."

"You have the evidence you need for the courts, milord. Be grateful this thorn in your side is forever clipped."

Regarding the viewscreen, Silver gasped. Multiple gunships converged on their vector. The Marauders buzzed them like angry wasps.

"Do we have any firepower left?" Jace's brow folded in concentration as he worked the controls.

"That shot depleted the pulse cannon. Our defenses won't hold them off for long," Silver replied. "We're still close enough to the sun, if you could get us into position again."

"You're right. Everyone, listen up," he announced on the speaker system. "Brace yourselves. We have some sharp maneuvers ahead."

His fingers danced over the helm panel as they dodged blasts from enemy ships. The motion would have sent Silver flying if she hadn't gripped a hand rail for support. Jace flew them to the far side of the raider ships and the gaseous star.

She pushed the matrix lever two notches forward to accommodate for their change in position. Since their new target was wider than one ship, she set the beam for a more diffuse field. Her display showed the giant reflective surface outside tilting to catch the rays. One more adjustment and the space mirror reflected the energy back at the ships ranging between their Corvette and the sun.

Tyrone's Marauders went out in a blaze of light so intense she clapped her hands over her eyes. The deck slanted underfoot as Jace veered off. She peeked from between her splayed fingers, noting sparks of light diminishing in the growing distance.

"We are saved," Mixy cried, embracing Silver. His joy turned his robe a deep honeybell orange.

She hugged him back, feeling a sense of satisfaction so deep it brought tears to her eyes. Revenge felt good, but even better, she didn't feel guilty about killing Tyrone Bluth. Mixy had taken that burden from her.

She understood what he'd done. Jace had wanted Bluth dead but couldn't act on it because of his moral standards.

Mixy detached himself and offered her a wan smile. He looked tired, now that the action was over.

Jace got up and faced his valet. After a long moment of weighted silence, he embraced Mixy himself and patted his back.

"Thanks, my friend. You had the courage to do what I couldn't. I'm glad we no longer have to worry about that scourge of the galaxy." Jace sprang back, his face red.

Mixy's robe infused with streaks of scarlet and tangerine. "I didn't do it for you, milord. It was the only way to gain some peace in here." He tapped his forehead.

Jace's mouth curved upward. "Why don't you get some rest? It's been an eventful day."

After Mixy left the bridge, Silver lowered herself into the copilot's chair. What would happen now? Eliminating Bluth had been her purpose for so many years, even if she'd only recently been sanctioned for the job. Yet the void she'd feared after completing her mission didn't materialize.

Because of Jace. That realization made her inhale a sharp breath. He'd filled that empty place in her heart.

"I'm setting a course for Kurash, unless you want me to drop you off with Gruber?" Jace asked, resuming his pilot's seat.

"You're not getting rid of me so fast. You still need my help."

"Oh?" He spared her a glance.

"You asked me to examine your crops. They have some kind of blight."

"Ah, yes. We've lost valuable acres to the disease."

That's not why I'm really coming along. "There's another reason why you need me. You're a fugitive with a price on his head. How do you expect to get clearance from Kurash Space Command? I'll have to fly this baby in." *Not to mention this is my ship, not yours.*

Jace locked the controls and swiveled to face her. "Did you ask your uncle to send the proposal to my government?"

"Yes, he supported my idea one hundred percent."

Jace grunted. "Do you really think the Parsate will accept you as Earth's acting ambassador when we're on the verge of war? Our peoples have broken off diplomatic relations."

"Your ruler might think twice about trusting Garth after Kira's transmission. When she boosted our signal through the amp buoy, she sent copies of the files we acquired to Uncle Manny. He'll compress the stream and forward it to Ruler Hurat."

"What good will that do?"

"If we're lucky, Hurat will grant you an audience and hear your version of the story. We have to hope he isn't so far gone that he'll turn down this last chance for a peace agreement. Kira will be sending Bluth's confession ahead, too, once we're within range of the next buoy."

Jace's shoulders slumped, as though he dared not push his hopes too far. "We still have time before the Incantation Ceremony, but if Garth gets wind of this before we reach Hurat, we're finished."

"Then let's hope your king receives our messages on his private channel. If he's a staunch follower of procedure, he'll reconvene the court."

"Unless he's committed to war. In that instance, we'll be arrested and thrown into prison."

"Where does Gruber want to be dropped off? He doesn't need to be part of this."

"You go ask him." Turning away, Jace bent his head over the blinking lights on the command board.

She found Gruber in the galley, polishing off a sandwich.

"Where do you want us to take you?" Silver filled a glass with cold water at the dispenser and gulped greedily.

He gave a nonchalant shrug. "I'll stick with you kids for now. You don't wanna waste time taking me to a transit station. Besides, I gotta keep my nose down for a while."

"You think the remaining Marauders will be searching for you? They'll have better things to do if they decide to reorganize. Like finding a new leader."

"I'd rather take my chances on Kurash." His ears turned red. "Anyway, I need a new job. Everything I had was back on that moon."

Why, you old farlett, you like being part of the team.

She poked him. "Hey, when I get a bigger ship, we could use a tactical officer like you."

"If we survive Kurash, and your new boss at S.I.N. approves your request, then I'll consider it."

Jace swaggered in and poured himself a mug of ale. "None of you have to come with me, you know. This is my battle."

Silver sensed his resentment through their mental link.

Didn't he understand why she was accompanying him home? It wasn't to satisfy her curiosity as an agronomist and examine his wilting crops. She wanted to be with him, to see his title and lands restored, his sister whole again. She'd been through tragedy and knew how important loved ones were for support. If only she'd realized that when her cousins welcomed her, she might not have felt so alone.

Now Jace needed her. She wanted to stand by his side as he fought for justice, rebuilt his estates, and guided his world into an age of peace and progress.

Stars above, she wanted to grow old with him. She couldn't imagine continuing on by herself.

He was part of her universe, her life. But was she part of his?

Uncle Manny had said Dash wanted to speak to her about transferring to Intelligence. Together, she and Kira and Gruber, if he chose to join them, would make a good team. She needn't carry on alone if Jace chose to go his own way.

So with those happy prospects, why did she find herself swallowing back a sob?

Jace glanced at her, startled. She plunked down her water glass, sloshing the liquid. He opened his mouth, but she couldn't bear to hear what he had to say in front of Gruber. She muttered an excuse, stumbled toward the door, and fled.

****

Jace paced the corridor, shaking his head. Women. Silver should be elated over Bluth's demise, yet he felt sadness emanating from her in the galley. Why wasn't she thrilled with their success? She'd even requested a new ship, one bigger and faster and better armed. Obviously, she couldn't wait to resume her work for S.I.N. So what was bothering her?

He couldn't worry about that now. The shackles of his criminal status restrained him. Until he freed himself from the yoke of his past, he couldn't offer her anything. And truth be told, he feared her rejection when he did ask her to stay by his side.

At least Mixy, his one true friend, would stand by him.

Stopping in front of Silver's cabin, he knocked on the door. Despite the frenzy of battle, he hadn't forgotten his sister.

"Who's there?" Shanna's voice squeaked.

"It's me, Jace. Can I come in?"

"Of course you can."

A swell of relief hit him to find Shanna alone. His sister laid on the bed, arms folded across her chest like a corpse. Her skin had the waxy, pale look of one, too.

"Why didn't you get something to eat? You must be hungry," he said, his tone sharp with worry.

"I don't have much of an appetite."

"You'll need your strength for our arrival on Kurash. I can have Mixy bring you a snack."

Shanna struggled to a sitting position. She wore a clean shirt and a pair of pants, obviously borrowed from Silver. She'd needed a belt to cinch the trousers at her tiny waist. Her hair, a dull black, was tied in a ponytail. Shanna looked more like a child than a woman of twenty-four.

"Jace," she said in a small voice, "I'm still trying to cope with the fact that you're alive. Bluth told me you'd been killed along with our parents."

"It must have been terrible for you."

She shivered. "You have no idea."

He waited for her to say more, but her face shuttered with private memories. "When you're ready to talk about it, I'm here to listen. In the meantime, I need your help." Leaning against the wall, he explained how he'd been accused of murder, tossed into prison, and escaped with the help of Connor, Yvette's brother.

"Oh, dear. Poor Connor. What are we going to tell him?" Shanna asked.

"We could tell him that his sister is dead. That's not far from the truth. Her old life is dead to her now." He hoped his voice didn't betray his anger. It was still hard to believe Yvette had chosen to stay with Wagun. Or was his ego bruised because she'd rejected him?

"You think Connor won't believe Yvette chose to stay behind? She enjoys the luxuries Wagun gives her and ignores the conditions under which the slaves are forced to live."

"Yvette told me she'd improved things for the captives. She insisted she could do more good by remaining there."

"That's rubbish, Jace, and you know it. She likes being in control, which is more than most women get to do on Kurash."

"Nonetheless," Jace said, "Connor doesn't have to know everything. If you insist upon telling him a partial truth, just say Yvette found happiness with her mate and sends her loving regards."

"As you wish." Shanna cast her gaze to the floor.

He stalked over and tilted her chin up. "Look at me. You're no longer a slave. Don't act submissive, understand? Not to me, and not to any man. I need you to be strong." *Like Silver.* The thought came unbidden to his mind.

Shanna's eyes moistened. "I'm sorry."

"Don't be sorry. Be angry." He clenched his teeth. "You should be cursing Tyrone Bluth for what he did to us. And cousin Garth… he stole our lives."

"You're right, of course."

"We've lost our estate, our seat in the Parsate, and the confidence of our ruler. The Incantation Ceremony will seal our fate unless we stop Garth, now. He'll be shocked by your appearance. We can use that to our advantage."

****

Their chance came sooner than he'd expected. Ruler Hurat agreed to a private conference at the palace just before the

318

ceremony that would swear in the new Parsaters for a life term. Connor told them the news at the spaceport, where he'd met them at their assigned landing site. Jace embraced him, thankful he still had a few loyal friends and that Hurat was willing to give him an audience despite his failings. Hopefully, his leader had received the communication from Mans Lyonus, Maxima Chancellor of the Terran Consortium.

"I knew you'd return one day to clear your name." Connor stood back to study him. His blond hair gleamed in the sunlight, while his sharp blue eyes perused Jace. "We've been gathering your supporters. You'll have whatever help you need."

Jace's throat clogged, and he took a steadying breath of pine-scented air. "Thanks, my friend. How go your parents? Are they well?"

Connor's face fell. "I guess you haven't heard. My father died in a hunting accident, and my mother passed soon afterward. She couldn't bear so many losses."

"I'm terribly sorry."

"The girls are aboard, yes? You wouldn't have come back without them."

Connor lifted his hopeful gaze toward Shanna who descended the boarding ramp. Mixy didn't have any gowns suitable for a Kuraski noblewoman, so he'd improvised by providing her with a Mynoran dress.

Shanna approached Connor, her emerald eyes glistening and her dark hair arranged in glossy waves. The gown swished at her ankles as she strode forward.

"My lord." Shanna dipped her head at their friend and neighbor.

Connor bowed, then kissed her hand. "Shanna, I am overjoyed that you have returned safely to us."

"Thank you. Forgive me, but I have news of your sister."

She moved off with him, out of range. As she spoke, Connor's consternation grew. His expression changed from disbelief to anger.

Meanwhile, Jace grew aware of Silver's presence from her vanilla scent and comforting mental touch.

He turned, struck dumb by her appearance. No feminine, frilly gowns for her. She wore a silver jumpsuit, utility belt, and knee-high boots. Great Cosmos, what was she thinking? His glance swung to her hair, neatly twisted into a braid, and her defiant face.

"What?" she snapped at him. "I'm not one of your dolls, to be dressed up and hung on your arm. This is me. I can fight better when I'm in my own skin."

"You're not fighting anyone here. Is this how the Terran Consortium's ambassador approaches her first diplomatic mission?" His pitch rose but he couldn't help himself. They needed to make a good impression on Ruler Hurat. His entire future—no, his life—depended on it.

"I'm on your side, Jace. I'm only using the title of ambassador to get an audience with your king. Maybe if your people see me as someone they can't bedazzle, they'll be more respectful."

Respectful, my ass. She'd be the laughingstock of his peers. It wouldn't matter that she came from another world. Visitors were expected to follow their customs.

"I don't suppose I could change your mind?" he said in morose tone.

"No time." She tapped her chronometer. "We'd better go."

The rest of their team followed. Gruber had cleaned himself up to the best of his ability, which meant trimming his scrubby beard, while the Elusians appeared in their ubiquitous robes.

"Don't you dare think about shopping," Kira chided Mixy after he'd closed and sealed the hatch. He punched in the lockout code, securing Silver's ship.

"Preparations must be made for Master Jace's homecoming. I'll have to replenish the food stocks at his estate. We will hold a great feast in his honor." Mixy's hands fluttered in the air while his cobalt robe exhibited tinges of gold.

"Not yet," Jace said with a grim smile. "I know you share my hope that this meeting will go well, but let's not jump the gun, as the Earthlings say. We'll have plenty of time to notify the staff we're home, once our lands are returned. At the moment, Garth holds the deed."

"The traitor. The murdering son of a yellow-bellied snortface." Mixy's robe blackened. "We'll execute him for his crimes. I'll string him up myself. He'll rue the day he set his path against ours."

"Stuff it, Mixy. First we have to convince Ruler Hurat to believe us. You're all coming with me. I may need you as witnesses, and besides, we stick together from now on."

Chapter Twenty-Five

Silver's concern heightened when an armed escort met them outside the security gate and directed them to a waiting vehicle. She plunged inside the ground transport, ignoring the hand Jace offered to assist her.

Not only did he tolerate her presence just to treat his sick plants, but he'd criticized her choice of clothes. It hadn't bothered him before when she'd worn a jumpsuit or pants. Now, when she was being presented to his leader, he expected her to dress like a lady. Did she really want to live among people who held such a provincial attitude?

They rode in silence past suburban developments into a city with narrow streets. She peered out the window, hoping for a glimpse of the capitol building, but they drove to a side door at the ruler's palace.

Inside the massive structure, their escort led them into a spacious room with a high ceiling and ornate furnishings. Before she'd had a chance to admire the paintings on the silk-covered walls, an older man entered wearing a black robe and a solemn expression. He dismissed the guards, who assumed positions outside the room.

"Your Honor," Jace said, looking startled. He gave a deep bow, while Silver sensed his grave apprehension.

She wanted this to turn out well for him. His happiness meant everything to her, despite the distance that had sprung between them.

"This is Chief Magistrate Omar," Jace said in a tight voice. "He presided over my trial."

Omar surveyed him with a stern glare. "Mr. Vernon, I hope this interview leads to a better conclusion than our last." Turning to Connor, he nodded briefly. "Lord Blackstone, it is always a pleasure to see you."

Connor regarded him somberly. "As I am pleased to stand by my neighbor and friend, Lord Vernon. May I present his sister, Shanna? She will vouch for his innocence in the crimes for which he stands accused."

Omar kissed Shanna's hand, while she lifted an imperious eyebrow. Silver was glad to see she wasn't cowed by the judge. Perhaps she'd already regained her confidence just by being home.

Jace presented the rest of them. "Mixy is my personal valet. Kira is my, uh, financial advisor. Gruber is a… bodyguard. And here's Silver Malloy, the ambassador from Earth."

"The ambassador? I thought they'd sent a woman." Omar stared at her. "Great Creator, it is a lady. Pardon me, madam." He swept her a courteous bow, his robe of office sweeping the floor.

Silver stuck out her hand in the customary manner of her people. "How do you do?"

To her surprise, he took her hand and kissed it. Her face flushed, while Kira's robe steaked with scarlet.

"His Eminence told me you have new evidence to reopen your case," Omar said. "You and your sister will accompany me to see Ruler Hurat. As for the rest of your friends, they'll remain here until summoned."

In the empty silence that followed their departure, Mixy stood ramrod straight, his lips pursed and his robe presenting an ever-changing rainbow of colors. Silver couldn't imagine the strain Jace must be feeling under his king's interrogation. Her muscles tensed and her stomach roiled, as though she were there with him. Kira's robe segued into jade, reflecting their mutual anxiety.

Had Hurat received the uplink with Bluth's confession?

The copied files showing Garth's connection to the Marauders and to Fester Niles on Earth? Was Jace even now telling him about the worse threat from the Weavers?

For what seemed like an eternity, she paced back and forth on the polished wood floor, listening for shouts from outside that might indicate things had gone badly. Her auditory sensors didn't pick up anything out of the ordinary.

A servant entered bearing a tray of refreshments, and she finally sank into an armchair. Connor consulted Mixy in a corner, while Kira amused herself by fiddling with her personal reader. Gruber munched on an apple, chewing loudly.

At last, the door flung open, and a uniformed page motioned for them to follow.

Silver balked when they neared an outer door. "Where are we going? Why isn't Jace here?" She refused to budge until they got answers.

"Madam Ambassador, I presume?" said the youth. "I've been ordered to escort you to the Incantation Ceremony. You will rejoin the rest of your party there. It is already past time for the event to begin."

"But what's happened to Jace?" Nothing came through her link, and Mixy's robe had gone neutral. Either Jace was concealing his feelings, or he'd been executed for his crimes. Surely she'd have felt his loss?

Her heart racing, she climbed into the waiting vehicle and vowed revenge if he was dead. This time she wouldn't fail. As soon as someone pointed out Garth Vernon to her, she'd kill the bastard with her poisoned stick pin.

No, you won't.

Squashed between Kira and Gruber on a passenger seat, Silver glanced about. Who'd said that?

Justice shall prevail.

Elation filled her. Jace's triumph came through loud and clear, meaning Ruler Hurat must have accepted his plea.

Breathless with anticipation, she tumbled out as soon as the car stopped. They faced a courtyard filled with people, bleachers seating thousands, and a domed white building with columns.

"This way," their guide said, creating a path through the crowd.

They approached a dais with a single throne on which sat the potentate, his identity obvious by his rich ruby robe, gleaming medallion, and gold crown.

Silver liked his face which reminded her of Uncle Manny. Its many nooks and crannies spoke of years of experience, while the crinkles framing his eyes spoke of wisdom.

She peered around, but Jace and Shanna were nowhere visible.

About a dozen men wearing fancy capes and feathered hats stood on each side of an aisle leading to the raised platform.

"Lord Blackstone, you may take your position," the young man told Connor. "The rest of you will please wait here."

"What's going on?" Silver asked Connor.

"Three new Parsaters are being appointed for a lifetime term. Garth intends to take the vacancy left by Jace's disgrace. He's responsible for my sister's abduction. I won't let that happen."

"What do you mean?"

"If Jace doesn't give Garth what he's due, I will." His lips taut, Connor took his place in line with the other aristocrats.

I don't think so, Silver thought. *It's my job to finish this if anything bad happens to Jace.*

She barely heard the opening remarks, her mind recalling the recent sequence of events.

Tyrone Bluth had conducted the attack on Roth Colony where she'd been researching a potential new fuel. Her discovery might have turned the tide in the Consortium's favor in the event of war. Assuming Fester Niles had been the snitch who leaked information about her work, had he also ordered the assault?

Or had Garth been the one to pull the strings? He could have done it to keep the balance of power in Kurash's court.

The notion of a third party alarmed her more, especially if the Weavers were involved. Clearly Dash needed to send someone to investigate the activity on the rim.

Maybe she should lobby to make her ambassadorial appointment a permanent one. Peace with the Kurashki Alliance would be essential for a united defense should the Weavers become a real threat.

Trumpets sounded, and her attention shifted. Three men emerged from the glittery white building. At the base of the dais, they bowed before their leader. Each man wore a small coronet instead of a feathered hat.

These must be the candidates for the Parsate. That meant Garth was among them. She turned to Mixy, who'd made a choked sound.

"Which one is he?"

Mixy pointed a trembling finger. "The man in the bronze cape. Curse his name forever."

"Where's Jace? I don't see him anywhere, or his sister. And notice how all those officials are men?"

Kira pressed her lips together. "This society is so backward, it's a wonder they have space travel."

Silver gave her an appreciative grin. She could get used to having a friend who shared her opinions.

Ruler Hurat rose to address his people. As a hush fell over the assemblage, he spoke about their system of government, their prospering economy, and their strength at arms.

Silver admitted he was a charismatic leader, punctuating his speech with forceful gestures and moderating his tone to set the mood. But she didn't hear a word about how their failing crops were raising prices, or how a traitor had infiltrated their court and sold them out.

"Step forward," Hurat commanded the candidates at the completion of his speech.

Reporters aimed holovid cameras in their direction. Giant mounted screens broadcast the ceremony to the crowd and presumably to the millions watching at home.

"Lord Cameron, kneel before us. We bestow upon you the honored title of Parsater, so that you may serve the Kurashki Alliance with loyalty to your Ruler and your people. Do you swear to abide by our laws and to die should you knowingly betray us?"

"Yes, Your Eminence, I swear to do my duty to king and country, to put my peoples's needs before my own, and to forfeit my life should I willingly subvert these goals."

"Then we grant you this badge of office." Hurat took a feathered hat from a page and offered it to Lord Cameron. The nobleman stood, exchanged his coronet for the hat, then joined the row of staid Parsaters.

The other Lord went next, and soon it was Garth's turn. Surely Ruler Hurat didn't plan to award Garth this honor? Yet as Silver watched in horrified dismay, the king proceeded with the ceremony until Garth had sworn his fealty. However, when Garth stood, Ruler Hurat did not offer him a hat. Instead, he held out a sword.

"What is this?" Garth cried, his face stunned.

"My people, we wish to replay a message we received in secret from the leader of the Terran Consortium," their monarch proclaimed. "All this while, we have been preparing for hostilities between our federations, because we believed our enemy meant to go to war. We were fed a bunch of lies. Earth's people are our friends. They seek peace and trade agreements, not combat. Our enemy lies within."

The crowd gave a collective gasp while Silver's jaw dropped. Onto the monitor screens came their recording of Tyrone Bluth's final confession, a message from Mans Lyonus, and a statement made by Shanna and Jace Vernon about events that had transpired.

And then Jace and Shanna were there bowing before the king, accompanied by the Chief Magistrate.

Facing them, Garth paled and his eyes bulged.

"Jace Vernon," said Ruler Hurat, "you are hereby given a

formal pardon and absolved of any guilt in the murder of your parents. Lands that were taken from you shall be restored along with your full titles and other properties. In addition, you are to be compensated for the injustice done you. I cede you all that belongs to your cousin, Garth Vernon, including his life."

Garth turned to run, but guards quickly moved into place, blocking his flight.

"This man is our enemy," Hurat's deep voice boomed. "We have received copies of financial transactions between him and other conspirators. This heinous crime reaches beyond our borders, and we will need help to mend the breaches. The Terran Consortium has sent us an ambassador. Lady Silver will act as liaison between our governments so we can forge a lasting peace. Madam, please step forward."

Silver strode to a spot beside Jace, who sent her reassuring vibes. Unsure of the proprieties, she gave an awkward curtsey to his leader. Maybe a gown would have been more appropriate, but they might as well see right off the bat that she had a brain and the guts to use it. She expected equal treatment and wouldn't accept anything less.

She held her head high while Hurat regarded her with an amused twinkle.

"Lord Jace Vernon, before you can be named Parsater as is your rightful place, there must be a vacancy. Accept the boon that we gave you."

"I will not take my cousin's life." His spine stiff, Jace shot Garth a venomous glance.

"He has sworn his oath. Give him the sword so he can carry out his own sentence."

Garth didn't accept the proffered instrument of his death. He uttered a strangled cry, and in the next instant, lay on the ground, writhing. Foam issued from his mouth, his eyes wild.

"Poison, eh?" Jace scoffed. "Even now, you take the coward's way out. Die quickly, cousin."

Soon it was over, and the body removed. Silver stood by,

stunned at the rapid turn of events. She stepped back while Jace was sworn in as the final candidate for Parsater.

At last, he'd gotten everything he had wanted—justice for his parents, the safe return of his sister, an honorable title for himself, and his estates restored to the family. She couldn't be happier for him.

But not for herself. She'd keep her promise to examine his crops and to open peace negotiations with Hurat. But then she would leave, soaring off to her next adventure with Kira and Gruber for company. Her heart ached for missing Jace and Mixy. Already Jace was so caught up in his world that he'd left her standing alone.

"Sire, since I was unable to take advantage of your generous boon regarding the traitor," Jace said, "I wish to request another."

Ruler Hurat smiled. "We might allow this slight diversion from protocol. What is it you desire, Lord Vernon?"

"The Lady Silver's hand in marriage, Your Eminence," he said, while murmurs arose from the assemblage.

Silver gasped, her heart skipping. Jace turned to her, and she saw in his eyes what he had never said aloud.

"This would be an important alliance between our races," Hurat mused for the benefit of the microphones. "I understand the lady is niece to the Maxima Chancellor. Will he give his consent?"

"Excuse me," Silver interrupted, "but we don't ask permission of guardians on my world. Women have the right to choose their own husbands, to vote, and to dress as they please, I might add."

Hurat's grin broadened. "Are you sure you wish to contend with this feisty female for the rest of your life, my lord?"

"Oh yes," Jace said, capturing her gaze. "We'll need her input if we're to face those threats on the horizon. Our women can no longer stand in our shadows. We must work together to defend ourselves, and that means everyone. Lady Silver will help us take the first steps toward a new future."

"May I have a word?" she said to him. At Hurat's nod, she drew Jace aside.

"Is this an actual proposal? You realize I'm no ambassador. It's a temporary role. And I wouldn't be a very docile wife."

Jace took her hand, swirling his thumb in her palm. "That reminds me, deermin. We received a communication from your cousin, Dash. He's sending you a GW Magnus VI Corvette with an ion cannon, antiflux missiles, and a chameleon device, in addition to the standard weaponry."

"What about a crew?" While grateful, she couldn't operate a ship that size on her own.

"Fifty people, some of whom are ex-military, to support your missions. And get this, Dash offered me a job as a S.I.N. operative."

"That's absurd. You have too much to do, between getting your estates in order and meeting with the other Parsaters and such."

He shrugged, while she resisted the urge to hug him. "Oh, I don't know. I like roaming the stars and getting into trouble, especially with you. Just think how much fun it would be if we worked together—a trained assassin and a former felon in covert ops."

"You're joking."

His expression sobered, while she was aware that everyone strained to overhear them. "I'm deadly serious. We're a team, remember? And I love you more than life itself. I can't imagine going forward without you at my side. Will you marry me?"

She looked into his warm, hopeful eyes. Joy buoyed her, lightened her spirits, and made her want to leap with happiness.

"Yes, I will be your wife. But only if I don't have to wear a skirt or call you my lord."

Laughing, he caught her in his arms and kissed her, as cheers erupted all around.

The End.

Author's Note

Thank you for taking the time to read my book. If you enjoyed the story, please consider writing a review at your favorite online bookstore. Reader recommendations are critically important in helping new readers find my work. Find links here - https://nancyjcohen.com/silver-serenade/

I loved creating Silver and Jace's story and following them on their out-of-this-world adventure. I hope this tale provided you with several magical hours of escape. If you want more in this genre, check out *Keeper of the Rings*, another futuristic standalone novel. See the excerpt below.

If you like mysteries, check out my Bad Hair Day cozy mystery series. These are available in print and digital editions, and some are in audiobook as well. They're also bundled as box sets.

****

For updates on my new releases, giveaways, special offers and events, join my reader list at https://nancyjcohen.com/newsletter. Free Book Sampler for new subscribers.

Keeper of the Rings Excerpt
Copyright © 1996 by Nancy J. Cohen

Chapter One

"If we don't start soon, I'm going to faint. Dear deity, what if I trip over this thing when we're called to the dais?"

Leena adjusted her royal blue robe with trembling fingers. Unaccustomed to its length, she grimaced at the sight of her satin slippers peeking out beneath the hem. She couldn't believe she'd earned the privilege of wearing the sacramental vestment.

Karole patted her shoulder. "You'll do fine. You always appear so well poised."

Leena met her friend's gaze. "Today is different. My father is in the congregation, and I don't want to embarrass him. And where's my brother? It's unlike Bendyk to be late."

"He could be seated with your father in the Inner Sanctum. They're not allowed back here." Karole swept her arm in a broad gesture encompassing the Robing Salon. Their fellow initiates stood around fidgeting like lower school graduates.

"You're right." Leena placed the ceremonial headdress over her head of blond hair.

Soon she and her newfound friends would become official members of the aide corps that served the Synod, the ruling body of priests on Xan. They awaited a signal from Dikran, the Arch Nome, who would begin the annual Renewal service. At its completion, Leena would assume her honored role as a Caucus delegate.

Her pulse raced with excitement. Ever since she was a child, she'd wanted to learn more about the Apostles who had established the religion of Sabal on her world. Her father, a high-ranking Candor, had inspired her interest in archeology by his study of ancient religious texts.

Growing up beside a crumbling ruin had sparked her imagination as she thought about life in days of old. Where had the Apostles originated? They'd established the magnificent reign of Lothar, their god, and then vanished. Why did they leave, and where had they gone?

Craving knowledge of her forebears, Leena realized the Synod held the key to wisdom. The ecclesiastical leaders were privy to secrets known to no one else. Joining the Caucus was the swiftest route to enlightenment.

A solemn bearded figure marched into the room. Planting himself firmly in the center, he peered around at the young initiates, waiting until everyone fell silent.

"It is time," Zeroun intoned.

"Holy waters." Leena's knees quaked. "I can't believe we've made it this far. May Lothar guide us."

"You're supposed to be near the front." Karole prodded her. "Get in line."

Leena wiped her sweaty palms against her flowing robe. Not even her graduation from archeological college had made her this nervous. Was it because Malcolm was in the congregation?

Her wealthy neighbor had been after her hand in marriage for several years now. Lately Leena had been inclined to accept, mainly for the security he could offer. She felt mildly affectionate toward him, but something made her hesitate.

Lining up behind the others, she tilted her chin in the air and marched forward with Zeroun in the lead. Leena had been in the cathedral-like Inner Sanctum many times during the past six weeks of training, but it hadn't prepared her for the sea of faces that greeted them in the cavernous hall.

She took a seat along with the nineteen other initiates in the front row that had been reserved for them. The members of the Synod filed in, claiming their spaces on the dais.

Arch Nome Dikran sat on a throne-like chair, wearing his gold robe with the dignity that befit his eighty years. A towering headdress covered his head, and it was much more resplendent than the simple ones Leena and her friends wore.

She may not care for formal dress, but because her father held a high position, she was accustomed to elaborate affairs.

As she settled the robe about her legs, she wished for the comfort of the breeches and short-sleeved shirts she wore on her archeological digs. There was no pretense when you scoured a site for ancient treasures.

Malcolm didn't approve of her career. He would expect his wife to stay at home and manage his household. Leena had plenty of experience in managing her father's property, having done so ever since her mother's death five years ago. That tragic accident had given her brother his true calling.

Where was Bendyk? She craned her neck, searching for her brother's familiar face, but she didn't spot his blond head anywhere in the crowd. Returning her attention forward, she mentally checked off the dignitaries on the dais.

Sirvat, the most prominent woman on the Synod, looked stiffly proper in her white robe tied with the gold sash of office. Magar sat beside her, his eyes twinkling beneath a crop of white hair. Karayan, a family friend, caught Leena's eye and smiled. Flushing, she looked down at her blue robe, eagerly anticipating the moment when she would be given the gold cord signifying her as an ordained servant of Lothar.

She shifted impatiently, watching Dikran rise and approach the podium. His shuffling gait proclaimed his age, but his dark eyes were sharp as they pierced the crowd like orbs of glowing embers. The service began with a hymn praising Lothar for his beneficence.

"We come here today before the face of our deity, the miraculous Lothar," Dikran spoke into a microphone. "Together in worship, we sanctify our existence and praise Lothar, ruler of Xan. Who is like unto you, O Holy One, majestic and awesome in splendor? Who can compare to your generosity? Let the name Lothar be hallowed unto the world for all time. Let his name be glorified and exalted although he is beyond praise, because he is so mighty and powerful."

The congregation raised their voices in a hymn, and Leena's song joined them. The familiar melody brought her the same calm serenity as it had throughout her life at similar services. Renewal was a time to recall one's past deeds, one's joys and triumphs, one's tragedies and sorrows, and to look ahead to the new year with reborn hope.

"May the coming year bring us peace, joy, and exaltation." Dikran raised his arms toward the vaulted ceiling. "May you bless us, O Lothar, with plentiful rains so our crops may grow bountiful and our fields be fertile. May our rivers flow and our lakes remain unblemished.

"We count on you, O Holy One, to maintain our land and to provide us with your blessing that keeps us from ill health. May our redemptive labors make us happy and our struggle for purity not fail. Let us toil at our work to the best of our ability. Blessed is the vision of holiness that exalts us from on high."

Leena joined in a series of responsive readings. Her heart opened to Lothar and his generosity to her people. Truly they were blessed to have such a wonderful god looking out for them. He provided them with fertile soil with which to grow adequate foodstuffs. Xan was a rich, bountiful world. The lakes and rivers teemed with fish. The land blossomed with fruit, and the air was pure and clear. Truly, what more could anyone want?

Zeroun got up and exchanged places with Dikran. Minister of Religion, Zeroun's presence was powerful, the hunch of his shoulders indicative of his forcefulness.

"Praised be Lothar who unifies all creation." His gaze pierced the congregation as though he would read their souls. "May the Holy One fill our minds with knowledge and our hearts with wisdom, and praise those who labor to bring harmony to our world. Let the next year be a fruitful one for us. Be gracious, O Lothar, and treat us generously. Be our teacher and guide." He raised his hands toward heaven.

As the choir began to sing, melodious music filled the clerestory. Leena's heart soared with faith and love for Lothar. *Please help me clear my father's name*, she prayed. *I know the answers are here in your Holy Temple. I vow that I will find them before the next Renewal.*

The communion of those around her filled her with comfort and peace as she followed the service.

"Let us bend in humility before Lothar." Zeroun bowed low, his headdress dipping. "Let us give praise unto the one who established our land."

"May the Holy One be gracious and bring us peace," the congregation intoned in unison.

"As the new year begins, so is hope reborn," said Zeroun. "Lothar has been resting after the toil of the harvest, but now is the time for Renewal. We must blow the sacred horn to awaken our god from his rest so the life cycle may begin anew. Behold the vessel for summoning Lothar."

Karayan, Minister of Justice, and Eznik, Minister of Labor, rose and approached a set of immense carved wooden doors at the rear of the Grand Altar. Uttering incantations, they reached out to draw the doors apart in front of the awed congregation.

Leena held her breath. The sound of the horn was more than a symbol for ushering in the new year. It summoned Lothar, and when he awoke, he reset the climatic cycles of Xan for another year. Without his beneficence, her world would revert to the wild, untamed fury of the past. No one ever wanted that to happen. It would mean the end to civilization as they knew it. Renewal was the pinnacle of all the seasonal holidays.

"Show us the horn," Dikran shouted as he faced the rear.

Karayan and Eznik drew the doors apart, and a collective gasp went up from the congregation.

Emptiness yawned from within the richly lit interior.

"Dear deity," Leena whispered. Where was the sacred horn?

Dikran had a stunned look on his face, while the other members of the Synod wore horror-stricken expressions. Dikran cast a quick glance at Zeroun before indicating the doors should be shut.

As he stepped forward to the podium, he signaled the choir. A trumpet always played after the horn to reflect the holy voice. Now the trumpet player began a haunting melody that reverberated throughout Leena's soul. When he finished, the congregation remained mute.

Dikran, his expression stony, spoke into the microphone. "Our opening of the holy chamber this year was symbolic. The sacred horn, after so many years of continuous use, has required a cleansing in sacramental water. We have blown the trumpet in its stead. It is Lothar's will that this be done. Hear us, Holy One, and awaken from your rest."

He raised his hands toward the congregation. "Bless our people and grant them freedom from sickness and sorrow. Let us love our neighbor as ourselves, walk humbly with our god, and convert our thoughts into faith and our words into good deeds. And so we say, Mahala."

He beamed pontifically. "And now, it gives me great pleasure to call upon our initiates. These young people have dedicated their lives to serving the Synod. By their faith, they serve Lothar and thus you, the people. Treat them with the respect due their station. You may step upon the dais." He gestured to the trainees with an imperious wave.

Holy waters, it's time. Leena trembled as she made her way to the elevated platform. On the dais, she faced the congregation in line with her fellow initiates. One by one, Zeroun called them by name. He gave each candidate a lit candle and a gold sash signifying their station. Holding their candles, they repeated the words they had rehearsed.

"We pledge ourselves to serve the members of the Synod

in good faith, with loyalty, dedication and compassion, and in so doing we pledge ourselves to you, O blessed Lothar. Praised be the power that brings us peace and prosperity. Praise Lothar, who sanctifies us all. Mahala."

They blew out their candles to denote the end of the Renewal ceremony. The congregation remained in place while Dikran, the Synod members, and the new Caucus filed from the sanctuary to head for the reception hall.

A huge feast had been prepared, for Renewal was a happy, joyous occasion. Lothar was awakening. He would provide for them for another whole year, a year free from ill health, a year blessed with bountiful fruit and produce of the land.

Leena's heart soared with joy as she followed her robed companions through the nave toward an archway at the rear.

Someone planted a hand on her shoulder in the reception hall. He whirled her around and planted a firm kiss on her lips.

"I'm proud of you." Malcolm flashed her a grin that showed his white, even teeth.

Leena scanned his handsome features. His brown eyes reflected warmth and something more when he looked at her.

"Thank you," she murmured, pleased by his sincerity. "Have you seen Father?"

"He's over by the refreshment table. Can I get you a drink?"

"Yes, I'd like that."

She glanced around for Karole, wanting to introduce her friend to Malcolm, but couldn't locate her in the crowd. People stood about in clusters, drinks in hand, chatting and laughing. Friends and relatives had come from miles away for this special occasion.

Most people attended religious services in their hometowns or at the regional worship centers, but guests of the elite were invited to participate in services at the Holy Temple, and such invitations were highly coveted.

Leena wondered where Dikran had gone. She wanted to

put in a good word with the Arch Nome for her father. But Dikran was nowhere in sight, and neither were the top members of the Synod. Where had they gone?

Dikran should be here to give his blessing to the bread so they could eat. But it was Jirair, Minister of Agriculture, who offered the prayer. A moment of doubt overwhelmed her as she recalled the stunned looks on Dikran's and the others' faces when they noticed the horn's absence.

Had it really been intentional that the horn not be here for Renewal, or was this a surprise to the Synod that Dikran had hastily covered up? They were certainly experts at cover-ups, as she well knew.

Malcolm interrupted her thoughts by returning with a cup of fruit punch.

"Thanks." She gulped the drink down, her throat dry.

"What's the matter? You look worried."

She lowered her voice. "The sacred horn… do you really think it's being cleaned? This seems an odd time to be doing a chore like that. We need the horn blown for Lothar to reset the cycles."

Malcolm raised an eyebrow. "Are you calling Dikran a liar?"

Leena's heart skipped, because it *was* Dikran's veracity she questioned. Fortunately, she was saved from a response by her father's arrival.

"Congratulations, my dear." Cranby embraced Leena in a huge bear hug. He was a large man, and his crimson robe of office made him even more imposing.

"Thank you, Father." Sliding back, she gazed at him with loving affection.

Gray sprinkled his blond hair, receding from a high forehead. Years of grief over the loss of his wife had dulled a set of blue eyes similar to her own. Clearly a pressing matter weighed heavily on his mind as he regarded her with an anxious expression.

"Have you heard from your brother?"

"He's not here? I tried to contact him earlier, but communications to Amat were out. I can't imagine what might have happened. He should have arrived by now." Her stomach churned. It was unlike Bendyk to be so late.

Malcolm raised his hand. "I'll go make inquiries. Amat is located in Seacrest Bay?" At Leena's nod, he hastened away.

"Malcolm is a fine young man," Cranby said, eyeing her carefully.

Leena lowered her lashes. "I'm still not sure about him, Father."

His look grew stern. "You've achieved a great deal for a woman of twenty-five years, daughter. Now it's time to think about your future."

"I've just been admitted into the Caucus. My immediate future is here." Her heart sank, knowing where this conversation was leading, but she tried to head him off regardless.

"Do you hope to be promoted to Docent, as do many of your peers?" Cranby pursed his lips. "I hadn't known you to be so religiously inclined."

Leena guarded her expression. Her father didn't know the true reason she'd joined the Caucus, and it was best he remain ignorant. Otherwise, he'd warn her against her course of action.

She didn't mean to stir up trouble but meant to uncover the truth about her religion's origins to quell the doubts in her heart. Leena wasn't the only one questioning their faith. The Truthsayers protested rule by the Synod. They demanded reforms, claiming Lothar was a false god created by the priests. The spate of recent weather disasters gave solidity to their words and shook the credibility of their religion.

The Synod proclaimed Lothar was angry at the people and punished them for their doubts, but Lothar was normally a god of compassion and mercy. There had to be some other reason for the climate changes on Xan, something only the Synod knew. That was another item of information she hoped to discover.

Her father shook his finger at her. "Mark my words, not another Beltane will pass with Malcolm and you unpledged. I shall speak to his father myself. It is still within my authority to troth you a husband, miss, and so I shall."

"I don't want a husband right now. I have too much to do in my new role."

"Nonsense, that's just an excuse. You dilly-dally too long, and this indecisiveness is unbecoming in a lady. You'll lose the young man if you don't snare him now."

"I'm not ready."

"You'll never be ready at your pace." He glowered at her. "No more arguments. The matter is settled."

Leena bit back a retort as the Minister of Justice bore down on them.

"Cranby, my old friend." Karayan slapped a hand on Cranby's shoulder, then vigorously shook both his hands as was the custom. "How good to see you again, and what a thrill to celebrate your lovely daughter's success." His pale grey eyes swung to Leena, expressing approval.

"I'm looking forward to serving the Synod." She smiled warmly. Karayan had always supported her father, even during his censure.

Karayan gave a slight bow. "You honor your family by your service." He tilted his head at Cranby. "I understand your son Bendyk is earning a name for himself as a missionary. We have word that requests are pouring in from the villages for his counsel. If he keeps going at this pace, I see him being appointed soon as a Docent. Where is the young man?" Karayan glanced around. "I thought he was supposed to join us today."

"Bendyk never got in. I called Amat earlier but couldn't get through." Leena adjusted her headdress, which had begun to tilt. The heavy piece made her temples ache. When could she get away to change into more comfortable clothes? Probably not until this reception was over.

Karayan's eyes widened. "Did you say Bendyk was in

Amat? We've just received word that there's been a terrible disaster at Seacrest Bay. A tsunami struck last night. There have been massive casualties, and a rescue effort is underway. I'm uncertain of the details."

"Dear Lord." Leena's knees quivered. "Bendyk was supposed to leave last night. I hope he made it out."

Karayan laid a hand on her arm. "The Synod has called an emergency meeting to deal with the tragedy. Come with me."

She gave her father a brief kiss and hurried after Karayan. Muttering a quick prayer that her brother would be found safe and unharmed, she followed Karayan through the maze-like corridors of the Palisades complex.

Order Now: https://nancyjcohen.com/keeper-of-the-rings/

Glossary

Abrasor: A medical instrument.

Aircar: A form of low flight transportation using antigravity technology.

Al'ron: A dusty planet where outlaws come to buy arms, men, and equipment.

Altuis Three: Colony where Silver grew up until attacked by Tyrone's Marauders.

Amp Buoy: Communication amplifier in space network.

Anhunda: A type of meaty fish, usually farmed like tilapia.

Anriat: Mining Colony.

Antiflux Missiles: A concussive weapon that carries an armor-piercing warhead.

Aromatic Sphere: A round aromatherapy air diffuser.

Atrani: Bond-mate to an Elusian.

Attocaine: An injectable painkiller.

Autorama: Meal-ordering device at Stacktown.

Avenger: Silver's scout ship, a GW Nova 14 built for speed and evasion.

Balak Province: A territory on Kurash ruled by a landholder.

Basic: A universal language.

Bellamia: A term of endearment.

Bangleberries: An edible fruit.

Bartlett Station: A space station with a scientific outpost that offers ship repairs, dining, and a merchant corridor.

Biodromes: Biosphere settlements in the outer colonies.

Blaster Bomb: A concussion device.

Botdrone: An automated attendant.

Bramblejuice Bushes: A prickly shrub.

Branna Leaf: An herb used in a healing potion.

Brookworms: A food delicacy from Elusia used to make mog soup.

Bulkhead: A barrier between separate compartments on a ship.

Bunger Snake: Poisonous snake on Kurash.

Capsilon Spice Sticks: A valued spice used for flavoring.

Carolla Nuts: A rare nut found on Stacktown, harvested every five years, and used to make carollium oil.

Carollium: A valuable fuel made from carolla nuts.

Chaklah Bread: A loaf of egg bread like challah.

Chameleon Device: A technology that creates a warp in the fabric of space surrounding a vessel so energy slips around it as though the ship weren't there.

Cilica Crystals: A luminescent mineral found in caves.

Clastine: A hard plastic-type material.

Comax System: A star system located in neutral space.

Communicor: Communication device in Stacktown.

Conduser Platform: A component of ship-to-ship communications.

Coolant Generator Coils: Cooling mechanism for ship's reactor.

Corvette: A mid-size ship with six double turboboost laser batteries.

Crawlers: Ant-like insects on Kurash.

Crockers: A reptilian carnivorous race from the Raptor star system.

Delium: A strong painkiller.

Deermin: A term of endearment.

Dingbat: Flying rodent.

Disruptor: A personal energy weapon with settings from stun to vaporize.

Dockwing Formation: An attack strategy.

Dorians: Tall and rangy aliens with speckled skin from Dorius. They fought against the Kurashki Alliance in the recent conflict.

Duranium Alloy: A metal alloy.

Elusia: A planet whose people have the capacity to form a mental bond with another. Their race has slight builds, delicate features, and no sex hormones. They reproduce by budding.

Elusian Robes: These garments reflect the emotions of its wearer and, if bonded, of the *atrani*.

Blue—neutral

Amber—sad

Tangerine—affection

Orange—happy

Pink—sexual attraction

Rose—love

Scarlet—embarrassment

Purple—lying

Gold—excitement

Green—annoyance or disdain

Jade—agitation

Black—anger or fear

Expansionist Party: Political party on Earth that wants to expand colonial influence.

Falkner's World: A neutral planet known as a financial haven.

Farlett: Someone who kvetches a lot. A whiner.

Feeder Conduits: Part of a ship's drive system.

Findale: A planet whose people have bony foreheads and shimmering hair.

Formatron: Fingerprint security device.

Foticular Shield Generator: Generates a shield that protects a ship against energy beam weapons but does not stop matter. Emits omincron particles.

Fried Sorgut Bellies: Popular junk food.

Grappling Locks: Used in docking maneuvers.

Gravicom Wells: Well-known shipyards near Earth.

Gunship: A heavily armed ship used for combat.

Hakah Pipe: Curved pipe used to smoke pungent grasses.

Holoflicks: Holographic Movies.

Hoatch Foundation: Organization that supports scientific research.

Hyperdrive: Form of propulsion that uses a fusion generator to enable faster-than-light speeds through hyperspace, a distortion of the space-time continuum.

Hyperdrive Actuators: Parts needed for hyperdrive to function.

Inox Truffles: An underground fungus with a rough skin that is eaten as a delicacy.

Ion Trail: Ionized particles left in the wake of a ship.

Jalobies: Tight-fitting leather pants.

Jinars: A currency exchange like money.

Joyfa Bars: Outlawed weed that produces pungent smoke and euphoria.

Kaloran Sector: Charted space territory in shipping lanes.

Kelius Two: Planet circled by three moons, one of which is Bluth's hideout.

Kewl Sticks or Kewlwood Incense Sticks: Wood tapers that give off a foul smell when lit.

Krellian Steak: Tender meat from range-fed Krellian cattle.

Kurash: Jace's home world.

Kurashki Alliance: Kurash and its conquered worlds and satellites ruled by a hereditary potentate.

Kurl Vines: Gnarled vines close to the ground.

Landrover: A form of ground transportation using antigravity technology.

Levelator: A form of transport like an elevator that goes horizontal as well as vertical.

Lillysnort: Fool.

Lupella Blooms: Lilac-type flower that grows in mountain valleys on Kurash.

Magna Beam: Generates a magnetic field to tow another vessel.

Mantay Fish: Tasty wild fish caught at sea.

Marlberries: A juicy berry like a mulberry.

Matue Pot: Incense burner.

Medivac: Medical evacuation vehicle.

Melarian Brandy: A prized brandy from the mountain province on Melaria.

Mog Soup: A nourishing soup on Elusia made from brookworms.

Mok Tay: The instant when an Elusian bonds to a human during a moment of extreme duress.

Molecular Unit Matrix: Also known as MUM, this device mixes molecules into desired configurations to make food, clothing, and other basic supplies.

Molecular Transport: A rudimentary transporter system that dissembles molecules at one terminal and reassembles them at another.

Monduran: A scaly-faced mercenary.

Mynorans: Merchants who dress flamboyantly and trade high tech goods.

Nacosian: Humanoid alien with eyes on flexible stalks.

Nav Computer: Navigational system.

Omnicron Particles: By-product of foticular generator.

Optiplex: Retinal scanning device.

Orelian: Tall, brawny race with tanned skin from the Menagua system.

Parsate: Government system on Kurash like Senate or House of Lords.

Parsator: Representative of above.

Pava Melon: A sweet fruit grown in tropical climate on Stacktown.

Pedway: A moving walkway.

Peratoes: Root vegetable like a potato grown on Kurash.

Pickled Ochart's Tongue: A delicacy made from the tongue of an ochart beast found in the outer provinces.

Predator-Class Starship: A battleship used for ship-to-ship combat.

Quantum Grenade: Grenade that produces a concussive blast.

Realspeed: The Kittering-Bosch ion engine moves ships through real space by breaking down fuel into charged particles. The resulting energy vents from the vessel, providing thrust.

Rec Bot: Robot programmed for recreational pursuits.

Rejuv Treatments: Rejuvenation procedures to erase signs of aging.

Remnant Two: A moon with a trading post and repair station.

Repellant Shields: Provides added reinforcement to armor plating on a warship by strengthening adherence of molecules.

Repository: A private reserve bank.

Reverrock: A reddish rock on Al'ron.

Roth Colony: Settlement where Silver did her research until destroyed by Tyrone's Marauders.

Rothgut Bait: Worms used to bait a rothgut fish.

Rubilite: A valuable red-colored gemstone.

Sarcoid: A native of Sarcoidonia. They possess blue skin and emit an electrical charge.

Sawbone: A freighter converted into a hospital ship, commanded by Captain Keelo.

Scout Ship: A small vessel built for speed and maneuverability with limited armaments.

Secondary Drive Modulators: A backup system for the realspeed engines.

Sela: Lady.

S.I.N.: Security Integrated Network is the Intelligence division for the Terran Consortium.

Sirrah: Sir.

Slicer Disk: Curved blade weapon.

Sonic Grenade: Grenade that produces a disabling sound wave blast.

Stacktown: A mysterious planet that is the source of carolla nuts.

Stemlings: Pre-teen on Elusia.

Stentorian wine: A common label red wine made from a blend of grapes and other fruit from Stentoria.

Stinger: Jace's ship, a KDY Model 10 Torris with a laser cannon and antiflux missiles.

Takeover Bids: A card game played in the Terran Consortium.

Talusican Ale: A popular type of ale.

Tangleberries: A type of berry that grows on a shrub on Al'ron and emits a spicy scent.

Terran Consortium: A confederation of Earth and its colonies.

Tiger Gnats: Flying insects with orange and black spotted wings.

Trona: A durable metal used in construction.

Turanium: A valued metal like platinum.

Turbo Scooter: A flying scooter utilizing antigrav technology and turbo boosters.

Tyrone's Marauders: Space pirates who terrorize outlying colonies and shipping lanes.

Vector: Heading.

Vidcam: Security camera.

Viewscreen: Clear screen viewport on the bridge of a ship.

Weavers: A mysterious race reputed to live beyond the Wolf's Tail Nebula.

Wonkby: A horned wild animal.

Wyndcor Particles: Air pollution found on Elusia.

Xerxes Imperialate: Empire bordering the Terran Consortium on the opposite side from the Kurashki Alliance and Dorius.

Yagith Perimeter: An area in neutral space.

Yamens: An ally in the Terran Consortium.

Yurb: A serf in the Xerxes Imperialate.

Zeeworm: A large worm-like creature that lives underground.

Zolifar: Hell.

Weapons and Warships

Weapons

Antiflux Missiles: Concussive weapons that carry an armor-piercing warhead. They cause blast damage to targets. Favored on small vessels for surface assaults.

Blaster Bombs: A concussion device.

Chameleon Device: A technology that creates a warp in the fabric of space surrounding a vessel so energy slips around it as though the ship isn't there.

Ion Cannon Batteries: Highly energized ion particles used to disrupt electronic systems.

Laser Cannon Emitter Arrays: Deployed on lightly armed vessels.

Magna Beams: Used to generate a magnetic field and tow another vessel.

Proton Torpedo Launchers: Used to launch proton-scattering energy warheads effective against shielded targets.

Turboboost Laser Batteries: Heavy lasers equipped with turbine generators and capacitor banks to build and store energy for a powerful laser pulse burst. Can penetrate planetary defenses, plus shields and armor plating of military vessels. Lower firing rate than ordinary lasers.

Personal Firearms

TechVix LD-6 Sharpshooter Special: A laser rifle with a multi-spectrum targeting sight.

Laser Carbine Rifles: Laker G6; TechVix B460 (Silver)

Laser pistols: TechVix KL-24 (Silver); Zed CX 920; Laker Super 7 Special produces blue laser fire.

Disruptor: Personal energy weapon that can range from stun to vaporize. Z-Max 580.

Sleeping Gas: Break a rod and gas is emitted

Sonic Grenades (disabling sound wave blast) and Quantum Grenades (concussive blast)

Slicer Disk: A small curved blade. Jace carries one up his sleeve.

Shields

Deflector Shield: Protects against lasers, missiles, and space debris, but it must be temporarily shut down to launch or receive shuttlecraft.

Foticular Shield: Protects against energy beam weapons but does not stop matter. Uses a lot of power so is mostly deployed as an extra layer of protection in battle. Emits omincron particles as a side product.

Repellant Shield: Provides added reinforcement to armor plating on a warship by strengthening adherence of molecules.

Ships

Scout: A small vessel built for speed and maneuverability with limited armaments.

GW (Gravicom Wells) Nova 14 has a large cargo space, 4 passenger cabins, a laser gunnery turret and a magna beam. Built for speed and evasion. The Avenger is Silver's ship.

KDY (Kurash Drive Yards) Model 10 Torris has a laser cannon array and 2 antiflux missile tubes. The Stinger is Jace's ship.

Corvette: A mid-size vessel with six double turboboost laser batteries. Can reconfigure for less cargo hold and more weaponry. Or more passengers. Its flaw is a stabilizer fin. Hits to this fin can cause heat build-up in the main reactor located directly below. Can upgrade the shielding to protect the fin.

Length: 160 meters

Crew: 35-165

Passengers: Up to 400

Cargo: 3,000 metric tons

Weapons: 6 double turboboost laser batteries

Bluth's ship at Al'ron is a Pamorian T-80 Corvette equipped with a foticular field generator.

Silver gets a GW Kelvin Class IV Corvette to go to Stacktown.

New ship Dash sends her is a GW Magnus VI with a crew of 50.

Gunship: A heavily armed ship used for combat.

Length: 120 meters

Crew: 25

Cargo: 300 metric tons

Weapons: 14 turboboost batteries (8 doubles + 6 quads); 4 antiflux missile tubes. Batteries are manually operated and cannot be controlled from the bridge.

Frigate: A warship with mixed armament, lighter than a destroyer. Escort Frigates are larger and better armed but slower than a Corvette.

Destroyer: A small, fast warship. Orion-Class Destroyers are designed for planetary defense and attack.

Length: 1000 meters

Crew: 5100

Cargo: 8200 metric tons

Weapons: 50 turboboost batteries (10 quads + 40 doubles); 80 antiflux missile tubes; 10 magna beam projectors

Cruiser: A large, fast warship; smaller than a battleship and larger than a destroyer.

GW Tag 120 Star Cruisers

Length: 1400 meters

Crew: 5600

Cargo: 20,000 metric tons

Weapons: 48 turboboost batteries; 20 ion cannon batteries; 6 magna beam projectors

Fitted with the new hyperdrive upgrade, a chameleon device, 40 antiflux missles, and reinforced repellant shields.

Battleship: A heavily armored warship with large-caliber guns.

Predator-Class Starship is used for ship-to-ship combat.

Length: 1700 meters

Crew: 35,000

Cargo: 38,000 metric tons

Weapons: 60 turboboost batteries, 60 ion cannon batteries, 10 magna beam projectors

Other Transports include Space barges, light freighters, bulk freighters, container ships, passenger liners. Patrol craft are in-system only. Sawbone is a cigar-shaped Class II Foxhorne freighter.

Engines

Hyperspeed: A fusion generator enables faster-than-light speeds through hyperspace, a distortion of the space-time continuum.

Realspeed: The Kittering-Bosch ion engine moves ships through real space by breaking down fuel (i.e. liquid reactants, heavy metals, energy conversion cells, or ions from ion-collector scoops) into charged particles. The resulting energy vents from the vessel, providing thrust. Change direction with lateral thrusters or by altering levers on exhaust emission.

Antigrav Engines form a field of negative gravity that pushes against the natural gravity field of a planet. Examples of vehicles: (Royce Manufacturing) R-14 Aircar, R-25 Turbo Scooter (also has turbo boost); (Vixton Motors) VM-180 Airbus, VM Cloud VI Air Tram; VM-1080 Personal Landrover.

Turbo Drive: Engines used in surface vehicles along with antigrav technology for extra maneuverability.

About the Author

Nancy J. Cohen writes the Bad Hair Day Mysteries featuring South Florida hairstylist Marla Vail. Titles in this series have been named Best Cozy Mystery by *Suspense Magazine*, won the Readers' Favorite Book Awards and the RONE Award, placed first in the Chanticleer International Book Awards and third in the Arizona Literary Awards.

Her nonfiction titles, *Writing the Cozy Mystery* and *A Bad Hair Day Cookbook,* have earned gold medals in the FAPA President's Book Awards and the Royal Palm Literary Awards, First Place in the IAN Book of the Year Awards and the *Topshelf Magazine* Book Awards. *Writing the Cozy Mystery* was also an Agatha Award Finalist.

Nancy's imaginative romances have proven popular with fans as well. These books have won the HOLT Medallion and Best Book in Romantic SciFi/Fantasy at *The Romance Reviews*.

A featured speaker at libraries, conferences, and community events, Nancy is listed in *Contemporary Authors, Poets & Writers*, and *Who's Who in U.S. Writers, Editors, & Poets.* She is a past president of Florida Romance Writers and the Florida Chapter of Mystery Writers of America. When not busy writing, Nancy enjoys reading, fine dining, cruising, and visiting Disney World.

Follow Nancy Online

Website – https://nancyjcohen.com
Blog – https://nancyjcohen.com/blog
Twitter – https://www.twitter.com/nancyjcohen
Facebook – https://www.facebook.com/NancyJCohenAuthor
LinkedIn – https://www.linkedin.com/in/nancyjcohen
Goodreads – https://www.goodreads.com/nancyjcohen
Pinterest – https://pinterest.com/njcohen/
Instagram – https://instagram.com/nancyjcohen
BookBub – https://www.bookbub.com/authors/nancy-j-cohen

Books by Nancy J. Cohen

Bad Hair Day Mysteries
Permed to Death
Hair Raiser
Murder by Manicure
Body Wave
Highlights to Heaven
Died Blonde
Dead Roots
Perish by Pedicure
Killer Knots
Shear Murder
Hanging by a Hair
Peril by Ponytail
Haunted Hair Nights (Novella)
Facials Can Be Fatal
Hair Brained
Hairball Hijinks (Short Story)
Trimmed to Death
Easter Hair Hunt
Styled for Murder
Star Tangled Murder

Anthology
"Three Men and a Body" in Wicked Women Whodunit

The Drift Lords Series
Warrior Prince
Warrior Rogue
Warrior Lord

Science Fiction Romances
Keeper of the Rings
Silver Serenade

The Light-Years Series
Circle of Light
Moonlight Rhapsody
Starlight Child

Nonfiction
Writing the Cozy Mystery
A Bad Hair Day Cookbook

Order Now at NancyJCohen.com/Books

www.ingramcontent.com/pod-product-compliance
Lightning Source LLC
Chambersburg PA
CBHW072010190726
48293CB00001B/217